Dedicated to my mother Jean

Chapter One

Hartford, Connecticut May 1885

Jessica lay on the chaise in front of the tall windows in her parents' bedroom, waving a paper fan to cool her flushed face. This was her last attempt to change their minds. "Megan and Sarah have both been to Europe." She snapped the flowered fan closed and slapped it on her lap. "Everyone's had a chance but me!"

Her mother, Bethany, sighed as she folded another shirt. "You know very well your father will have no time to entertain you," she said. "He's there strictly on business."

Jessica perched on an elbow. "But I'll entertain myself with the art museums. Father said Liverpool is a marvelous city. I could sketch the architecture. I'd love to try my hand at the surrounding land! Professor Fields said it would greatly advance my education." Her professor had been a student at the Hudson River School, where landscape artists rendered ethereal paintings of the world around them. He taught the value of a grand and inspiring landscape. Although she appreciated the work of these men, what truly inspired her were the paintings done by female artists such as Cecelia Beaux and Rosa Bonheur. Jessica would get lost in Bonheur's realistic paintings of sleeping sheep and muscular horses, Beaux's captivating portraits. She yearned to express herself in such a way.

"Your professor has too much to say about what you should be doing," her mother shot back. "It's time you settle into a good marriage and direct your attentions to a home, children, and your place in society."

Jessica puffed out a breath of air. "I haven't the slightest interest in any of it." She looked out the window at the street beyond the expansive lawn. Through the manicured hedge that lined the inside of the tall black iron fence, she caught glimpses of people walking by; they seemed to be going nowhere important. "Someday I'll be famous and I won't need to be married."

"That's quite enough of that kind of talk," her father said as he entered the room.

Her shoulders slumped. "Professor Fields says that a beautiful rendition of the outdoors can inspire us to appreciate and preserve our lands. He says my landscapes create such a feeling."

"There's plenty of land to paint around here," her mother said, hanging a pair of her husband's trousers in his stand-up trunk.

Jessica leaned back, muttering, "It would only take *me* minutes to pack my own cases." She had arranged her closets and chests ready for the invitation to sail to Liverpool, England. She looked forlornly at her father, but he did not return her gaze as he inspected his trunks. She knew the time had come to accept the verdict. Her father, a lawyer, had taught her never give up on a case until one was certain there wasn't a sliver of hope remaining. She huffed slightly and returned to the window. *Someday,* she thought, *I will travel to far off places.* She waved her flowered fan across her face.

A scent of the spring air floated into the room, past the yellow brocade curtains, reminding Jessica of last year at this time. Her high school diploma had lain neatly on her lap, its leather bound contents acknowledging the completion of her education. The graduation from an all-girls school in Hartford, Connecticut was a heady experience. She thought she was leaving to join a world of opportunity. If only her parents understood her true desires. The small art school she was allowed to attend and the few hours a week she spent working at Mr. Cromwell's gallery were hardly the exploration of the world she had in mind. Her first choice, The Pennsylvania School of Art, was met with a quick dismissal by her father as a place for bohemians, not for a daughter from good society.

Jessica's thoughts found their way to her cousin Jacob, as they often did. The way he had looked at her as she left the graduation stage. He'd seemed impressed. His smile was one she would like to have tucked into her diploma to keep forever. She waved her fan more vigorously to relieve the heat blooming in her neck and chest. Her emotions rocked like a boat on the ocean; their last horseback ride together was too brief, and she hadn't seen him in over a week.

Her father's agitation interrupted Jessica's daydream. It was just as well, for even thinking of Jacob in front of her parents felt risky. Her father searched through his clothing, pushing aside the clothes on the bed.

"What is it, Thomas?" her mother asked.

"My best tie, the one I had planned to wear on my first dinner with the Moores. It seems to have disappeared." Her father flung his hand up in disgust.

"I'll help you look, Father," Jessica said. When she stood, the white satin tie fell from the back of her dress and onto the floor. Her mother retrieved the wrinkled strip of material from the thick carpet with a cluck of annoyance.

"Oh, now that's a fine thing," he said.

Jessica turned to peer at the back of her full blue-plaid skirt, feeling terrible she'd upset him. "Oh, Father, I'm sorry! I'll have Winnie press it for you right away!"

"As if Winnie hasn't enough to do," her mother sighed.

Jessica left the room just as her brother Will was about to enter. She stopped short, then continued past him. He didn't acknowledge her. His clothes were untidy and his hair was disheveled. He had one hand on his head as if trying to hold back a painful headache. She knew what this was about and rushed down the stairs.

"Winnie!" she called, in search of the family's housekeeper. Once on the main floor she arched her back to peer through the stair rails. His tall body leaned in the doorway, he hadn't entered the room; this was not a good sign. She continued her errand. From the laundry room she heard the rumbles of an argument above her. "Oh, no," she whispered.

Winnie entered from the backyard with a basket full of linens, freshly picked from the clothesline. She stared at her young mistress, then looked up to the ceiling where muffled shouts filtered down. She set down the basket. "What you got there in your hand?" Winnie made quick work of ironing Jessica's father's evening neckwear and sent the young woman on her way.

Returning to the kitchen, Jessica was surprised to see her mother at the sink, washing a dish. "What are you doing, Mother? Winnie will get that."

"Please stay downstairs for a while," her mother replied.

Without warning a voice boomed from above, breaking the uneasy silence. "How am I supposed to have confidence in you when I'm away? This damn habit of yours has got to stop!"

Jessica rested against the counter, her arm extended with the white piece of material hanging over it. "What's going to happen to Will?" she asked quietly.

"Never mind," her mother snapped.

"How will he overcome his gambling problem?"

"Jessica!" Her mother whispered so loudly, Jessica's arm jerked. "How would you know of such things? I do *not* want you repeating any of this! Do you understand?"

"Yes," Jessica answered. "Is he in trouble?" As much as she was concerned about her brother, her thoughts were more on Jacob; he and Will were inseparable.

"No," her mother said. "This does not concern you. Now, that's enough talk, go find something to do."

Relenting, Jessica pushed herself from the sideboard and placed the tie over a chair. She was too old not worry about her brother's behavior and too young to have any say in the matter. "I'm sorry," she said, and made her getaway into the family's smaller parlor. Uneasy, she wished she could gather her pencils and paper from her bedroom upstairs, but she had no desire to hear her father and brother argue.

Drawing and painting always relaxed her, taking her away from her present life of duty and obedience. Often she would have to be called several times to dinner before she became aware of the room around her, and then was scolded by her mother for coming to the table with paint-stained fingers. It wasn't something she could help; if given her way, she would do nothing else but create art. She was reminded almost daily that young women her age were married or engaged. She didn't lack for suitors, and each one had presented himself in a likeable manner, but she had no feelings for any of them. Her heart was full and had no room for Holland James, or Carl Whitman, or God forbid, the Fletcher's skinny and pale son, Andrew.

What a conundrum you have here, Jess. She sat down heavy on the green upholstered settee. Jessica raised her soft brown eyes to the chandelier, which vibrated with slight tings as the rumblings above continued. She decided to visit her Aunt June. Perhaps Jacob would be there—he'd likely be off work by now and surely change her mood.

"Mother, I'm going to Auntie's," she called out from the foyer. Her mother's swishing skirt could be heard before she was seen. Jessica waited.

"Now remember, not a word of this," her mother reminded her in a loud whisper. "I don't need your aunt's opinion on the matter. And arrange your hair before you leave the house."

Jessica swept up her dark, silky locks into a loose chignon that she secured with a large hairpin she retrieved from her skirt pocket. When she stepped outside, the cool early evening air penetrated her day dress and she returned inside for her blue waistcoat. As she did Will walked past her, out of the house, without a word.

"Are you coming home for dinner?" she called after him. He merely raised his hand and headed down the wide gravel path that led to the iron gate and onto the road. She shook her head.

As she walked to her aunt's, Jessica began to feel familiar flutters in her stomach. She slowed her pace to a graceful stroll to calm herself. She passed the Fletcher's home and noticed beyond their low fence the buds and blooms of so many daffodils and irises. Clumps of them circling each oak tree, heralding spring and the fullness of summer that would soon follow. Her heart felt in the same state of bloom. Something wonderful seemed about to happen, but it was not as certain as the seasons. It was a game playing out in her mind—a sort of hide and seek.

"Hello!" Jessica sang out as she entered the back door. The front of the Stanford estate was reserved for guests; family came in the back way. Though still formal with a bright, tidy foyer, it was far less grand than the front of the house, with its large white pillars and expansive veranda.

A plump, redheaded woman with bright green eyes came out of the kitchen. "Jessica! What a nice surprise," she said, wiping her hands on a small tea towel. "Oh, tell your mother that I have a new recipe that she must copy in her beautiful handwriting so we can present it at the Lady's Recipe Exchange."

Jessica greeted her Aunt June with a kiss on a rosy cheek that smelled of cinnamon and ginger. Her aunt looked more like the hired help than the wife of a successful attorney. Her hair was tucked under a flowered kerchief and a matching apron was tied around her thick waist. Jessica visited June often, if only to have a sympathetic ear or a break from her social duties. Today, however, she had come to see Jacob. Her secret weighed more heavily with each visit. She put her guilt aside, next to her growing feelings for her aunt's son.

"Is Jacob here, Auntie?" Jessica asked, nonchalantly sweeping a loose strand of hair from her cheek.

"No, he's off doing something, don't ask me what." June waved her hand in the air. "What do you want with him? Come sit at the kitchen table with me," June continued before Jessica could say a word or control the flushing of her cheeks. "I'll make us a pot of tea and we can talk. The oatmeal cookies are cooling. I'll fix up a plate." Her aunt scurried around her kitchen with such delight Jessica had to smile though she was disappointed at not seeing Jacob. "Let me tell you all about my new recipe. It's certain to be the envy of all the women at the club." Jessica took a seat at the small kitchen table so familiar to her over the years. The yellow printed tablecloth and white porcelain napkin holder gave a simplicity to the space she cherished.

"How is your father's packing coming along?"

"Fine." Jessica pursed her lips and tilted her head. "I was feeling underfoot, to be honest."

"This has taken such a toll on your poor mother. She'll be happy to have him off on his trip and even happier when he returns. I don't know why they haven't hired someone to do all that packing. Oh, I can't imagine being without your Uncle Burt for an entire month. And now my poor husband has to take on the whole responsibility of the law firm. My goodness!"

"I'm sure he'll be fine, Auntie. He does have help," Jessica inserted softly.

June chatted on and Jessica drifted, hoping Jacob would come home. As she served tea, June recited her recipe step-by-step. Jessica patiently listened, but when it grew close to her dinnertime, she said her goodbyes. She had lost all hope of seeing Jacob today. She stepped into the back foyer and there he was, his tall body against the frame of the door, his back to her. He was bending down to remove his riding boots.

"Hello," she said. The pounding in her chest was thunderous.

"Hello, Jess," he said cheerfully. "I should have taken these off in the stables, but I couldn't find my walking shoes."

She gave a small laugh. "Yes, it wouldn't be very comfortable to be in the stables barefooted." She wished for something wittier to say.

He dropped his boots on the outside porch and stood full height in front of her. It sent her into a state of nerves. "I … I was just visiting … your mother. She has a recipe for my mother." She stumbled over her words.

He smiled down at her. "How have you been, Jess? We haven't been riding in over a week."

His smiling eyes and tousled hair didn't help to calm her. "Oh, has it been that long? Well, you know how busy one can get with all the social events of spring and all that." *What was she saying? Why was she being so formal?*

"Yes, I suppose," he replied with a furrowed brow.

"How was your ride?" she asked.

"Good. Teddy Barker is a better rider and wants to prove it every time we go out."

She felt indignation rise like a tide, but before she could denounce Teddy he touched her arm. "You were just leaving. I won't keep you. Have a good evening, Jess."

Her stomach churned as she returned his pleasantries, then all too soon she was out the door, heading home. Her feet felt inches off the ground. The spring breeze played with her hair and she tucked a strand behind her ear with a slight shaking in her hand. Her nerves would settle once she and Jacob were with each other for more than a few minutes, but these brief encounters sent her blood racing through her body.

As she turned the corner, the sight of her family's three-story Victorian peeking through the maple trees calmed her spirit. The amber light in the windows glowed in welcome. Her bedroom, her retreat, faced the front yard just above the long, white painted veranda and when she wasn't writing her thank you notes and RSVPs, she would daydream from her cozy seat tucked into the window or sketch the scenery of the two-acre estate. It all looked especially inviting, with the birds singing their end-of-day songs in the sun-dappled trees.

She left the wooden sidewalk to enter through the gate. A man whistled behind her. Her heart leapt to her throat. She glanced over her shoulder, hoping it was her cousin. Perhaps he wanted to tell her something, alone. "Darn," she whispered. It was just an older boy with a spirited gait. She watched him slide a stick along the black iron pickets of their fence, as so many children did on their way down the sidewalk. It drove her father into a state of indignation each time he heard the hollow clanging, but he never did anything to stop them. She wondered if he would be concerned about it tonight with all he had to do before his trip.

She went straight upstairs, passing her parents' room on the way. "Jessica, you're back," her mother called out. "How is your Aunt June?" Jessica paused in the threshold. They had resumed packing, but tension from the father and son argument still hung in the air. Jessica's heart swelled with sadness at the thought of her father so far away, and now Will had upset him.

"Oh, fine. She wants you to pen a new recipe for her," she said, then excused herself. Once inside with the door closed she climbed onto the bed, hiking up her skirt and crossing her legs. She stared at the pink flowered wall in front of her, then plopped backwards onto her bed. She placed a hand over her stomach and gently rubbed her belly, but nothing could soothe the turmoil in her gut. The very thought of Jacob made her nauseous. Her heart and mind were in a tug-of-war. She knew it was unorthodox to fall in love with her cousin, but still she dreamed of his full lips and his manly hands. The way his hand lingered on her back when they were alone, then the wink he had given her last week when the family wasn't looking. Their vigorous rides through the expansive meadows off of Blake Street. On their last ride her horse had come up lame just as they were heading back to the Stanford stables. She had to ride with Jacob. They laughed as she squeezed in behind him. She held on tight. Now only moments ago, the way he touched her arm. "Oh!" she yelled into her pillow.

"Your father is finally packed," her mother announced as the trio sat down to dinner. "Let's have a nice meal and give him a good send-off tomorrow." Then scowling she asked, "Where is that brother of yours?"

Jessica knew exactly where he was. The family pretended that he was an upstanding young man, the son of a highly successful attorney. Yet, it was hardly a secret where he spent his time and money. She had heard the whispers coming from the gilded society ladies when she passed them in the park or at the theater. The hushed tones of sympathy were like an unseen cloud of dismay. She would walk through it with her head held high, but secretly her pride was wounded. She often thought of what they would think and say about *her* if they truly knew what she carried in her heart. The love for a cousin, the son of her mother's brother—a partner in the well-established law firm of Messing and Stanford. That would truly give them something to cluck about.

She mused for a brief moment at the worldliness of such a scandal as she ate her buttered boiled potatoes. She knew her family would never hold up under such shunning from society nor would Jacob ever allow it. Her brother had already put her at risk for becoming an old maid. The high morals of her parents' society would not tolerate an alliance with a family whose member was a chronic gambler. Her life was dictated by others in a circle of should and should-nots with little in between.

Jessica's father laid his knife on the side of his plate and took a bite of pork smothered in gravy. She felt his eyes bearing down on her. "What is it, Father?" she asked. Her parents exchanged a look of understanding.

"Jessica," he began. "You may know that my purpose for this voyage is two-fold. Besides visiting my friend Charles Moore and his family, I wish to invite his son, Frederick, to come back with me. In fact, it's already been arranged."

Jessica looked at her father with curiosity. This had been common knowledge since his decision to take the steamer to Liverpool. She waited for more. He chewed on another piece of meat and before swallowing he glanced up at her mother.

"My dear," her mother began. "What your father is trying to say is that he considers Mr. Moore's son an asset to Messing and Stanford as well as to our little family."

"Yes." Her father swallowed and took up where her mother left off. "An alliance with the Moore family is important to us," he said. "And we would like you to consider Charles' son Frederick as a friend. More than a friend. A suitor."

Jessica was relieved she had not continued to eat, for she would have surely choked on her food. "A suitor?" She turned to her mother with a panicked plea on her face.

"It's just a thought, my dear, nothing more. Let's see how it goes," her mother said.

"A thought worth considering," her father said. "He is after all an English gentleman of good breeding and astuteness. A fine Liverpool attorney."

Jessica looked back and forth at her parents. "I don't want to marry. I thought I had explained myself."

"Marriage? Who spoke of marriage?" her mother chirped. "We're getting ahead of ourselves." She dabbed at her lips with her napkin, then laid it back in her lap and continued to eat. Her father continued his meal as well. They had said their piece and there was nothing more to discuss. Jessica felt adrift. She certainly knew about arranged marriages, but she never thought her parents would subject her to such a thing. Was this their plan all along? She pushed her plate away. She'd lost her appetite, even for Winnie's maple syrup dumplings with cream.

After dinner, Jessica took up her needlework in the smaller parlor. Embroidery was nothing like painting; the tedious in and out of the needle was too slow for her hands and mind. She sighed. Her mother, who was already seated in the grey linen armchair next to the fireplace worked her knitting needles. She stopped and placed the half-knitted sweater on her lap.

"Jessica, it's only a suggestion. Your father means well. The news from your uncle Burt of his retirement came as a shock to him. I feel he may be trying to tie up too many loose ends with this trip."

"I'm a loose end?" Jessica asked quietly as she threaded the blue-color crewel wool through the taut fabric.

Her mother picked up her knitting. "Why do you twist his

intentions, our intentions? You *will* marry soon, and we only desire the best possible situation."

"Yes, mother," she replied. *The best situation is to allow Jacob and me to live our lives together. To allow me to take art classes in Philadelphia.* The room felt stuffy and she needed to be alone with her thoughts. She rose from the settee. "Mother, I think I'll go upstairs now. I wish to be fresh for our farewell to father tomorrow."

She kissed her mother's cheek and as she turned for the hallway she heard her mumble, "I wish your brother had half a mind to do the same."

Jessica wanted to yank Will out of the haughty place she knew he had gone to. She took each step up to the second floor with a grin as she imagined the look on his face if she performed such an unspeakable act. Then she thought of Jacob alongside her brother. She clutched the banister and stomped up the remaining stairs.

She went to her desk and laid out her paint tray and brushes. She dipped a glass into the basin of water on her nightstand. Her recent drawing of a robin perched on a blooming branch waited for her attention. She swirled her brush in the water and applied just enough to the squares of color to create a reddish orange puddle in the shallow wells of her palette. She touched the brush onto the textured paper and spread it across the robin's breast. Controlling the water contained in her brush she wiped the excess on a towel. It was one of the more challenging parts of painting in this medium. The last piece she did ended up a soggy mess, the colors running together like mud. She would be more mindful this time. Her shoulders relaxed as she lost herself in her art.

Chapter Two

Jessica's brother headed down the dirt road, a mile to the cross section at the end of town. A right turn led to the bustle of downtown Hartford; the opposite way led to its underbelly, where the Palace Hotel stood, waiting for its prey. Will turned toward the unseemly hotel with the money he had just argued out with his father.

Jacob entered the front hall of the Palace Hotel and paused to look up. Dozens of his reflections danced across inlaid mirrors bordered in gold leaf that lined the high domed ceiling. The dark wood-paneled walls and large crystal chandelier gave the small entrance where Adele Harper greeted all her guests a grand feel.

However, this evening Adele was absent from the front desk, and there were no patrons loitering on the purple velvet ottomans and settees. He slid his lean body behind a heavy ornate door at the far end of the lobby that stood slightly ajar. He looked around the large, square, windowless room that was hazy with cigar smoke and held the sharp odor of alcohol. The painted ladies of the Palace, wearing frilly lace dresses, were mingling with the men seated at the card tables. Some of them stood close behind their chosen players, hoping to enrich their own pockets with the men's winnings. The low hum of male voices mixed with the soft tones of the women lending a musical tone to the room. And there was Will at the far end, waving him over.

He made his way through the dozen or so round card tables. Once at Will's table he noticed the pile of bills and coins in front of him. "That's mostly mine you know," Jacob said to his cousin with a smirk, reminding Will of the many loans he had advanced him in this very room. He grabbed a stool nearby and sat by Will's side. His cousin's light brown hair was slicked back and caught the light of the candelabra above their heads. Jacob smiled to himself at the thin golden mustache Will now sported to make himself look older.

As the game progressed, Jacob watched Will's luck begin to slide. Finally, he stood to leave, whispering into his cousin's ear, "You've only lost my half. Why not call it a night?"

Will grabbed his arm. "Hey, you're my good luck charm!" he insisted.

Jacob shook off his cousin's grip, but reluctantly returned to his seat. One of the ladies approached Jacob and was about to sit on his lap but he waved her on.

Will turned to him with a raised eyebrow. "What's the matter? Are you getting that picky?"

"Play your cards and never mind about me," Jacob replied.

Miss Harper appeared at their table. "You too high and mighty for one of my girls, Jacob? By the way, I didn't see you come in. Where's your dues?"

Jacob presented a silver coin from his pants pocket and put it into her waiting hand. "Why you even come here we can't figure," she said. "But you sure have the money and we sure have your entertainment, so if you show up, plan on being respectful."

"Maybe later," Jacob replied. He patted his shirt pocket then reached in for a rolled cigarette and match.

"Tish," Adele Harper scoffed as she slid the coin down the bodice of her dress and turned away.

Jacob lit the cigarette and turned to watch his cousin. He couldn't explain his lack of desire for the Palace ladies or even for the place itself. He didn't want to think about it. He cursed to himself and gave a grunt.

Will tilted his head. "Shh, I almost got this guy beat," he said with a whisper out the side of his mouth. Jacob dismissed him with a curt wave of his hand.

Within the hour Will had lost all but a few coins. He tipped back on his chair with a curse. The winner stood up and collected the soft bills and mound of coins. He touched the brim of his hat to Will, then bent down to Jacob. "Your cousin is a lousy cheater," he hissed in Jacob's ear. "He best watch his back. I'll bring my gun with me next time and a few of my friends." Jacob pulled on his cigarette and let out the smoke as the man straightened his vest and walked out of the room.

Will spat as he slapped his measly winnings across the table.

Jacob's stomach turned, and not from the greasy supper he had eaten earlier. It wasn't because his cousin had been threatened, again. No, it was something else. His mind whispered her name and he quickly dismissed it. He coughed to release the tension in his chest. Jessica was not going to impede on his thoughts again, not in this place. His head hurt, he needed fresh air.

As the cousins walked along Washington Street to their family's respective homes, Jacob felt a sense of urgency in his belly. Again he dismissed it. He lit a cigarette and took a long drag then handed it over to his cousin. "Geez, Will, are you sure you want to make a living at this?" Jacob asked through the stream of smoke releasing from his lungs. "Think twice, before you get yourself killed."

"Ah, Saul's a jackass, I'll beat him next time." Will handed the cigarette back to Jacob and wiped his mouth with his sleeve. Jacob looked away with disgust. Who had Will become?

Who had *he* become for that matter? He tossed the cigarette in front of him and stepped on it as he walked. "I'm not making a living out of it anyway," Will added.

"Aren't you?" Jacob asked. "Give up that place," he said and stopped, forcing Will to turn around.

"What in God's name is wrong with you tonight?" Will asked. "No one had to twist your arm to be there."

"Why are you wasting your money?" Jacob argued.

"I've got the skill, that's all." Will continued walking. "Besides, tonight was going to be different. My win was going to get me on a ship."

"A deck hand? Where?" Jacob asked.

"I heard that one of the last whalers is taking off soon from New Bedford, Massachusetts."

Jacob couldn't believe what he was hearing. "Do you have any idea what you'd be getting yourself into?" He'd read about the whaling ships and the terrible conditions for the men who worked on them. Calming himself, he gave Will an impish grin and raised eyebrow. "I've got something better in mind, Cousin. I need a partner ..."

"No, Jake. I'm not working for Hank," Will blurted out. He kicked up dirt from the road. "It's bad enough working for Cunningham and that damn roofing company. I need something more than pounding nails on a steep slope. Saddles and spurs are not my idea of progress."

Jacob felt Will's jab. He knew that his cousin had always placed higher expectations on him than Will did for himself. After a year at Yale Law School, Jacob had decided that the law was not his calling and working with his hands suited him better. There had been lengthy discussions about his future with his father Burt. Finally, he was allowed to put his academic life on hold, giving him one year to explore his desires. Now two had passed. Will had also given Yale a stab, but he'd been expelled for gambling before he could quit.

"Sorry, Jake."

"Yeah, yeah." Jacob dismissed his apology. "I'm not talking about Hank," he replied. "I've got something better in mind." He had found other employment besides working at The Tack and Saddle

Company, one with cash rewards and just enough adventure to satisfy his lust for a life much different from his father's.

Chapter Three

After many days on the ocean, Thomas Messing welcomed the solid ground beneath his feet. His first steps on English soil. The harbor was filled with all sorts of boats and ships overflowing with commerce, the docks bustled with travelers and workers. He looked around for his connection and soon spotted a thin young man underdressed for the windy and cool spring air. He held up a sign reading, "Mr. T. Messing." Thomas approached the youth.

"I'm Mr. Messing."

In a thick Irish accent, the boy replied, "Right, Mr. Messing, you follow me then."

Thomas put his handkerchief to his nose against the smells of rotting fish, brined pickles, and animal dung as he began to weave through the crowd of humanity, trying to keep up with the youth. Three small boys followed behind, carrying his trunks. He passed finely dressed women with fluttering fans and capable looking men shouting instructions to servants carrying trunks of varying sizes. Commoners sold all types of wares and services, from women extending parcels of food to the shoe shine claiming his expertise. He had no time for charity and turned away from a legless man with a cup who sat on the wet pier and the shabby children begging for food.

The wind picked at his coat and he gathered his collar and continued to follow the young man. Finally, he stopped in front of a carriage parked on a street filled with carts, carriages and buses, horses and people.

The driver quickly loaded the back of the coach. Thomas watched the young boys waiting with anticipation on their dirty little faces. The driver threw them each a coin and they ran back to the docks. Before Thomas entered the coach, he searched his waistcoat for a coin, and handed it to his guide.

"Thank you kindly, Sir," said the young man, then ran off to follow the others.

"I assume you know where to take me," he said to the driver who was now in his seat arranging the reins. The driver nodded. Satisfied, Thomas put one foot on the iron step and entered the coach. Jostled about as the horse drew the carriage down the cobbled road, he peered past the black velvet curtain at the brick buildings crowned by smoke stacks. The sky was overcast and the gray left him feeling lonely. There was little vegetation and so many people to get through. A woman knocked at the carriage door begging for money. Thomas's patience was tested; irritated, he snapped the curtain shut.

After a while he noticed the noise had diminished. He drew back the curtain. The landscape had changed and to his relief there were trees and shrubs and green pastures. He lost count of the parish churches along the way.

He was dozing off when he felt the driver take a turn. He saw they were traveling down a narrow tree-lined road and then into a courtyard with a large stone water fountain in the middle. The four-story house resembled a small castle. Statuesque topiaries stood on either side of an impressively carved wooden door, green vines climbing up the grey brick and bushes of azaleas in full bloom sat under tall windows. The steps leading to the entrance were long and grand. The gloomy sky lifted and a bright ray of light shot through the fog, lighting the courtyard. Thomas felt he had stepped into a fairytale. He was handed off by the footman, then to the doorman, and finally to Jason, the butler.

Thomas reflected on the entrance to his own estate, it had its own grandeur but wasn't nearly this ancestral and ornate. He vowed to have more authority over his staff and his household in general, especially his son. At the thought of Will, acid rose from his stomach, searing his throat. He coughed into his handkerchief. He followed the butler through a great hall, where giant palm plants reached to the high ceiling. The walls displayed dream-like landscape murals and he thought of his daughter. *She would love these.* He struggled to take it all in, then realized he stood alone in a large bluish room. The expanse of windows revealed a carefully landscaped property. Not one leaf seemed out of place in a maze of bright green boxwood and animal-shaped topiaries surrounding a large, square gazing pond.

The large, beautiful room seemed to resent the intrusion of an American. The unlit fireplace added to the chill that had seized him on the carriage ride. He hugged himself as he marveled at the room's majesty. He wondered what he and his friend had in common after all.

Charles Moore came through the door at that very moment, a spring in his step.

"My dear Thomas, I'm so pleased you are here at last!" Charles exclaimed. He took hold of Thomas's hands. Even at sixty, he had the robust appearance of a much younger man. At forty-seven, Thomas forced himself to equal Charles's vitality.

"It's wonderful to be here, Charles, thank you for your invitation," Thomas said as he returned his friend's grasp. He began to relax into their familiarity.

"How was your journey, my man? As you know, I loathe the voyage myself. Come my friend, this is the parlor where my wife greets her guests." Charles led Thomas from the room. "Jason insists on seating all my company this way. My study is down the hall—we'll be more comfortable there."

Thomas followed, taking in the long hallway that led away from the blue room and grand entrance. Floor-to-ceiling windows encased in heavy dark-stained wood and gas sconces lined the hallway on one side. Larger than life-sized portraits on the other side gave the impression of the subjects gazing out to the world beyond. A slight breeze funneled in from a few open windows, chilling the vast hall. Charles opened a heavy wood door at the end.

"Now, here is a room!" he exclaimed. He fixed drinks from the well-stocked bar and the men settled into the overstuffed furniture. The fire in the great stone fireplace was crackling and soon its warmth made Thomas feel at ease.

Not more than an hour had passed when there was a knock on the door. "Yes?" Charles sighed, as if expecting the intrusion. A crisply uniformed young woman stood in the doorway, her hands folded in front of her starched, white apron in a way that was neither subservient nor authoritative. Charles rose from his seat. "This is my good friend Thomas Messing. Thomas, this is our head housekeeper, Anice Mills."

Miss Mills curtsied. Thomas simply nodded his head. He couldn't help but think how her sweet and youthful looks belied what would be an important position in a house this size.

"Anice means grace in Scottish," Charles announced and smiled at the blond-haired beauty. Thomas again nodded politely. It was odd to be introduced to the help in such a familiar fashion. "Anice will show you to your rooms, my friend. You can rest and refresh yourself before dinner."

Thomas agreed and took the lead toward the door. When he turned back, he saw Charles carefully tucking a strand of the young woman's hair inside her white bonnet. He turned away. Once in his rooms, he relaxed. He hoped he wouldn't have to deal any further with Charles's indiscretion. He stood in the middle of the lavish room. Heavy red and gold patterned drapes hung from two large windows. The cloth covering the canopy bed matched the drapes and looked fit for a king. He noticed his trunks had been unpacked and his clothes and accessories were neatly arranged in the polished walnut bureau and armoire. Weary, he took a deep breath.

After a short nap, Thomas dressed for dinner. Looking at his reflection in the standing mirror, he parted his straight brown hair down the middle, ran the comb over his tidy mustache and through his full brows. His formal dark tailcoat with satin lapels and matching waistcoat fit well on his trim body. He wrapped his white satin tie around the stiff winged collar of his shirt and tied it into a neat bow. Once done, Thomas knew he looked more than suitable.

Fredrick Moore opened his appointment book. Scribbled on today's date was *Thomas Messing/ Dinner.*

He sat at his heavy wooden desk in the highly coveted office he inherited from his father when he joined the family law firm and thought of the evening ahead of him. Though Frederick had a natural curiosity about his father's friend, he felt indifferent toward meeting Thomas Messing socially. He was more interested in what the American could do for him personally. He placed an elbow on his desk and cupped his chin looking out of his office window. His father had mentioned that Mr. Messing had a son and daughter. Frederick wondered what obstacles the son would present and what opportunities the daughter could offer. The sun pierced the clouds and he took the light as a good omen for the evening ahead.

He returned to his paperwork and finished several files before leaving for his quarters in the left wing of his parents' estate. He was as ready to meet the challenge of convincing his father and Mr. Messing of his sincerity to learn from the Americans. He knew his plan to become independent of his parents and free from the confinements to his routine was indeed unusual, yet the thought thrilled him to no end and he couldn't wait to begin. He placed the rest of his papers in his leather case then looked at the room he had worked in since his early twenties. At thirty-two he was ready to move on. His father's business lacked the excitement he craved.

Thomas observed his hosts, Charles on one end of the polished walnut dining table, his wife, Lillian on the other, and Frederick across from him. It felt slightly forced and he sensed that this may not be a nightly ritual for them. Or was it just their formal British way? He caught Lillian's eye. Her stoic, pleasant expression did not mask the sadness in her eyes. He thought of Charles and the housekeeper and diverted his attention to the line of silverware on either side of his plate.

The dinner conversation flowed easily through several courses. Thomas noted that Frederick was as much of a proper gentleman as he had expected and knowledgeable on many topics. He resembled Charles in stature, but Thomas could also see the fine features of his mother Lillian. Frederick was a handsome man; he hoped Jessica would think the same.

After dinner the men went into Charles's study and Frederick began to pepper Thomas with questions about his law firm and life in America. He stood by the fireplace mantle, a drink in his hand. The older men were seated as they enjoyed brandies. At one point Charles had to remind his son that their guest was not a witness on trial, and the three men laughed.

"Excuse me, Mr. Messing," Frederick apologized then added sardonically. "Actually, I haven't been in a courtroom for some time. My father keeps me busy with the shipping companies we represent. It's mostly a matter of keeping them from entering the courtroom."

Thomas looked at Charles for a reaction to his son's remark, but noticed no change in his demeanor. "Tell me more of your intentions in the States," Thomas finally asked.

"Yes, of course," Frederick began. "I'm interested in becoming more familiar with how law is practiced in America."

"And in the financial markets, your father tells me."

Frederick took a sip of his drink before answering. He began to pace the room. "I've been studying your markets. I'm intrigued."

Thomas noted how measured he was with his answers. Perhaps the younger lawyer felt he was being interviewed. Naturally he'd be a bit nervous. "I think you will find a good deal of difference in the way we approach our business affairs."

"I'm sure I will," said Frederick. "I'd like to learn as much as I can."

"That sounds possible," Thomas said with a smile. "Indeed, quite possible," he repeated. "Now, gentlemen," he continued in a serious tone. "I must remind you that I cannot make a contract of agreement here for Frederick's employment. However, once you arrive in the States, it would be perfectly legal for you visit our law firm as our guest. We don't want to get ourselves in hot water at the start. I assume you are gathering the necessary paperwork needed for you to work in America?"

"Yes, of course," Frederick replied. He looked into his glass and swirled the liquor.

Thomas felt satisfied. "It would be an honor to show Frederick the workings of our business," he said, easily assuming the role of mentor. It was one he sorely missed with his own son. "Is your intention to continue as a financial lawyer only?" he asked.

Frederick paused. "Yes. My father tells me that you have a good number of clients who require legal financial assistance."

"Indeed," Thomas replied. "Although we have a diverse clientele, we would surely be able to steer you in the direction you are most interested in."

Charles cleared his throat. Frederick chuckled. The tension between them was obvious. "My son believes he can broaden his knowledge, making himself a better lawyer for our company," Charles said. "I believe that may be true, but we have many fine opportunities here for his expansion."

"Father, we've talked about this," Frederick said through tight lips.

"However, I believe that you, Thomas, will give him the experience he desires," Charles continued.

Thomas was uneasy. The conversation had turned sour, but he smiled graciously. Charles changed the subject and the three men discussed the business of law, opining how it could be improved in both countries. They solidified Frederick's plans to return to America with Thomas.

Later as he lay in the large bed reflecting on the evening, Thomas felt that things had gone well. The tension between Charles and Fredrick was not his affair. He would take Frederick on the man's own terms. He found the attorney had great confidence and intellect, along with an ambition surprising for someone already steeped in wealth and recognition. He was also convinced Frederick would make an ideal husband for his daughter and he was willing to push the matter to its conclusion. He rubbed his chest vigorously in an effort to remove the nagging pain he had felt in the weeks leading up to his arrival in Liverpool. He thought of Will and determination swelled in him. *I will not let you ruin this family, my son.* Was Jessica his only chance to secure the family's fortune?

His chest continued to throb and he regretted indulging in the rich food and liquor this evening.

Chapter Four

Two weeks had passed since her father's return from England. His presence at home both relaxed Jessica and kept her on edge. He reminded her frequently that Mr. Frederick Moore would soon be joining them for dinner.

To Jessica's great relief, Will and her father hadn't argued once. She had enough to worry about; her relationship with Jacob had grown more serious in the month her father had been absent.

With the June heat came a rise in their usual flirtations. Without any formal recognition of their unique circumstance, they saw each other beyond the normal Sunday family dinners and their frequent, early morning rides. She would make time for him even if it meant canceling her afternoon social events or skipping a class at school. She explained her tardiness to her mother with a variety of excuses, such as having to work late on a project in one of her classes or that her duties at the gallery ran long. She would steal away to the path that led to the secluded Mary's Pond, where Jacob waited each time. They sat under the tall oak tree. The sturdy oak became *their* tree. Jessica didn't know how it had come this far. The nerves that kept her from thinking beyond her own desires had evaporated replaced by a confident devotion. First there were long looks into each other's eyes, then another day, another look. A touch of an arm, a smile that spoke, a brush of their hands. The chill of the morning air on their last ride he had warmed her hands between his, one at a time. Their conversation held more value and she felt that alongside him she could truly escape her confined life and find a great and glorious purpose. Their rendezvous were the respite from her daily routine, an acknowledgement of life's tide rushing towards her instead of slipping away under the layers of social obligations as a young lady in Hartford, Connecticut. The freedom was palpable and tasted delicious.

This morning was already warming uncomfortably when she took the omnibus downtown to Main Street. It carried her as far as Clifford Street and she had to walk the rest of the way. She was hoping to gain practical use from the public summer classes Mr. Cromwell offered to her without charge. However, her mind was on Jacob, thoughts which added to the burden of the corseted dress and waistcoat she wore over light stockings. Even her shoes felt leaden on her feet. The humidity growing, she wiped her damp brow.

Minding her pace to avoid becoming overheated, she made her way down Clifford Street then on to Benton trying to stay in the shadows of the tenements and shops lining the street. She pulled at the band of lace on her high collar to let air reach her neck, then looked around to make certain no one had noticed her unladylike gesture. She had enough to carry with her art box and paper, but she was remiss in not bringing her parasol. She let her body suffer as her mind whirled with the thought of her last rendezvous with Jacob. His kisses remained on her lips. She touched her mouth, but felt only the sweat from her upper lip. She smiled anyway for the memory was as heady as lilacs in summer.

Just a few days ago they had rested their backs against the base of the oak as they talked about the possibility of living abroad. Unexpectedly, his hand slipped over hers and their fingers curled together. Without looking up at him she let her body draw closer. Her chest contracted as her heart expanded. What was happening? Then his finger lifted her chin and his lips were on hers. His full and tender lips. They felt warm and soft. She touched his clean-shaven face. He felt as magnificent as he looked. His fingers left hers and his hand was on her waist, then her bodice. Her breasts tingled as he cupped one and gently squeezed it. She had fallen off the edge of the world. He came away, his lips parting from hers with a slight suck. Still close he touched her cheek and she wanted to swoon. It was official, she thought. He loved her as much as she loved him. From this day on they would be a secret couple. She had the love of her life; she certainly had no use for any other. Then Jacob sat back. His expression no longer loving, but anguished. "I shouldn't have done that, Jess. I'm sorry. I … I just couldn't help it."

Jessica stepped off the sidewalk and crossed the street. Thinking of his guilt tortured her. A horn blared and she pulled herself back up the curb as a hackney went by. She stopped and caught her breath. She searched her mind for a way to soothe his feelings. The truth between them had been revealed in this forbidden act. Yet all she could say that day was, "Kiss me again, Jacob." The memory made her head swim. She made sure to look both ways this time when she crossed the street.

In spite of Jacob's uneasiness and her own anxiety, her commitment to their relationship did not waver. While her feelings for him occupied her heart, her college studies and gallery work filled her time, and she had to be cautious not to ignore her social obligations. She knew her mother wouldn't tolerate it no matter how plausible her excuses. She attended the theater and ballet with her friends, making sure she was seen, and spoke only when spoken to. No loud laughing or silly giggles at the social dances she attended with other wealthy young women, those who pined for a rich husband and a life of children and duty. Jessica wanted nothing of that life. A few young men in her circle called her "High and Mighty" after she refused their advances. It didn't bother her and she liked the thought of being above them. No, she knew what she wanted. Her husband would be Jacob and they would live in New York City or even Paris. She would paint his portrait, and … that was where her daydream came to a dead end. She mourned a life she had not lived. She shared none of it with the other girls, for when she tried to explain her plans to her closest friend Sarah, without mentioning Jacob's name, she was met with wide eyes and a gaping mouth. Jessica laughed to ease the tense moment and tucked away any further thoughts of confiding in anyone.

She sighed deeply as she entered the gallery. She came in through the back door and walked quickly past the storeroom and into the small darkish lesson room. It offered cool relief from the outside. There were six worn wooden desks from a school no longer in need of them and a steel stool with a round wood top accompanied each one. At the front of the room a blackboard was attached to the wall behind a teacher's desk. It was cruder than the college art rooms she was use to but it didn't matter to Jessica, she was here to take in any bit of knowledge she was given while on her summer break. She settled at a desk by an open window. A soft, welcoming breeze floated in and Jessica embraced the sweet fragrance of early summer bringing with it the scent of roses hanging heavy on a bush just outside. A perfect subject. She laid her art box on the top of the desk and raised the lid. As always her supplies were in impeccable order. She organized her brushes by size and each square of color was wiped clean from her last practice. The pencils were sharp and a cotton cloth was at the ready. Her mother let her buy a small sea sponge, which had greatly enhanced the texture of some of her work. She examined the colors deciding which ones to mix to duplicate the pinkish, apricot blush of the delicate layers of the rose petals. She took out her tin palette and was ready to mix her paints on it. Mr. Cromwell had told her this lesson would be on the study of the glazing process and how to better make use of it. Although she had studied it at college and practiced it many times she had to admit she was not as good at layering her colors as she would like to be.

While she studied the rose she chose to paint, the other students took their seats. A man stood at the front of the room and called for attention. Jessica looked up and saw that it wasn't Mr. Cromwell. Instead, there stood a man with an extremely large and curly mustache that stretched beyond his face. His baggy beige suit coat matched his pants. It was casual attire for a teacher making it difficult to take him seriously.

"Mr. Cromwell has been detained in New Haven," said the man. "He asked me to teach the class in his stead." His tone was formal and condescending. "My name is Mr. Layfette. I am the Art Professor at Bristol College. I hope I may offer you all a bit of inspiration in your artistry."

Well, this does sounds promising.

Mr. Layfette turned to the blackboard and began to write. He then stepped aside. "Techniques used in 16th Century Art," he stated, reading what he had written.

Jessica raised her hand. "Excuse me, Mr. Layfette?"

Layfette looked stunned at the interruption. "Yes? Stand up, young woman. What is your name?" he asked.

"Jessica Messing," she stated. "I believe today's lesson was meant to be about glazing and choosing our own subjects to practice with."

He looked down at his notes. "I'm sorry, Miss Messes, but I don't see that here. Please sit down and refrain from further interruptions. Thank you. Now, as I was about to say-"

"It's Messing, Mr. Layfette." Jessica was compelled to continue. "I think this lesson has been taught already."

"I beg your pardon?" His voice raised in pitch and volume. "What makes you think you can disrupt my class like this, young lady?"

An older woman stood, her attire and demeanor noticeably that of a wealthy matriarch. "With all due respect Mr. Layfette, this young woman has a point. We are here taking time out of our busy days to learn about techniques and acquire, as you say, "inspiration for our artistry" and we *have* had this lesson in the class prior to this one."

Mr. Layfette inspected the woman. "Very well. You may pick your subjects." He pointed to the table at the front of the room covered with artificial flowers and fruit, scarves and vases.

As Jessica prepared to sketch the rose outside the window, Mr. Layfette added, "When you are done constructing your still life portraits, I will come by to approve or make improvements, whichever the case may be."

The five other women in the class hurried to the table, their bustled skirts competing with each other as they grabbed for the pieces they fancied. Jessica ignored the scene, searching for the right color for her rose. She worked for several minutes until it was time to apply a light wash. Having cleaned this room many times as one of her duties at the gallery, she knew she would find a small glass by the sink at the back. When she returned with the glass of water Mr. Layfette was standing by her desk, his arms folded in front of him.

"And where is your composition, Miss Mess*ing*?" he asked, drumming his fingers on his upper arm.

"Oh, it's right here," she replied, showing him the beautiful rose bush. She took her seat and placed the filled glass next to her brushes.

In a voice loud enough for all to hear and with considerable condescension he announced, 'Still life' is just that. Not moving. Maybe a few more technical lessons might do you well, Miss, even if you seem not to think so."

Jessica looked around the room and noticed each desk had a variety of fake flowers and fruit on it as the others began to arrange gaudy-colored scarves in artistic fashion. It was one of her least favorite ways to express her art, but she was willing to compromise. "May I snip a rose from this bush and arrange it with a vase?" she asked hopefully.

"You've been provided the necessary material on the table at the front of the class," he replied. "I suggest you make the most of that. A true artist is able to create from what is given to him." He walked away from her as he spoke.

Jessica felt the heat rise from her blouse. This was not the lesson she had expected. This was for wealthy, idle women to while away a summer afternoon. "Mr. Layfette, please may I paint this lovely flower?" She waited. He turned to her and huffed. "As you wish, but I will inform Mr. Cromwell of your disrespectful behavior. He may want to bar you from further lessons." She lowered her head and smiled. Her paper waited for the first wash, her favorite moment, when the pencil drawing came to life. She would give this portrait of a rose to her mother.

During the lesson Mr. Layfette walked about the room considering each student's work. He came to her desk and she raised her head from her painting. His brow was arched and his mouth held a smirk. "I see you have some talent. Yet, you lack discipline. You'll never amount to anything in the field of art. I suggest you stick to what most young women aspire to. I'll wager your needlework stitches lack the same discipline."

Jessica neatly tucked her supplies back into their places in the wooden art box and took up her damp paper. She stood from her seat and cleared her throat. Her face flushed.

"I've decided to look elsewhere for my inspiration," she announced. "If you'll excuse me, I will spend my day exercising my artistic abilities alone." She couldn't help herself. It was a terrible habit of hers, this speaking up. She turned and walked to the door, her art case under her arm, her head held up as if a princess walking away from her subjects.

When she stepped outside the heavy heat and burning sun accosted her. She winced as she walked to the street and kicked up the dust. She was shaken by her own actions. Mr. Cromwell would surely give her a reprimand and she didn't want to think what her father would say if this got back to him. She knew what consequences might arise from her vanity. She didn't want to lose her job, yet her anger dominated her reasoning. She clenched her art supplies and took a deep breath. The sweat trickled down her back and into her pantaloons, the discomfort almost unbearable. She wished to escape the confinement of her clothes as much as she wished to escape the confinements of society. She settled her nerves and declared, "The devil with it!" As she stormed off, a bone from her corset poked into her ribs. Was it the finger of God reminding her to behave?

She would have to explain to her mother what brought her home so early. Any of her excuses might be unacceptable, so she decided to meander down the side roads leading back to Main Street. However, the heat would not allow such luxury and she began to compose her alibi. Mr. Cromwell became ill and was forced to cut the class short. She agreed with herself that it was clever and not overdone. She walked on and began to contemplate her life and future. Not having the ability to decide what she wanted to paint annoyed her. "Why should I have to comply to so many rules?" she lamented aloud. "It's bad enough my college lessons have to be so strict! Now this!" She lowered her head and looked from side to side. No one had heard her. A rider and his horse trotted by and she coughed from the dust left in their wake.

"Oh!" she barked at the man holding the reins. She stamped her foot and her box fell to her feet, the latch opened spilling its contents. "Darn!" she shouted. A woman passing by gave her a disapproving look. She settled herself and wiped the dust from her damp face, and quick as she could she collected the now soiled supplies.

"Darn!" Soon she could hear the clip clop of another horse with a buggy. She prepared to give this driver a disapproving look but to her surprise, Jacob smiled down from the top of his runabout. "Why hello, Jess. Were you painting today?" he asked.

Her heart skipped a beat. "Jacob! What are you doing here? Why aren't you at work?"

"Too hot. Hank let us off early. I'm going for a swim; would you like to come along?"

She hesitated and looked at her disarrayed art box. She took a breath, struggling to keep the composure she was sure to lose at any minute. His handsome face and smiling dark eyes led her to abandon her mood. "Why not?" she replied, her legs quaking.

She handed him her art supplies then grabbed her skirt and hoisted herself up to sit beside him; it was a much nicer place to be than that old stuffy classroom. He gave her a wink and commanded the horses to trot on.

As they made their way down the street she caught him looking at her art box not resting near her feet.

"I was supposed to be in a lesson at the gallery but it went quite awry," she said.

He chuckled. "You can tell me all about it after we've cooled off."

She smiled and settled into her seat.

Chapter Five

The glistening water moved slowly from the pond down the stream, eventually finding its way to the Connecticut River. Jessica closed her eyes and took in a deep breath. The grasses and wildflowers mixed with the thick aroma of maple and oak and the clean scent of the pond. It filled her head with pleasure.

She opened her eyes and caught a glimpse of Jacob's naked chest as he stripped down to his long johns. She turned away, but from the corner of her eye she watched as he walked into the pool, then dove under. She looked around; no one came to this end of the pond. It was hidden among the trees. She slowly removed her dress and hung it on a branch. She untied the side laces of her corset and the release from its confining stays made her feel as if she would float into the sky. She loosened her hair and the dark, shiny tendrils fell around her delicate shoulders. A soft breeze wafted over her exposed limbs. As she inched her way into the refreshing water a sharp chill ran through her. Self-conscience in her white cotton pantaloons and ruffled camisole, she bit her bottom lip and refused to let her timidity ruin this luscious moment. Her rebellion in the classroom had momentarily awakened a spirit that took her from her restrictive shell. As she walked deeper into the pond, the light cotton pantaloons bubbled up around her. Jessica forced the garment down until it finally clung to her skin. The water embraced her and she relented.

"Jess, let's swim to the middle so you can get on my knees and I'll throw you over my shoulder!" Jacob called to her.

"Come and get me!" she shouted. They played like young children. She laughed, trying to swim away from him, but he grabbed her by the waist. She broke free but could barely escape with her fit of laughter. "Twirl me around," she ordered him.

Jacob grabbed her hands and stood up, dragging her in a circle. She threw back her head as her body swirled through the water releasing the day's troubles. Jacob pulled her towards him and gave her a quick wet kiss and she splashed him for it. He slowly fell back into the water as if shot. After some time of playful seduction, they lifted themselves out of the blue-green water and into the heat of the sun, its warmth embracing her body.

Jessica's makeshift swimsuit clung to her. She tried in vain to pull the material away, only to have it suck against her skin. Jacob laughed and took her hand, drawing her down to the soft grass under the oak tree. He put his arm around her shoulder, closing the gap between them and she nestled her head in the crook of his neck, feeling lightheaded. Touching his damp skin, she felt they were one; dangerous and forbidden, she no longer cared.

As they relaxed together, she began her account of Mr. Layfette and the art lesson. As she talked, her body touched his; the wet, light sheer material filmed over her pink breasts; her hands in animated gestures increased their movement.

"So, do you not agree it was right for me to leave the class before it was over?" she asked, awaiting his judgment.

"Yes," he answered.

Satisfied, she stopped talking and rested her hand on his smooth, tanned chest. She could feel the pulse under his tight abdomen beating strongly. While she had been ranting about her lesson, part of her mind was taking pleasure in his half-naked body and part of her was abashed she was seeing and feeling him in this way. Surely the weather and her tainted lesson had compromised her reasoning, or was it her feelings for him that allowed her to abandon her modesty? She only knew her desire was growing with every second that past. The pleasant dizziness she felt in her head was love, no matter what society would have to say about it.

"Jess ...," Jacob said. His voice was low and hoarse. He placed his hand atop hers to stop its motion. "I should take you home. This may lead to something you're not ready for."

She looked up at him. "Do you really want to take me home, Jacob?"

His expression was serious. He kissed her mouth. It wasn't the first time, but Jessica felt something different from him. Jacob's breathing was audible as he moved his body over hers. She felt herself become weak, her mind flooded with waves of ecstasy mixed with fear. He pulled down her pantaloons then her silk under pant while he kissed her lips, then her neck. He peeled back her wet camisole to taste her soft, round breasts and she moaned helplessly. Soon she was helping him remove his pants, the strings of her camisole hanging loosely, her breast exposed. The blood rushed to her head, she was enthralled with each touch of her hand on his tight body. She laid back in surrender.

The sharp and painful penetration made her cried out. She hadn't expected this. She felt him slip out of her.

"Jessica," he whispered. "Look at me." She looked away. "Jess." he repeated. She faced him, the tears running down her face. He wiped the wetness from her cheeks. "I'll stop," he said.

The air was thick around her but his heavy breathing hit her face like a soft breeze from heaven. It filled her with courage. "No ... no." she said. Her throat was tight with emotion. She would cross this threshold with him.

He kissed her cheeks, and slowly moving his lips to her ear, he whispered, "I love you." He repeated it and soon they were breathing in harmony and she felt her body relax as he tried again. This time she embraced him within her; the pleasure mixed with pain. She felt as if she was about to lose her mind as the smell of his sweaty chest threw her into an explosive state of ecstasy. Before she realized what was happening he was removing himself from her with a moan of agony. A silence followed.

Jessica waited. The air grew thicker. She felt the world become a bubble around them. It encompassed the sound of her heart beating in every part of her body along with the soft waves of the pond lightly cresting the pebbled shore and the wind barely a whisper through the leaves. She meekly cleared her throat. "Are you all right?" she asked shyly.

"Mmmm," he answered.

She lay still, waiting for his next move. After a while, he rolled over and began to kiss her as if she were some kind of dessert. She was confused, but relieved. His kisses made her laugh now. "Stop, that tickles." She giggled.

He laughed and gently placed his hand onto her cheek. She was lost in his eyes, the deep brown with just a speck of yellow in one of them. He moved his lips to her mouth and they lingered there. Jacob slowly pulled away and spoke quietly. "Are *you* all right, Jess?" he asked. "Was that too much? I mean ... did I hurt you too much? I know it was your first time."

Jessica gave a half smile. "I'm fine." She really had no other words for it. Maybe in the future she would share with him the tremendous feeling she had experienced, or maybe not; a part of her felt protective of it. She moved the lower half of her body. It felt different. She felt different. She wondered about his actions. She moved slightly away from him. "Jacob?" she began. "Did I hurt *you*?"

He chuckled. "No. Why do you ask?"

"Because you sounded and acted as if —"

He interrupted her with another short laugh.

"What?" she asked, feeling as if he were making fun of her.

"What do you mean, *what*? You're twenty years old, Jess. Don't you know about the 'birds and the bees'?"

"Well of course I do," she answered. "Mother told me. Some things, at any rate."

"Such as?" He gestured for her to continue. Jessica remained silent. "Oh," he said.

She raised her chin. "Mother said that the act of love between a man and wife is sacred."

"Is that all she told you?" he asked. "We are not a man and wife."

Jessica wrinkled her nose at him and he kissed it. Her friend Sarah had filled in some of the gaps of her education on the subject, but she could see now that it was not as helpful as she had thought it to be at the time.

"Jess, I didn't want you to become pregnant," he said bluntly.

"I see. Of course. I understand that," she replied as her fingers slid her wet hair behind her ears. "I still don't know why you ..." Her embarrassment surfaced. She knew she was not his equal, and as a male he would be worldly than she, even if he was only three years older. It had never seemed to matter, until now. She wanted to run away and hide. She reached for her pantaloons and adjusted her camisole then she rose and retrieved her corset, fighting with the side laces.

"Girls aren't told about these things. Perhaps some are, but most aren't," Jacob explained while he struggled to get his pants back on over his wet long johns.

Finally, she placed her dress back on and drew her heavy hair up and firmly clipped it back into place then grabbed her waistcoat. She held it in front of her.

Jacob reached out his hand to her. She paused then took it and he led them back under the large oak, her wet underclothes feeling cold and foreign to her skin. He put his arm around her and she leaned into him. "I'm sorry, Jess."

She barely heard his apology over her own feelings of inadequacy. She closed her eyes and noticed that her body was unusually calm. She decided to embrace the pleasure of it hoping it would ease her disturbed mind. She stared out onto the water.

"Where are you, Jess?" She heard him whisper. She felt his warm breath through her hair, touching her head. She pushed aside her embarrassment.

With determination in her voice she asked, "Will you tell me more? Will you tell me everything?"

Jessica hung on his every word, stopping him now and then

to make sure he wasn't just making some of it up to tease her and he assured her it was all true. He wrapped up the lesson in a professorial voice saying, "So in conclusion, my dear, whenever a man and a woman copulate it could result in a child. The End."

Jessica was a bit dumbfounded and couldn't respond right away to his glibness. She never knew exactly how a child was conceived and the truth seemed more impossible than any of her own imaginings. Then she wondered, did her mother know all this?

They made love again that afternoon and the sweetness of it gave Jessica a sense of belonging to him in a way she had never experienced with any other person. She embraced this blooming of her womanhood; it belonged to her and no one could take away.

When the daylight began to change, Jessica knew that time would not stand still. She had to return to her life, and where this afternoon would lead her and Jacob, remained a mystery.

Chapter Six

Jessica tried to pass the kitchen without her mother noticing her. She was tired and her head felt fuzzy. She wanted to go to her room and sleep for a week. Her mother met her at the bottom of the staircase. "Where have you been? What happened? Are you not well?" Her mother came forward to inspect her closer.

"Yes. I'm . . . I'm just tired," Jessica replied, pulling away.

"Have you been swimming, instead of your lesson? Was that Jacob in that old rig? And since when does your cousin kiss the back of our hand? What game is this?" her mother pressed.

"Mr. Cromwell wasn't there." She began making her way up each step. "He had a substitute who wasn't familiar with the lesson, then Jacob got off work early, so we went over to the pond, I mean the canal, for a quick swim." She winced, chiding herself for bringing up the pond, almost divulging their secret hideaway.

"And do tell, what did you swim in?" her mother folded her arms over her ample bosom.

Jessica looked down at her dry dress. "I didn't want to get my dress wet or wrinkled," she said, keeping her head lowered.

"And your corset?" Her mother's hands were now on her hips. "Oh, never mind. You are too old to be swimming in your undergarments around your cousin! My goodness, why you insist in doing such activities is beyond me! What if someone had seen you? Next time ask Sarah or one of the other girls to go swimming with you, and wear the proper dress!"

"Yes, Mother. It's just that he invited me, and it was so hot out and Sarah wasn't around and I didn't think you'd want me to go alone," she replied, her excuses ringing in her ears.

"I don't care. As a young lady, you should know that your actions were inappropriate. These types of things have consequences."

"Consequences?"

"Never mind!"

"Yes, Mother, I'm sorry. I think I'll just go up to bed now. Would you save me some supper, please?"

"Oh, I should say not," said her mother in a firm voice. "Take a short rest my dear, then fix yourself up fine. Mr. Moore is coming to dine with us!"

Oh no. She had forgotten about tonight. "Can you please say I'm not well?" she pleaded from the stair landing, a safe distance from further appraisal. "I do feel as if I'm catching a cold." She only had to look at her mother's expression to know she had lost the battle. "Yes, mother." She dragged her feet up the rest of the way.

In her room, Jessica changed into fresh cotton undergarments. She noticed a stain of reddish pink on her underpant. It wasn't her time of month. Did their lovemaking damage her? Then she recalled with great relief the virgin's show of blood after the Duke, *or was it the Emperor?* had deflowered her. She had read it in a scandalous novel borrowed from her friend Josephine last winter. She decided she would have to take care of this without Winnie's notice. She placed the garment under her bed, and then opened the window wider to release the stifling heat. At last she fell onto her bed and into a deep sleep.

A knock on the bedroom door woke her. The light had changed in the room and the breeze from the open window felt fresh on her face. The heady smell of lilies and dried hay wafted in. The nap had refreshed her and she was ravenously hungry and thirsty.

"Jessica, are you awake?" her mother asked softly as she entered the room. "Oh, I see that you are. Here, I brought you a nice glass of iced tea." Her mother handed her a tall, cold glass; it was just what she craved.

"Thank you." She gulped it down. After coming up for air she asked, "Do I really have to meet Mr. Moore tonight?"

Without hesitation, the answer was a firm, "Yes."

Jessica fell back onto her bed, holding the glass straight up so as to not spill the tea.

"Get up now, that's enough. Mr. Moore will be here by seven. Be ready and downstairs by quarter of." Bethany rushed from the room. "Oh my, did Winnie remember the rosemary?" Her words trailed behind her.

Jessica rose and drank what remained in the glass. She sat on the soft cushion in her bay window where the early evening air floated in, bringing with it the sweetness of her afternoon. She brought her knees up to her chest, closed her eyes and relived the moments with Jacob. Soon her lovely remembrance was replaced by her fear. *What if they were found out?* The scandal this would bring about made her stomach turn into a knot almost bringing up the tea. Perhaps meeting Mr. Moore might be a good distraction.

Like a thud it came to her that her father suggested him as her suitor. She straightened her legs and sweep them to the side. With a great sigh she decided she would make a minimal effort to look appealing tonight. She was curious why Mr. Moore would come all this way to Hartford when there were so many fascinating cities to be explored. It couldn't possibly be to find a wife.

She entered the bathing room attached to her bedroom. A white tub with brass feet sat on a white tile floor. Ornately framed portraits of dogs and landscapes hung on every wall. The water closet was separate and a small sink sat on a pedestal near the tub. The high window let in the right amount of light without exposing the room. In the winter an embroidered rug gave the warmth to the cold tile, but today Jessica let the coolness of the floor relieve the heat Jacob had ignited. She filled the tub the five inches her mother had allowed with tepid water. After bathing, she put on a light evening frock. The pale yellow silk with gold satin vertical panels tied with a matching sash fit snuggly to her corseted undergarments while the high-neck lace bodice modestly covered her chest. She brushed her hair, and waited for Winnie to come up and style it. Jessica's mother popped in to remind her that Winnie had too much to do and Miss Hargrove, the friseur, would be around shortly.

After Miss Hargrove had arranged every curl with precision, leaving some to fall over the shoulder, Jessica inserted a pin to the side of her head. The bright yellow butterfly hairpin was one of the gifts her father had brought back for her from his trip.

"Thank you, Miss Hargrove, I can manage it from here." When Miss Hargrove was completely out of sight, she leaned in close to the decorative brass rimmed mirror over her dressing table and tugged on the curls around her face; Miss Hargrove always twisted them too tight. She smoothed out any remaining wisps of hair with a dot of scented pomade. The smell of the lavender calmed her. Then finding the little pot of lip stain she had received from Sarah, she dabbed it on as they had practiced several times, judging each other's lips. *"It can't look too obvious,"* Jessica heard Sarah saying. She gave herself a once over and proclaimed, "Done!"

Chapter Seven

Frederick's voyage from Liverpool, first by ship to New York, then by train to Hartford, was uneventful. Except for the occasional dinner with Thomas, he kept to himself. He and his father had one thing in common: they both hated taking the steamship to the States. Frederick had been to New York City with his father twice before. He was twelve the first time and had become wretchedly seasick, confined to his cabin for the entire journey. The second time he was twenty-one and the seasickness wasn't nearly as bad, but he still felt unwell. This time he felt no nausea, yet his head ached dully. He vowed to never take this voyage again. If his plans went as he hoped, he would be able to keep his vow. This first step had to be handled with care — a marriage to an American girl. Then the move to San Francisco. He believed he would be successful in convincing the wealthy to invest through him.

Frederick reveled in the idea of leaving his parents and his onerous life in Liverpool. Although the bustling city offered more than enough to entertain him and his father had provided great opportunities as Charles's own father had done for him, it wasn't enough. His father also kept a close eye on his every move, which Frederick had come to resent. When he had grown bored with being a solicitor for the shipping companies, he became interested in the financial part of the business. Frederick soon learned how to manipulate the books to allow a cash flow to him without anyone's knowledge. It calmed his wanderlust for a time until that too became routine. Even his longtime romantic interest, Molly Ambers, no longer satisfied him. America had always called to his sense of adventure, and he was eager to be free to exercise his own will.

The First National Bank of San Francisco had responded favorably to his request for employment in their investment department. He felt that luck and good fortune were with him and Thomas Messing's invitation solidified his feelings.

On his arrival in Hartford, Frederick settled into a suite of rooms at Victoria House. The upscale hotel on Main Street was modest by his standards, but comfortable enough. It would be his temporary home until the money he'd wired to himself arrived.

Yes, Messing and Stanford will be a brilliant starting point, he thought as he prepared to meet the rest of Thomas's family. Frederick had grown weary of the man's blatant referrals to his unattached daughter. He wasn't ruling anything out to further his plan, but wanted to be the judge of her first.

As he was about to leave for the Messing estate, he absently brushed by a stack of books near his dressing table knocking one to the floor. It fell open, exposing a small cream-colored envelope. Frederick picked it up. His name and the date of his departure were on the front. The handwriting belonged to Molly. The fact that she'd likely bribed one of the household staff to insert it into his private book collection irritated him. He tore it open to find a brief note inside.

My Dearest Frederick,

I miss you already. I wait impatiently for your return. What good this will be for you and our future! Think of me, as I will be thinking of you always. Your devoted, Molly

He ripped the paper in two and threw it into the fireplace. He had no time for her now.

Yet, if Thomas's daughter were completely without merit, he

would confess he'd been previously engaged to a young woman back in England all along.

The inevitable loomed over him this evening. His stomach ached at the prospects of having to marry someone below his standards. He rallied his spirits with the thought of fulfilling his dreams.

Chapter Eight

The smell of roast beef pulled Jessica into the kitchen. Her brother was already there and Winnie had to work around the siblings as they ate leftover ends of bread and speculated what this Mr. Moore might be like. Jessica leaned against the counter near the sink under the open window. The evening breeze tapped the lust for Jacob in her and she went for a glass of cold tea.

"Suppose we can't understand a word he says? He could be a short, fat, stuffy sort of man. No, father said he was tall, intelligent and well mannered," she speculated.

"Well, no matter," Will replied. "Your future husband will be impressed by you. You look very grown up tonight."

Jessica felt exposed by his insinuation. She'd been pleased to learn that Will would join the family for dinner. His good humor eased her tension. Now she felt self-conscious. *Could a man tell if a woman had been deflowered?* She cringed and swallowed hard on a crust of bread, leaving the kitchen, longing for the sanctum of her window seat and sketchpad.

Will joined her and mother in the large parlor where most guests were greeted, but her father remained in his study, hiding from the preparations. Though an intimate dinner, Jessica noticed her mother had taken the extra effort to impress Mr. Moore. The table was set with their finest china and cutlery and Winnie wore a formal uniform, matching those worn by the hired servants. Most of these dinner parties were so staid. She took a deep breath and looked over her dress. It would be over soon and she could return to her life.

As the time grew nearer to Mr. Moore's arrival, her nerves teased her. The room felt smaller this evening. She stood by the windows behind the grand piano and tinkered with the keys. The open bay of windows gave little relief, the heavy cream drapes barely moving.

"Sit down, Jessica," her mother said. "You may play after dinner. I think that would make a good impression. A piece from Bach, or perhaps something from Mozart?"

"I prefer Strauss," Jessica said flatly. She wanted to play Stephen Foster's "*I Dream of Jeannie with the Light Brown Hair*", but that was a song she only dared when she was alone. She sat down beside her mother on the walnut framed Chesterfield near the massive white stone fireplace and tried not to fidget with the silk bow at her waist. The deep blue fabric she sat upon clashed with her yellow dress. She stood again by the piano, not touching the keys.

Will looked into the large gold-framed mirror hanging over the fireplace mantle. Jessica saw how casually he brushed back his hair with his hand. If only it was so easy for her. He laughed sharply, as if reading her mind.

"What is it, William?" Bethany asked her son.

He faced his mother. "We look as if we're waiting to meet the King of England."

Before any of them could speak, the doorbell chimed. Her mother hurried out of the room and she heard her father's voice. "Calm yourself, Beth," he said sternly. Then they were both in the parlor. Jessica smoothed her bodice, fluffed the layers of fabric on the back of her skirt and straightened the gold panels in front. She stood by Will. Her mother and father sat by the window in matching maroon damask-covered chairs. They stared at the entrance.

"I feel like a prize cow ready to be judged," she whispered to her brother.

"Well, Bessie. Get ready for the show," he replied.

Jessica made a face and they both laughed quietly. She moved to the entrance of the room to hear what she could from the foyer. It was difficult to see anything from where she stood and she stretched her body to get a better view. She caught a glimpse of one of the servants with his coat and hat. Were those a pair of white gloves she held?

"Jessica! Stand back!" her mother hissed.

The next voice was Winnie's, presenting their guest.

"Mr. Moore, we are so pleased you could join us tonight," her mother announced floating across the room her hand extended.

"Thank you so much for the kind invitation, Madame." His accent had a certain charm. He bent down and kissed her hand. Jessica looked at her brother for his reaction, she hoped he wouldn't give her a fit of giggles. He was staring at his shoes, his face ashen. "Will?" she asked under her breath, but received only a quick shake of his head.

Her attentions went to their company. She was stunned to see a young, handsome man before her. She knew Mr. Moore was nearly ten years her senior. His cutaway coat revealed a slender figure and his brown curly hair complemented his hazel eyes. He was attractive. Their eyes met and he lingered until she looked away. Her heart pulsated unnaturally.

"Frederick," Thomas began, "May I present my son, William, and my daughter, Jessica."

They exchanged polite greetings. A servant entered the room with a silver tray of canapés and the conversation began. Jessica listened, nibbling on a triangle of bread topped with black caviar. She disliked the fishy taste and smell, but she ate it with dignity, washing it down with several sips of champagne. As the evening progressed, she ignored Frederick's glances, though it took some restraint. She was drawn to his manner and expression.

The men discussed the politics of the ongoing post-war agenda in Washington and the laws now being strictly instated in the West to control the Indian population. They talked about the financial problems facing the country, and even covered the unlawful trade of gun-running, her father ranting about the "filthy business." She couldn't care less about any of it, though she noticed her brother become flush and agitated when asked by Mr. Moore if he had heard about "the filthy business." Her brother had his own opinions on most everything, yet he simply shook his head.

Frederick's attention during dinner made Jessica uneasy. She hoped her politeness would not be construed as an invitation. He was far more than she had expected. His intelligent views and insights held her interest. He was a grown man and he seemed to regard her as a grown woman. She liked the feeling and let it linger in her head, but only for a moment. Soon her mother was talking nonstop about her daughter's standing in society, making Jessica feel as if she were on display. To her great relief, her mother changed the subject. "How is your Yorkshire pudding, Mr. Moore?"

Jessica sat in one of the high back chairs in the smaller parlor. "Well, I'm happy that's over." She sighed. "And I'm even more pleased that mother didn't make me play for him." Her brother had already made his way to the green settee. His legs stretched out in front of him.

"What do you think of your future husband, Jess?" he asked teasingly.

"Oh! What can Father be thinking?" she exclaimed. "What do *you* think of him, Will?"

"I like him," he said.

"Mother seemed to like him," she commented mischievously.

"Good God, that wasn't obvious," Will replied. They laughed at their secret. Will rose from his seat with a moan. "I'm meeting Jake in town tonight, so I'll leave you to dream about your new beau." He kissed the top of her head.

"You're seeing Jacob?" she asked quietly.

"Yes, why?"

"At the Palace?"

"Jessica," Will said her name sternly. "That's not a name to cross your lips ever again. Do you understand?"

"Yes," she answered. "Father will be furious if he finds out."

"And let him find out," Will mumbled. "Goodnight, Sister."

She slumped back into the chair, hurt and betrayed. She rallied at the thought that Jacob was going there to protect Will. Then she cursed her lack of freedom and envied her brother and cousin. It had become sadly apparent to her that she might never achieve the sense of ownership of the world they so casually took for granted.

She knew her longings for freedom must remain a secret in her heart. Tired and discouraged, she decided her only relief was bed. She dragged her body upstairs.

Jacob ordered another drink while he waited for Will. He couldn't get the afternoon out of his head. What he and Jessica had done changed their relationship forever and the implications of it weighed heavily on him. His love for her was making him careless; he had to go away, and soon.

Will appeared, a drink in his hand. "Sorry I'm late." They clicked glasses as he sat down. "We had the famous Frederick Moore over for dinner. What a performance my parents put on."

"Oh? And how was Mr. Moore? My father says he's a model gentleman." Jacob could feel the effects of the alcohol.

"He's not a bad fellow, actually. I've seen him in here a few times, and I know he saw me, but he gave no sign of it tonight. Thank God," Will said.

Jacob studied his glass. "I think you both had a stake in that one, my friend; after all, he's here to make a good impression."

"What have *you* got against him?" Will asked.

"Huh? Uh nothing." He turned away, looking mindlessly around the room.

"Is it Jessica?" Will inquired.

"What?" Jacob returned to stare blankly, denying the turmoil between his heart and mind. The cousins had a way of reading each other like an open book. He was counting on the liquor to dull his anxiousness.

"I just think it's time we let her go. Maybe Frederick would make her a good husband," Will explained.

"Oh ..." Jacob's heart sped up and he calmed himself by draining his glass. He set in down with a thud. He didn't want to think about what he and Jessica had done, especially not while seated across from her brother. Yet, the afternoon played over and over in his head, sending heat to his belly.

"So, what's the plan for tomorrow?" Will asked.

Jacob motioned to the bartender for a refill. He could feel the world close in around him. The bartender delivered his drink and he made quick work of emptying the glass.

"Hey, Jake, take it easy with the booze. We have a big day ahead of us. What the hell is up with you anyway? I haven't seen you drink like this, since I don't know when."

"Nothing, I'm just tired." His words were slurred and he avoided making eye contact with his cousin. "So, cuz," he said, speaking louder than necessary. "We gotta take this other route and get up pretty early so that bastard, Big Larry, doesn't shoot us for showing up late." Jacob felt his eyelids close then a hissing sound in his face. It was Will shushing him and at the same time grabbing his arm and shaking him. "All right, all right, I'll be quiet! Leggo of me." He pulled away. "Merle found out the other trail was being worked on for a road. Sons-a-bitches, why don't they just gravel the whole goddamn country and —"

"Jake," Will interrupted. "Let's get you home."

Jacob confirmed with a nod, his head falling forward. He raised it back up slowly and asked, "So, is this Frederick fella good looking?"

Will paused. "I guess, yeah, he's pretty good looking ... why are *you* interested in him?"

Jacob laughed loudly and reached for his glass again gesturing for a refill. Will stopped him, and took it out of his hands. "You've had enough."

"I can have whatever, how much I want." He stood but lost his balance, sitting down hard. He grimaced then turned to his cousin. "William, I think it's time we move on."

"Oh, is that so?" Will deigned, raising an eyebrow.

"Yep." Jacob leaned forward and stared into nothing. "I can't stay here any longer."

"I agree. I'll take you home." He began to rise.

"No! I mean I have to leave this damn city!" Jacob shouted, again attempting to stand.

Will glanced around at the other men taking notice of Jacob's behavior. "We can talk tomorrow, Jake. Let's go."

Chapter Nine

As Jacob finessed the leather strap around another polished stirrup he caught a glimpse of Merle Kingston walking into the back shop of the Tack and Saddle. He kept his anger in check while Merle talked to Hank about ordering a special bridle for one of his new saddles. The day had been long, and sweat was running down Jacob's face. He thought briefly of the pond and Jessica. Playful and … he dismissed the trail of passion that followed.

Taking his handkerchief from his back pocket, Jacob wiped his brow, thinking about the clean office his father sat in. A suit and tie, a fan to cool him, surrounded by stacks of papers and briefs. He knew his life would not be as predictable as his father's. His yearning to see what the country held could not be eased by leather chairs and ceiling fans. He glanced over his shoulder at the heavy man from Atlanta. He was a wealthy Southerner who didn't spare any cost for his horses and the tacking of them. Hank's storefront inventory did not include brass ornate spurs and saddle horns. Merle said he knew a man who made such finery and suggested Hank use his services.

Merle Kingston did not trust the mail service, so his orders were picked up personally by an employee of Hank's. Jacob had been chosen to carry out the task.

The man Merle had suggested was an artisan by the name of Lawrence Carson — Big Larry — whose foundry was on the border of New York and Connecticut. He was larger than most men and as mean as a teased grizzly. Jacob was given another task but without Hank's knowledge; he was to deliver two rifles and six pistols to Big Larry. Although hesitant at first, Jacob was soon running guns and ammo, using the foundry as a front. Sometimes it was cash only, other times it was guns with cash. Since he began back in March, he had figured out what routes to take to stay clear of suspicion. With heavier loads he opted for an open carriage and a rifle over his lap at all times. When Will agreed to join him he was able to double the amount of inventory and increase the profits. Jacob liked having Will by his side; both cousins enjoyed the tease of adventure. However, their latest run didn't go as planned.

Jacob sensed Merle approaching. He completed his task and began to put away his tools. He glanced over his shoulder; Hank was at another employee's workbench. The hum of activity would shield conversation.

"How's it going, Jake?" Merle's jovial attitude added fuel to Jacob's anger. "You're doing a fine job retrieving the ornamentations for my saddles."

Jacob answered flatly, "Yes, Sir."

Before he knew it, Merle was in his ear. He smelled of sweat, peppermint and booze. "What the hell happened out there? My people tell me you were nearly robbed. You and your cousin better watch your backs. This is not some fuckin' game!" His voice was low and intimidating, but Jacob wasn't backing down. He jerked away and began his own interrogations.

"Yeah, what the hell *did* happen, Merle?" he asked through tightened lips. "I thought you told me no one knew about that trail. Someone must have tipped them off. What kind of game are *you* playing?"

"What are you implying, boy?" Merle snapped.

"First, don't call me boy, and second, those men knew exactly what they were looking for," Jacob replied, the muscles working in his jaw.

After a few tense moments, Merle pulled away and gave out a hearty laugh, slapping Jacob on the back. "Good work, Jake! You passed my test. Sonny and Clyde are employees of mine. I sent them after you boys to see how you'd do when faced with a little trouble." Merle laughed again, his large belly shaking. "Didn't expect you two would be that, well, assertive, boy. I mean Jake. Sonny is still nursing that gunshot grazing on his arm. Your cousin's fast on the trigger. And my man Clyde can't get over the shakes. They're passed their prime, but I thought I'd give them a bit of an adventure. You know what I mean?"

It took Jacob a minute to take all this in. He stared at Merle, then threw down his tools and stormed out of the shop.

"Jake, Jake, I had to see if you boys were trustworthy, if you could handle the pressure," Merle wheedled. "Come on now, we're still friends!"

Jacob had to walk off his anger. His wounded pride convinced him of what he had been thinking for a while; he and Will could make better of this gun-running game. He'd heard rumors of Indians in the Indian Territory needing weapons to defend their assigned government land from homesteaders, as well as the homesteaders who wanted to protect themselves from the Indians. He was under no illusion they could manage it alone. They'd have to seek out help. Jacob knew he was getting deeper into a way of life that could send him to an early grave, but Merle and the city of Hartford were closing in on him.

He mounted his horse and slapped the horn in anger. *Ornamentations, my ass!*

He rode down the side street then headed to Mary's Pond outside of town, past a wooded area, down a narrow, bumpy path. He could smell the water, he closed his eyes and shook his head. She was with him again. He sat with the large oak tree at his back, contemplating his next move. He was still angry with Merle, but mostly he thought of Jessica. He couldn't free his mind of her. His guilt fought with his love and desire. Jacob knew that the easiest way to solve his problem was to leave Hartford and his feelings for her well behind. He had fallen in love with his own cousin, had taken away her virginity. He felt foul. After such a dip into hell he was ready to throw himself into a life beyond the borders of society.

Chapter Ten

Jessica sat on the settee in the small parlor room waiting for Frederick Moore's arrival, nerves on edge. Her mother had insisted on a low fire to dry out the room from the oppressive August humidity. She also had one set in the dining hall, and in the kitchen. Jessica fanned herself as she considered the night ahead. She would be polite and try not disrupt the family's plans, while making it perfectly clear to Mr. Moore that she was not interested in him. She longed for the evening to be over, with the Englishman in his place.

She waited patiently, distracting herself with thoughts of Jacob. In spite of the risks, they continued to meet at their usual place by the pond, where she felt as if they were the only two human beings on earth. They satisfied their longing with touching as much of the other's skin as they dared. Jacob would not allow them to go any further and she knew it was to protect her. Yet, his passion for her came through and it was all she needed to confirm their feelings for one another were real. Yet when Jacob talked of leaving, she felt the vulnerability of their tender relationship. She put it out of her head, letting his last kiss replace any doubts.

The minutes felt like hours. She adjusted the strap on her new shoes, which already pinched her feet. She inspected the lace and satin around the square neckline of her bodice. The deep red dress with strips of cream lace running down the skirt was her favorite. It should have been worn for a more important occasion, but her mother insisted that this was the dress to wear tonight, with a small crinoline, not just a bustle. "It will show off your figure," she advised.

Jessica didn't care for the stiffly structured undergarment. Her corset was enough. The latest fashions had neither, but her mother would hear nothing of it. Jessica much preferred the softer bustle when sitting for long periods of time. She stood and smoothed the back of her dress and heard her mother rushing down the stairs.

"Jessica! Jessica!"

"I'm in here, Mother, no need to shout." The sharp chime from the front door set her heart racing.

Her mother's skirts swished as she turned to stand by her daughter while Winnie answered the door. "Oh, I only wish your Father were here!"

"He said he would meet us at the restaurant, Mother. Please calm down."

"Calm down? I think you are too calm!" her mother replied. "Yes, yes, well, let me take a look at you." Bethany gave her daughter a once over, then stood as rigid as a solider.

Jessica held her breath, closed her eyes and practiced again, in her head, how she would avoid showing any interest in Frederick while entertaining his every word. Her insides twisted at the thought of having to go through a long, dreadful evening of pretense. She thought of the day she and Jacob would be together in front of her family and the world.

"Good evening, Mr. Moore," Jessica began formally.

"Good evening, Miss Messing," he replied, his English accent enhancing the formal air between them. "It's a pleasure to see you again."

"Don't you look very handsome tonight," Bethany remarked.

"As do you, Madame," Frederick said.

"Oh, why thank you, Frederick."

Jessica cringed at the note of girlishness in her mother's voice.

Yet, her mother was right; he did look very handsome. She tried to rekindle thoughts of Jacob but was interrupted by Mr. Moore's deep, melodic voice. "And may I also say that you are looking especially lovely tonight, Miss Messing." He dipped his head.

An unwanted blush warmed her cheeks. "Thank you. You may call me Jessica."

Frederick nodded politely. "I have a carriage and driver waiting for us," he said, gesturing for the ladies to go before him.

He had indeed arrived in one of the finest hackneys in town. Bethany gleefully exited the house, while Jessica walked by him without a glance.

The restaurant her father had chosen was a favorite place for engagements, weddings, and anniversaries. Now they could add *arranging marriages* to the list, Jessica thought ruefully. Thomas was waiting at their round white-clothed table, which was lit only by candles in the center and a gaslight sconce on the wall. Jessica felt uneasy at the intimacy of the space.

"My dear," Thomas said, greeting his wife with a kiss on her cheek, then turned to his daughter. "Jessica, my girl, you are looking well tonight. Please forgive my meeting you here. A difficult case had me stuck at my desk. I had to rearrange everything my clerk had …" Thomas turned to Frederick. "Thank you for delivering our beautiful dinner companions."

Jessica was embarrassed by her father's suggestion that she was somehow already attached to Frederick. It made her acutely regret agreeing to this evening. *Maybe, I'll be sick and we'll have to leave.* She held steady, hoping the time would pass quickly. Frederick waved on the maître d'. She watched with wide eyes as he offered her a chair. She sat and he gently helped her push in closer to the table. "Thank you," she said quietly.

His hand swept lightly over her shoulder and brushed her

cheek, sending a tingle up her spine. Jessica sat up straighter. Her parents didn't seem to notice and Frederick was now in his own seat. She focused on the menu, ordering the most delectable items. She would indulge as much as her corseted waist would allow.

As the evening wore on, Jessica was drawn to Frederick's maturity and confidence. The way he included her in the conversation made her feel like an adult, something she rarely experienced with her own family. She had to admit it satisfied her. Though with every bite of food, she pushed down any further attraction to him.

"I would love to see your paintings," he said "Your father tells me you're quite good."

With little enthusiasm Jessica answered, "If you stop by Cromwell Gallery on Benton, you'll see a small painting of mine in the window. Mr. Cromwell, the owner and my employer, said it is better than average. He displays it to encourage other novice artists to take his classes. It isn't one of my best works. I'd be glad to show you my recent landscapes." She returned her attention to the filet mignon, slicing it into small pieces.

"You're *employed*?" Frederick turned to Thomas. The pause in the conversation was palpably awkward.

"It's only temporary," her mother said. "The gallery is nothing more than a hobby."

Jessica placed her utensils to the sides of her plate. "Yes I do work, Mr. Moore. My art is my work and spending time at the gallery is inspiring." That would do it. He would be turned off her for sure.

"Well, I would enjoy seeing your work," he answered. His large hazel eyes lingered on her and she became uncomfortably self-conscious. *What were his intentions? Was a relationship already decided?* A feeling of dread entered her body. She brought her hand up to her lower neck and held herself in check as she nodded to him, and then to her parents.

Frederick's hired carriage awaited them at the restaurant. The ride back to the Messing's home was relatively quiet except for a comment on the excellent meal and the weather. The horses clattering on the graveled drive came to a stop in front of the large veranda. The men stepped down and helped the woman exit the carriage. Before Frederick bid them all good evening he asked Jessica's parents if he may have the honor of accompanying their daughter to the opera or theater in the near future. They cheerfully gave their approval and their eagerness agitated her. She stepped onto the first landing, needing air. She felt as if she were a little girl with no power in her life whatsoever. She imagined tearing the shoes off her hurting feet and throwing them at her parents, with one ricocheting and hitting Frederick in the head!

To her surprise, Frederick looked up. With soft eyes and a clear voice, he said, "Of course, if that is to your liking, Miss Messing."

If not for his genuine consideration of her own opinion, she was ready to have this evening come to an end, with no more talk of Frederick courting her. Instead she found herself saying, "Yes, that would be fine, Mr. Moore."

"Very well, then I shall call on you soon. Good night, *Jessica.*"

"Good night," she answered with a slight dip of her head, which she immediately regretted.

She went directly up to her room, queasy from the food. Or maybe it was something else. She changed into her nightclothes and got into bed. Tomorrow she would write a note to Sarah, telling her about Mr. Moore. It would amuse her friend to learn she'd been treated like an adult, even by her parents. She enjoyed feeling as if she were on equal ground with Frederick, despite their age difference. She was caught between two worlds and she was anxious to cross the threshold into the future one. As she fluffed her pillow and tried to get comfortable, she heard her parents enter the house.

"That went well," Thomas exclaimed. "But we must encourage her to be even more gracious next time. Jessica? Well, where is she? Jessica!" Her father called up the stairs.

She pressed her pillow around her ears, then sat up and gave out a great belch. Relieved, she lay back down, hoping to escape into sleep. Her parents crossed the threshold of her bedroom door and she heard her mother say, "You know this is her first experience of this nature, so we must tread lightly."

Jessica felt a daughter's guilt. Her mother knew nothing of her unspeakable behavior. Tears welled in her eyes as she mourned her lost childhood. She ached to call her mother "Mommy", to sit on her warm lap while she hummed a lullaby as she had so long ago. Her desire to separate from her parents left a great void in her heart. She wiped the tears from face. Somehow the void would be filled. Somehow she would find her way.

Chapter Eleven

Frederick arrived at the hotel he had made his temporary home. The Victoria House was growing on him. His cozy rooms of upholstered chairs and thick rugs, the brick fireplace in the parlor and one in his bedroom welcomed him back each time, promising warmth once the season changed. Knowing these rooms would not be his residence forever added to their appeal.

"Good evening, sir," the desk clerk said. "We started a fire in the hearth. Your bed has been turned down and the bar has been refreshed. Would tea or coffee suit you this evening?"

"Nothing, thank you," Frederick replied. He headed for the comfort of his rooms.

"Oh, sir." The clerk stopped him. "This came for you this afternoon. I meant to deliver it to you earlier, but it got buried under some of my papers."

"Very well," Frederick said impatiently, taking the small letter from the man's hand. Molly's handwriting. His head began to pulse painfully. Upon entering his suite, he placed the letter on the polished end table in the sitting area. After fixing himself a nightcap, he picked up the letter and relaxed into one of the winged-back chairs that sat in front of the fireplace. He watched the flickering flame and wondered what possessed the maid to start it; the August heat was stifling. He sniffed his brandy and let out a sigh, letting his mind lift from all worry. His thoughts drifted to his evening.

He knew he would have to pursue Jessica or move on to someone else. She was a little headstrong, but generally obedient. He liked her rebellious side. She was a clean slate. He could teach her a thing or two. Her beauty aroused him. He noticed her reaction to his touch at the restaurant and imagined how smooth her naked body would feel.

He turned the letter over in his hand as he drifted further into his fantasy. It slipped and the corner of the envelope hit his foot. Molly was in the room demanding his attention. He cursed and tamped down the fire. He then settled himself to open the letter. She'd sealed it with red-stained lips and a brief scent of perfume came from its contents. "You harlot," he whispered. She knew exactly what he liked. It took him back to their intimacy, stirring his feelings for her. Remembering how freely she gave herself to him tested his resolve. Her love and devotion were his for the taking. He had tried to get her out of his mind and out of his heart. It was easier with her so far away, but as he looked at her handwriting and smelled her scent, he was pained with regret and longing. He wanted to toss the letter into the dying flames. Instead, he took a good swig of his drink and read her words.

My Dearest Love,

Have you abandoned me?

Frederick went to the next page to read the final line.

Please, let me hear word from you, or I shall imagine the worse. My heart is in your hands. Yours Always, Molly.

The in-between contained the pouring out of her love and faith, the celebration she was planning for his return, and her sincere hope that his feelings for her remained true. He dropped it to the floor.

"Bloody hell!" he cursed.

He knew what he had to do.

It took little time for him to pen the note. As much as it was insufficient for their years together he could not suffer her pain, or allow her to intrude any further into his future. He decided to send it to his mother and have her present it to Molly with the thought that she would be able to soften the blow. His purpose was twofold: Molly would have a shoulder to cry on and his mother would feel needed by her son.

He left the letter to Molly unsealed for Lillian to read. As he looked at it, he knew he was solidifying another piece of his life. He pushed away his feelings, and returned to his thoughts of Miss Jessica Messing.

Chapter Twelve

Liverpool, England, Early September 1885

Molly Ambers stood at the door of the Moore mansion. She tugged the hem of her grey-striped waistcoat and smoothed the creases in her matching skirt. Her long red curls were drawn up and secured by a large pheasant-shaped pin studded with tiny diamonds. She wore one of her small afternoon hats and short, cream-colored day gloves. The weather had turned cooler in the waning summer and a slight chill ran through her, mixed with nerves. She was confident she had made herself presentable for her visit with the mother of her future husband. She had little reason to worry, yet a sense of foreboding haunted her.

The invitation from Lillian Moore stated there was news from Frederick. At first Molly wondered why he had sent the correspondence through his mother, and then she concluded that it was good news for them to share together. Her heart swelled with love at his thoughtful gesture. She relaxed her shoulders as Jason opened the door.

Molly knew exactly where to go, but she dutifully followed the butler to the small drawing room. She swept through the expansive entry hall, past the large potted palms and gilded mirrors. The thick luxurious rug beneath her feet gave her a heady pleasure; someday she and Frederick would be master and mistress of this most beautiful manor. What a pair they would make. She had been told many times that she possessed all the grace and manners of royalty; her breeding was upper class if not royal. She would finally be the lady of her own estate, presiding over grand parties and lavish meals. She would be kind and gracious, not like her mother, who snapped at the servants over the smallest mistakes.

As she entered the room, Frederick's mother came away from the expanse of windows. The skirt of her light blue dress swept gracefully across the floor. "Hello, Miss Ambers," Lillian Moore said, extending her hand to the young woman.

Molly examined her face, but Mrs. Moore gave no sign this was anything other than a friendly visit over tea, to share in the correspondence from the man they both loved. A puffy white cloud drifted over the sun and the room's light dimmed. Molly's emotions moved in that direction, as well.

"Hello, Mrs. Moore. Thank you for your invitation." She greeted the tall, slender matriarch. Lillian was much younger than her husband, Charles. She could almost pass as Frederick's older sister. Molly removed her gloves from her perspiring hands.

"I thought it would be nice to have tea here today," Mrs. Moore began. "Please sit down. How was the ride over? I hope the weather didn't give you any trouble."

"No, it was pleasant, thank you," Molly answered.

Molly watched patiently as Lillian turned to the small cart next to her. It held delicate china cups and decorative saucers, along with a hand-painted porcelain teapot and sweet biscuits on a tray. She poured the hot steeped liquid into a cup and Molly caught a whiff of the Earl Grey. It brought her back to the many times her and Frederick sat in one of the parlors of her parent's estate and shared tea and conversation. Lillian placed the cup on one of the saucers with a biscuit to the side and handed it to her guest. Molly received the pretty cup, which rattled in the saucer, revealing her nerves. She was relieved that Lillian poured a cup for herself, seemingly unaware of her anxiety. She waited for the ritual to find its end. Finally, she was able to ask, "Did you say you had news from your son, Mrs. Moore?"

"Yes," Lillian answered. She paused before taking a small note from her skirt pocket and extending it to Molly. Molly took the envelope from Lillian and was just about to open it when Lillian placed a hand over hers.

"Dear, it's … not what you might expect," she said gently. "You may want to read it in private."

Molly looked at Lillian's hand preventing her from indulging in his words. She slid her hand away while grasping the note. "Oh, of course." Reluctantly she slipped it into her dress pocket, where it seemed to whisper to her. Knowing that his mother had read the contents rattled her further. Her only thought now was to drink the tea, eat the biscuit, and politely leave so she could be alone with the sentiments of her beloved. Lillian took a sip of tea then placed the cup and saucer on the small table between them.

"Molly, I'm afraid I have some upsetting news for you," she began.

"Is he well?" Molly asked. She kept her hand over her pocket to reassure herself that he had written only of his love and devotion.

"Yes, he's fine. But he has decided to stay in America," Lillian said. Then added in a solemn tone, avoiding Molly's eyes. "Permanently."

Molly looked at Lillian in disbelief. "Oh, that can't be," she said, smiling to cover her shock. "He must have been taken by the novelty of a different country and it's just turned his head for a bit. I'm sure he'll be back, if only to claim me. Liverpool is full of our past and present, our future. Why, would he give all that up?" She put her cup down and clasped her hands close to her stomach and took a breath. "I suppose I may have to adjust to living in that country, if that's what he truly desires."

Lillian leaned in. "No Molly, I'm afraid that's not it. He won't be back for you, or for any of our sakes."

"What do you mean? I don't understand." Molly rose and

began to pace in front of the unlit fireplace, wringing her hands in dismay. "We were; we *are* getting married." She stated, losing a battle with her tears. "Have I done something wrong?"

"No, no. Please, dear. Do sit down. Have some tea."

Molly remained standing. "I'll be myself soon, Mrs. Moore. Please forgive my outburst." Her face felt hot and the room began to spin. She sat down and gripped the arm of the chair.

"Of course, you will be yourself," she heard Lillian say.

Molly swallowed as the voice came from a distance.

"And I'm quite sure it will be sooner than you believe. I heard you recently turned twenty-one years of age. Why, you have the world at your feet, my dear," Lillian stated. She softly cleared her throat. "May I ask if there was a promise of marriage between you and my son?"

Molly's thoughts were muddled. He hadn't formally proposed but it was certainly an understanding between them.

"Forgive me, I must go," she said, pressing her palms on her cheeks to stem the flow of tears.

Lillian embraced her, reassuring her that it was all for the best. Molly felt the hollowness of her words as she sped from the house.

Safely in the coach, Molly pulled the note from her pocket with a trembling hand. She examined the front, but it gave no clues of the contents. With trepidation, she opened the letter and began to read:

Dear Molly,

Forgive me for what I am about to write. My circumstances have dramatically changed and I fear I can longer continue our friendship. I have decided to make a life here, and will not be returning. It is my sincerest wish that you find happiness in your own life.

I will forever think fondly of our time together,

Frederick

She turned the paper over, searching for any fragment of Frederick she knew, but found only the cold little note. She shivered with finality of it. A jolt of the carriage took her attention to the window. She stared out as the driver rounded the corner from the circular courtyard and headed for the road, taking her farther and farther away from her once-future home.

"This will not due," she said aloud. "I will have you, Frederick. I will not be treated this way." Breathing heavily, she sat back and began her plan. She would be the mistress of his house no matter where that led her.

Chapter Thirteen

Throughout the summer Jessica accepted many of Frederick's invitations. He took her to the theater, the ballet, on strolls in the manicured park where she often painted the scenery, and several dinners at the restaurant where they had first dined. They were chaperoned by her parents, Mrs. Hargrove, or Winnie. Often they strolled the Messing's two-acre estate unchaperoned. It was her parent's plan and she felt caught in their web. Yet, she enjoyed the freedom from watchful eyes. Whenever she met Jacob, she avoided any talk of Mr. Moore. When he pressed for an explanation on the state of her relationship with the Englishman, she replied, "My parents think they will gain much in society with our association. It's good for the family. Nothing more."

It wasn't until the end of the season when she finally invited Frederick to dine with her family. Jacob and Will had been out of town for nearly a week and they weren't expected back for a few more days. She hoped to keep Jacob and Frederick apart as long as possible, at least until she could sort out her feelings. Jacob's abrupt departure couldn't have come at a more vulnerable time and lately, she had begun thinking of Frederick more often than she cared to. It unnerved her.

This evening, while she and Frederick strolled the sidewalks of Washington Street unchaperoned, the pink and cream waist jacket she wore failed to keep the chill away, but it complemented her ruffled blouse and matching striped skirt so well that she was willing to endure some discomfort. It wouldn't be long before she would have to put it away as the season changed. She knew they made an elegant portrait strolling arm in arm. Jessica took a moment to admire the large maple trees lining the street, sprinkled with orange, yellow and red leaves. Autumn would not be in full bloom for a few more weeks. She loved the fragrance of fall and its hint of winter's approach. Looking around gave her time to construct an invitation that would not encourage Frederick's eagerness; he tried to kiss her on the lips the last time they had returned from dinner after her parents went inside the house.

"Frederick, as you know, my family dines every Sunday at my Aunt June and Uncle Burt's home. Our family would like to have you join us this coming Sunday," she said.

"I look forward to joining the rest of your family for dinner," he replied.

Jessica gave him an approving smile. She felt it was sufficient. The street lamps were being lit and the sun began to fade; she would be home soon.

"Tell me, my dear," Frederick continued. "Does this invitation come from your own desire to have me at your family's dinner?" he asked.

Without looking at him she replied, "We all desire your company."

Frederick stopped in front of her, taking her hands in his. "Jessica, I would like to know where we stand with one another. Are you as drawn to me as I am to you?"

She looked at his strong hands grasping hers. For a moment she felt as if she were being held captive. Why such a thought entered her mind she did not know. Before she could answer, he pulled her away from the lamplight. Jessica glanced around. No one else was on the road. Frederick came closer to her and brushed his lips against her cheek. She felt the warmth from her body rise up from within her jacket. She stepped back with a flush on her face.

"I ... I haven't made up my mind, Frederick," she began. Her body wanted to flee. Instead she smiled and held her pink silk purse in front of her with both hands. "I think you should know that I want to do more with my life than most other women. I want to be an artist. It's not just a pastime. I also want to travel and … all sorts of things." She felt her words catch in her throat. This was the first time she'd spoken of her desires to him.

"I expect only that you stay true to your passions," he interrupted her. "Allow me to be one of them." He looked deeply into her eyes with a most engaging smile. Jessica stepped further away. "You have a very modern attitude, Frederick," she said. "I think, however, that you will expect much more from me, but as a friend, I will surely remind you of your words in the future."

Frederick gave a jovial laugh. "I can see you'll not make this easy for me. Very well then, until Sunday."

They walked in silence until they came to her home. He took her hand and bowed his head. His eyes stared up at her as his lips touched the back of her glove. "Your coyness is fine for now, but I will expect a more mature answer from you in the near future."

She whispered good night and hurried inside. She stopped in the foyer and wiped the back of her hand on her skirt. Her thoughts were confused. The grandiose feeling of being an important lady whenever in his presence withered under his sudden scrutiny.

Frederick accompanied Jessica along with her parents to the Stanford's home that Sunday evening. "Here they are!" June sang. "Welcome, Mr. Moore!"

The ballooning skirt of her aunt's dark violet dress filled the space between her and Frederick. Jessica glanced at Frederick with an apologetic look and he smiled with understanding. She hoped her aunt's exuberance would be short-lived. After a drink, they all preceded to the table where June's hired servants had set a feast.

"Now, Mr. Moore, I will seat you next to my niece where you may converse easily. I'm so pleased you and Jessica are becoming friends," June chirped. "I knew the first time I saw you at the offices, well, I'm just very pleased." June gave a dimpled smile to Jessica.

"I'm very fond of your niece," Frederick replied.

Jessica noticed the wide grin on her father's face. She sat and arranged her skirt, then folded her hands on her lap. She held her breath when her father began to speak. However, he was interrupted when a noise erupted from the back of the stately home.

"My goodness! Burt, go see what that's all about!" June exclaimed, then turned to her guests. "I don't know what it could be, the stablemen have all gone home." She stretched her neck in the direction her husband was now taking. He disappeared down the long hallway.

Burt returned with Will and Jacob following behind. Jessica's relief at the disruption turned to panic. "Well, what do you know! Here are two hungry travelers," he boomed. "We didn't expect you two back for a few days. And just in time for dinner. They must have smelled June's cooking from the road," he added, laughing.

Jessica fidgeted with her blouse and hair. How did she look? Would Jacob find her beautiful? She had dressed plainly to discourage Frederick. Why should she care now? She felt Frederick's hand take hers and she withdrew it sharply, then checked herself. She gave him a flash of a smile and turned her full attention to Jacob.

He stood at the head of the long dining table, nearly as tall as the curved entrance. Jessica was taken by his looks; he was perfect.

Her brother walked around his cousin and sat beside their father. "Father, Mother," he greeted his parents. "Mr. Moore, what a nice surprise."

"You and your cousin seem to be the surprise tonight," Frederick replied.

Jessica heard only a mumbling of conversation. She tried desperately to rein in her emotions. Finally, she felt a small sense of calm. The confinement of her corset would be her brace; it would keep her steady. Jacob smiled at her with a wink and a fresh wave of nerves flew up into her chest. She felt Frederick's glance and turned to him with another smile, then touched her hot cheek with her clammy hand and looked away.

"Frederick, this is my son Jacob, and you already know William," Burt said.

Jacob nodded to Frederick. "A pleasure to meet you." He sat across from Jessica.

An odd tension enveloped the room until June broke it with a story of finding a frog in the bucket of greens she had brought in from the garden and what a time she had getting it out of the house. Soon, she had everyone laughing, Frederick remarked on making frog leg soup, to which she teased, "Well, I'm always open to new recipes."

Jessica noticed Frederick's scrutiny of Jacob. She looked down at her plate and played with her silverware. Might something slip in Jacob's behavior that would expose their relationship? Frederick had a keen sense of judgment and seemed to know the inner workings of others. It made her acutely self-aware when she was with him. She couldn't look. What she heard was reassuring, however, and she finally felt at ease. Jacob was as clever as any lawyer and knew how to steer a conversation.

As the dinner progressed, Frederick remarked to Jacob that it was a shame he had not followed in his father's footsteps. "You would have made a fine attorney."

Jessica looked up from her brandied scallops watching for Jacob's reaction. He remained composed. "I've made a fine choice for myself even if it is not in the law profession."

Will coughed and the conversation turned. Frederick spoke quietly into Jessica's ear. "You and your cousin could pass for siblings," he said. She nodded, her mouth too full to answer. Her father took Frederick's attention away with other conversation. She swallowed and let out a sigh. Jacob caught her eye with a soulful look and she wanted to melt. Was he thinking the same as she?

That they would take each other's hand and run down the road in the twilight to the path that led them to their romantic spot? The very place they continued to meet even as the summer turned cool and the autumn brought out the chill? The place where they could shut out the world as they embraced and kissed and stared into each other's eyes?

"So there it is," Frederick proclaimed.

Jessica was startled from her dream. "There is what?" she asked placing a hand to her chest. A servant refilled her wine glass and she took more than a sip.

"I was just saying to your dear mother that I see the resemblance between her and her brother, and now you and your cousin."

"Oh," she replied and pushed her dinner plate away.

"Now, no one is allowed to leave the table. The *piece de resistance* is on its way," June announced at the end of the meal. "And that means pie. Bethany, dear, would you lend me a hand? You always get the cream just right." The women excused themselves from the table and cheerfully walked through the arched entrance and turned into the kitchen off the hallway.

"Your aunt serves her own pudding?" Frederick leaned over to ask Jessica.

"Yes, she likes to serve the desserts she's made," Jessica answered. "I should go help them." She rose to join her mother and aunt. To her astonishment, Jacob excused himself and followed her. She glanced back to see Frederick scowl. Her heart thumped in her chest.

Her mother and aunt each carried out a sliced pie and a dish of clotted cream. "Don't be long you two," her mother said as the swinging kitchen door came to rest. They were alone.

"Hello," Jessica said meekly.

She saw before her a grown man. His hair was a bit shaggy and a light beard lined his chin and jaw. His clothes were more rugged than refined. She didn't know what to think.

"Hello, Jess," he replied. "How are you?" He touched her hand and she wanted to collapse into him. Tonight the large white kitchen seemed to have eyes and ears. Her back found the counter and she placed her hands on its edge. "What's all this? Has he caught your fancy while I was away?" he asked.

"Don't be upset, Jacob. It's only for my parent's sake, as I've told you before." she looked down at her shoes.

"Your parents behave as if they've found you a husband. I thought this might happen."

"Now, it's not like that," she replied, looking up at him.

"What's he doing here then?"

Jacob's accusing tone put her on the defense. She crossed her arms over her chest. "He's just here for dinner. You know he's important to the firm now that your father is thinking of retirement. Are you jealous?"

"No. The way he attends to you makes me wonder what his intentions are though. What *your* intentions are." Jacob replied. Before she could response his arms reached around her waist and he drew her from the counter. "Jess, meet me at the pond tomorrow," he said.

"Of course," she answered as she gently pulled away, his breath still warming her face. "They could return at any moment," she whispered.

He moved forward and pressed his body into hers. Her defenses melted. His smell was intoxicating. She wrapped her arms around him. He kissed the top of her head. With watery eyes she looked up and found his expression one of sadness. He wiped a tear from her cheek, and then walked out of the kitchen, the door swinging behind him.

Jessica cleared her throat to make the lump in it go away. She found a glass and filled it with water. She drank heavily and pressed a towel to her eyes trying desperately to control the waves of emotion. She took another gulp, then held up the crystal glass and took a moment to reflect on their relationship. Like the clear liquid in it, their love would be impossible to hold without the proper support. Her heart felt heavy.

At the end of the evening Jacob gave Jessica a polite kiss on the cheek. He then offered to walk her home. Frederick stepped up to her side. "My dear," he said. "I would be most honored to walk you back home." He placed a hand against her back. She turned to her cousin. "Thank you Jacob, but please don't go out of your way."

"It wouldn't be at all out of my way," Jacob insisted.

"Oh, don't be silly," Jessica's mother chimed in. "Frederick will escort her."

Jessica saw her mother's eyes darting wildly from Jacob to Frederick, stopping at Jacob with a disapproving look. She felt claustrophobic, her waistcoat tight around her stomach. Aware of everyone's eyes bearing down on her as they waited for an answer, Jessica stumbled over her words. "I … um, I came with Frederick and we'll be walking back to the house with Mother and Father," she said. "Thank you, Jacob." Her insides were in turmoil.

"Well, that's settled," Will said. "Let's go, Jake."

"What the heck was that all about?" Will asked Jacob as they started on their way to the Palace.

"What?" Jacob asked in return.

"You know what I mean," Will insisted.

Jacob came to an abrupt stop. "Look, I can't stand seeing Jess pushed into something she doesn't want so your parents can feel that they've made a good match," he declared. "Who knows what he's really doing here. You should be even more concerned than I am; she's your sister."

"How do you know if she's being pushed or goes willingly?" Will asked. "Frederick seems to care about her."

"I have a feeling it has more to do with your father's pursuit of happiness than Jessica's. He's been after this match before he even set sail to England," Jacob said sourly.

"All right. But what can we do about it?" Will demanded. "We'll be gone soon and she's going to have to figure things out for herself. Damn it, Jake, you're going to have to let her go. She's not going to marry someone she doesn't love. I know you've been just as much of a brother to her as I have. It's time we let our little sister grow up."

Jacob walked away with Will on his heels. He couldn't look at his cousin. The clarity of Will's statement sounded a bell for Jacob. If she truly didn't care for Frederick, she would have put an end to it right away. At the same time, he tried not to think about Jessica as his sister. Although she was in the background of his life growing up, she lived in her world and he in his. She was far from being a sister or even a cousin to him. His heart felt like a lead ball in his chest, his fate was sealed. She had made her choice. He would leave her and their relationship behind him. It would be better for both of them. He would make a life for himself, but somewhere else, somewhere far from her and Hartford.

Jessica glanced over her shoulder to see her parents walking a respectful distance behind. Frederick had wrapped her arm in his and spoke softly as they strolled. "My dear, you didn't tell me that you were so attached to your cousin."

Jessica brushed a stray wisp of hair from her cheek and shivered. Frederick offered her his woolen overcoat. "No, I'm quite all right." She searched for a subject far from Jacob. "I heard there may be a frost this week. The sidewalks will be slippery." There was an uncomfortable pause.

"Have you always been close?" he persisted.

She brought her hand across her neck. "No, of course not. We had very different childhoods, as you would expect, him being a male and me a female."

Frederick chuckled. "Yes, that would be the case. Yet, I saw this evening a certain ... well, if you weren't related, I would be very jealous indeed." He drew her closer.

"Oh, you have little to worry about," she said with a feeble laugh.

"I hope that is the case," he replied.

Jessica winced at the flatness of his voice. They walked the rest of the way without a word until they came to the gate of her home. What was always a short walk seemed like a mile tonight. Jessica was eager for her parents to catch up. "Father, Mother, wasn't it a lovely supper?" she called out to them.

Her parents seemed anxious to say goodnight and before she knew what was happening, she and Frederick were alone.

"It's been a lovely evening, Frederick. I should go in." She turned for the safety of the door when his hand grasped her arm. She turned with a start and looked up into his eyes.

"In such haste?" he asked. "I thought we might sit for a while. Perhaps discuss our ... association."

With a generous smile she replied. "I really must turn in early tonight. I fear I will be too tired to get through my day tomorrow." She slowly slid her arm out of his hold. She could feel his eyes reading her face as the corners of his mouth turned down.

He dropped his arm and stepped away. "Am I to take it that you no longer wish for us to be friends?"

"No. I feel ... that." She was caught. A few polite words and she would be done with him, but the words stuck in her throat. She had enjoyed his company more than she realized. "We will talk again soon, Frederick. I'm so tired and find it difficult to think."

"Yes, I see," he replied. "Good night, Jessica." He stepped into his carriage without looking back. The carriage lurched and with the spewing of tiny pebbles it was swiftly away.

"Good night, Frederick," she heard herself say.

Chapter Fourteen

Jacob's inquiries into gunrunning led him to Jones Keaton, originally a businessman from Cincinnati, Ohio. J. Keaton, as he was known to his men, was experienced in underground gun selling and trading, as well as dealing with the Indians and the homesteaders in the Western Territories. Jacob was relieved to find out Keaton and his team avoided territories such as Texas where up until recently there had been news of Indian raids. Although they were sparse and most of the Comanche and Arapaho had surrendered to live on the land allotted to them, he was disturbed by what he had read. Keaton told him they also steered clear of the Indian Agents set up on the reservations; their power to undo his business, according to Keaton, made them as much of an enemy as anyone.

"The homesteaders are the most grateful people for the guns. The stories of Indian raids have them scared and paranoid," J. Keaton had said. "But I'll sell and trade to anyone as long as they have the cash and behave themselves." He'd added under his breath. "Still, it can be a daunting task at best, and worse, leave you dead as a door nail. He had looked Jacob up and down. "We're heading to Colorado and then to the coast. I'll need a few young, strong men."

Jacob wasn't sure if he and Will had the guts for the job, even with their previous experience. Perhaps they were just being naive and would find themselves back where they started in only a month or two. He was ready to take that risk. Seeing Frederick with Jessica last night strengthened his resolve.

Jacob rested his back against the oak tree, its once welcoming trunk now strangely annoying. The water at Mary's Pond reflected his melancholy mood. The dark green pond looked murky under the overcast September sky, creating a sense of foreboding. He searched the gray vastness beyond the tree tops. The scent of the dying oak leaves heralded change. He'd always loved this time of year, but today he wanted to go back to the simplicity of summer. He heard a small bird chirp from a tree limb above and wished he could be that bird and simply fly away. Just then it took flight and he watched it with envy. It darted the sky as if mocking him.

His heart began to beat faster as he heard Jessica approach. She came around the tree. He sprang to his feet.

"Hello, Jacob," she said.

Her pretty face and innocence grabbed his heart and he faltered.

"Jacob?" she asked.

He gathered his courage and taking her hands in his, he began to speak the words he had practiced. "Jessica, we can't continue to see each other," he stated quietly.

"Is it Frederick?" she asked. She shifted her weight and tilted her head. "It seems he'll be staying so I don't know why he and I can't be friends. That doesn't change anything between us, I mean we can still—"

"No," Jacob stated sharply, and held on tighter. "Listen to me, Jess. I'm leaving. Will and I found employment that will take us far away from here and for a very long time."

She stood motionless. Her large brown eyes turned sad; testing his strength. He steadied himself. "This is silly. You're just jealous of Frederick," she said.

"I'm telling you, I'm leaving," he replied.

"Why?" she asked, searching his face.

"I just told you, damn it."

"You didn't explain why," she pressed.

"Jess." He avoided looking at her.

"Tell me!" she demanded.

His insides jumped. His mouth felt dry as a desert. "I can't be the cause of ruining your future and I can't watch you marry Frederick. I've made my decision."

"What about me?" she asked taking her hands from his.

She stood before him, her slight figure, her sweet face and shapely, trembling lips. He wanted to make love to her, and then run away with her to some distant place where no one knew them.

"What about us?" she pleaded. "*We* could marry." The words held in the air as if they were searching for some valid place to land.

Jacob stepped back and ran his fingers through his hair studying the ground. "Jess, you know that's not possible, you know we'd be breaking the law and hurting our families for … forever." Jacob said.

"It is possible," she implored him. "Look at me. It is possible. We could run away and live in another county or state or even another country where no one would be the wiser. New York, Paris. Remember, Jacob?"

He looked at her. Her words striking him deep inside, her willingness to abandon everything frightened him. He closed his eyes and lowered his head. "I don't want to marry you," he said quietly. His own words felt as if he had been punched in the gut. When he looked up his heart broke to see her expression. "I'm sorry Jess. Jesus, I didn't want to hurt you. I love you, but this is impossible. If I could, I'd make it work, but I can't. We have to accept it." He embraced her and could feel their hearts beating against each other. "I'll write to you as often as I can."

"No," she cried and pulled away. "I don't want your letters. I want your courage, for us."

He grabbed her and they stood together, her sobs muffled in his coat. His feet felt leaden but he finally let her go and walked away, quickening his pace to escape her weeping.

Jessica watched the love of her life go, each step more determined than the one before. This couldn't be the end. She had just begun to convince herself that their future was possible. That someday, not now and not next year, but someday they would be able to marry. She touched the oak's rippled bark, the bark of their tree. A violent feeling of betrayal welled up inside of her and she pounded her fist on its unyielding surface, over and over, until her skin broke. The blood ran down into the lace cuffs of her waistcoat. She had let Jacob break her heart. This was all her fault. She cursed herself for letting it go so far. How was she supposed to stop it? What training had she missed? The tears stung her eyes and moisten her cheeks and neck. She sat down at the base of the tree and stared through her misty vision into the placid pond. Eventually the cool late afternoon air and dimming light warned her to be on her way. She walked home in a daze, Jacob's words ringing in her head. *"I don't want to marry you."*

Jessica slowly climbed the stairs to her bedroom. She closed the door behind her, aching to be alone with her grief. But tonight she had to face another evening out, this time to a dinner for the Junior Ladies' Auxiliary Guild. She looked at the dress she had carefully chosen earlier in the day; it and the event had lost their appeal.

She washed her bloody hand and arm in the basin of water Winnie set out for her. The sting from the liquid pierced her heart. The pinkish water was almost pretty and she wanted to paint a heart with it, a symbol of her pain. The ghoulish thought frightened her and she quickly covered the basin with a towel. She undressed and put on her cotton nightgown. Sitting at her desk she penned a short note of apology to her hostess. She had become ill and regretfully would be unable to attend. Nothing her mother would say could change her mind tonight.

Before the sweet summer air was nipped by the coming fall, Jessica took her art supplies to Mary's Pond. She walked the full mile and a half by herself. Her melancholy draped around her heart. She sat away from the oak tree to get a better view, and began to compose her subject: Jacob and her under their tree wrapped in each other's arms gazing out onto the water. Her tears dropped onto the paper and she mixed the color into them.

Chapter Fifteen

The aroma of cigars and sweet liquor permeated the air in Burt's study. Jacob sat uneasy. His cousin had a defiant look on his face. His uncle Thomas stood with his arms folded across his chest, a raised brow indicated his skepticism. The heavy dark green and gold furnishings around the wood and marble fireplace gave a formality to the room which felt unusually intimidating to Jacob. Although he and Will had hinted to their fathers of their plans, the time had come to explain in more detail. He began to lay it out as plainly as he could. "An opportunity has come our way. A fine opportunity. A respectable tradesman, Jones Keaton, has hired us to travel with him and show us the financial side of his business. However, it will take us far out west."

"Jacob, before you continue, I have something to say," Burt stood in front of the seated cousins. "Thomas and I accept that you boys want nothing to do with the law firm that we have worked so diligently to preserve for your futures. But we do feel that gallivanting into unknown territory with some trading company is a foolish endeavor."

Jacob looked at his father. "At our ages you were both well on the way to making the law firm a success. We have chosen differently. J. Keaton is a good businessman and we can learn a great deal from him. It may lead to something very prosperous."

He was trying to do his best to sound convincing. He knew his cousin would have sold it better — his gambling skills had given him a keen sense of negotiation — but he wanted it to be sincere and not a sell. He couldn't risk their fathers' doubt of their ambitions.

Thomas stood to face his son. "William, since that reckless gambling stint of yours at Yale you have been a disappointment and embarrassment to me and this family. Your pursuit of a career has been to work in labor as a roofer and a delivery boy for a saddle shop. Law school was not your calling, but this is unacceptable. A folly."

"Would you have me run away as I once planned to do?" Will replied.

"What? Such nonsense! Run away from what?" Thomas replied.

"Now, now," Burt said. "We've been all over this. Water under the bridge."

Jacob rose, a pillar of confidence. "I mean to find my way in this world, on my own terms, Father."

"As will I," Will said as he too stood tall. "I'm sorry to have disappointed you again."

Jacob sensed another argument brewing between his cousin and uncle. "Excuse us," he said. "We have much to do." The two young men left their elders to discuss and judge.

Early October 1885

The family gathered in the Messing's carriage house. The large four-stall structure was damp on this cold and drizzly day. The smell of hay and horse dung surrounded the group, who stood with solidarity to face the difficult task of saying goodbye.

This setting had been chosen because it was far from prying eyes. Jessica had heard rumors concerning Will and Jacob. Their dealings with Keaton were as dirty as their nights at the Palace Hotel. No one had dared approach her with such accusations, so she had no way of denying them. Her mother's instructions were to inform her friends and anyone who asked that Will and Jacob were going into high finance, taking them to many regions of the country. "And then you will gracefully change the subject," said her mother.

Jessica knew only that the man she loved was leaving and taking a piece of her heart with him. She felt empty as she stood alongside Frederick. She wanted him to stay away, but he had insisted on being there to comfort her. His comfort meant nothing.

As Jacob and Will said goodbye to their parents, Jessica walked to Jacob's chestnut quarter horse and began to stroke its cheek and forehead. "I'll miss you, Otis." He snorted, breath visible in the cold air. She buried her face into his long silky mane, the musky aroma bringing to mind Jacob's soft, tanned neck. She pulled away, swiping at the tears stinging her cheeks.

Jacob came up beside her. "He's going to miss you too," he said. "More than you know," he whispered. Her tears flowed as he hugged her, then kissed her on the cheek. She closed her eyes and leaned into him, ever so briefly.

"We'll be back this spring, Jess. I promise," he pledged. "May I write to you?"

With glassy eyes and a quivering lip she responded with an affirmative nod.

Will was the next to say goodbye. "Take care of yourself, Jess. You're finally rid of me; for a while anyway."

She put a hand over her aching heart. He embraced her as her tears flowed freely. She straightened her back and stepped back courageously. "I'll miss you, Will."

Will pinched her chin and went for his horse. "Take care of my sister, Frederick," he said from atop his mount. Drake whinnied and shook his head tossing his mane about. It was as though the horse knew he was being taken away from his home.

"Most certainly, Will," Frederick said. "Let us know how you get on."

While he and Will exchanged pleasantries, Jessica went to Jacob who sat astride Otis. She looked up at him and their eyes locked for a moment and in that instant her mind and heart raced for the truth to be revealed. She turned her head and her eyes darted from her parents to Frederick to her uncle and aunt then back to Jacob. She lifted her chin and raised herself for him to hear her whisper. "I'm going to tell them."

He leaned down from his mount. "No," he insisted. He resumed his seat and looked straight ahead. She watched helplessly as the two young men rode down the long, gravel entrance and onto the road. She brought her heavy skirt up from the dirt floor raising it ever so slightly as if to take flight but she froze and dropped it back down. Her heart pounded and her hands shook from her brief madness.

June and Bethany walked arm in arm into the house, their heads together.

Thomas turned to Frederick. "Stay for a drink," he said.

"Yes," Burt agreed. "We'll adjourn to your study, away from this dank stable."

"Thank you, gentlemen. May I have a word with Jessica before I join you?"

Jessica's father paused, then replied. "Why, of course."

Jessica stood at the wide entrance of the stable watching her brother and Jacob slowly disappear. From behind her back she heard Frederick's request and her father's blessing. Her breath caught. She remained still, waiting for Frederick to make the next move, but her true desire was to run to her room and stay there until Jacob came back to her.

He cleared his throat and she turned around. He approached her with large softened eyes and a tilt of his head which made her bristle. "I don't need your pity," she said.

He took her delicate, ungloved hands in his. "Let me be your comfort, my dear," he said. He brought them to his mouth and blew warm air onto her cold hands. "Let's get you in before you catch your death."

She slowly withdrew from him. His words seemed shallow and she was in no mood to be courted. "I'll be along shortly. I'd like a moment alone if you don't mind and I wouldn't want my father to get any wrong impressions."

Frederick seemed amused as he pulled her into him. She brought her arms to her waist to stop any closeness. He smirked. "You'll not have to worry about your father. I will make you a proper lady soon enough." He kissed her squarely on the lips and walked away.

Jessica wiped her mouth defiantly. The pressure of his lips hurt her mouth. She rushed out of the stables, following the indents from the horse's hooves, which created small puddles dotting the path her brother and cousin had just taken. Stopping at the gate, she looked down the road. They were nowhere in sight. The road she had walked so many times was deserted. The road that Jacob had rescued her from when last March the snow hurled at her as she made her way home from the gallery. He had lifted her onto his horse in one swoop. The road she wanted to skip upon after one of their rendezvous. The road she and Jacob had walked upon together as they talked about art and books and things she could not remember, only the joyous feelings they left in her heart. That same road seemed tainted to her now, marred by his exit, or was it his escape? Despair overtook her as the rain cried down, its tears mingling with her own. A stern hand grabbed her by the arm. She turned with a start to find Winnie by her side.

"My Lord, child," Winnie exclaimed. "Whatever you doing out here?"

Jessica looked sadly at the housekeeper her voice even and unapologetic. "Life will be different now, Winnie. Nothing will ever be the same again."

Chapter Sixteen

Spring was upon her and the time had come to let go of the last remnants of childhood. Jessica inhaled deeply then exhaled, releasing her tension. She sat at the kitchen table with only a candle for light. Winter had been harsh and Frederick warmed her cold, lonely days. By Christmas they were engaged. Soon after, every waking moment was spent preparing for this day. She held a piece of paper up to the dancing flame and read the events for tomorrow. Her wedding day. She wrapped her shawl around her nightdress. The warmth had gone out of the house and wouldn't return until the fires were lit again in the morning. April nights still brought out the last bit of winter chill.

Every detail for her wedding had been carefully planned and she merely had to make her appearance. First on the list was the ladies' breakfast, consisting of her girlfriends and their mothers. Second was the afternoon tea with her mother and future mother-in-law; it would be attended by women from the most respectable society. After the tea, she would retreat to her room where she could rest before she would be transformed into a virginal bride-to-be for the biggest event of the day and of her life.

If they only knew. She brought the paper closer to the flame. All of the arrangements had been made for the one hundred and twenty-four guest event. The very house felt as if it were filled with the anticipation. Yet Jessica was ready to have it over with. She felt as if she were a complete fraud. A young maid could go in her place and be more truthful in her vows to Frederick than she would be. She swore, however, to keep Jacob in her heart where no one could take him from her. This was her vow on the eve of becoming Frederick's wife. She knew it would be a profound moment as she said the words while Jacob sat looking on. She held the piece of paper to the candle and watched it burn. She blew out the small flame and sighed.

Jessica awoke, not having recalled falling asleep. The day dawned as new as the spring flowers in the garden outside her window. She stared at nothing then slowly lifted her body from her cozy nest. She bent over the basin of water by her bed and brought the cool liquid to her face. Butterflies swirled in her stomach. She stood still not wanting to move. A knock on the door and her body jerked. Winnie entered with a tray filled with tea and pastries.

She sipped the tea and started on an apple tart when she noticed an unaddressed envelope tucked under the plate. She wondered who would write to her today. She took the note out and read.

Congratulations, Jess. Your happiness will always be my wish. Love, Jacob.

She placed it back on the tray. *How dare he write to me!* He had written so sparingly since he left. The letters were so brief and only contained talk of the weather in New Jersey, or of good trade in Pennsylvania. How could she let him know that her happiness was with him and not Frederick? Perhaps he didn't want to know. She went straight to her writing desk and before letting the ink hit the paper, she thought of his eyes peering into her soul on the day he departed. She wrote:

You hold my heart, no other.

Jessica called Winnie back into the room. "Please be sure my cousin Jacob receives this before the wedding," she said.

"You have no time to be writing notes, child. Get dressed now, and I'll make sure this gets to him. My Lord," Winnie answered and pocketed the note.

Jessica began to dress for the lady's breakfast. She mindlessly put on the modern gown she herself had chosen. She wanted to look stylish for her contemporaries. The royal blue ensemble had a natural form; no bustle. Instead the silk and satin skirt was heavily pleaded. The front and back panels of the bodice complimented her slight figure. She especially liked the cream colored tiers of organza lace on the sleeves and hem. The light sheer shawl that flowed from her shoulders and down the back of her gown gave a light and airy feel to the rich color of the dress beneath it. Her mother had scoffed at the idea of such a dress being worn on this important occasion but Jessica had begged to be allowed to buy it with her own earnings. To her surprise her mother had given in.

Winnie returned to the bedroom to style her hair. Jessica asked about the note and Winnie assured her that indeed she had given it to the postman to run it over to the Stanford's. "I got him just in time, but had to wave him down. He was crossing over to the next street." Jessica wished she had expressed to him more of her love.

She looked at the more formal dress she had chosen for the afternoon tea. Its deep red satin bodice and high collar matched the bustled skirt. More lace adorned the ends of the long fitted sleeves. Winnie had stuffed the sleeves and bodice with lightweight paper so as to keep their form. Jessica looked at it hanging on her door. It seemed to be alive. Indeed, she would have preferred for the dress to go on without her. The thought of it made her chuckle as Winnie put the last touches on her tight chignon with curled tendrils around her face.

"What's so amusing?" Winnie asked her. "Or are you just happy to be getting married today to that fine gentleman, Mr. Moore?"

"I just imagined my dress going by itself to the afternoon tea," Jessica replied.

"Whatever for?" Winnie asked.

"Oh, ever since meeting them last week, I get the feeling the

Moores don't approve of me, especially Mrs. Moore. She makes me nervous," she answered. "I have to sit near her and be pleasant and engaging. I wish it was done with, or that my dress would go without me."

"Don't be talking nonsense on your wedding day," Winnie scolded.

She mindlessly played with the jewelry on her dressing table. "Why? Is it bad luck?" she asked, then said under her breath, "I can't imagine having any worse luck."

"What did I just hear you saying?" Winnie asked.

"Nothing. Are you almost done with my hair, I don't want to be late."

While his bride-to-be was fulfilling her duties, Frederick waited for his mother's arrival. He fixed himself a stiff drink; one of many he knew he would pour as the day progressed. He stood in front of his dark gray morning suit, which was supported by a sturdy wooden hanger in back of the heavy walnut floor-length mirror. He gulped his drink, the fire from the liquid burning his insides. He gasped as he went for another. The knock on the door distracted him from his objective of becoming sufficiently intoxicated. He opened the door to find his mother standing in front of him. "What a pleasant shock," he said.

Lillian entered his modest hotel suite. "Don't be insolent, Frederick," his mother replied as she removed her gloves, one finger at a time. She surveyed the room.

He offered her a drink, forgetting the time of day. Noticing his mother's look of disapproval, he pulled the rope that rang for the bellboy. He would have tea brought up for her and strong coffee for himself. "Have a seat, Mother."

Lillian looked at the chair before she sat in it. "Well, my darling, the first thing we have to do is find a decent home for the two of you. I saw a few impressive estates as we were out with Mr.

and Mrs. Messing." She sat down as she continued speaking. "Of course it would be a temporary dwelling."

"Temporary?" Frederick asked. He stood by the fireplace, an elbow on the mantle.

"Why, yes. I can't imagine you'd want to raise your children in this country. My grandchildren must be born and raised in Liverpool. It's disturbing enough that you've chosen someone from here. Your father is even more insistent on it. He's quite upset and expects you back at the offices no later than June."

Frederick thought of the dismal, polluted docks of the city. His office by the sea. As much as he loved the ocean and the impressive ships that sailed across it from New York and many other ports, he loathed the smell of the commerce that went on, the hordes of people and their constant noise. Not to mention the endless, boring paperwork. "Liverpool, Mother?"

"England." Her allegiance to her country spoken in one word. He would have to be extremely careful fighting for his freedom.

"Grandchildren?" Frederick said without emotion. He turned away and finished his drink in one easy gulp, then coughed and wiped his mouth.

The bellboy was at the door and Frederick gave him his request and the boy was off. He turned back to his mother.

"I remain hopeful. The doctors don't know everything," Lillian argued.

"I thought I had made it clear that I would not be returning," Frederick stated, changing the subject. "Is that why you came? Did Father send you here?"

"I came here, on my own, as you can well see. I want to know, are you truly in love with this young woman? Does she know about …? She is most likely to want a family."

"Of course I'm in love," he spouted. "And the rest of it is my business to handle as I see fit. Why would you question my intentions?"

Lillian examined her hands. "At one time you claimed to be in love with Miss Ambers and I saw firsthand how you dealt with that, or I should say, left it for *me* to deal with," she stated.

"Good God. Why bring that up now?"

"I want you to know the consequences of your actions, Frederick."

"My actions are none of your concern." The anger rose in him, as it did each time his mother reprimanded him. He let the liquor sooth his emotions. "I'm truly sorry for involving you in that business with Molly, but for God's sake, that was months ago."

The temperature in the room increased and Frederick helped his mother remove her structured wool coat. She turned to face him. "There's a big difference between being sorry and feeling regret," she said. "The latter seems to be more of the truth for you. The way you informed Molly of your change of heart was a cowardly way of breaking things off with her. Your father and I didn't imagine it meant that you would truly be staying here for good. How could you lead that poor girl on? And now, all of us, apparently."

Frederick raised his voice to meet his mother's acidity. "You know little of it, Mother. Do not confuse my choice not to fill you in on every detail of my life with leading you on." Then he added, with genuine regret, "I haven't been your little boy for some time, my dear, so please." His mother's expression silenced him. An uncomfortable stillness filled the room. "Mother, let's not do this. Today should be one of the happiest days for us all."

Lillian stood still and stately; her eyes had softened to the point of tears. *Bloody hell,* Frederick cursed to himself. She began to put her gloves back on. He stopped her and took both her hands in his. He looked down at his mother's face. She was still beautiful, yet he could see her age. She was no longer the strong matriarch he had tried so hard to please. Her pale face and light colored hair framed the blue eyes that reflected the years of unhappiness he knew she had lived. His heart ached. What could he do now? His life was not going to be marked by misery and unfulfilled dreams. He would not suffer in the way she had. He had goals. He would not be compromised.

"I'm sorry, my son," she said, softly. Then she stiffened, erasing her vulnerability. "I see now where we stand with each other. Just as I know where I stand with your father."

"Don't, Mother," he said and turned from her. "Do not compare me to my father for your own satisfaction."

"Well, I hope you treat your wife with love and patience and never find your affections wandering outside *your* marriage bed, causing her to do who knows what," she warned.

It was the most unsavory part of his parent's marriage. His insides churned. "Oh, for God's sake . . ." He fixed himself another drink.

"Frederick, I hope this will be a sober affair. At least wait until after you are married."

They were interrupted by a knock on the door. The waiter placed the tea and coffee on the banquette.

"Mother, please stay. We've had no time to visit since you got here and after the wedding we'll have even less. As you've brought up the subject of residence, I have some news."

Lillian sat down, once again removing her gloves. She placed the brown leather pair neatly on her lap. Frederick prepared his mother's tea; he knew just how she liked it. He handed her the cup and saucer then sat in the chair next to her. The coffee he poured for himself didn't smell as strong as he needed it to be. He pursed his lips and looked down at the floor. As he raised his head he blurted out. "My wife and I will be moving to San Francisco soon after the wedding."

"Where?" she asked. Her blue eyes sharp and defiant.

"San Francisco, California."

"I know where it is, Frederick," she snapped. "Why in God's name would you want to live in that wilderness of a place?"

"I'm going to practice financial law and investments and I think it would be a perfect place to start something of my own. Jessica has relatives nearby, so we won't be completely on our own." His mother was still. "I know it's a shock," Frederick continued, "but I would like to have your and Father's blessing, though I will go there with or without it."

"Frederick how could you do this to me?"

"Mother, I don't mean to hurt you." He had the urge to kneel down beside her. He wanted to comfort her as he did when he was a child and she wept for reasons he could only guess were due to the actions of his father. The feeling abruptly passed as her expression of sorrow changed.

"And I suppose you expect us to help you finance this little adventure of yours?"

Frederick heard the disapproval in her question. "No. I have my own money. I had it wired to me several weeks ago."

"And will that be enough to settle you and your wife in that city?" she inquired.

Frederick fingered the rim of his cup, "I have other resources," he replied quietly.

"What other resources?" she asked.

"My other accounts," he replied.

"Those other accounts are under your father's name and authority. He has many more years to live before he releases them to you along with the company."

"He can give the company to his brother's son. I want only my inheritance, in cash," Frederick stated bluntly.

"Your cousin is an idiot. He wouldn't leave anything to be run by Albert. And I state again, only your father has final approval of the withdrawal of those funds," she said. "He hasn't informed me of any arrangements you've made with him. Or am I completely useless to the both of you now?"

Frederick ignored her plea for his pity. "Please don't concern yourself with this."

"You mean to say, just look the other way, Mother."

He leapt from his chair. "It doesn't matter! Do whatever you wish, just don't dictate my life anymore!" Lillian sat back as if he had struck her. "Mother, please," he begged. He heard his tone become that of a little boy and he resented her for bringing him to such an infantile state.

"Frederick, calm yourself," she stated firmly. "Now then, what have Jessica and her family said about this move?" she asked.

He took a sip of the coffee. His head was beginning to spin. "They don't know."

"Not even your future wife?"

"My wife will go where I go."

Lillian shook her head. "Well, I suppose if she loves you that much. But why have you not told her?"

"She'll find out soon enough. I didn't want to bother her with it, before the wedding."

The subject was closed, but only for now. To Frederick's advantage, the distance from which his mother would be making her remarks in the future would dilute their impact. It gave him the kind of excitement he had experienced when he first decided on his new life. She stood, signaling their visit had come to an end.

"I must go to your bride and her mother. An intimate afternoon tea, although I hear there will be some twenty women there. My Lord, how involved do they expect me to be? Isn't it enough that your father and I and several of our servants have traveled all the way from Liverpool?"

"Thank you, Mother. I know these gatherings are not to your liking," Frederick replied as he helped her on with her coat.

"They are not. As you know I can only take small groups. Anything more encourages over indulgence and gossip."

"Yes, Mother."

"I will let your father know of your plans. I'm certain he'll be less accepting of the idea than any of us. He will be outraged, Frederick."

"Let me tell him."

"Very well," she said. "I will see you at the wedding."

"I'll be very happy to have you there. Truly I will."

She paused at the door. "I hope these tracks you lay will not lead you off a cliff."

Frederick accompanied his mother to her waiting carriage. He kissed her on the cheek and waved goodbye. When he returned to his rooms he sat down heavily in the winged-back chair. He felt drained of emotion by her practiced way of drawing him in, then coldly rebuffing him. Her words rang in his head; he took them as a challenge, fueling his determination.

Chapter Seventeen

It was nearly four o'clock and time to dress for her wedding. Jessica opened her bedroom window and looked out at the expansive lawn. The birds sang their merry tune and the air smelled as sweet as the world she dreamed of living in. The green grass, so neatly trimmed beckoned her to run barefoot upon its lushness. She felt melancholy in the pit of her stomach. Soon this would no longer be her home, this room would no longer be her sanctuary. She blew out the air in her lungs. The day had made her weary and there were hours yet to get through.

Before she could dwell on it further a flurry of women filled her room. Her mother and Aunt June, the maid of honor Sarah, and bride's maid Megan. Winnie, Mrs. Hargrove, the hairdresser, and Mrs. Delanie, the dressmaker. Arms and hands were all around her body, lacing up her corset, and attaching the padded bustle to her waist, helping with her white stockings and guiding her into the heavy gown of cream colored silk satin. Sarah's nimble fingers worked the fifteen satin-covered buttons on the front of the fitted bodice. Her mother smoothed the rose point lace collar that draped on either side of the square neckline.

"Mother, is the collar too—" Jessica began.

"Keep still, Jessica," her mother interrupted. She turned to the dressmaker. "Are the sleeves the correct length?" she asked.

"Mother, please, we've been over this," Jessica implored. "Look the lace covers my arm below the elbow, just as I wanted."

Her mother went to the back of her gown, with Mrs. Delanie close behind. The same lace trim that adorned the sleeves finished the edge of the skirt and long train. The dressmaker smoothed the many pleats on the back of the dress then adjusted the folds of ruching in the front. She dared not move while the woman examined the fit and gave her approval. Jessica's petite but shapely figure was accentuated by the snug waistline. Her aunt remarked how she could practically place her open hands around it. Jessica felt as if she couldn't breathe. Mrs. Hargrove stood on a small stool to style her long silky hair into an upsweep atop her head. She then took the hot iron rod from its perch by the small fireplace to touch up the curls around her face.

Jessica stooped down to allow the hairdresser to affix the long organza veil into her hair. She winced as the teeth of the tiara of encrusted pearls scraped her scalp. "This will stay in place now," the hairdresser remarked. Then the women each took an end of the veil to drape it ever so carefully around the bride.

Her mother took a handkerchief out from her sleeve to dab her wet eyes. "You look so beautiful, my daughter. I am truly happy for you"

Jessica smiled and thought how sad her mother would be if she knew her daughter's true feelings. It was her Aunt June who gave her courage. "You'll be fine my dear. Just remember, you are never alone, even in marriage."

Soon only Jessica and Sarah remained in the room.

Jessica regarded her reflection in the mirror. She had transformed into a fully-fledged woman, at only twenty years of age. "Sarah, do I look as if I'm wearing my older sister's frock?"

"Jess, you look positively radiant!" Sarah exclaimed. "And if you had a sister she would be as jealous of you as I am right now."

"I feel odd. I don't look like myself," Jessica said.

"No, you don't look like yourself, simply because you are now going to be a wife," Sarah replied. "A wife, Jess. What more could we dream of?" she gushed. "And such a handsome husband you will have. So worldly!"

"Yes. So worldly," Jessica mused. She turned back to the mirror. "I suppose I must look the part."

The church was filled to capacity. Towers of white and pink roses stood on either side of the altar. The pews were adorned with white ribbons at each end and the heavy scent of frankincense and sandalwood filled the air. Jacob joined his parents, who were seated next to Jessica's parents in the front row. His formal coat felt constricting. His top hat sat in his lap where a rifle had lain only days ago. When he had sent his latest post to his mother informing the family that he and Will would not be able to make it back as they had promised, he hardly expected a response for them to return immediately for Jessica's wedding. He could have ignored it, claiming they had left the area before her letter reached the post office in the little western Pennsylvania town, but he knew it would cause a great embarrassment to both families. His sense of decency overrode his hesitation and Will was anxious to see his sister wed.

He looked up at Will, who stood stiffly at the altar alongside Frederick. His cousin gave him a nod and Jacob shook his head; this was the last place Jacob wanted to be. He sat back on the hard wooden pew. His hands became clammy and his heart began to race as the keyboardist struck the sharp notes on the idiophone. He looked at Frederick, a proper Englishman in his grey morning suit. Jacob moved uneasily in his seat. He entertained the idea of getting up and leaving soon after the ceremony. He sat back as the shrill music and low humming of the crowd threatened his sanity.

"What's wrong?" June whispered.

Jacob became aware of his restless behavior. "Nothing," he answered.

"Are you as excited as I am to see Jessica?" she asked.

Jacob looked at his mother's plump face. It seemed as if it was about to burst. "Yes, of course," he replied. He composed himself. He would get through this. Just then he caught Frederick's eye and quickly looked away. At that moment the keyboardist stopped playing and the three-piece orchestra began with a great flair its introduction of the bride and her maids. Jacob stood with the rest of the family and guests. He watched Jessica enter the hall arm in arm with her father, who gently escorted her down the long, red-carpeted aisle to the altar. She was the essence of beauty and elegance. His emotions rose in his throat and he swallowed hard. When they stopped in front of the family, her father kissed her on the cheek. Jacob ached to look into her eyes. Jessica touched her mother, who wept into her handkerchief. She then touched her weeping aunt. Jessica turned to him and her eyes pierced his heart. He held her gaze, but for only a second, his own eyes misting over. She stepped to the altar and Jacob felt his loss deeply. He looked down and ran his hand through his hair.

Jessica stood as steady as she could in the heavy gown and held tight to the cascade of roses and greenery. She not only felt the weight of the garment and flowers, but the weight of the audience seated behind her. Jacob's eyes spoke to her of his pain and she accepted it into her heart as a reminder of his love.

She recited her vows as if Jacob, not Frederick, were standing before her and they rang as true as anyone who was in love. Afterwards she turned and slowly handed her flowers over to Sarah so as Frederick could bestow upon her finger his late grandmother's wedding ring. She turned to Jacob and to her dismay his expression was unreadable. Her attentions were back with Frederick; offering her hand to him and in so doing, her life. The ring felt clunky on her delicate finger. It was made of ivory surrounded by gold and had a carving of a face on it. She felt the weight of it as if it was keeping her from flying away. A shackled bird.

The Hartford Country Club greeted the wedding guests. Hothouse white and pink roses and pink peonies accented with sprays of green fern and peacock feathers were arranged in ornate golden urns on linen draped tables. Swaths of white satin hung in great billowing clouds from the ceiling. Hundreds of candles and gas lit sconces gave a surreal ambiance to the hall. There were a few new electric lights by the long table of food, giving the banquet an unnatural brightness. The band performed a melody of soft tunes as the guests mingled to find their assigned seats. A buzz of chatter, and soon all were assembled, awaiting the bride's arrival.

Sarah helped Jessica to the rectory of the church where Frederick and Will and the priest waited. The witnesses watched as the couple signed the document that made them a legally bound entity. Jessica's shaking hand made for a scribble of a signature. It was invalid in her eyes.

Frederick took her hand. "My dearest wife, we are one," he said.

She no longer held back her emotions. She answered through soft sobs. "Yes, Frederick."

"Oh, Jessica," Sarah cried. "You are the happiest bride I have ever witnessed. Congratulations, Mr. and Mrs. Moore."

Will shook Frederick's hand, "Congratulations, Frederick, take care of her." Jessica hugged her brother, her emotions still unchecked.

"Don't cry my love," Frederick said as he took her by the arm. "The guests are waiting."

Will stepped back. "I will join you at the club," he said.

"Frederick, I will need a moment to compose myself," Jessica said. "Would you mind if Sarah and I excused ourselves? We won't be long."

Frederick looked displeased. "Of course, but the guests await our arrival, my dear. Do not keep them, or me, waiting."

"I won't. Sarah will you accompany me?" Sarah gathered the long train and guided her from the room. Once she was out of Frederick's sight, Jessica instructed Sarah to go ahead without her. "I can manage. Truly, I just need a moment alone."

Sarah reluctantly left and Jessica was finally by herself. Her wedding dress was cumbersome when she had help, but to manage it alone was quite a chore. She lifted the heavy skirt and made her way into the church; perhaps a prayer would help. She took off her veil and placed it on one of the back pews. As she turned to sit down she noticed a man sitting in the front row. Then he turned.

"Jacob, whatever are you doing here?" she asked, the acoustics of the church making her voice louder than she intended.

"I could ask you the same thing," he answered.

Her instincts cried out *Run to him*, but she was imprisoned by her dress. He approached her, a handsome sight in his dress clothes.

He bent down and kissed her cheek. "I have to leave now, Jess," he said.

Jessica touched his face. "I had no choice."

Sarah came rushing into the church. "Jessica, your mother has scolded me for leaving you," she exclaimed. "Oh, hello Jacob. You're holding up the festivities."

"I will be there shortly, Sarah," Jessica replied.

"I can't go back without you, Jess. Your mother …" Sarah implored.

"Yes, of course," Jessica said. "Would you help me with my veil?" Sarah reattached the veil to Jessica's head.

"I'll say goodbye now, cousin," Jacob said. "I'll be leaving early tomorrow."

"Jacob, you must stay. Will is staying." Panic ran through her. This couldn't be goodbye.

"Sarah, please wait outside for me. I would like to have a word with my cousin in private."

Sarah gave an impatient look at Jacob. "Very well," she said and left them alone.

"Did you get my note?" she asked feeling out of breath.

"Yes. You married him, there's nothing more to say or do. I wish you well, Jessica. Remember be true to your dreams."

"You are my dreams," she heaved in a wave of emotion.

He kissed her lips and walked away. The sound of the heavy door closing behind him echoed in her ears.

Chapter Eighteen

"Good evening and congratulations," the man at the front desk of the Belmont Hotel said to the newly married couple. "We are so pleased to have you with us this evening."

The Belmont Hotel was a grand mansion in Hartford, located on a hill overlooking the river valley. Once a private residence, it had been turned into an exclusive hotel after its bankrupt owners fled the city soon after the Civil War. It boasted serene views and spectacular sunrises, but with its comfortable beds and rich linens, it was a rare guest who awakened so early to witness the very first rays of daylight. A sturdy young man lifted their cases and led the way to the luxurious honeymoon suite on the third floor.

Jessica had often wondered what the hotel was like inside. At every turn she was more impressed by its beauty and elegance. Layers of lace curtains covered the many large windows. Satin and velvet seating adorned the grand lobby, and delicately painted blown glass lamps sat on the dark wood tables. The walls were made of intricately carved walnut and burl panels. Gold fixtures were everywhere. It exuded such richness, Jessica felt as if she had stepped into another world. She pictured her brush stroking the paper with colors of rose and peach, creating the lovely images she saw before her. Soon the smell of faint perfume mixed with the gas lighting made her head hurt. Perhaps the thick carpet under her might be a safe place to faint. She took a breath.

Once in the room she set her eyes on the ornate bed with its soft yellow linens. She was exhausted and the thought of lying down was more inviting to her than anything else. Her wedding day had been filled with highs and lows throughout, though she gave no sign of her troubled heart. The high points were that of family and friends uniting joyfully for the occasion. The low was saying goodbye to Jacob at the church. The lowest, she had married a man other than Jacob. She felt only a hint of possible happiness with Frederick. If she tried, if she gave in, maybe she could be a contented wife. She blamed herself for finding interest in him. For letting him court her. She wanted to be strong and resist, but the tide was against her and now she was in the middle of the ocean.

The grandfather clock in the corner of the room struck one. She had never been awake at this hour. She wanted to go home to her bedroom and sleep until noon. She had never fallen asleep next to a man, and she knew before sleep there would be the consummation of their marriage. It was only yesterday that her mother took her aside to explain, or tried to explain, the marriage bed. She listened while her mother stumbled over her words and wrung her hands. Jessica had nodded her head and smiled. A kiss on each cheek as if to wish her good luck and the conversation was over. If she hadn't already experienced sex this would have left her quite confused. *Oh, Mother.* An acute feeling of guilt and loneliness engulfed her. She quietly began to unpack her small overnight case.

Frederick came up behind her, putting his arms around her waist and kissing her cheek. "Shall I leave you to yourself for a while, my dear?" he asked. "I know it's been quite a day for you." He turned her around and she looked into his hazel colored eyes. She did not reply. "You are the most beautiful bride any man could ever hope for." He paused, then said, "Thank you for marrying me."

Her heart was touched and she truly saw him for the first time all day. She shyly offered her lips. He didn't hesitate and she felt the force of his passion. He led her to the foot of the stately bed and began to undress her. As he slowly removed one layer after another, she could feel the weight of the world literally being peeled away.

His lovemaking felt foreign. His larger frame seemed to consume her as she lay underneath him. He brought her arms up above her head and smothered her breasts with kisses. She didn't know how to react. She closed her eyes and waited for it to be over.

Jessica remained still, wondering if she had met his standards. She hoped he wasn't put off by her lack of experience. Yet, Frederick seemed pleased. She was relieved that she had successfully fulfilled her wifely duties. There would be no hiding in certain places or catching a moment here or there, as it was with Jacob. She and Frederick had announced their union in front of everyone and did what was naturally expected of them, not what would be abhorred and unlawful by society, yet she felt dirty and ashamed; she gathered up the sheet and blanket to cover her naked body, her eyes lowered; a tear or two escaping.

"Jessica, my love, what is it?" he asked.

"I'm fine, Frederick."

"Are you sure?" he asked.

"Yes, yes. It's been a grand day."

"Then why the tears? Did you not find it, or rather, *me* … satisfactory?" he asked.

"No. I mean yes, it was, more than ... satisfactory. And was I?"

Frederick grinned and leaned into her ear, "I will ignore the fact that you are not a virgin. It will be our little secret." He came away from her and sat up. "If I'd known, I wouldn't have married you. I will not ask about the circumstances. Your fall from grace is safe with me."

Jessica's body stiffened and a sharp ripple ran up her spine.

Frederick's mood quickly changed. "Now, dry your eyes. I have some news. It's my wedding present to you, my darling."

"What is it?" she asked meekly, barely comprehending his knowledge of her body.

"We're moving to San Francisco!" he announced.

"San Francisco?" she sat up straight. "Whatever for? Why didn't you tell me this sooner?" *He must be mad.* "When?"

"Very soon. I know it's a shock, but I didn't want to burden you before the wedding. I thought it would be a brilliant surprise!"

Jessica searched for the proper response. She was afraid to refuse him his joy. Then, like a flash of light, her thoughts went to her brother and cousin. She knew they were headed to California and perhaps would visit Aunt June's brother and his family, who lived not far from San Francisco. She popped up on her knees and blurted out, "Jacob will be there … and Will of course. They said that their business would take them out West." She sat back regretting her outburst. She had angered her new husband.

"Jessica, that is *not* the reason for our move. I think you ought to know the truth: most men in the *business* your brother and cousin have chosen don't always make it all the way out West." Then he said under his breath, "And from what I've seen of those two, they'll probably have a slimmer chance than most."

Jessica was appalled by Frederick's assumptions. "Why would you say that?" Her regret fell by the wayside as she came to their defense.

"My dear, I'm sure you've been kept in the dark, as you should be, of the antics of your brother and cousin."

"What do *you* know about them?"

"Let's not argue over such nonsense," he said with a raised voice. He left the bed and swung his robe around his body. "The whereabouts of your brother and cousin have little to do with our lives now. Especially your cousin." He lowered his tone, but remained defiant. "We will move to San Francisco, where I will start work as a financier."

She held the blanket tighter. "I'm sorry," she began. "I was feeling homesick, and now this."

Frederick came back to bed. She felt the warmth of his body on her skin. He slowly swept a lock of her shiny, dark hair off her bare shoulder. "I'll protect you, my sweetheart," he said with quiet gallantry.

Jessica witnessed his sincerity, along with his ability to change from a puppy to a beast then back again. He could decide her life in an instant, giving him a power over her she had not expected. She searched his eyes while his hand caressed her cheek.

"Hadn't you considered making a home with me after our marriage?" he asked. "Or was your mind simply set on finding a way to be free from your parents? And now on our most precious wedding night, you say you're homesick?"

She stirred uneasily. She took his hand, intending to ask for his forgiveness. Frederick kissed her forehead, then her lips, giving her no chance to speak. He gently pulled the blanket from her grip.

She surrendered to him again, suppressing her own feelings. He had seen through her and it put her on guard. She was determined now to follow his lead and show him that she had no other motive for marrying him than true love, telling herself that the lie would somehow serve a higher purpose.

June's table was never so quiet. Frederick had left them all speechless with the news of their move to San Francisco only days after the wedding. Finally, Charles spoke.

"We'll be discussing this between ourselves after dinner, Frederick."

"There will be no discussion," Frederick stated firmly. "My mind is made up."

Again there was silence. Jessica watched the exchange of looks between the father and son. "Pardon me," she said, then cleared her throat. "We are aware of the suddenness of this news, and we respect your concerns, but this is something my husband has chosen for us and we hope to have your support in it." She looked at Frederick and although he didn't acknowledge her she noticed the corners of his mouth turned up in a devilish grin. She lowered her head and stared at her folded hands; her integrity now compromised.

"Has this been your plan all along, Frederick?" Thomas asked.

Charles interrupted, "Excuse us please. Frederick may I see you in the next room?"

Frederick followed his father down the hall and into the first open room, on their right was the home's library. Jessica waited with the others for the muffled rumblings to stop. Charles returned seething with anger. He turned to his wife. "Did you know about this?" he asked, accusingly.

Lillian paused before answering. Her loyalty to her son over her husband would not be appreciated. "Yes, but only recently," she stated quickly.

"Father, this has nothing to do with her," Frederick asserted.

Jessica's mother turned to her. "Jessica, do you want to move so far away? Maybe take some time there first to see how you would like it. You can return and make a more rational decision."

"Yes, yes," her aunt chimed in, "And perhaps Uncle Burt and I could escort you both to my brother's home in Clermont City. It's across the bay from San Francisco. I've mentioned it many times to you, Jessica. He could show us around. Get the lay of the land, so to speak."

"We've made our plans," Frederick interrupted. He turned to Thomas and Burt. "I'm grateful to you both for allowing me to work with you. I feel the time has come for me to expand my potential. The arrangements have been made for our leave." Frederick looked at his father, then offered Jessica his hand. "Please, excuse us," he said to June and Bethany.

Jessica slowly took her husband's hand. She stood by him now, her heart beating hard. She had never treated her parents with such disregard. She ached to tell them that this was a misunderstanding, that she and Frederick would surely consider all of their views on the matter. Her loyalties were ripped in two and she wanted to quickly stitch them back together. Her wide brown eyes darted around the room seeking some alliance, but she found none. Frederick tightened his grip and soon they were out the door.

"What do you make of all this?" Thomas asked Burt.

Sitting in an overstuffed leather chair Burt tipped his head and shrugged, then sipped his brandy. Thomas sat in a gold-striped high back, brandy in one hand, thin cigar in the other. They had left teary-eyed Bethany and June in the parlor. The men smoked in quiet contemplation.

"I don't know what to make of a man who says he's going to do one thing, then pulls the rug out from under all of us," Burt answered, as he puffed his cigar.

"Now I'm not sure *what* his intentions were," Thomas wondered aloud. He feared his own perceptions may have prejudiced his judgment.

"Had Jessica spoken to you about these plans?" Burt asked. "Surely he would have let her in on it before the marriage took place."

"No, not at all, this comes as much of a shock to me as it does to you. Charles was quite put back as well," Thomas replied.

"Yes, he and his son seem to have a troubled relationship," Burt noted.

"I see that now," Thomas replied. "And to think I once envied it."

"This could go very badly," Burt stated.

"I agree. Frederick may have money, yet we've both heard stories of the rich being bankrupted in the West by unbridled greed."

"With all due respect for your new son-in-law," Thomas's brother-in-law paused and swirled the amber colored liquid in his glass.

"Let's not stand on ceremony, now, Burt. We've known each other too long for that, tell me what you're thinking."

Burt looked up at him beneath his brows. "I'm thinking that Frederick seems more of the type who would be doing the taking, instead of the one being taken."

"You're just seeing the lawyer in him," Thomas assured. "I feel whatever he has in mind will be legitimate. I'm grateful that June's family is close to San Francisco. At least they will have some connections there."

Burt walked over to a tin plate and rested his cigar. "Well, since June sort of let the cat out of the bag, I guess I will tell you."

"What cat out of the bag?" Thomas asked.

"About us going to Clermont City ... for a visit," Burt began.

"Oh, yes. I recall she jumped to one of her solutions before thinking it through. Just like our June," Thomas said as he raised his glass to his lips.

"We *are* going to Clermont City," Burt said, then added, "We are moving there."

"Moving?" Thomas sprang from his chair and began to pace. "I knew you wanted to travel after retiring, but move? How could you even consider it?"

"We want to be in a more temperate climate and away from all the busyness of a city. June wants us to get some land. She misses her brother and his family, and now with Jacob heading that way," Burt tried to explain, adding, "we thought that you and Bethany would come out to visit and maybe ..."

Thomas rubbed the back of his neck. "Yes, well, I suppose I saw this coming. I didn't think you'd move to the other end of the country. You know this will break Bethany's heart."

Burt looked at Thomas, "It will be difficult for us all. We feel it would be the best time to do this; we're not getting any younger."

Thomas never considered either of them to be old, but now he felt he had aged with Burt's statement. This large, sentimental and gracious man whom he trusted as a brother was telling him they were no longer in their prime. They returned to the parlor where Bethany and June quietly sat, sipping their tea. Their silence disturbed Thomas. The two couples said good night. Jessica's father felt the future weigh heavily on his heart and he rubbed his chest to disperse the dull ache.

Chapter Nineteen

Frederick and Jessica sat in the intimate parlor of his suite of rooms, each sipping their chosen nightcap. His, a bourbon and tonic; hers, a sweet red wine. The fire crackled in the hearth and the room smelled of burning pine.

"I think you should discuss this further with our fathers and Uncle Burt," Jessica suggested.

"Why, so I can change my mind and forget my dreams, our dreams?"

"*Our* dreams?" she asked, unable to stop herself.

"Yes, *our* dreams! I thought you wanted to travel and paint and do "all sorts of things". Have you changed your mind?" His eyes bore into hers.

"No, but I had expected to be in on the plans, not to be told of them out of the blue as you saw fit to do. What else is there that I've not been informed of?" she asked. The wine had loosened her tongue.

"Since you asked, my dear, I will be leaving early tomorrow for California, alone."

"What? What do you mean?" She placed her wine glass on the table by her chair and looked at him, her mouth agape.

"I'll need to travel ahead and prepare everything for our lives in a new city."

"Why can't I go with you?" she asked. "I'm sure you don't mean to have me travel by myself?" She wrung her hands, his unexpected news alarming her.

"Of course I don't," he replied. "I've hired a man and wife from the help my parents brought with them. Their names are Kevin and Hannah Rolland. My mother agreed to let go of them as somewhat of a wedding present to us. I am now their benefactor. It's been all arranged," he said.

"Your mother knew?"

"No, it was simply a gift. Where we choose to employ the Rollands is up to me now."

Fear coursed through her. "How could you?" She rose and walked to a window, then turned to face him, her cheeks flushed with anger. "How *could* you?"

He stood and approached her. "Calm down," he demanded as he raised the back of his hand.

She instinctively jerked backwards and closed her eyes, bringing her arm up and across her face. Then his large hand was on her arm, gently lowering it.

"My love, my love," he said. "Come sit down."

Jessica moved from the window and slowly seated herself. She reached for her glass of wine, her body trembling. She finished what was left of it.

"You're no longer a spoiled child, Jessica. You are my wife and as such I need you to behave as an adult. From now on we will discuss our affairs calmly. Do you understand?" She nodded. He leaned back in his chair considering his drink. "I'm sorry I lost my temper, but you provoked me, my darling. This is a very difficult time for me. Unfortunately, you're seeing me at my worst." He turned to her and Jessica could only nod again.

"I thought you would be pleased about this," he went on. "I have tickets for you and the Rollands. You will be well taken care of. Take this as a sign of my love for you, instead of jumping to your own selfish conclusions."

She searched his face for the truth, but she wasn't sure how to recognize it. She decided she would have to tread lightly with her new husband for her own protection.

"Please sweetheart, don't be angry." He took her hand. "This is all for the good. You don't want to live in a hotel in a strange city while we look for our own home, do you?"

Jessica took a moment to think. She looked down at his hand holding hers, the same one that nearly struck her. "I don't know. I suppose. I've heard of husbands going out West first, then having their wives and children follow, but I thought with your standing, with money and all, that we wouldn't need to do such a thing. I'm sure my father would be willing to help …"

"Your father?" Frederick's anger flared. Do you take me for some idiot, some incompetent idiot? I can take care of my own affairs and that includes my wife!"

"All right, Frederick. I'm sorry I said that. Please, calm down." Jessica placed her trembling hand over his. "Forgive me. This has all been so much for me."

His eyes were watery from the alcohol. "I forgive you," he said. "You must understand that it is prudent to let me go first, and make it as comfortable a move for you as possible."

She raised the corners of her mouth. "Whatever you think is the best for us," she said.

The next morning Jessica heard Frederick collecting his things. She left her warm bed and wrapped her robe around her. She stood in the doorway of the bedroom as she watched a man determined to get out of town. His haste made her cold. She would prepare herself for the good-bye at the train station.

Seeing that she was awake, Frederick went to her and kissed the top of her head. She felt like a child. "Good morning, my love," he said cheerfully.

"Good morning," she answered quietly.

As if sensing her disappointment, Frederick said, "My love, we must be brave. We shall be reunited soon and have a wonderful life in our new home. This simple hotel will be a distant memory. I shall acquire a fine house for us."

Jessica wiped her moist cheeks. "Yes, Frederick, if you say so. I promise I won't make a scene at the station. When will the carriage arrive?"

"It will be here shortly, and I'll be going on it alone. I couldn't bear to see you off at some lonely, dusty train station. Let's say our goodbyes here. I've arranged for you to be taken to your family later this morning. Go to them, my dear, and explain our plans. Don't forget to let them know I've hired the Rolland's to accompany you on your travels."

He kissed her again, and then he was gone.

Jessica watched from the window as his suitcases went onto the back of the hackney. Frederick climbed into the passenger seat without looking up. She followed the carriage until it was no longer in view. A feeling of despair overtook her. The rooms she had begun to call home now felt foreign and uninviting. She lowered her head and sobbed on the sill. Her thoughts instinctively went to Jacob, but she found no comfort in them. She came away from the window and dressed. She would go to her family as Frederick had instructed.

Chapter Twenty

Jessica heard a loud knock on the door. "Yes, I'll be down in a minute," she called out. She had dressed herself in a simple ensemble and was just putting on her hat. She knew her parents would be shocked by the news that her new husband had left town without her. The carriage had arrived too soon for her liking.

More pounding on the door, followed by a hoarse voice. "It's Mr. Moore. Let me in!"

She rushed to open the door. Her father-in-law stood in front of her, his face a flash of red as if he had run all the way up the stairs. Jessica was forced to stand back as he entered; he could not be stopped. She watched while he searched the rooms.

"Where is my son?" he shouted.

"Frederick is at the train station by now, I'm sure," she answered.

"Train station?" he asked, indignantly.

She put her fingers to her lips. By his expression it was clear she had given away her husband's secret. It also occurred to her that Frederick was leaving town without saying goodbye to his own parents. Something was terribly wrong.

"What do you know?" he asked her accusingly.

"I … I don't know what you mean."

"The money! Were you in on this?"

Jessica pulled together all the courage she could muster. "What has happened?"

"He drained his inheritance without my knowledge or approval! That's what has happened!" Charles blared in her face.

"Oh, dear," Jessica replied. "I'm so sorry. All I know is that he's on his way to California to set up a home for us."

Mr. Moore grunted, then left in the same manner he had arrived, without so much as a hello or goodbye. She rushed to the window to see an expensive hackney leave in a cloud of dust. Her own rented carriage waited just behind to take her to her parent's home. With a racing heart, she grabbed her waistcoat and handbag and ran downstairs. "To the Valley Depot, please," she instructed the driver.

The morning sun exposed the haze around the large, whitewashed building, the movement of people and horses stirring up the dry dirt around it. Jessica watched her father-in-law enter the train station. A few minutes passed. He stepped out, frantically looking up and down the platform. He stared off into the distance at the empty train tracks, then slowly walked away. She contemplated whether or not to approach him, but it was too late. He got into his carriage and was gone before she could come to a decision. Her driver stood at the door, ready to help her out.

"Madame?"

She held onto his hand as she gingerly stepped down. "Please wait, I won't be long."

She entered the station where dozens of people sat and stood in anticipation of the next train. The smell of old leather, worn wood, and the sweet aroma of a man's pipe made her think of distant places; the convergence of people from all over gave this simple space an atmosphere of worldliness. She searched each row of wooden benches, some empty, some filled with families, others dotted with lone travelers, then made her way to the ticket counter.

"May I help you?" the man asked from behind a small window.

"Yes, my husband was on the morning train. When did --?"

"Name," he asked abruptly."

"Oh, Mr. Frederick Moore," she answered.

"Don't see him."

"Could you check again, please? He should have been here just a little while ago. Maybe he got on the last train."

"The *last* train left three hours ago, Ma'am."

"But, he couldn't possibly be on that one. Is the next train coming soon?"

"Cargo or Express?" he asked.

"Why, Express of course."

"Here, this is our schedule," he said. He handed her a small cardboard paper with dates and times on it.

"The next train doesn't leave for another two hours," she said to the man. "Could you please check the list of passengers once again?" she pleaded.

"Madame, you can check for yourself," he said impatiently. "Here's the manifest."

She went over the lists of names, but Frederick's wasn't on any of them. She handed the paper back to him. Her mind couldn't reason with her findings.

"Maybe he went down to the station in New Haven," the clerk said. "It's a good ten hours by coach, he'd have to overnight along the way. Middletown would be my guess."

"Why would he do that?" she thought aloud.

The station worker shrugged his shoulders and returned to his paperwork, clearly bored. Jessica reluctantly turned and left, bewildered.

From the coach station Frederick hired a carriage to take him to his destination. It stopped in front of one of the brick buildings lining the tidy South Main Street in Middletown. He stepped out and stared at the hotel's many windows. The cool air drifting off the Connecticut River did not relieve the heat of nerves rising in his body. He'd tried to calm himself during the journey with the liquor that filled his silver-tooled flask, but it hadn't stopped the terrible flutters in his stomach. His plans had recently taken on a much deeper meaning. The flutters now felt like hot pokers stinging his gut. A vendor offered him a warm biscuit, jolting him out of his thoughts. Frederick waved him away, steadied his nerves and reminded himself of his pride and position.

He entered the modest lobby, where few chairs and a desk sat on a worn red-flowered rug. He turned to his right and saw his purpose for being there. The sunlight streamed in through the lace-draped windows, lighting Molly's red hair as it fell across her back. She slowly turned, her face as familiar to him as his own. He took a moment to take in the sight of her. The soft grey two-piece flannel attire flattered her tall, curvaceous figure, the skirt flowed pleasingly over her hips. The fitted front lifted her bosom high on her chest, giving her an even grander appearance. He took note of her forgiving green eyes. Molly offered her hand. Frederick rushed to her and lifted it to his lips, the smell of her perfume made his head swirl. "My dearest, I can hardly believe you are here. Thank God."

"I'm here, my love," she replied.

He embraced her and whispered hoarsely as his lips caressed her cheek. "I will never again let you go."

Jessica sat silently on the green settee in the parlor, her hands folded on her lap. Her father paced in front of her, her mother sat, dabbing her eyes with her handkerchief.

"This is intolerable!" Thomas boomed. "Charles must have a reasonable explanation for all of this. If not, we will certainly consider annulment." Jessica's heart felt the loud bass of her father's voice and she sorely wished Will was there to bring some levity to the room. She spoke quietly. "I don't think you'll get much information from Mr. Moore," she began and looked down at the floor. "He came to our suite this morning, quite upset. He didn't know Frederick had left."

"What?" her father asked. "Why didn't you say something about this?"

With the tone in the room intensifying, they hadn't heard the front doorbell chime, or noticed Winnie entering the parlor with a telegram in her hand. "This just came," she said. She handed the yellow piece of paper to Thomas.

"What is this?" he asked, snatching the paper from her. Winnie ignored his impatience and returned to the kitchen with slow dignity. Jessica's father began to read the message to himself, while Bethany and Jessica stared at him, waiting for what news it held.

"Well, I'll be damned." Thomas held the telegram out for his wife to take from him then he sat down. Jessica thought if that chair hadn't been right next to him he might have sat directly on the floor.

"What is it?" Jessica asked, looking back and forth between her parents.

"The Moores are on their way to New York, then back to England," her mother said. "Mr. Moore states they are returning on some urgent business and will be in contact with your father as soon as they are able to."

Jessica was shocked by their lack of respect for her family. "I'm truly sorry," she said. Her mother's voice was low and distant. "What will we say?"

Jessica took a deep breath and decided it was time to take matters into her own hands. She stood up and smoothed her skirt. "I'm leaving in a week's time to be with Frederick."

"I should say not. Sit down," Thomas commanded rising from his stupor.

"With all due respect, I'm a married woman now. I will follow my husband. I need you to see me off at the train station, Father. Otherwise it will be as if I'm running away. Please do not bring that shame onto us. Father?"

Thomas looked at his daughter. "Yes, we wouldn't want that," he said flatly.

Was it resignation or sarcasm? She couldn't tell. "Don't forget that Uncle Burt and Aunt June will be moving there shortly."

"Yes, the fools," he replied.

She hugged her mother then her father and walked to the front door. Her hands shook and her heart lost its rhythm. She swallowed her emotions and opened the door to her childhood home; it felt heavy and she thought for a brief moment that it might not let her go. She stood on the veranda and looked out on the manicured lawn. She heard a child at play across the way and it brought her back to the many times she played among the flower gardens so lovingly attended by her mother and their gardener. She took comfort in knowing she had painted many renditions of them to take with her. Winnie came into sight and Jessica called to her. Winnie approached the bottom of the veranda.

"I heard everything, child," she said.

Jessica ran down the steps to the housekeeper. "Oh, Winnie, I will miss you!" she cried as they embraced.

Winnie took her by the shoulders. Jessica looked into the dark eyes of her friend. "Be brave, Mrs. Moore. I have faith in you. Keep your temperament strong, but think before you speak, now."

"Yes, Winnie," Jessica answered. Winnie took up a corner of her apron and gently wiped the tears off of Jessica's cheeks. Her heart swelled with remembrance of Winnie doing the same thing when she was a child and skinned her knee or someone wasn't playing fair with her.

"Work calls me, now. Be on your way."

Jessica turned to the road as Winnie went back to her chores. A sweet breeze swept across her face, the intoxicating smell of spring, of new beginnings, the promise of summer's warmth. She took it as an invitation from the world to go forward into the unknown.

The envelope Frederick had left for her revealed tickets for three passages and also a sum of cash, but she was sorely disappointed to discover that he had booked them on a cargo train and not the luxury passenger train.

No matter, she thought. She held onto the tickets; the lightness of the papers disguised the importance they represented. *I will be as worldly as Jacob.*

Chapter Twenty-one

Molly Ambers entered the luxurious compartment on the passenger locomotive in New Haven, Connecticut. It would take her back up to New York City and then on to San Francisco. She was enthralled. The lush velvet green curtains in the window matched the velvet on the ceiling, where a small glass chandelier was mounted. She could feel the plush carpet under her feet even with her shoes on. The polished walnut table for two held a spray of white blooms in a light blue vase: lily of the valley, her favorite flower. She bent to inhale the delicate scent, then spun around and wrapped her arms around Frederick and kissed him on the cheek.

"Will this do for your journey to the West, my love?" he asked her.

"Oh, yes!" she replied. She crossed the small suite to a wall-mounted bed and ran a hand over the satin cover; the invitation to lie in it delighted her. A square box with a yellow ribbon tied in a French bow came from behind her. She turned to face Frederick. "What is this?" she asked, her eyes gleaming with anticipation.

"Open it," he replied.

She untied the ribbon carefully; it would be her keepsake for life. She sighed deeply as she smelled the contents and saw the treasure it held. "Candied citrus! Where on earth did you find it?"

"I have my sources," he replied. "I had a few dipped in your favorite chocolate." She began to delicately pick one out of the box. "Ah no, my love," Frederick softly reprimanded her. "These are for me to feed to you, later tonight."

She closed her eyes with a sigh of contentment as he proceeded to feast on her lips and neck. "Can we close the curtains and pretend it's nighttime?" she asked in a faint whisper.

He cupped her face in his hands, kissed her again, then still holding on to her, he reached over and undid the black braided ropes that held the window curtains apart. She felt dizzy as he devoured her lips as if *they* were made of chocolate. She held still as he moved from her mouth to her neck and slowly and methodically began to unburden her body from its heavy skirt, letting it fall down around her silky body.

She in turn began to undress the man she had waited so long for. His defined, broad chest showed his racing breath. She slowly unbuttoned his shirt and he moved to kiss her. She coyly backed away, fueling his lust. He tore off his shirt and pulled her closer to him. They stood quietly for a moment, then she brushed her soft, round hip against his flesh, and backed away, until he pulled her to him. Molly melted into submission. He laid her on the bed, turned her over and had his way with her. She groaned into the satin pillows as he reached his climax; her body shook from his might. When it was over she lay limp. She remembered how forceful he could be; she was hoping he had softened. Frederick's new wife came to her mind; had she been a virgin, poor girl? But Molly had no intentions of dwelling on Frederick's marriage. She was pleased she had aroused him to near-violent ecstasy, even if it had frightened her a little.

The bright morning sun found its way into their nest, waking Molly. Their room smelled of citrus, chocolate and flowers, mixed with the heavy scent of their satisfied bodies. She yawned and stretched, then slipped out from under the satin sheets. She pushed back the curtains, welcoming in the bright light, only to wince from its intensity. Before she could close the curtains, she felt Frederick's naked limbs surround her own. He helped her shut out the world. She found herself back on the fluffy warm bed as the locomotive rocked.

"I wanted to see the countryside, my love," she said in faint complaint.

"There will be time for that my beauty," he said. He made love to her, more gently this time. She consented with pleasure, but her thoughts were on what delicious delights she would have for breakfast; she knew Frederick had paid the porter to bring the morning meals to their compartment.

When they weren't making love, Frederick read aloud to Molly from the newspapers he picked up along the way.

"I will know more about this country, and how to behave in it, through these papers; much more than I ever would by reading from our own country's sheets," Molly commented as she gazed out the window at the passing landscape. It seemed dull to her and she hoped that San Francisco would provide a more interesting scene. She hadn't had time to study more on the place beyond the small brochure in the lobby of her hotel. Too nervous to read as she waited for Frederick, her eyes just wandered over its contents. She wished she had informed herself better. Frederick's voice broke into her thoughts.

"Yes, I suppose they tell the story of certain parts of this land, but remember, my dear, we'll be living in a modern city, where you will be revered for your English beauty and manners."

"Oh, yes, of course, Frederick."

In the late afternoon of their sixth day of travel they peered out of the small windows to catch a glimpse of the Oakland Train Station. It was unremarkable to Molly. "Don't worry, my love," Frederick began. "Wait until we get into the heart of San Francisco. It will surely change the look on your face."

"Oh Frederick, I *am* excited," she replied, although Molly was sad this part of their journey was over. She loved playing the wife of Mr. Frederick Moore, however brief. In the dining cart she had noticed how the other passengers looked at them with smiles of approval. She knew they made a fine looking couple. One woman even asked if they were newly married. "Yes," she replied, and it gave her a thrill. Molly wondered what future this place held for her. "But I thought this train went all the way to the city."

"We'll take the ferry by coach into the city," he replied. "Come away from the window and finish packing your bags."

Frederick stopped her as she was about to place her feathered hat on top of her loose chignon. "Are you ready to live here as we agreed?" he asked.

"Yes," she answered quickly.

"Are you sure? It's a dangerous game we'll be playing."

"I know, my love, but I would gladly do as you say to be with you," she answered.

After writing to Frederick to congratulate him on his marriage, Molly announced her engagement to a colonel in the English army. Frederick began his pursuit of her not long after. She wasn't about to let his marriage of convenience to this American girl or the fact that she had to play a game of charade deter her from being with him. He was hers now. She had already begun the charade with her family. She schemed to convince them of her plans to travel to America to visit a wealthy friend in New York City; a young woman she had met at one of the many summer balls. With the help of a few confidants, who were in on her mischief, she set sail with her parent's reluctant approval. Her mother's tears and her father's flexed jaw could not deter her from her destiny. She promised to write.

"I must warn you, if my wife finds out about us it will go very badly for me. I may even have to send you back."

Molly nodded. Her insides stirred nervously. "Frederick, how could that happen? You can merely tell the story you told me, that I am the widow of a dear friend of yours and I needed to get away. Since you are here it made perfect sense for me to travel to you, my benefactor. Is that right?"

"Yes, that's it exactly. Well done." Frederick replied. "But are you still resolved to being my mistress, instead of my wife?"

"I've told you already. If this is what I have to do to be with you, then I shall," she answered confidently. "Because I love you. Besides, I will be very happy if you continue to spoil me like this."

Frederick laughed. "Then you should be very happy." He took her in his arms and kissed her lips lustfully before they parted from the train to begin their new lives of pretense.

The late April breeze coming off the bay was cooler than Molly had expected. It reminded her of the weather back in Liverpool. She smelled the air that held the scent of salt water mixed with a hint of fragrant flowers. It mingled with the stale odor of travelers and their luggage and Molly was keen to be out of the crowded, stuffy corridor. She pushed through the crowd and was helped off the train by the porter. She took in the Spanish-style depot. The glare from the white stucco stabbed her eyes. She searched her handbag for her shaded spectacles.

The ferry ride turned Molly's stomach and traveling through the city of San Francisco proved to be very annoying as the coach tipped to one side and the other, hitting various potholes. She didn't care for the rows upon rows of houses on dirt streets. The ferry station was dismal and the hordes of people reminded her of the docks of Liverpool; a section of that city she and her family managed to stay clear of. She put a handkerchief to her nose. "Are we almost there, my love?" she asked him.

"The Grand Hotel is in sight, my dear," Frederick proclaimed.

The impressive hotel improved her mood and she anticipated the home Frederick had promised her. She was relieved that the hotel was to her standards. The quaint gingerbread façade and the elegant interior décor charmed her. She felt like royalty.

Frederick's much-anticipated arrival to this wondrous place, once only a dream, gave him an overwhelming sense of accomplishment.

The great city of San Francisco, where I will begin life, on my own terms!

To Frederick the city was a marvel of architecture and people. He was as a child looking in every direction to catch all views at once. For all his studies of the place, he was truly taken with its modernity and diversity. Though it was not nearly as impressive as the city of Liverpool he found it suited his needs very well.

He wanted to explore every inch of it. Yet, there was much to be done before his wife arrived. His nearly-perfect plan had one glitch: Jessica's own travels with the Rollands would get her here sooner than he would have liked even with the slower cargo line.

He left Molly to settle into her room at the hotel, then he went to his own room to begin his task of finding a home for him and Jessica. He wanted to impress her. He searched through the city's directory to find a manager of properties. As for Molly, he felt that the hotel would have to do for a time, though he was keen to find a secluded place for her, one he could visit regularly without being noticed.

Tomorrow he would go to the First National Bank of San Francisco to verify that his funds had transferred from the Bank of Connecticut, and to secure his employment. Mr. Harding was his immediate contact at the bank. He had assured Frederick of a position in the investments department. Frederick's thoughts turned to his father. He could almost hear his outrage at the missing funds. He knew his nearly perfect forgery of his father's signature would be to his benefit one day. He calculated again. It would have to be enough. There was no turning back now.

Frederick found the name of a property manager and wrote it down on the small pad on the desk he sat at. Then he took up the newspaper, stopping at the society page. He was eager to learn about San Francisco's elites and how they spent their money. His pulse quickened as he thought of manipulating the wealthy into investing with him personally, with the legitimacy of the bank to ease any of their concerns; it would take every bit of his English charm.

He dropped the newspaper on the desk and laid his body on the bed. His mind was in a whirlwind yet his body begged for sleep. His body won out and he fell deeply into rest.

Chapter Twenty-two

On the day of her departure, Jessica's stomach ached dully. Her anxiety was high and her head felt light. She tried to eat, but it only worsened the discomfort in her belly.

Her parents were waiting at the Valley Depot, alongside Burt and June. A few of her friends from town were also there. The Rollands stood at the corner of the building. She swallowed hard, straightened her back, and walked over to her family with the confidence of a woman who knows exactly what she's doing.

"Thank you for coming, Father."

Her father ran his hand through his slicked-back hair. "I'm sorry that we didn't have a proper good-bye the other day." Jessica smiled as the sound of the passenger train came closer.

"Is it here already?" Bethany asked. She wiped her eyes.

It was time for Jessica to tell them. "My train is on the other tracks," she said.

"No, Jessica that other train is for cargo," her mother corrected her, then added in a whisper, "and for the less fortunate."

Jessica played along. "Yes, of course," she said. "Good-bye, Mother, Father. She embraced her parents, then her aunt and uncle. June handed her a small sack of biscuits as she dabbed at her eyes. "I will telegram my brother Austin. If you need family, my dear," she said.

"Thank you, Auntie," Jessica replied as she accepted the sack. She looked around nervously. How was she to get out of this? Then a thought came to her. "It will be awhile before we can board," she said. "It's perfectly fine with me if you don't want to wait. I would prefer it. It's too heartbreaking to say goodbye." To her relief, they all agreed. Minutes later, she faced her future alone. She closed her eyes and lifted her shoulders then released them with an exhale. Before she could dwell on her fear, the newly arrived passengers crowded the wooden sidewalk. Noise and movement filled the area. The flurry of activity swept her up, exciting and new. She looked frantically around for The Rollands. They approached her at last. "We'll be boarding now, Mum," Kevin said.

Jessica winced. "That is not our train. Our train is the cargo one. It will board shortly."

"Oh," said the Rollands. They looked at each other then back to Jessica.

"It will serve our needs, I'm sure," Jessica said.

The couple smiled in unison and nodded their heads. "No doubt it will," said Hannah.

She sat on the edge of her seat and looked out the window. The small compartment was stuffy and smelled of old clothes and wood that had taken on the stale body odor of so many travelers. She trembled, her heart beating as if it were trying to keep time with the click-clack on the rails. Her luggage had been placed in cargo and she had only her ticket, the large satchel she clutched and the cash she wore safely in a pouch sewn into her undergarments, along with the thoughts of her future, to cling to. It barely kept her from running from the train before it picked up too much speed. She placed her bag in the overhead shelf then sat back on the thin cushion that laid across the wooden bench. The back of the bench had a similar cushion attached to it with small black tacks. The seat felt reasonably comfortable. At last she settled in as the large, steel locomotive took her through time and space to her new home.

The rail station quickly became a distant place and the future lay ahead. Jessica turned away from the window. She smiled at the Rollands seated across from her. They looked content. They weren't much older than she. Kevin was tall and thin, but he appeared strong. With his short, thick strawberry blonde hair and ruddy complexion, he looked more Irish than English. Hannah was shorter and broader, but looked just as capable. Her wavy blonde hair half of it in a bun atop her head and round face complemented her husband's appearance. Jessica was relieved by their youth. They couldn't act so much as her guardians, and she could be free to exercise her adulthood.

The first leg of her journey took her to New York City where she and her companions were obliged to change trains. A steward approached Jessica as they all waited for the next cargo train.

"Miss, you're in the wrong area," he said. "I'll be happy to direct you to the Express."

Jessica handed him their tickets. He sized them up with a steady gaze. "Very well, get along."

Jessica's cheeks flushed with embarrassment. She rushed to the ticket agent's window. "How much for the Express to San Francisco?" she asked.

"Ninety-five dollars, Madame," he replied.

Frederick had given her only forty dollars and her own money came to less than that. She walked back with her chin up and waited with the Rollands to be loaded onto the cargo train.

The locomotive chugged out of the city and into the rural landscape. The hours passed. She was exhausted, almost as if *she* had been moving the train along. At nightfall, the thinly padded benches became their beds and Jessica bunched her skirt underneath her body for more comfort. She soon resented Fredrick's choice. She learned the cargo train took nearly four days longer to reach the cost then the Express, the thought of nearly ten days of this made her weary.

She tried to sketch as much of the changing views as possible. From the vast rolling hills of green, yellow and brown to the dipping valleys seen from their vantage point atop a winding ridge. Her fingers worked feverishly to capture it all on paper. She looked forward to every stop, hoping it would offer something more than a quick stretch and a local newspaper, but each one seemed just the same as the last: little groupings of houses around a depot, one saloon, maybe a church, and a small general store with nothing worth looking at. Always cargo being unloaded from the train and other cargo being loaded onto the train. Lumber for new houses, housewares, stoves, grain, people. She felt more like cargo with each passing day.

The next stop was coming up and Jessica brushed her wrinkled skirt and redid the pins in her hair. She was pleased to see that this depot had an eatery alongside what looked like a larger than most general store. She wasn't the only one. The excited passengers swarmed toward both, leaving Jessica, Hannah and Kevin to fight their way to the first open table they spied in the small café. The food on the train was barely edible, and the aroma surrounding them smelled like home cooking. Jessica could feel the juices in her stomach churn. She had long gone through her aunt's delicious biscuits.

As the three savored boiled potatoes and slabs of ham, a man announced that the train would be leaving from the Cheyenne, Wyoming station in one hour. Jessica finished eating first and decided to sketch the scenery. It captured her imagination, which was filled with the lives of cowboys, pioneers and Indians. She was amused at the large straw-like balls tumbling at the winds bidding. She had never witnessed such open land without trees. Only a few rocky hills in the distant gave a break to its vastness.

She wondered how anyone could survive out here. She also wondered about the Indians. Would she see any? The conductor had instructed the passengers not to wander too far from the train or station on their recent stops. Her heart quickened, but she felt perfectly safe.

Jessica stood by the train, the shade of it providing relief from the searing sun. She fell easily back into her relationship with pencil and paper. The air was dry and dusty, and without the stifling humidity that accompanied this sort of warmth back home. As she sketched she made references to color on the side of her tablet so she could put paint to it in the future. She loved organizing her subjects for later, when the memory of the moment would be revisited and the pencil drawing would come alive with color.

"That's a fine job you're doing."

The baritone voice startled Jessica. She turned around to find a large man leaning over her shoulder. She had to tilt her neck to take in the full height of the rugged cowboy. She'd heard about these men and what they were capable of doing. Her instincts were alerted and she immediately felt frightened and vulnerable. She folded her paper around her pencil and looked around for other passengers.

"Sorry, ma'am. Didn't mean to catch you off guard like that," he said, tipping his hat back. His face revealed a deeply tanned and creased complexion behind a full beard and heavy brows. He squinted his eyes and examined her face. "Say, you look just like a fella I met down in Colorado. It was in a saloon. Mighty fine poker players, him and his friend. I mean you're a heck of a lot prettier, and I'm sure you've never even been near a place like that. I'll be a monkey's uncle though; you could be his kin for sure."

Jessica didn't wait to hear more. In her fright she fled back to the café, clutching her paper to her chest. She stopped in her tracks, her skirt bringing up a whirl of dust. "Kin?" She wheeled around, looking one way then the next. The man who seemed to come out of nowhere had disappeared.

As the train slowly labored out of the station, Jessica felt as if she were leaving Jacob behind. She was sure, if she hadn't been such a mouse, she could have learned the whereabouts of her cousin and brother. She wanted to scream in frustration. Just then the train whistle did it for her. She tried unsuccessfully to settle into her seat. Hannah asked if something was wrong. Jessica jabbed her skirt underneath her as she explained the story of her brother and cousin leaving to go west with a trading company.

"They may be heading to some relatives of mine," she said. She told them about the cowboy who might have had some information for her.

"Oh, you were right to get away from him like you did," Hannah began. "I've heard about these American cowboy types, and they are rogues to be sure!" Her eyes were round with horror.

"I agree," Kevin said. "Seems like a long shot for him to be talking about your kin. This country is a whole lot bigger than I expected. It would be like finding a tiny piece of straw in a huge heap of dung." He sat back and crossed his legs, satisfied he'd said his piece.

"A needle in a haystack, Kevin!" Hannah quickly corrected him. "Excuse him, Mum, he thinks he's just among his own sometimes and forgets his proper speech." She gave her husband a warning look.

"If your kin are heading in the direction we're heading then I'm sure you will meet up with them again, sooner than later," Kevin assured her.

"Kevin, you shouldn't raise her hopes like that!" Hannah scolded.

"Now I'm getting her hopes up! You're impossible, woman," Kevin argued.

"Thank you both," Jessica cut in. "Hannah is right; I'm making something out of nothing. I know I'll see them again someday. I just miss him so much."

"You mean to say, *them*?" Kevin asked.

"Yes, yes, *them*," Jessica corrected herself. She closed her eyes bringing the conversation to a close.

She was awakened by the conductor announcing the next stop. She and the Rollands would remain on the train, so she sat up slowly and stretched her arms and legs and rubbed her stiff back. She smiled at the young couple across from her, leaning on each other as they slept. It made her long for the closeness she hoped for with Frederick, and was missing with Jacob.

When the train came to a stop, she peered out the window looking at the passengers disembarking and the large crates leaving the train. She wondered for a moment what these particular ones held. She sat back and prayed they'd be at their final destination soon. She noticed the newspaper beside Kevin, it had last week's date at the top. Old news was better than no news. She gently picked it up.

She came to an article with the headline "Illegal Gun-runners Scorched". She recognized the name Keaton. She had overheard her father and uncle Burt talking about J. Keaton being their sons' new boss. *Could this be him?* She read about the raid on a camp of outlaws who covered their actions under the title of a trading business run by one Jones Keaton; a wanted man. The sheriff of the small Colorado town claimed they had killed all the outlaws and confiscated many of the illegal weapons and ammunition then set the camp on fire in the dark of night. The bodies of the men taken to the pauper's cemetery for burial without informing next of kin; for sanitation and safety. The paper slid out of her hand and fell to the floor; she needed air. As she struggled to open the window, Kevin stirred, then quickly rose to help her. She stuck her head out and gasped.

"Mum, steady yourself," he said. "Hannah, wake up!"

"What is it?" Hannah exclaimed, seeing Jessica's pale face hanging out of the window. "Oh, dear, I'll get her some tea," she said and rushed out of the compartment.

Kevin helped her back to her seat. Once she had restored her breathing she broke down and began to cry. He sat with her, trying to console her. He looked down at her feet and picked up his newspaper; their eyes met. "It said they were all dead," Jessica whispered. Her hands began to shake and she felt faint.

"Mum, that article was about some lawbreaking cowboys. Couldn't be your kin. Your mind is going in all different directions. The tea will help."

Jessica trembled. "I guess the traveling has gotten the better of me," she said. "I'll be fine. Yes, some tea would be nice, thank you. And Mr. Moore need not know about this. Do you understand? He worries so."

"Of course, Mum," he replied.

She stayed awake that night, putting together a timeline for her own comfort. As she grew wary of her mind's endless pursuit for answers, she concluded that Will and Jacob had abandoned the unlawful Keaton to go off on their own, long before this terrible tragedy.

Chapter Twenty-three

The heavy rain pelted the compartment window for the second straight day. By late morning it showed no sign of stopping. Jessica shifted restlessly in her seat, unable to get comfortable. Her bottom was sore and her bunched-up skirt and the thin pad on the bench had long ceased to offer any comfort. Kevin rested a hand on Hannah's knee as she worked her knitting needles, he in a light snooze. The passenger who had joined their compartment in Laramie City read a book, ignoring them all. Bored and sleepy from the rocking of the train, she fell into a fitful rest.

Without warning a loud crash of steel and a violent jolt threw her and the stranger into Kevin and Hannah, whose own bodies were slapped against their seats with the same great energy. The car lit up, struck by a bolt of lightning. Screaming steel penetrated their compartment and they were thrown onto the floor like rag dolls, amid the broken glass and their belongings. Cries and shouts sounded throughout the train as Kevin and the man helped the women to their feet.

"What happened?" Hannah cried out.

Jessica's head was spinning and her whole body hurt. She shuddered uncontrollably as she quickly gathered up the scattered contents of her large satchel. Shards of glass pricked her fingers and her skirts were stained with her blood. Kevin dragged open the wooden door of their compartment. Jessica followed Kevin, with Hannah close behind. The cries of the other passengers, crowded in the narrow corridor, rang in her head. *This must be a dream.* She wiped her face and came away with more blood — her head had a small gash. She reached in her pocket for her handkerchief and held it to her wound.

Squeezing and pushing their way through the chaos of panicking people, Jessica and her companions made their way off the train. The mid-morning sky was dark. The smell of rain mingling with the burning coal filled her mouth with an acrid taste. Her feet immediately sank into the soft mud and silt. Making every effort not to slip, she labored to higher ground. She glanced back to see Kevin helping Hannah up the steep bank. When she returned to her own struggle she lost her footing and plunged into the soupy earth. She jerked herself upright again and continued to the top of the hill. Having lost her handkerchief in the fall, she found a clean corner of her waistcoat and wiped the mud and blood off her face.

From the higher vantage point she could see what had happened. An avalanche of rocks and mud across the tracks had caused the train to derail. Some of the cars were on their side, their cargo spilling out. It looked like a toy that a child had carelessly played with. A small fire ignited in the second cargo hold. The flames hissed under a deluge of rain.

Assured that she and Hannah were fine, Kevin joined the other men in offering assistance to those still trapped on the train. The folks walking from the wreck looked dazed. Her mother's words came to her mind … *"and for the less fortunate"*. She felt no different than any of them.

The merciless rain beat down. Soon she and Hannah were standing in pool of water. She had to shout to be heard over the downpour. "We can't stay here! We have to find our luggage! I'm sure there's another station not far from here!" She hoped she was right.

Hannah refused to move. "No, we have to wait for Kevin!"

"We'll find him, Hannah! We can't stay up here! The ground

isn't stable!" Jessica gripped Hannah by the arm. The others began to move from the rain soaked hill, crowding around them. The young English girl stopped abruptly. One of her shoes had been sucked into the mud. "Oh! My boot! Mum! My boot!" Hannah cried.

A stranger pulled the shoe out from the muck as he rushed by, his wife clinging to his side. "Thank you, sir!" Hannah called. She held onto Jessica as she stepped into her sodden shoe.

"Come on!" Jessica pulled her along.

The ground gave way beneath them and they were thrown into a large black pool alongside the tracks. Jessica pulled herself out of the mud, coughing up the dirty liquid that splashed into her mouth. She scrambled around for her satchel. Although soaked, it wasn't damaged. She clutched it to her chest; inside were her paintings of a place and time she needed to have with her.

With one hand holding her heavy skirt high above her ankles and the other holding on to Hannah and her bag, she searched for Kevin through the chaos. He was helping the injured to higher ground. The other passengers huddled together waiting for instructions from the conductor and his crew, stunned into silence. The dark clouds drifted to the east yet the rain continued. After what seemed like hours, Jessica heard horses neighing in the distance. Several buggies and flatbeds dropped toward them over the ridge. Her shoulders relaxed; someone had found them.

Jessica helped place a young woman with an open gash on her neck into a flatbed. She wasn't sure if the girl was dead or unconscious. Staring down at the woman, helpless in her horror, she felt a tugging at her sleeve. It was Kevin, his face flushed, rain dripping off his nose. In a hoarse voice he said he had secured passage to the next station. She and Hannah hurried alongside him in the direction of a man who was speaking to a small crowd. "I've got a horse and flatbed on my ranch not far from here!" the man shouted. "I could get about twenty of you in it. Only the able-bodied. Can't care for the injured. You'll have to walk the mile or so to get to my place, but I can take you from there to the stage coach station."

Jessica turned to the baggage car where the rest of her luggage was stored. "I'll ask the conductor if he knows where my cases are!" she called to Hannah.

Kevin jerked her back. "No!" he exclaimed. "That man is leaving *now*. We have to go!"

She was forced to walk away from the disabled train and its forlorn passengers, and somewhere in it all, her baggage and the rest of her art supplies. But how could she grieve her loss? She was alive, after all. And uninjured.

The rancher rode ahead of their weary group in a small covered buggy, his horse splashing its way through the muddy grassland, leaving a dismal path for them to follow. Though none of the twenty passengers spoke a word, they could be heard by the sucking sounds of their shoes stepping through the mud. Soon Jessica couldn't feel her feet; any daydreams she had entertained of her future now turned to thoughts of survival. Once at the rancher's stables, they piled into the back of his open wagon, each finding a tiny bit of space on its slatted bottom and between the straw bales. Some women had to sit on their husband's laps. The rain finally let up.

Jessica sat beside a bale of straw in the corner at the back. Kevin in front of her and Hannah curled up next to him. She leaned into the bale to avoid touching the man to her left. The look and smell of the wagon reminded Jessica of the hayrides she would take with her friends on clear, crisp fall evenings. She let her mind wander as the flatbed tossed her about. Sometimes Will and Jacob would join in those hayrides. Her memory fell on one occasion when she was fourteen. Jacob had brought a red plaid wool blanket with him, which he draped over her shoulders. She ached for him to be with her now, keeping her warm. The wagon jerked violently and she got tossed to the side into the man next to her. She pulled herself upright. The man said nothing and she didn't apologize. Feeling embarrassed and humiliated, she swore she would never again take for granted a decent carriage or hackney. Her impulse to ride a horse as fast as she knew how and find a way out of her predicament was a mere fantasy. She looked around at the others and sighed. The landscape was flat and dotted with cattle offering only boredom and the reminder of why she was there.

When they finally reached the Brice Ford Stage Coach Station, about ten miles from the train wreck, the rancher undid the board from the pen-like enclosure they had travelled in for nearly four hours. Jessica was one of the last to climb down, her legs cramped. She felt dizzy and held to the wagon to get her balance. The sun piercing through the clouds gave little warmth. A chill ran through her entire body and she rubbed her achy, stiff shoulders.

As she came around the wagon, Jessica took in the mob of people surrounding the stagecoach office; no doubt word of the train wreck had already reached the waiting crowd. The long, low building was neatly painted white and several coaches were parked in a graveled area to the side. She looked at the large round clock hanging outside the station. Seven-thirty. It would be dark soon — they needed to find a place to stay. The station manager was doing his best to give out his limited information above the shouts of questions and cries for loved ones. Kevin helped to push them to the front and after some time they were issued tickets for tomorrow morning's stagecoach departure, which would take them to the next train station.

She came away from the crowd and looked around the small street for lodging. There wasn't much to see. A few commercial buildings lined either side of a dirt road. The usual saloon and sheriff's office, along with a small general store. A few houses in the distance. Then she spied a hotel sign at the edge of the town. She let out a breath. Her legs would make it to what she hoped would be a hot meal and comfortable bed.

Although she had once thought her money would fund her purchases of souvenirs along the way, Jessica now felt it couldn't be used for anything better than two clean rooms with a soft bed.

Alone and disheartened, she removed the mud-encrusted dress from her body. She looked at her bloodied waistcoat and examined her forehead. Her head and fingers throbbed. Blood streaked across her skirt as well. She thought of the injured woman she helped into the flatbed and her stomach churned. She could have been that woman. She shook her head to dislodge the memory. Finally, with a thin towel in hand, she entered the communal water closet down the hall. Once the large copper tub was filled she slid her aching, weary body into the hot bath. She closed her eyes and let the warm water take the chill and dilute the day's events.

She inhaled deeply and let out the sobs that could no longer be held at bay.

Chapter Twenty-four

Jessica and her companions waited at the ferry dock in San Francisco. The boat ride had been rough, adding to the discomfort of their long journey. A cool April breeze nipped at her and she crossed her shawl over her chest. The water wasn't as fragrant as the seaside back in Connecticut, but this was the *Pacific* Ocean and she felt as if she were truly on the other side of the world. She tried to take it all in. The docks were filled with men loading and unloading the many boats and ships at the end of grey and worn piers. A whiff of kerosene filled her nostrils, then fish, and finally another breeze brought back the salty air. She noted the wooden crates of cargo were similar to that on the train. More crates coming from ships she imagined had traveled from other countries, places she could only dream of. Perhaps filled with silk scarves from the Orient and exotic trimmings for ladies' hats. Sarah had made a request for a pair of earrings. In the distance a fine carriage caught her eye. It pulled up near the docks. It looked odd among the everyday workers and dirty boardwalks. Out of the coach stepped her husband. *"Frederick!"*

Frederick approached. The look of disgust on his face spoke for him. She looked a fright. Indeed, the dress Hannah had lent her was wearing her more than she it. Her hair was a heap of tangles, far from the neat bun she had at the start of her trip, and she was damp with sweat.

"Oh, Frederick," she said. "It's very good to see you. Very good!"

"My dear, what in God's name have we here?" he asked. "We must get you out of those clothes." His lips did not touch her cheek even as he bent down to kiss her.

"Yes, a bath and some fresh clothes would help."

"Come along then," Frederick said. He gestured to the fine carriage. "How on earth could you be in such a state?" he asked.

"You haven't heard of the derailment?" She had to quicken her pace to keep up with him.

"Yes, of course," he snapped. "How would I be here to meet you otherwise?" He softened his tone and continued, "My dear, I thought I gave you enough money to keep yourself well." Jessica walked on without a word.

"Here we are." Frederick motioned her to the carriage. She stopped to wait for Kevin and Hannah. Frederick sighed with impatience.

"It's been a pleasure traveling with you, Mum," Kevin said. Hannah wiped away a tear.

"Thank you. Both of you. Under the circumstances, it's been my pleasure as well."

Frederick handed Kevin a piece of paper. "Here is the address of our home. You can find transportation at the station house. I will expect you both to be clean and in uniforms by tonight. You'll find your quarters in the back. The door is unlocked."

"Yes, Sir." Kevin bowed.

She watched them go, knowing it would be inappropriate to say anything more.

Frederick helped her into the carriage. "Leave your feelings for them here," he said sternly as she glanced back at the young English couple. "It does no good to befriend the help."

She nodded and found her seat. Another means of travel; she was just about undone. She peered out the window, but she was too tired to take any of it in. She would venture out when she was rested. She recounted the story of her harrowing experience, realizing Frederick had chosen to sit across from her, his hands clasped in his lap. Finally, he spoke.

"My poor darling!" He reached over and touched the bruised cut on her forehead. "I will make this up to you my love, with everything it takes. I hope the home I've chosen for us will begin to lessen your grief. We'll get a doctor to examine you. I need you to be well."

She offered a weak smile, then ventured to ask him about his own journey.

He sat back in his seat and examined his nails. "My own days of travel were somewhat boring. I managed to keep myself entertained, however."

"I'm happy you had a good trip," she replied. "But why didn't you go directly to the train station the morning you left? I went there to look for you and . . ." She caught herself as his demeanor changed. His eyes squinted at her as he folded his arms across his chest.

"Why were you looking for me?" he asked.

She swallowed hard. "It was your father. He was looking for you and I . . . Well, he was so upset when he left. I followed him to the Valley, and they told me that you might have taken a different train."

"My father, yes, I'm sure he was upset. I'm sorry you had to be on the receiving end of it. Frederick relaxed. "I took out a large sum of money from my accounts back in England without telling him. He's had a fierce grip on me all my life, Jessica. I couldn't let him know too much about my plans. You understand, don't you?"

She watched his expression as he gave his side of the story. It touched her, but she still wondered about the nature of his departure. "I don't mean to question your intentions. I'm wondering why you didn't say good-bye to him."

"We said our goodbyes in our own way," he answered. "You don't understand my family and I don't expect you to. I just hope your loyalties lie with your husband."

"Frederick, need you ask? I'm sitting here with you, aren't I?"

"Forgive me," he said. "Talk of my father tends to bring out the worst in me."

She nodded. She carefully worded her next question. "Did you make a mistake with my ticket? I was on a cargo train."

Frederick looked away. "I thought the adventure of travel would be greater for you that way. The Express I found to be quite boring."

There would be so much more to learn about this man, and she still questioned the nature of his departure. She felt she may never know.

"Never mind all that," he said. "How nice it is to have my wife by my side." He leaned forward with a mischievous grin. She didn't dare move. He slowly came off his seat and sitting beside her she felt his warm hand sliding up towards her inner thigh. With a smile she gently moved away from his advances. "Are we nearly there?" she asked sweetly.

He straightened and sat back. "Yes, my dear. Nearly there."

The horses clopped onto a brick courtyard and stopped in front of the stately house with sumptuous two-story curves on either side of the entrance. The wooden French door was adorned with brightly colored stained glass windows, like jewelry on a woman's bodice. Pristine white columns on each side of the dark wood porch held a soft turn of light green ivy, making a lovely contrast to the winding, red and yellow flower beds along the skirt of the enchanting home. It stood off the road, but its grandeur could be seen by passersby.

"Oh my goodness!" Jessica stated. There were similar houses back home, but this one was so richly adorned. It looked more like a dollhouse; one she couldn't wait to play in!

Frederick beamed. "Is it to your liking?" he asked.

She embraced him tightly. "It's lovely. I can't wait to see the inside."

The grandeur flowed into the two-story high foyer. The sun filtered down in soft beams of light from the windows above them. A white staircase wound up to the second floor, with the balcony waiting for someone to gaze down from it.

She slowly spun around, feeling as if she were in a fairy tale. She walked into the parlor. The furnishings were simple and the room was airy and bright. The columns on the large fireplace mimicked the ones on the front of the porch. In front sat an ivory-colored chesterfield with two chairs, their legs looking as if they could get up and walk away. She delighted in the artistry of such furnishings. Now, they belonged to her. Inside one of the bay windows was a charming writing desk and low back padded seat, waiting for her future letters, RSVP's and thank you notes. Rich walnut tables sat next to the sofa and between the cushioned chairs. Jessica was grateful Frederick had chosen a comfortable and warm décor for them. It was as if he had read her mind.

He escorted her to her bedroom. They passed another bedroom she assumed would be his and a finely appointed bathing room with a water closet. In her room, there was a large four-poster bed with a footstool to step up and into its luxury. She laughed as she plopped onto the voluptuous feather mattress, where the silk duvet and large pillows enveloped her. Frederick followed and hungrily began to remove her clothing; his heated strength welcomed her, yet she felt no desire. She gave into him, not wanting to spoil the moment; she buried her rising feelings of loneliness, unlocking her desire for Jacob.

Chapter Twenty-five

In his tent in the foothills of Clear Creek, Colorado, J. Keaton counted money on a small, uneven table. In the dim light, his shadow loomed larger than his thin, 5'6" frame. The campsite was nestled in an area surrounded by mighty firs, spruce, and pines. It was a sufficient camouflage.

Jacob watched from his perch against an old fir tree. He lit a cigarette, wondering how much of the cut he and Will would receive this time. Keaton's math differed from his own. He looked at the tired and dirty faces of the men sitting around the campfire. Will was breaking a small branch into pieces to be used as chips for a poker game.

It had been nearly seven months since he and Will met this motley crew of men. The ten of them got along fairly well. The occasional fight broke out, but everyone knew who to avoid after a long day. The sale of weapons and ammo had been good, a fair amount of Indians, farmers and cattlemen had done business with Keaton's group, and one lawman who said he lost his rifle and needed to secure another without anyone finding out. Last week the crew raided an old farm about twenty miles away. Rumor had it the farmer had a store of black-market guns. It was clearly by luck that no one was around at the time. They took what they could carry and galloped away as fast as their horses could take them. Tempers were always on edge. Transporting the rifles, pistols and boxes of ammunition to various points of trade while dodging the law wore hard on the men. The poor pay and lack of decent lodging added to their strain. Their boss spent most of his time giving orders and collecting the spoils, showing little concern for his crew, except for one: Caleb Cantrell.

Caleb's long blond hair made it easy to spot him in a crowd. Tall and lean, his liquid blue eyes and fine features, belied his ability to be as intimidating as any who had traveled in this rugged wilderness. Jacob admired Caleb's intelligence and self-assuredness.

Keaton consulted with Caleb on every move the outlaws made. To Will and Jacob, Caleb — who wasn't much older — was just as much their boss as J. Keaton. He rode the cousins hard. Whispers circulated early on that he disliked the pair and had claimed he wouldn't be surprised when they went running back to their mothers, tails between their legs.

Jacob was offended by the rumors at first, but he knew he'd prove to be as worthy as the rest of the group, so he leaned in and did what was expected of him. He strove to outdo Caleb. From scouting out new trails and customers to a friendly hand of poker, he silently competed. This did not go unnoticed by Will. His cousin joked to him one night. "I'd hate to see you two in a fight over a woman; the poor gal would end up with two dead suitors."

"That will never happen," Jacob had replied.

Among the group was Levi Landsburg, a small spitfire of a man. His generous smile revealed dark, crooked teeth and his thick brown hair was always dishevelled. Caleb towered over him, but only in stature; he treated Levi with all the respect and trust due an old friend.

Levi had revealed to Will and Jacob that he'd once seen Caleb kill two men when they had tried to rob him after a fair deal had been struck. Jacob thought it was probably just gossip, but he took it as the warning it was clearly meant to be. On another occasion, Jacob had asked Levi about the stick up Caleb's ass, sending the small man into convulsive laughter.

"You be not the first to inquire that, Jake," Levi said still laughing. He quieted for a moment. "You know, some of us have had it real hard. And some of us can handle it being that way. Not him though. He has to carry around his past like a mule carrying a pack. That's okay with me 'cause I got some packs to carry myself, so him and me, we get along just fine."

"Yeah, but you always seem to be in good spirits," Jacob remarked.

"True. My nature is what it is, but I didn't lose all my kin in an accident either."

"Is that what happened?" Jacob asked.

"Yep, when he was fourteen, or thereabouts. Upstate New York. A carriage accident in the dead of winter. He was the only survivor."

Jacob remained silent. He didn't want to give too much sympathy to Caleb.

"He went to live with his grandma, but left right after he graduated from school," Levi said. "He joined a bunch of wild fur traders and grew up mighty fast: gambling, women, you know what I'm talking about." He laughed, then spat brown liquid from the tobacco lodged in his cheek. "We met about three years ago. In a saloon in Mississippi. I was just a wandering at the time. I spotted him right away, which wasn't hard to do!" Levi shook with laughter. "The women just flock to them good looks! He was surrounded! I guess I made for somewhat of an escape, 'cause he started to talk to me as if he knew me and well, don't you know, we hit it off. Been friends ever since. We traveled a bit looking for work, did some odds jobs here and there. Then two years ago we met up with Keaton and he hired us. That brings you up to date."

He spat again, as if trying to hit a target in the distance this time. "He lived a pretty lush life there in the big city before it all changed that terrible day, I mean with proper schools and tutors and all that regal stuff. I bet he could sit at the table of kings and queens and know just what to do." Levi puffed with pride, as if Caleb were his own son.

Jacob smiled. "He's lucky to have you as a friend."

"It's me who's the lucky one." He examined Jacob carefully. "You remind me of him in a way. I mean you two look like night and day, to be sure, but I think you're cut from the same kind of cloth. Am I right?"

Jacob chuckled. "I attended school, if that's what you mean."

"Me, too. The school of life!" Levi said. He gave a wink and slapped himself on the knee.

Levi's information gave Jacob more reason to stay on guard around Caleb. Now he sucked on his cigarette and waited for his share of the money. Perhaps this time he and Will would have enough to strike out on their own. He looked over at Caleb seated on a tree stump. They exchanged a cool glance, each playing his part in their rivalry.

Keaton stepped out of the tent and handed everyone a small fold of cash. He finally got to Jacob and said, "Good job, Jake." Jacob casually stuck his cigarette in his mouth while he counted his share. To his surprise, he was given what he had expected. He figured Keaton had sensed his unhappiness with the way the profits were divvied-up and was now making amends. He looked over at Caleb. The blond man touched the brim of his hat and smirked. Jacob snuffed out his cigarette and folded the cash inside his pack, next to his other earnings. The pack doubled as his pillow and also held his pistol, buried deep.

"So, the bastard can count after all," Will whispered as he sat down next to his cousin.

"What do you know," Jacob answered.

"What's the plan for tomorrow?" Will asked.

"Haven't heard yet, but I know one thing. Those fools over there are going into town tonight to spend all their money. Damn if they don't get us caught."

"Hey, I was going to be one of those 'fools' if we didn't have a job tomorrow," Will said. "This cash is already burning a hole in my pocket. I need to keep my skills sharp."

"Right. Which ones?" Jacob jested. He knew full well that his cousin was talking about cards and women, in that order.

"Jealous?" Will tossed a coin in the air and tried to catch it behind his back, but lost his balance and keeled over.

Jacob laughed. He didn't reveal to Will that very soon, he too would have to go into one of these small towns and get lost in a card game, and a roll in the hay. Since he'd left Jessica that day, which seemed so long ago, he'd tried to avoid thinking about her. Sometimes when he was in bed with another woman he would pretend it was her, the image leaving him physically satisfied and emotionally empty.

He grabbed his pack and folded it behind his back, making the tree a little less uncomfortable to lean against. His recent dream of Jessica came flooding back to him: *Her body was close to his. He looked into her eyes and touched her soft, pink lips. He was in heaven. She reached up and touched his hair as he went to kiss her. Then she was on a train speeding away from him and towards him at the same time.* He awoke, sweating and anxious. wishing he could hold on to the warmth and satisfaction of her face, her smile, her lips.

"Jake!" Will called to him.

Jacob was rudely pulled back to his reality. "What?"

"Are you listening to me? Caleb's telling us to join him over there."

"All right, all right." Jacob made no excuses for his daydreaming. It was one of the few comforts left to him.

Caleb laid out the map of the Colorado hills to show Levi, Will and Jacob where the next deal would be made. He warned that some of the Arapahoe and Ute were in alliance with the government and may cause them some trouble. "Or they could be escapees from the reservation and gun-runners themselves," he explained. "Nevertheless, this will be a cash for guns deal only, no trading. It's the biggest one we've done so far and if all goes well each get a good deal of the profit. More than you fellas have seen so far," he said as he looked at Will and Jacob.

Jacob wanted to get his hands on some real cash, ready for the day he and Will could be free of this band of outlaws.

"Where did you get your information?" Will asked.

"I traded in these parts before. I know who to ask," Caleb answered. "What's your concern about, Will?"

"Just want to know what I'm getting myself into, that's all."

"It's a little late for that, don't you think?" Caleb remarked.

"Just get on with it." Jacob felt Caleb's hard look, but he didn't back down. "What kind of haul are we loading?"

"All the guns and ammo we got outside of Evansville. Between the four of us, we can manage it. We'll be on the trails for half a day." He assigned each their roles. "Get some sleep now, dawn will be here soon enough."

Several men left the camp to go into town. Will lay in his blanket, snoring rhythmically. But Jacob couldn't find sleep. He turned over and thought of Jessica and tried to reclaim his dream of her.

Chapter Twenty-six

The spring morning was cold and damp. Caleb, Levi, Will and Jacob headed out after a quick breakfast of hot coffee and cold biscuits. They each packed a few in their bags and poured the rest of the coffee into a canteen. They brought water and a few other supplies in case they decided to overnight on the way back.

The band of four rode on throughout the morning, the rising sun warm on their backs. They broke from the well-worn trail to blaze their way through the thick brush, dismounting from their horses to chop through the berry vines and low branches with their knives.

They stopped only once on their nearly eight-hour trek. Jacob felt Caleb's tension. Indeed, this was the most out of the way trading spot they had ever ridden to. His mouth was dry and he took his canteen to his lips. The refreshing stream of water brought Mary's pond to mind "Damn," he said aloud. Will turned to his cousin with a questioning look but Jacob dismissed him with a shake of his head and continued riding behind Caleb and Levi. Finally, they came to a clearing in the woods where a shabby cabin stood alone.

Waiting for them on the dilapidated porch was a man with a rifle. His grey scraggly hair stuck out from his tattered cowboy hat. His clothes were frayed and he looked weak and haggard. Jacob assured himself this would be easy. With pistols at the ready, he waited with Will and Levi for Caleb's instructions. Their horses shifted uneasily from the weight of the weapons.

"You took your time, Cantrell."

"We're here, Leon. Let's get this thing over with," Caleb responded, dismounting.

"All right, come on in."

Caleb signaled Jacob to follow. Jacob dismounted, his gun by his side. They cautiously entered the rundown cabin.

Two men with drawn rifles waited inside — one in the back left corner of the room and one by the front window. He instinctively placed his hand on his holster. The man at the front window was an Indian, dressed in worn military garb in odd contrast to his long black braids. He recognized him as one of the Mohave Indians. He knew that the Colorado River Tribe had some renegades and he wondered if this might be one of them. His attentions then went to the other man who stood in the corner of the small room. He was a white man, dressed like a farmer, his finger on the trigger of his gun. Jacob's stomach tightened.

"Did you bring the load we agreed on, Cantrell?" Leon asked.

"You know how this goes Leon. Show us the cash first," Caleb said.

Leon went to a floorboard and with some effort raised it. He pulled out a burlap sack, nervously looking out the window. Beads of sweat dotted the forehead of the man in the corner. Jacob felt in his gut that something wasn't right. He stood by Caleb as he counted the cash.

"Is it all there?" he asked.

When Caleb looked up, Jacob lifted his chin toward the Indian craning his neck as if looking for something, or someone. Caleb returned to counting the crisp, new bills. "You expecting anyone, besides us?" he asked Leon.

"These fellas never done anything like this, nerves that's all," Leon explained.

Caleb sensed the old man's own nervousness. He finished

counting their pay and returned it to the bag and said simply, "Get the load."

Jacob fought the urge to pull his gun out of its resting place. He stepped off the porch his hand on the holster.

"What's going on?" Will asked as Jacob approached.

"I'm not sure, but something's not right. They're acting a little squirrelly. Let's get this thing done and get the hell out of here."

"How many are there?" Levi asked.

"Counting the old man, three," Jacob replied.

"Well, at least we outnumber them," Will said.

The sun lit the dusty little room of the cabin and Jacob saw fear on the Indian's face as he peered out from behind the dirty glass window. Anxiety flared up in his bowels. He removed his gun. Will dismounted and took his own pistol from its holster. Jacob cocked his gun. He heard the clicks of his cousin's own gun echo beside him.

Levi loaded his arms with three rifles and told the boys to cover him. As he got closer, the cabin filled with more sunlight. Levi halted at the foot of the porch. He turned his head slightly to the cousins and said in a low, deep voice. "There's a gun to Caleb's head."

At the pop of gunshots within the cabin, Levi dropped his load and begin shooting. Jacob hunched down and followed behind, Will by his side. Levi jumped on the porch and shot at the window, then burst into the cabin with a mighty kick to the door. Jacob ran in his gun hot in his hands. The farmer slumped in the corner. Levi had shot the Indian before even entering. Leon crouched above Caleb, the barrel of his gun pushed under Caleb's chin. Jacob's blood ran cold and his mind sped in ten different directions. He forced himself to focus, but before he could think his gun went off, the bullet speeding into Leon's back. The outlaw coiled up and fell on top of Caleb, who immediately pushed off the sprawled body. The room fell silent.

Caleb slowly lifted himself and grabbed his shoulder. Dark blood stained his shirt and canvas coat. He up-righted the stool and sank heavily onto the seat. "Jesus Christ," he hissed in pain as he looked at his wound.

Levi tore the shirt off of Leon's still warm body and wrapped it around Caleb's shoulder and upper arm. He took the guns from the dead men, then the bag of cash. "Let's pack up the horses and get the fuck outta here," he said to the cousins and went for the door. Will followed him outside, gagging into his shirtsleeve.

Caleb looked up and for the first time Jacob saw in his transparent blue eyes and the pallor of his face the heavy consequences of this man's choices. "Thanks," he heard him say. Jacob nodded and the two men left the grisly scene.

No one spoke as they repacked the guns and got onto their horses. Levi gave Caleb a leg up. Caleb grabbed his reins with one hand while keeping his bloody arm close to his chest. Jacob wondered how far they could get with a wounded man.

The little cabin, shot up with bullet holes, its window shattered, told of the trouble left inside and the tomb it had become. The men rode away, but not in the direction of Keaton's camp. Caleb led them further west and without question, they followed. No one wanted to go back and explain this. Eventually Caleb spoke. "It'll just be a matter of time before whoever paid off Leon will come looking for us. By the look of those bills, I reckon it'll be the government."

Jacob and Will exchanged a knowing glance; this could be the end of their association with Keaton's group. They rode in the shadow of the full moon, stopping by a river for the night. There would be no campfire and their meager packs had to keep them warm, with only the light of the moon reflecting off the water to see by.

Before they bedded down, Caleb spoke to Will and Jacob. "Tomorrow, we'll divvy up the money, and you two can do whatever the hell you'd like. Just get out of Colorado as soon as possible. And for Christ's sake, keep your mouths shut. Levi and I will do the same." Caleb removed his coat and shirt and reapplied Leon's blood-soaked shirt tight to his arm and shoulder, wincing, he turned away.

"Wait a minute," Jacob said. Caleb turned slowly, his hand clutching his arm. "So what do you mean by divvy up the money?" he asked.

"Levi and I will get most of it and you two can split the rest," Caleb answered sourly.

"You think we'll just go our merry way with nothing but a damn thanks for our troubles?" Jacob shot back.

Caleb spoke calmly. "It'll be enough to get you started on something of your own. Isn't that what you fellas have been planning all along?"

"It better be enough," Will said, "or you've got two *fellas* stuck to your ass."

Caleb's laugh was short and sharp as he walked away. "Levi, you got an old shirt in that saddle bag?" Jacob heard him say. Then, "I need reinforcements here." He saw by the thin light blood running down Caleb's arm.

"I've got some liquor," Will said.

Caleb gladly took the flask of bootlegger's whiskey. "Thanks. Thought you might have something to ease the pain." He took a hearty swig and handed it back

"Keep it," Will said. "You need it more than I do."

It was barely the break of dawn when Jacob awoke from a fitful sleep. Despite the sheltering trees, he felt unsafe. Caleb, too, was awake, but he was motionless and his eyelids drooped. "You need a doctor," Jacob said.

"Yep," Caleb answered. "Do me a favor, look at my arm, will you?"

Beyond the pain, Jacob saw something else in Caleb's eyes.

Sorrow. Surely this warrior of a man couldn't be sad by his fate in the cabin. Angry. Vengeful. Yes, but not sad. Jacob went to his pack and took out a clean shirt. "Let's go down to the water," he said. "Your shoulder probably needs a good rinse."

At the water's edge, Caleb rinsed his shoulder and arm of crusted blood. His moans of pain rattled Jacob. He winced and looked away, spitting out the bile that rose into his mouth. Then he steadied himself to take a good look at the wound, his insides turning upside down.

The bloody gap in the lower part of Caleb's shoulder held no lead—the bullet had gone through, tearing up the muscle and skin. "I can't see it," Jacob said. But … I should make sure." He searched the ground for a sturdy stick. He found one and handed it to Caleb.

Caleb grabbed the stick from Jacob's hand. He closed his eyes and bit down on the wood.

Jacob's fingers met no resistance as he probed the area. He tried to be gentle, but Caleb hollered and cursed. Finding no bullet, he washed his hands in the river, leaving Caleb to catch his breath.

The two men were the same height and their eyes met on a level plain. Jacob marveled at Caleb's steady gaze. It was as if he were in a trance. Jacob tightly wrapped his shirt around the wound. "That should be fine for now. I hope you're heading to a town with a doctor. This thing could turn pretty quick." Caleb nodded and Jacob watched the tall proud man walk back to his horse. "Where are you headed anyhow?" he ventured to ask.

"Southern Oregon," Caleb answered without turning around.

The men were preparing to leave when the sound of an approaching horse caused them to reach for their guns, yesterday's adrenaline still fresh in their veins.

"It's me, Cork!" the stranger shouted.

They lowered their weapons. Cork was one of theirs, but they were shocked to see him. He came around a stand of trees. "What the hell are you doing here?" Levi shouted.

Cork approached cautiously, then slid off his horse. "I took off after I seen what they did to Keaton and the camp. Me and Harper were still in town when it happened. We came back to a real bad scene. Damn Harper took off on me. They killed all that was there, including Keaton. I crouched myself behind a tree way off in the distance." He petted his horse. "Luckily 'ol Jake here kept quiet or I'd be with 'em. I saw 'em takin' the bodies away. Then I looked 'round for y'all and remembered what you told me Levi. I figured I'd take my chances with my map and look for the cabin you told me 'bout."

Caleb gave Levi a hard look. "Who else did you tell?"

Levi removed his hat and placed it over his heart. "Only Cork. I swear it."

"I seen what went on over there, don't even want to know," Cork continued. "Then I tried to follow your trail, thought I was going on a wild goose chase until a few minutes ago. Sure glad to see it's you boys here instead of them in that cabin."

"Who were the men taking the bodies?" Caleb asked.

"Looked to be the law, sir." He removed his hat. "Dead Keaton and the rest of them bodies lying there in the middle of all our belongings. After they took the bodies they burned everything we owned."

"Burned?" Jacob asked. He felt weak. *If Cork was able to find them* ... He turned to his cousin, but Will was still listening intently.

"Yep, all burned, saw the flames myself. And I had my momma's bible in my pack," Cork replied.

Caleb cursed. "What else, Cork? Do you know if you were followed?"

Cork shook his head. "Those dead men shot up like tin cans at a practice. They must've been sleepin'." He heaved a trembling sigh and wiped his eyes.

The early dawn chill added to Jacob's dread. "They'll be coming for us next," he said quietly.

"Glad to see you made it out alive, Cork," Will said. He solemnly led his horse to the river to let him drink while he filled his containers.

"Where ya headed now?" Levi asked.

"Nowheres in particular, I guess," said Cork.

"You can travel with us," Caleb said. "We're riding hard until we reach Oregon. Can you manage that?"

"Yes, Captain! Thank you, thank you! If you be needing any help there," he said as he gestured to Caleb's bloody wrapped arm.

"I'll be fine. Thanks just the same, Cork."

They all joined Will by the water's edge. It was clear and ice cold. Jacob splashed his face and let out a whoop. He was alert and ready to ride. Caleb did the same with his good hand. He stood next to Jacob. "Thanks," he said in a low voice.

"You might not be so thankful once that thing starts to fester."

"I want to give you and Will a clean share of the loot. Each of us gets a fourth."

"All right. That's fair of you." Their horses drank from the water and whinnied. "So, what's in Oregon? If I may be so bold."

"My family," Caleb answered.

"I thought your family was —"

"There's a large tribe of Indians on a reservation in the south there. They are my family."

Jacob stooped down to top off his canteen. He wanted to ask about the tribe, but he held his questions in check.

"I'll get you back your shirt one day."

"Keep it, we both know we won't see hide nor hair of each other ever again," Jacob remarked. They each gave a short laugh.

"Just as well," Caleb said. He took his horse from the river and walked away. The rest of the men followed and each mounted his horse.

"I'm ready to get far away from here," Jacob said to his cousin.

"Yep," Will agreed. He turned to the others. "It's been interesting working with you men, and sure hope to hell I never have to do it again," he said with a smirk.

Caleb addressed the small group. "Before we go I want to take a moment to honor Keaton and the men we worked with." He took off his hat and put it over his heart his long blonde hair hanging down onto his leather vest, stringy with a few ends crusted with blood. He was barely able to keep his horse steady with his bad arm. A brief silence followed. Caleb placed his hat back on his head and took the reins of his horse with his good hand. "Good luck," he said to the cousins. He gave a nod to Jacob. Jacob touched the brim of his hat and nodded back.

"You boys take care of yourselves now until our paths cross again someday," Levi said.

Jacob had a feeling he would see them all again, but dismissed the thought as they went their separate ways. Caleb, with Levi and Cork, turned towards Oregon; he and Will deeper into the Southwest.

The sound of the horses in full gallop echoed through the hills

Chapter Twenty-seven

It took over a month before Jessica found a rhythm to her household, and with each passing day she felt more of the weight of her new responsibilities. Hannah was her main housekeeper. Frederick had allowed Jessica to choose the cook, though he insisted the woman must be able to prepare English food. It was a challenge, but after many interviews she hired Miss Benton, who agreed somewhat reluctantly to consult with Hannah for recommendations of Liverpool's favorite dishes. These included stewed meats and game pies, boiled chicken with vegetables and a jellied broth, tea service with the right biscuits and always a good and presentable pudding. To Jessica's relief, Frederick seemed very pleased with his meals.

Her next task was finding a kitchen maid for the cook. She hired a girl by the name of Gretchen Giles. Though barely seventeen years old, she seemed strong enough to handle the rigors of the kitchen and Miss Benton's authoritative personality. Her final hire was a helper for Hannah. Angie Greer was also young and sturdy and Hannah took to her immediately. Kevin worked with Frederick's choice of stable man, Sam Richards, and a gardener was hired to come regularly to tend to the grounds. Jessica's task was to keep her household running smoothly as she defined herself as mistress of the house. It barely gave her time to indulge in her artistic passion, but she managed to squeeze in a few painting sessions each week.

Frederick had surprised her with a small studio down a grassy hill from the main house. It stood like an eager child, ready to play. Glass French doors opened like welcoming arms. The gabled roof cottage was painted white with light blue trim. Inside, the high ceiling gave the space a palatial feel. Jessica left the doors open when she could; the cool, soft breezes were refreshing inspiration. She felt a sense of freedom here. Frederick provided her with the money she needed to make it her own and it became one of her favorite escapes. A wooden tabletop easel rested on a small desk. A soft pink chaise, her most prized possession, stretched against one of the walls. She would unlace her shoes, step onto the thick flowered rug and lie on the chaise while her mind wandered to Jacob and their time spent at the pond.

Today she retrieved the picture she had painted of Jacob and her by Mary's Pond and bravely hung it in her studio as a bittersweet memory. She gathered her art supplies and sat on the manicured grass outside her studio. She breathed in the mild sweet air. A large eucalyptus tree stood close by. The striped bark and draping branches filled with blue-green leaves intrigued her and she began to pencil in what she saw. A gust of wind blew its rich scent her way, making it all that easier to capture the tree's essence. Before long she was in her peaceful element and the painting came to life.

After a while she rose from the ground with a moan, her legs stiff. She was satisfied with the results of her efforts and brought the painting in to dry before she applied the final touches. She heard her husband's voice. She quickly washed her hands in the basin of water and hurried inside.

It wasn't long before Jessica was obliged to socialize with the wives of Frederick's clients. Teas, clubs, and dinner parties began to clutter her calendar. She longed to paint, but her dreams and aspirations had diminished while Frederick's career as an investment banker took center stage. She was expected to be the supportive wife and gracious hostess. Still, Jessica was determined to fulfill her desire to create art and discover her new world. While Frederick was at the bank, she would explore various parts of San Francisco with Hannah by her side. Yet, these places were the ones she was allowed by Frederick to visit; she wanted more.

The bright and warm July day made Jessica restless. She asked Sam to take her and Hannah into the city. The lanky, middle-aged driver was reluctant at first, but Jessica held firm. She handed him a small map on which she had circled several streets. "Make sure we see all of these places, and tell me if you know others I might like exploring." He took the map and securely fixed his cap over his balding head. "Yes, Ma'am."

On Battery Street, by one of the many wharves lining the bay, she and Hannah explored the merchants' wares. Everything from maritime supplies to ladies' gloves were sold in shops tightly strung together. The smell of the salt water on this morning helped to diffuse the strong odors surrounding the bustling area. Jessica held her handkerchief to her nose as they went by the shops and stales. The fishmonger cleaning a bucket of newly caught salmon, shouting "Salmon, just out of the sea!" Another market selling pig parts, and yet another had a vat of boiling meat, or something that smelled as such. Then Hannah pointed out an art supply sign. The small store sat cramped between the printer's and a woodworking shop.

Jessica opened the wood-trimmed screened door and her eyes lit up. She was like a child in a sweet shop. With the allowance Frederick gave her each week, a generous two dollars, she purchased a new brush and some paper. The storeowner suggested a few art galleries on Kearney Street, not far from where they were.

Sam handled the carriage with experience as he guided the horse along the roads, some laid with wood, others packed-down earth. Still the coach seemed unstable and she and Hannah held onto the handles inside the doors.

One of the galleries displayed unusual paintings: dark still lives of rotting fruit and bread, limp flowers and portraits of scruffy faced men. The most provocative art, however, was in a small room behind heavy black velvet curtains. They were allowed to go into the room with the gallery owner's consent and warning. The seductive art showed women and men with exposed bodies. Animals and ethereal ladies doing the unimaginable. Jessica felt her face heat up as she bravely took in the artist's techniques. Hannah turned away with a giggle and left the room, the black curtain falling heavily behind her. Jessica was glad to be alone. She came closer to the scandalous paintings. She wondered how they got the lines and shadows to work with such intensity. This was something she had never seen before. She went to touch the raised edges the brushstrokes had left behind when the curtain opened and the gallery owner gestured her to come away. The show was apparently over. She nodded graciously and she and Hannah left.

Next was a dry goods store that displayed various artists' works. The paintings moved Jessica in a most profound way. These paintings were optimistic and dreamlike. A dream of something good to happen and figures relishing in contentment; something she longed for. The warmth and richness of the colors spoke to her. Beautiful ladies in summer dresses standing on a seashore, the blue and green ocean dancing before them. The same lovely ladies lounging on a front porch, fanning their lightly dressed bodies. Families on ships crossing the vast Atlantic in hopes of a new life. Gardens rich in abundance. Each one beckoned her to enter its scene. She left the store doubting her own abilities and discontented with her life. She wondered if she would ever be able to create such graceful forms of art that moved the observer in such a way. The desire to improve her talents fought with her reality. After she returned home she felt eager to try her hand at creating folds of light fabric in sunlight. It wasn't easy, if only she could receive more training.

Whenever possible she ventured to other parts of the city, some less savory than others. If Frederick were to find out she would have to endure his harsh reprimand. Yet, her hunger to expand her view of the world kept her adventurous spirit from shying away from these places.

"Sam get my horse ready. I'd like to take a ride," Jessica said as she pulled on her leather gloves.

"Ma'am, I'd be happy to come along. The park is nice this time of day."

"No thank you, I'd rather be alone today, Sam."

Once on her horse she rode down the cobbled drive and onto the dirt street. She took out a map. The red line she had drawn directed her to the Tenderloin District. She'd heard the area was filled with a low-life society and determined that a quick look couldn't hurt. Then she'd ride back and stop at the park so she wouldn't make a liar out of herself when Frederick asked where she went today.

The dry, dirty roads and shabby buildings were indeed, an eye-opener to Jessica. She coughed several times to clear away the stench as she passed by the open sewage. A group of men stood outside a large gray building with the words "Salvation Army" painted on its face. Their sullen eyes stared past her. One gave out a sharp laugh as she rode by. She quickened her pace staying to the opposite side of the street. Once past, she dismounted and tied her horse in front of one of the shops. She was aware of the stares she received from the residents of the neighborhood as she carefully navigated the uneven sidewalk. She peered into the buildings whose patrons knew as little of her world as she knew of theirs. She smelled the aromas of baking bread and cured meats, and meals cooked from recipes she could only imagine — stews, chowders, soups. She thought perhaps this was not so different from her world as she first thought. Aunt June would be filled with curiosity from these various smells.

She entered a small shop. The shelves of freshly baked bread and seasoned rolls made her mouth water. She bought a loaf of the sourdough and a roll for her travels. Returning to her horse, she spied a woman carrying a burlap sack in each hand, the heaviness of the parcels obvious. Four small children followed behind her like little ducklings. Jessica offered to carry one of the bags. The woman looked at her suspiciously, then at her children dressed in worn, dirty clothes, the oldest without shoes. She politely refused and hastened on her way, calling to the young ones to hurry after her. Jessica watched silently as they practically flew from her. A lump thickened in her throat. She was acutely aware of her lace and silk dress, kid gloves and leather boots. She was a strange intruder in these lives. She mounted her horse and left the area, embarrassed by her attempt to use this place and these people for her own inspiration. Yet, she had a great urge to paint those faces and buildings and show this reality in her art. She wondered how she could replicate this scene with her innocent watercolors and limited techniques.

Her latest adventure, however, proved to be far more than she bargained for. Sam took her to Market Street. She instructed him to stay with the carriage while she went on her own to the shops. "I won't be long," she informed him. It wasn't meant to be anything more than an innocent day of shopping, distracting her from her dull life.

Jessica walked along the row of buildings, each with its own store on the street level and as she looked up she saw what seemed to be a residence above; curtains hung in windows framing a lamp or plant. The sight pleased her. Living right in the heart of it all, how exciting! As she explored, wandering from one street to another, she came upon a group of fifteen or so men and women. A few of the women held small children. They were gathered in front of a bakery. She stopped to listen to the most vocal of them; a man who looked as if he was the owner of the bakery, his white shirt and pants were stained with grease spots and dusted with flour. From what she could gather, he was talking, or shouting about Chinese immigrants taking over their neighborhoods. The bakery exuded the most delicious smells. If not for the intense mood of the crowd, she would have purchased some of his pastries. Her stomach growled under her fitted waistcoat. She felt the heat of the summer beneath her breast, the sweat running down her sides. As she fanned herself she asked the gentleman standing next to her, "What have the Chinese done?"

"They've taken our jobs!" he shouted. "They work for nothing, let them live on nothing!" The group cheered him on.

"We almost got rid of the wretches! How were they allowed to set up the damn village anyhow? They're a bad reflection on all of us!" another called out.

"I don't understand," she said, her voice rising over the clamor. "Everyone should be able to support their families." Her own bravery shocked her, but she embraced her boldness, which she soon regretted.

Another man poked his red face into hers. His long gray apron revealed the blood of a butcher's work. "What do you know about any of this? You with all your fancy clothes! What do you know of the opium dens? The gambling? It's against the law!"

"Not to mention the sewage problems they've caused!" a woman shouted, rocking her baby as it began to cry.

The butcher grabbed Jessica's lace collar and came in closer. His rotten breath made her stomach turn. "You gonna feed my five kids? Are ya?" he sneered, then spat on the ground in front of her. "Go back to your life of tea and needlepoint!" The crowd began to close in on her, some raising fists.

Jessica backed away, lifting her skirt to hurry down the sloped and narrowing street. She could hear him and others taunting her as she made her escape. Her satin and beaded purse swung from her wrist, her fan clutched in her hand. She ran blindly. Finally, she ducked into a shop with an open front door and peered out from the porch to make sure no one had followed her. She took a deep breath, straightened her coat and smoothed the skirt of her dress. She waved her fan in front of her face against the stifling heat. She wasn't sure how far she had come, but as she looked around she felt as if she had stepped into another world.

Aromatic bundles of herbs, whole fried ducks, garlic, onions, hung from the many storefronts of a large market. Barrels filled to the brim with potatoes and the pungent smell of brine. Across the dirt road was another such shop but this one sold silk scarves, brightly painted lanterns and baskets each filled with colorful trinkets the likes of which Jessica had never seen. She spied a pair of slippers and her mood changed. A line of such goods claimed both sides of a narrow road.

She became aware of three Chinese men in matching dark, baggy clothing, their long braids under small black caps. They bowed to her and began to show off their baskets of produce. One came rushing from the back of the store with a canister of powder. "You like this?" he asks as he raised it to her nose. The strong spice made her head spin with its exotic and richly layered scent. She recognized cinnamon and nutmeg, but the other notes were unfamiliar to her. When she asked about the ingredients she received an answer in Chinese. She smiled and nodded and bought a small bag of the unusual mixture. She tucked it into her purse and stepped onto the road.

Jessica wandered further into the village where the shops had colorful lanterns and banners with Chinese art and symbols hanging from their front awnings. She fancied them, but dare not bring a lantern or banner home. The colors fascinated her and she wanted to paint the scenes. The storekeepers called for her to buy their offerings. A few children ran out and tugged at her skirt, beckoning her to buy their trinkets. She smiled and patted their heads then continued along. She was fascinated by the sounds of the unfamiliar language, the music played by a man crouched over a gourd-shaped instrument with only one string, the heavy aroma of sweet and sour foods swirling among the taste of dust and the stink of sweaty bodies. A cooling breeze brought forth the water from the bay then retreated, returning the previous odors. She spied only one or two non-Chinese people beside herself.

She was in the Chinese district, the place she had most desired to visit. Surely, the people at the bakery were overreacting. What she saw was friendly and communal. Before long she had passed the merchants and there was a noticeable lack of women and children. The road narrowed further and a sharply aromatic smell hung in the air, like the incense from church, but not as appealing. It cut into her throat and she began to cough. She put her fan to her nose. She went around the corner, hoping to find more of the pleasant shops and owners but she soon found herself in a maze of square and squatty huts built from old lumber and scrap metal. Each doorway had gray smoke trailing out from the inside as if escaping some misfortune.

It came to her. This was the place the men were talking about. Prostitution. Opium. Gambling. Anxiety rose in her chest. Where was the road she had come in from? Where were the sweet and colorful shops? She walked on, looking from one side to the next. The air felt heavy and gray-blue shadows had replaced the bright sun. Chinese men sat outside the huts hunched over tables, scattered with cards and some with small whitish blocks. She turned around to retrace her steps. A young Chinese woman dressed only in a yellow silk robe with a painted purple dragon appeared from one of the small doorways of the low shanty buildings. Jessica pressed her fan to her nose and mouth, but the smell of dirty flesh, urine, and feces mingled with the acrid smoke bellowing out of the doorway, causing her to retch. She rushed from the scene just as a small woman grabbed her skirt. She tried to get away by slapping the woman's hand away with her fan. "Let me go!" Jessica shouted.

A man stumbled from an adjoining hut, a long black pipe in his hand. Jessica finally freed herself, but soon his hand was on her, pulling her into his den. He was not Chinese, but a tall white man with an ashen face. His hair fell haphazardly over his forehead. She fought with all her might, dropping her fan. The man set aside his pipe and grabbed her by the waist. He brought her hands behind her back. She struggled to get free in spite of the pain in her arms and shoulders. The Chinese woman came over and with a cackle picked up Jessica's white, pearl adorned fan and flitted it mockingly, then threw it on the ground and stepped on it. The man who held her captive gave a sinister laugh into her ear. His stench made her feel faint. His crusty lips were on her cheek and she screamed. Surely the others in the more civil part of the village would help her. Her throat went and she could barely let out a squeak. The man pushed her away, his laughter like the scraping of gravel. Jessica lost her balance, falling to her knees. The man simply retrieved his pipe and ducked back into the dark cavern.

Jessica picked herself up and ran, spitting out dirt, tears streaking her dusty face. Finally, she saw a familiar shop, then another and another. She ran for several blocks until the village was well behind her. She stopped to catch her breath, bent over, her hand clutching her stomach. Where was Sam?

She began to walk up a hill to get a better view of the city when, to her great relief Sam came running toward her. Jessica kept her calm in front of the flustered driver. "Ma'am, where have you been? I'll lose my job!" he exclaimed.

"Just take me home. Mr. Moore will know nothing of this, Sam," she commanded. "I simply got turned around."

"Your clothes, Ma'am. Your face!" He took out his handkerchief and offered it to her.

She waved it away. "I have my own, thank you." He helped her into the coach and she fought a desperate need to fall into his arms and weep with gratitude. Instead she gracefully entered and sat on the soft velvet seat. The carriage gave a jerk and she was headed back home. She took her handkerchief from her stained handbag that curiously had remained on her wrist. She let herself go and wept into the fine material. They were nearly home before she stopped shaking.

In the safety of her bedroom she sketched the faces of the people she had seen. First her hand would not keep steady then she began to recreate the scene without hesitation. Her pencil worked as if it had a mind of its own. The experience had delighted her then frightened her to beyond reason and she didn't want to forget any of it.

Chapter Twenty-eight

As the summer progressed, she eagerly looked forward to her Uncle Burt and Aunt June's arrival to Clermont City, the small town across the bay. She missed her family, and she keenly missed Jacob. She wondered if her cousin and brother were still alive and where they were. She did her best to stifle thoughts that they were in peril or worse, dead.

She wrote to her mother and to her aunt of her new life as if she were a contented wife. She wrote to them of Frederick's growing reputation and her good standing among this new society. Their letters in return were full of pride and excitement. She hoped that perhaps she could relay a few small truths to her aunt once they were face to face. She needed to tell someone of her discontent, if only sparingly.

Loneliness surrounded her with only her art to escape to. Conversation with Frederick centered on him and his clients. She had soon discovered that he and his business associates had a self-centered view of the world, one in which she was becoming less comfortable in. The women in her new social circle were very much concerned about how they appeared to others and where, and even more so, who did what and where they were seen and how they were dressed and coiffed and bejeweled. It was no different than the society back home yet in a strange way, less elegant.

Society bored her as much as it had at home. She wanted nothing more than to sit with Jacob and tell him about her views and opinions. What he once laughed at, she was sure he would find engaging. Every now and then the subject of the misfortunate came up at a dinner party or tea, but with no substantive conversation to follow.

"They should follow our lead," a woman had said at one such social gathering. "We must educate the poor," said another. A third woman had announced that the wretched underclass was meant to remain as such, and then quoted the Bible as proof.

Jessica kept her opinions to herself and she managed to blend in. Yet she yearned to break down the walls that separated the rich from the poor. She wondered what her parents would think of her more sympathetic views. They had always been charitable and often as a young lady she was obliged to attend the stuffy social affairs to raise money for the less fortunate. Yet, she had thought the poor as a problem, far away from her upper-class lifestyle.

The summer dinner party held in the home of one of Frederick's prospective clients was among the last of the season. The road leading to the small estate overlooking the city was daunting, but from the grand entrance, the sweeping view of the bay made the journey well worth it. An orange grove sat amid a carpet of green grass, the ripe fruit ready to pick. It was enchanting.

Once inside they were led to the ballroom through the grandest foyer Jessica had ever seen. The ballroom was gaily decorated with bouquets of hydrangeas, feathers, gilded pinecones, and lush greenery at every turn. Exotic fruits were piled on silver and gold trays that sat on small polished walnut tables strategically placed along the perimeter near towering potted plants and ornately decorated screens. A buzz of conversation with murmurs of awe and delight could be heard above the orchestra playing softly at the far end of the ballroom.

Although it was a magical setting, Jessica felt melancholy. Loneliness followed her even among all these people. After her brief experiences with the unsavory parts of the city, she felt compelled to enlighten the elite. She was certain they should be providing assistance. Perhaps she might form a committee. The thought gave her the courage to speak up. She looked down at the red skirt of her dress. It shone like a bright apple in the flickering light of the gas lamps. It felt a bit too much. Although the other women's dresses were formal, they didn't match the richness of her own. She would have liked to have worn something more fitting to the season, but Frederick had insisted she wear the red gown. "You must represent me in the utmost of good taste," he had explained. Adjusting her satin and lace bodice ever so slightly she observed the other women looking at her. She smiled at them graciously.

Margret Peterson, the wife of John Peterson, a rich landowner from Texas and one of Frederick's clients, approached her. "My dear, you look enchanting. Come join us and tell us where you got such a vibrant dress."

"I'd love to Margret," Jessica said. She turned to see Frederick giving her a nod to join him. "I see that my husband desires my company. Perhaps later."

Jessica stood with Frederick in front of their host, Mr. Kentfield, a successful merchant whose sole enterprise came from his trade with China. The potential client seemed a good person to begin her discussions concerning the unfortunate. Soon after Frederick introduced his wife Jessica began her cause. "Mr. Kentfield, what is your position on the plight of the poor in the Tenderloin, and the drug trade among the Chinese?" Mr. Kentfield stared at Frederick as if he had just been slapped across the face.

Frederick turned to Jessica and said, "My dear, Mr. Kentfield has much more important business to be concerned about." Mr. Kentfield raised an eyebrow at Jessica and puffed up his already protruding chest.

She swallowed her anxiety and continued. She couldn't help herself. "What is more important than one's fellow man?" she asked. "You of all men must be aware of the misfortunes befallen them."

"I beg your pardon?" answered Mr. Kentfield.

"We are all striving to make good and decent lives for ourselves," Jessica continued, her breathing becoming shallow. She placed the back of her hand to her neck, her blush surely making it red. She had plunged into the deepest part of a vast lake. Taking a step back she continued her misguided crusade. "Is it not right that we help those who are less fortunate and struggling with impairments such as addiction? And some of the Chinese girls are—"

"Jessica." Frederick spoke in a low, threatening tone, his hand gripping her arm. "Excuse us, Mr. Kentfield, my wife owes you an apology for her disrespectful comments."

Frederick's fingers dug into her arm. She had gone too far. Her heart beat fast and another flash of heat rose to her face. "I'm terribly sorry. I didn't mean to be disrespectful. You may already be donating, sir. I will assume that is the case. Now if you will excuse me, I will let you continue your conversation." Jessica's billowing dress rocked back and forth as she took large steps to escape. How could she have made such a terrible error in judgment? She felt ill. When she reached the ladies, she was out of breath.

"What is it, Jessica?" Margret asked.

"My, you are flush," another woman commented.

Jessica touched her cheek, "I think I'll step outside for a bit of fresh air."

"I'll go with you," Margret insisted.

Once on the terrace, Jessica felt more herself. She turned to Margret. "I've just made an awful fool of myself and worse, I embarrassed my husband."

Margret looked away. "Oh, dear." She turned back to Jessica. "What could you have possibly done to embarrass your husband? You're the model of the perfect wife."

Jessica smiled. "Thank you Margret, but I certainly don't feel that way this evening. Shall we go back inside? She courageously stood by the other ladies, her back straight, a polite expression on her face. She would somehow salvage this evening by being "the model of the perfect wife."

That night Frederick unleashed his anger. The parlor was lit by a few lamps and large shadows loomed across the patterned walls. "Because of your childish behavior I had to court Kentfield the rest of the night! Do you know how many other business men were in that room? That's how many you cost me!" This was the first time she had seen such rage come from him. She looked down.

"Look at me when I speak to you!" Frederick commanded.

She raised her head. Her body shook. "I will never interrupt again, Frederick," she said. "Please lower your voice, everyone can hear you."

Frederick lashed out at a large vase atop the table nearby, sending it crashing to the floor. Jessica's heart jumped and she rushed out of the parlor, fearing she would be next to experience his wrath. She found Hannah and ran into her arms, weeping convulsively and trembling with fear. Hannah held onto her until she was quiet. Jessica retreated to her bedroom without an explanation.

She locked the door and sat on her bed, pulling the covers around her. After a short while, just as she began to feel safe, she heard a knock on the door. Her body became rigid and her pulse quickened.

"It's me, my love," Frederick said on the other side of her barricade.

She hesitated, then crawled down from her bed. She stood at the door for a brief moment. Did she hear him breathing? Should she let him in?

"I'm begging you my dear," his muffled voice pleaded.

She opened the door. He stood in front of her, his arms behind his slightly bent body. He peered up from under his brows. It reminded her of a naughty child hoping for forgiveness. "Frederick, you frightened me," she said with a quaking voice.

"I know, my dear. I hate myself for it. Please say you'll forgive me." He drew next to her, his body was warm. With a single finger he lifted her chin then kissed her lips, enveloping them. His hands ran up into her neatly coiffed hair, then down her neck and onto her back. She whimpered.

He entered her room and closed the door behind him. He led her to the bed and began to kiss her softly as his hand caressed her breasts then slid down between her legs. She let him undress her and make love to her. He was gentle with his passions and affectionate. It almost felt romantic to her, yet his previous behavior had put her off and her trust for him had vanished. His display of rage troubled her throughout the night. She would talk to him about it in the morning.

The room was light with the first rays of a new day. Jessica turned to face her husband. He smiled and touched her cheek. "Good morning, my love." His voice was husky from sleep.

"Frederick." She sat up in the warm bed. He lay next to her, sliding his fingers up and down her arm.

"Yes, my dear," he answered.

Before she could continue, the knock on her door indicated that her breakfast tray had arrived. "Yes, come in," Jessica called to Gretchen.

The young woman entered and curtsied, as Frederick had instructed all of the female staff to do. With wide innocent eyes, the maid apologized for not bringing up a tray for him.

"That's quite all right, Gretchen," Jessica said. "Mr. Moore will be taking his breakfast in here this morning.

"I will decide." Frederick sat up. "I will take my breakfast downstairs shortly."

"Yes, Mr. Moore," Gretchen replied.

"Go." Frederick waved for her to leave. The maid curtsied, then scurried out of the room and closed the door.

Jessica inhaled. "Frederick, your manner with the staff …" she began.

"I've told you before, we do not make friends with the servants," he said, cutting her off.

"Being polite does not mean we are making friends with them," she insisted.

"Have you forgotten the limits of my patience?" he barked.

In an instant his mood had changed again. She grasped that the scope of his anger was something inherent to him and that she would have to protect herself by not provoking him. Her dual life would continue. He would have his dutiful wife while she took the risk of becoming her own person. Society and Frederick were on the same side. She shivered.

"What is it my love?" Frederick asked.

"Nothing, my dear. Perhaps the cool morning," she replied.

"The weather here is similar to England. You'll get used to it."

"Yes, Frederick."

Chapter Twenty-nine

Jessica sat in the women's dining room of the Palace Hotel. She thought of a different Palace Hotel, the one she was not allowed to speak of. This hotel, however, was indeed a palace. She waited impatiently. She had accepted the invitation from Margret Peterson, which stated she would be introducing Jessica to one Mrs. Randell Gaines, an art dealer in San Francisco. Jessica had arrived early, anxious to meet this woman. She took in the opulence around her. Each table had a white linen cloth cover and held a gold vase of fresh flowers. Gold accents were everywhere, from the legs of the chairs to the curtain ties to the chandeliers. Even the wall panels were gilded; she felt the glow of it on her face. A man quietly played a white grand piano in the middle of the room. The Palace Hotel would certainly be a place for wives of wealthy men to be seen. The hotel looked ready to welcome royalty. The impressive inner circular courtyard where her carriage entered gave her the feeling she should be wearing a tiara. Although Jessica wore her finest day dress, the one with the periwinkle blue lace that overlaid the cream-colored silk, she felt a bit underdressed.

Her anxiousness outweighed her self-consciousness. Jessica was excited to be meeting someone outside of her husband's financial circle, not to mention a person in the art world. She took out her timepiece from her deep blue velvet and pearl incrusted handbag. They were late. She looked around and noticed the dining hall filling up. The sunlit space was cool for the middle of August. Still she felt a wave of heat come over her. She hoped they would arrive soon — the other women were beginning to stare. Soon Margret and Mrs. Gaines were at the table.

After the formal introductions, Mrs. Gaines quickly said. "Please call me Jilly, everyone does." Jessica relaxed and decided to soak up as much from this woman's knowledge and experience as she could. She saw that the thin, and lively redhead was as equally enthusiastic about the topic. It felt exhilarating.

"We're a small community of artists and art enthusiasts right now, but my husband Randell and I are working to make our presence known and more importantly, to bring talented artists to the public's attention," Jilly said. "Margret tells me that you are an artist yourself."

Jessica felt shy. She hadn't given herself that title yet. "I have more desire than talent."

"Have you shown any of your works?" Jilly asked, ignoring Jessica's self-deprecation.

"Yes, a few, back home," she answered.

"Yes, Connecticut is it? And how were they received?"

Jessica moved in her seat and wished she hadn't had Hannah tie her corset so snuggly. "Rather well," she replied.

"Very good. Then I would love to take a look at what you do, your style, interpretation, use of the medium," Jilly said.

Jessica nibbled on a piece of bread, hardly touching the shallow bowl of bouillabaisse in front of her. *Style, interpretation, medium?* She had learned all of these things at college and with Mr. Cromwell but now came the real test and she wondered who she was as an artist.

Before she could answer Jilly continued. "If we find you have some talent you may join our association. We have a newsletter printed monthly. It may be helpful to you. The dues are minimal."

"Now that I've introduced you two, perhaps you may meet again to talk all about your mutual interest," Margret said.

Jessica smiled and looked at Jilly. "Yes, I would like that."

Jilly grabbed Jessica's hand. "I want you to come to a celebration with me."

"When?" Jessica asked. She flushed with anticipation.

"Tomorrow afternoon at the Billingston Gallery. It's not far from here. My husband and I are hosting a showing of Leo Gosselin's work. Invitation only. He's a notable artist from Quebec, Canada and we are very lucky to have him join our group," she stated with pride.

"I saw several of his paintings on Battery Street," Jessica began.

"Now that we've secured him exclusively, you will no longer be seeing his work scattered around town, but shown only in the best places." Jilly waved her arm. "For example, this grand venue, and of course, the Billingston Gallery.

Jessica was thrilled. She was already arranging her schedule in her head to make sure she wouldn't miss this opportunity.

It was a champagne reception. The gallery was packed with people wandering from painting to painting, holding fluted glasses filled with the effervescent wine. Shortly after Jessica arrived, Jilly and Leo Gosselin approached her.

"I'm so pleased you came!" Jilly exclaimed. "I have only a minute to introduce you to our guest of honor.

Jessica looked at the man before her. He was a slight man, and only as tall as she. His suit fit close to his body and the open coat revealed his high-buttoned waistcoat and watch chain. He had brown eyes, and brown hair parted neatly down the middle accentuating his round, pleasing face. A trim mustache barely covered his full lips. He looked much younger than she expected and she thought him quite attractive. "I'm honored to meet you, Mr. Gosselin," she gushed.

"Always a pleasure to meet a fellow artist," he replied in a thick French Canadian accent.

She had myriad questions for him. He stood close and leaned in as he spoke. "My studio is open to new talent. I most enjoy painting lovely women as yourself. We must get to know one another and share our …" He came even closer to Jessica and she had to take a half step back. She wished she hadn't noticed he smelled clean, like men's soap.

Jilly took him by the arm. "That's enough of your flirting Leo, say adieu to *Mrs.* Moore."

He bowed his head to Jessica. "*Nous nous reverrons.*"

Jilly turned back as she escorted Mr. Gosselin away. She mouthed, "I'm so sorry."

Jessica tilted her head and raised a shoulder. Disappointed, yet flattered, and somewhat aroused she turned to one of his large canvases, then another, studying his brush strokes, his use of color and light. The oil paintings intrigued her. The colors were soft and intricate and the subjects, mostly of women and children, were set in lush gardens, fields of flowers and seaside cottages. She marveled at his use of light, noting it for her future paintings. She was joined by an older woman who looked out of place among the highbrow crowd. Her plain, dark blue dress had no accents or lace and a large feather adorned a dark green hat tipped to one side. Unpolished lace-up shoes and thin leather gloves. Despite her bohemian dress, she exuded a regal manner.

"What a mess," she declared. Her baritone voice vibrated through the crowded room.

Jessica refrained from comment, not wanting to encourage the woman into a conversation. But she turned to Jessica and said, "It's a shame, such good talent going to waste on this imitation of life."

"I like the sense of calm conveyed in the scene," Jessica offered, folding her gloved hands primly in front of her waist, her ivory-colored bag hanging from her wrist.

"I told him to put his soul out for all to see," the woman continued. "No, he caved to the rich and painted these abominations for a quick sell!" She threw her hands in the air. Jessica began to move away, but the woman stuck out her hand.

"I'm Glendora Sangroven. People call me Lenny. And you are?"

Jessica politely shook Lenny's hand. "Jessica Messing. I mean Mrs. Frederick Moore. I'm newly married."

"Oh, you poor thing." Lenny laughed and shook her hand with the force of a man.

Jessica looked down at the woman's grip and slowly recoiled then fixed her eyes on the painting in front of her, searching for a way to make a graceful but quick exit.

"Are you an artist?" Lenny asked.

"Yes, I think so. I'm trying to be," she answered, flustered. It was the first time she had accepted the title of artist. She settled her nerves. After all she certainly didn't have to impress this woman, and she liked playing with the notion.

"What do you work in?" asked Lenny.

"Watercolors," Jessica replied thoughtfully. "Yet, I do like the look and feel of oils."

"Yes, that's my medium as well. Oils, I mean," Lenny said. She raised her chin and looked down her nose. "So, you're *trying* to be an artist? I got news for you: it's a difficult road for any artist. But especially for a woman." She turned back to the painting and shook her head.

"Yes, I'm beginning to understand that," Jessica said. She looked over at the woman who was now leaned towards the art in front of her with examining eyes and deeply furrowed brows. Jessica continued to speak. "But I can't stop painting. When I'm not painting, I'm thinking about painting and when I know I won't be able to for a day or so, I'm miserable." She felt she had said too much. The woman's attention was now on her. "I'm so sorry, I didn't mean to go on."

"Save your apologies!" Lenny exclaimed. "Tell me what you like to paint."

"I love to paint landscapes, faces, flowers and ..." Jessica stopped talking when Lenny closed her eyes and shook her head.

"Landscapes, faces," Lenny repeated. Jessica searched for a way to escape this pushy woman. Yet, she had nothing to lose, she could reveal to a stranger exactly what she wanted to paint and the artist she truly wanted to be with no apparent fall out. A waiter with a tray of fluted glasses came around and Jessica took one. After half of a glass of champagne she felt the words flow out of her. "The truth is I want to paint the world that no one sees. I want to paint with vigor! I'd like to show the world how I feel about it! And I want my work to hang in famous galleries and inspire other artist, women artist, to take chances with their deepest passions." She finished the bubbly wine, her cheeks warming.

Lenny's eyes widened and with a playful grin she said, "I can help you."

"Help me?" Jessica placed her empty glass on the waiter's tray as he passed by.

Lenny surveyed the room, then leaned into her. "I'm not what you call high society, but all these folks know me and know my art is worth its weight in gold. Several of my pieces hang in their homes. They just don't want to be seen around me." She turned to the crowd. "Hypocrites!"

"You're an artist?" Jessica asked.

"Don't I look the part?"

"Well, no. I don't mean to judge, but, no," Jessica said.

"Oh dear, you have been sheltered." Lenny took in a breath and exhaled. "That's fine if you want nothing more in life than to please a man. They prefer it that way." Before Jessica could tell her about her recent *unsheltered* adventures, Lenny continued. "I teach now. Mostly to students like yourself who have grand ideas and nowhere to put them. Who knows, you may get something out of it. I'll have to see an example of your work before I take you on. My lessons are seventy-five cents per hour." She reached into her pocket and came out with a small brown card and offered it to Jessica.

Jessica read the card: *Sangroven Art Lessons.* She also noticed the address was in the Tenderloin District. She wasn't sure about any of this. Yet, Jessica warmed to this spirited woman in spite of her rough exterior and condescending way. Jessica felt free to say what was on her mind. "That may work for me," she said. "Is it Miss or Mrs. Sangroven?"

"Miss. I prefer Madame, but please, call me Lenny."

"I would love to come by your studio and show you a few of my paintings, though I'm sure my husband would disapprove. I had planned to enter art school once we got settled, but that's been put to the side. I'm very busy with dinner parties and …" Jessica went no further as Lenny's attentions drifted to another piece of art. "He did give me a small studio to work in …"

Lenny returned her attentions with a frown on her face. "He has you captive? Are you even supposed to be here, talking to the likes of me?"

A small group of ladies passed in front of them. "Hello, Miss Sangroven," one said quietly, discreetly.

"Hello, Mable," Lenny answered. "Your son's improving. Give him some time, he'll grow into a decent artist." Shocked, the woman quickly caught up with her group.

"Hypocrites!" Lenny said to Jessica.

Jessica laughed and shrugged her shoulders.

"Does your husband have you captive?" she asked again.

Jessica hoped they had moved on to another topic. She paused before speaking. "I suppose you could say that, and I'm not supposed to be here, but I am." With a trembling belly she asked, "Does Monday at three work for you?"

Jessica braved the horse ride through the dusty alleyways of the Tenderloin District in the late summer heat. She secured her horse then pulled a small leather portfolio out of her saddle pack. She hurried down the back street and into the entryway of Lenny's building. She checked the map and address; this was the place. She knocked and looked in both directions for any trouble while she waited. The pungent odors of rancid meat, oily fish, and steamed potatoes invaded her nostrils. She waited for what seemed an eternity until finally she heard a commotion behind the dark wooden door. It flung open. "Welcome, welcome," Lenny called out.

Jessica peeked inside. Her fears vanished as she entered the colorful home. It reflected the person who lived there. The aroma of oil paints and thinner, and incense mixed with the sweet smells of lavender and gardenia erased the stench outside. It conveyed the vast world of art.

The small hall that led to the parlor had hooks for coats and hats and Jessica added her yellow paisley waistcoat to the others. It looked precious alongside the plain, cotton brown vests and newsboy hats; she buried it under the rest. She entered the parlor of mismatched furnishings. Another scent caught her by surprise, the sweet scent of pipe tobacco. She had to remind herself that it was Miss Sangroven, not Mrs. *Who could the pipe belong to?*

"You have an interesting home," she said, slowly turning about, taking in the rainbow of colors. In one corner there was a large, red striped chair next to a table draped in a silk multi-colored scarf. The rug looked Chinese with its painted symbols and pictures as if telling a story. To Jessica's envy, Lenny had a few Chinese lanterns hanging from the ceiling. A divan of purple velvet lay in front of three tall windows where gauzy curtains lightly shaded the view of the brick building next door. A pair of large, ivory elephant sculptures flanked the divan. The walls were crowded with paintings that gave their own color to the room. A cabinet painted orange, held plates, cups and saucers of creamy, almost yellow glaze. Jessica didn't know where to rest her eyes. Fringed lamps shades, lace pieces draped everywhere.

"I've traveled the world over and these come from my adventures," Lenny responded. "Come in and meet the other students. My studio is right through here."

She followed Lenny down a hallway; every inch of the walls filled with paintings in every size and color, a gallery in itself. Jessica entered the studio and stiffened. Leo Gosselin rose from leaning over a student's easel and rushed to her. "Ah, Madame, we meet again!"

Jessica felt him reach for her hand and it was at his lips. "*Vous êtes si belle.*" She looked at him bent over kissing her hand and gave a side look at Lenny. A tingle went up her spin. His touch was most intimate.

"Do not be persuaded to pose for him, my dear. He is a talented womanizer." Lenny turned to Leo. "Now, you have seen her, you may leave. I will meet you tomorrow and we can discuss your latest work."

"Oh, see how she treats me, Madame?" Leo scoffed. "Very well, I wish you both a pleasant afternoon. And do not let her intimidate you, *ma petite oiselle*"

Jessica smiled. She was now his little bird. She wondered what kind of cage he kept his women in. The thought disturbed her and she quickly dismissed it from her mind. She was here to become a real painter. She averted her eyes from his flirtatious stare. He snapped his cape over his shoulder and cracked open his top hat, bowing as he made his exit. Jessica returned to the room of students leaning into their works with artistic concentration. She wished to be doing the same.

Lenny turned to her. "Well, let's see what you have there." She pointed to a long, old wooden table.

Jessica placed her portfolio on it. She first took out the painting of the tree by her art studio. Lenny tilted her head but said nothing. Then she showed her the drawings she had done from the train and small renditions of the landscape around her home. Finally, she pulled out the painting of two people sitting under a tall oak tree by a sparkling pond. Lenny examined all of them, squinting with a hand to her chin. Jessica began to return the paintings to her folder. "Wait," Lenny said. "This one of the two under the tree. Are they lovers? It's very provocative." Jessica could not speak. "Never mind," Lenny said. "I see you have talent, my dear. It's a bit raw but certainly there. Grab an apron and find an easel. Let's get started."

Jessica unhooked a stained apron and sat at an easel. She was thrilled and petrified.

Chapter Thirty

Jessica was in a giddy state of discovery with each class she took from her new mentor. At first she was intimidated to be critiqued with four talented students, as Lenny stopped at each easel to give commentary on their works in progress.

"Too much blue, Kurt! I love your perspective, Delilah." And what seemed to be a constant statement, "Not so rigid, Jessica!" She once even took Jessica's hand and lifted it above her head, brush and all. "Now, make circles. Large, swiping ones! Good! Good! Now, slap the brush onto your canvas!" Although the other students didn't look away from their own pieces of work, Jessica sensed their amusement. She lowered her head into her work and tried to loosen her technique. After each session she would stay late scrubbing the paint off her fingers and from beneath her nails, while Lenny chatted away, cleaning up her studio.

"If you can become more fluid, you may very well develop into an artist of worth. We need more women painters to be recognized. I've done my part, Jessica. It's young women like you who can continue what I and other women artists have begun. Those damn men can't rule everything!"

Jessica would leave each time feeling inspired and honored to be a part of this women's art movement. She practiced Lenny's methods in her studio using watercolors, by adding small amounts of liquid so that they might resemble the thick, greasy, smelly oil paints she was falling in love with. She was saving her money to invest in the medium and its special brushes.

This afternoon, as Jessica scrubbed the oil paint out of her nails, with a cloth soaked in turpentine, she noticed Lenny watching her. "Is something wrong?" she asked her teacher.

"What would happen if your husband saw your hands?" Lenny asked.

Jessica turned back to cleaning her nails.

"I see," Lenny remarked. "I remember you said he wouldn't approve of you taking art lessons. Does he know?"

Jessica shook her head as she examined the last of the red stain on her finger.

"Hmm. Are you happy?" Lenny didn't wait for an answer. "Does he beat you?"

Jessica looked up at her in shock. "Oh my Lord, no! Frederick has a temper, yes, but he's never beaten me."

"When he does, Jessica, don't hesitate to come see me."

"Lenny, I ... I don't think that will ever happen."

Lenny nodded. "Yes, I know you think so. I'm just offering."

Jessica looked into the older woman's gray eyes. "Thank you," she said.

She entered the omnibus to return home. Her horse was being re-shoed today. The cab filled with people was stuffy and smelled of sweat mixed with odors from the various occupations of the passengers, mostly fish and sea salt. A few of the women had their handkerchiefs to their noses and Jessica took hers out as well. The horses drawing the bus had deposited their waste as the driver waited for the last passenger to enter. Jessica felt sick to stomach. It added to her already shaken insides. Lenny's keen observation disturbed her. Instead of preparing herself for dinner, she went directly to her studio. She opened the leather portfolio that held many of her drawings, including the series she'd done of Jacob. She held up one of her favorites and lost herself in memories of their many tender moments together. As she looked at the loving expression on Jacob's face that she had drawn from her memory of him, she wondered if she would ever be as free as Lenny Sangroven, to live her life and express her thoughts as she pleased. Mostly, would she and Jacob ever be together again? Her hopes were fading.

She heard someone coming and she quickly placed the paper back into the case. "Yes, Hannah, I'll be there soon," she said as she turned around. To her surprise it was Frederick. She stepped back her heart thudding in her chest.

"Why are you dressed so drably?" he asked. "It's nearly dinner. Where have you been?"

"I was just straightening up. I'm afraid I've lost track of time. Forgive me."

As she passed, Frederick grabbed her arm. "What's that smell?" He took her hand to his nose and winced. "My God, what is it?"

"Turpentine," she said. "It's used to dilute oil paints."

"What have you been up to?" he demanded.

Jessica searched for an answer.

"Well? What is this all about?" He shook her arm.

"Let me go!" she cried out. She released herself from his grip. "I want to study in oils and I've been taking lessons from an artist I met at a gallery," she spouted.

Frederick's expression went from anger to amusement. "Is that so? He folded his arms in front of him. "Hmm, let me think on this. Lessons? Where? From whom?"

"She's very good. Collected by some of the city's most famous art collectors. She has a lovely home not far from …"

"*She*? What would a woman know about teaching art? I will hire a professional to teach you. He will come to the house and you'll no longer need to travel who knows where for instruction. For God's sake, my dear, have you lost all sense of decorum? If you must have a hobby, I will personally see to it that you do this correctly."

"Yes, Frederick. Thank you."

"What am I to do with you? Have you not enough to keep

yourself occupied? Do I need to hire spies to keep an eye on you?"

"Of course not," she replied. "I'm not a child."

Frederick grabbed her arm again and brought her face inches from his. The force of his grip brought tears to her eyes. "You are not your own person, either. You are a part of *me*." He let her go and she stumbled backwards, just catching herself before striking the wooden table.

Jessica was furious. Her breathing became labored and she looked at him from under her brows. She lashed back. "I am not a part of you. I shall never be a part of you."

Frederick cocked his head. "Pull yourself together." He turned and walked away.

Her chest rose and fell with the heaving of her breath. She tried to settle herself as she paced, searching for a way to be free of him. She slumped to the floor in a heap of tears and hopelessness. "Jacob, where are you?" she cried.

Carson City, Nevada, September 1886

"Let him go, Jake. He's not worth it!" Will shouted at his cousin.

"You son-of-a-bitch. If I even catch you walking on the same side of the road as me, I'll beat you within an inch." Jacob shoved the man aside. The sorry traveler drew a small pistol from behind his back with a shaking hand. In a flash, Jacob drew his own gun. No one moved.

"Shit," Will mumbled. He knew it wasn't his cousin who would find his end this day. With a hand on his own pistol he said, "It's too nice of an evening to die. Now get!"

The vagrant shoved his gun into his thin worn coat. He slowly turned and scurried through the tall ponderosa forest and down a slope. Still Jacob did not relax his stance.

"Jesus, Jake," Will said. "He was just an old man looking

for food. How he got that gun, I'll never know. He'll probably kill someone before he gets it stolen from him. I hate that he stumbled onto our camp." He looked around. "Hope he keeps his mouth shut."

Jacob sat hard on the trunk of a fallen tree, still feeling his chest rise and fall. His cousin stood over him. "Let's go into town and rest up," Will said.

"No," Jacob replied. "I'm tired of it. I'm tired of the whole lousy business." He kicked his heel against the trunk in frustration. "And I'm sick and tired of watching you get plastered, then gamble away our money! Christ! We work hard for that cash and you treat it as if it's your last day on earth!"

"Well, maybe it is."

"Don't give me that shit! Rest up? I'm more tired from one of those 'restful nights' than I am riding next to your sorry ass all day, trying to figure out how we're going to recover the money you lost."

"Look, it's been a long hot day, and we've got little to show for it," Will said.

Jacob's nerves were on the edge and it only took one snap of a twig under the foot of an old man to unleash his anger and frustration. He was in no mood to prance around like a peacock in some saloon. He got up and walked away. After a while he heard Will behind him. "I'll stop being an asshole, if you will."

Jacob tugged on his cigarette. "Yep," he replied. Tobacco smoke swirled overhead before disappearing into the trees.

A long silence followed. Jacob, his back still turned to his cousin, spoke in a low voice. "I never thought of myself as someone who could kill another man."

The sentence hung in the air. "Ahh, you weren't going to kill that old man," Will said.

Jacob turned to him. "You *know* what I'm talking about."

"Look, it's done and behind us. Don't forget you saved a man's life," Will replied.

"Caleb?" Jacob asked. "*Shit,* it'll just be a matter of time before some other bastard guns down that son-of-a-bitch," he remarked.

"It could've been a lot worse and you know it," Will said. "*We* could be the ones lying in that cabin or shot in the camp. We did what we had to do, Jake. It's over and no one has to ever know about it."

Jacob faced his cousin and their eyes met in silent agreement.

"I think we should go to Clermont City," Jacob said. "I need to feel a real bed under me. We'll wire my uncle Austin and let him know we're coming."

In the early morning dawn of the following day, they headed out in the direction of Jacob's distant kin.

Chapter Thirty-one

The carriage came to a stop in front of Uncle Burt's and Aunt June's white bungalow in Clermont City. It sat on nearly an acre of land away from the tidy streets in the town of three thousand. It wasn't the stately house they had left behind in Hartford, but it was quaint and charming. Jessica felt right at home the moment she stepped through the doorway when she and Frederick visited almost a month ago. The edge of their land met a sweep of sun-scorched hill. It seemed as if the earth hugged their little cottage. She knew her aunt missed her sister-in-law terribly, yet she saw the gleam in June's eyes when she showed her the patch of land where she would cultivate her garden and the spacious pantry in the kitchen that would be filled with jarred vegetables by the end of next spring.

"Oh the climate was made for me, Jessica!" her aunt had exclaimed. Uncle Burt was equally enthusiastic. He had claimed the large shed in back of the house as his "workshop"; a word Jessica had never heard come out of her uncle's mouth.

"I'm taking up woodworking," he told her. Besides the hobby, he had also found employment with Dunbar's Real Estate Company as their legal advisor. Jessica was happy her aunt and uncle were content with their new lives and that they were so near. Or at least only a carriage ride, a ferry crossing, and another carriage ride away. It took nearly four hours from her home across the bay to reach Clermont City.

Now June stood uneasy on the front porch, wringing her hands. Jessica turned to her husband. "Aunt June seems unsettled. I hope it isn't bad news."

Frederick ignored his wife. The journey to her relatives had given him enough time to prepare for another weekend in the country. "Why must we see them this often?" he had complained to his wife. Her answer was what he had expected. "They're family, Frederick."

He detested having to leave his home and the stolen moments with his mistress for such a waste of time. Yet he conformed to his wife's wishes, if only to stay above reproach in the future.

Frederick had become fond of Burt and June, but the rest of the clan was uncouth. June's brother Austin, the schoolteacher, was gentlemanly enough, but his wife seemed to think of herself as royalty. Their daughter Sophie had an insufferable penchant for gossip. Her husband Carl was useless. He worked as a clerk at the town hall and rarely contributed to the conversation. His waistline showed his great interest in food and lack of exercise. Their two sons, nine-year-old, Billy and seven-year-old, Franklin were the most irritating to Frederick. Their lack of respect and rambunctious natures put him off them completely. He wondered how Jessica could have such unfortunate relations. His wife asked for his patience. He would obey by day but at night he expected to be rewarded generously. Sam came around to assemble their luggage on the walkway, as Frederick and Jessica greeted the rosy-cheeked June.

"Hello, Hello!" she sang out, wrapping her small, plump arms around them both in turn. Frederick smelled alcohol on her. "Come in, come in! Now you know where to put your things and if you want to, you can rest up before supper. I'm sure you're both ravenous from the trip." June prattled on without taking a breath.

They followed her into the dining room where platters held a variety of foods on a long, wooden sideboard. The aroma of biscuits, garlic potatoes and roasted beef stirred Frederick's appetite. He was very fond of June's cooking. Without warning, the stout woman stopped and the couple nearly collided with her. She turned and took her niece's hands.

"What is it, Auntie?" Jessica asked.

"Jessica, my dear. Your brother and Jacob are on their way to my brother's home as we speak!" June waited for a reaction with wide eyes.

Frederick's first thought was that alcohol had made her delusional. His second thought was a curse. He went for the food and caught the look on his wife's face revealing everything - her long lost lover was near. He picked up a fork, then set it down; his appetite abandoned him.

"Aunt June, are you sure?" Jessica asked.

"Of course I am. Your uncle Austin received a telegram a few days ago. I have it right here." She took the thin brown paper from her skirt pocket and handed it to Jessica who received it with a trembling hand. She began to weep. "They're alive," she whispered.

"Of course they are!" June replied.

Frederick tried to make reason of her stunned reaction. Perhaps her feelings for her cousin had long since passed and that she was simply overwhelmed by the thought of reuniting with family, yet her response and his intuition told him differently.

"Now my dear, you just let it out," June said, comforting her with soft pats on her back. "They're fine and we are all greatly relieved and grateful."

"Where exactly are they?" Frederick asked.

"We don't know for sure, but Austin thinks they may be just a few days away. Jessica, you must stay with us until they arrive," June insisted.

Later in the stuffy upstairs bedroom, Frederick watched his

wife quietly arrange their clothing in the tall cherry wood chest of drawers. A bank of windows let in the sunlight but no air. He turned and pushed up the sashes as far as they could go. A pocket of wind blew in making the white sheer curtains billow. He sat in a nearby upholstered chair, playing with the panel of curtain. "June certainly knows how to spring a surprise," he remarked.

"She's just happy about seeing her son." Jessica spoke to his reflection in the mirror. She placed her perfume, powder and brushes on the glass and silver vanity.

"And does *he* know that? Good God, they're in for a shock. When was the last time any of you had any news from them?" He moved to the bed and lay down on the large mattress. The wrought iron frame let out a screech. He bunched a pillow behind him. "By the way my love," he began as he studied the flower painted ceiling above him. "How do you feel about seeing your cousin again? He seemed eager to leave once we were married. Was it business, his pride or perhaps jealousy?" He was goading his wife; it was he who won her and not Jacob.

She remained at her task. "I'll be very happy to see him *and* Will, of course. What does our marriage have to do with it? Jacob was pleased for us. He just had to return to his business affairs. I'm grateful that my cousin and brother made the effort to return for our wedding."

"Look at me." He sat up and brought his legs to the side.

She draped a shawl over the bench at the foot of the bed. Her pretty brown eyes met his stare. He almost regretted what he was about to venture into. "I'm aware of your feelings for Jacob. It's hardly worth you hiding them any longer. I forgive your schoolgirl crush, and only hope you are thoroughly over it."

"What?"

"You heard me," he retorted, choking on his anger.

"I have been nothing but a good and loyal wife to you," she answered calmly.

"Are you denying your affair with him? Are you?" he asked. "Did anything happen between the two of you as I courted you? I know I wasn't your first."

"Please, Frederick, don't be vulgar."

He noticed the sudden flush of red on her cheeks. He rose from the bed and grabbed her shoulders. "Bloody hell! I'm talking about this childish affair the both of you carried on! How do you think that makes me feel?"

Her body stiffened as she pulled away. Then the words he knew he had forced to the surface came out of her. She peered into his eyes. "I will always love Jacob and be *in* love with him. That's something you can never take away from me." She blurted it out with a quivering chin. She went for the door and before leaving she said, "You needn't worry. You are my husband and I will continue to honor this marriage."

Frederick watched as the door shut with one click. He gave out a short laugh at his fit of jealousy. He finally got it out of her. It was in the open now and she could never take back what she had confessed. So why did he feel rotten inside? He sat on the edge of the bed and dropped his head in his hands, longing to be in the arms of his mistress. She would soothe his pain.

Jessica paused in the hallway, trembling. Her act of courage made her feel powerful. Having Jacob so close to her had sparked her braveness, yet she knew she would eventually have to pay the price for her honesty. She slowly took each step to the landing of the stairway, her heart strained in her chest. She caught her breath and rushed down to the parlor.

Chapter Thirty-two

Jacob stood at the front door of his uncle Austin's home, Will by his side. Travel-weary, he hoped that at least two nights' sleep and some home cooking would work some good. Austin opened the door, his wife Laura standing just behind him.

"Well, look at the two of you!" Austin said. "You're certain to be Jake." He shook his nephew's hand. "And you're Will."

Will shook Austin's hand. "Good to meet you, sir." he said.

From the shocked expression on Laura's face, Jacob knew their unshaven faces and long hair made them look like the outlaws they'd become. He removed his hat and elbowed his cousin to do the same.

"You must be hungry and tired. Come on in, we'll get you some food," Austin said. He was as short and round as his sister June, and had the same red hair, pleasant smile and bright eyes. "Now make yourselves at home," he continued.

Catching the dismay that flashed on his aunt's face, Jacob knew they weren't to make themselves *too* comfortable. Yet, she kindly offered to take their worn leather overcoats and boots. "We don't want to be a bother," Jacob began as he reluctantly removed one of his crusty brown boots. "Just a few nights until we find other accommodations. Maybe something in town for a while." He removed his other boot and placed it by the one his aunt had put in the corner of the vestibule; it looked as out of place on the scrubbed white washed floor as he felt.

Austin led them to the tidy parlor just off the main hallway. White crocheted doilies dotted every piece of furniture. He looked for the least ornate seat with no luck, so he sat on the edge of a small velvet sofa. His cousin was trying to get comfortable on a high-backed chair.

"I've made us some lunch," Laura said. "Excuse me while I see to it." Despite her hospitality, Aunt Laura's pinched expression revealed her disapproval.

The small sandwiches hardly met Jacob's appetite. He looked at the tiny quarter of bread in his hand with humor, remembering his mother's delight in serving tidbits of food before a big supper. His nose told him his aunt had no such plans; there were no smells of food cooking. "So, where have you fellas been?" Austin inquired. He leaned forward in his chair, clearly eager to hear their stories of adventure.

"For goodness sake, Austin, why don't you tell them our news!" Laura spoke just as Jacob was about to answer.

The room fell silent. Austin scratched his chin under his full beard, then clasped his hands in front of him. "I'm not supposed to let you know this," he began. "June will have a fit with me, but I just couldn't let you boys walk into it without warning."

"My Lord!" Laura exclaimed. "Burt and June moved out here this summer. They're living just at the end of town. Will, your sister and her husband Frederick are already living in San Francisco. We're to take you to your father's with the pretense of showing you the town, so they could all surprise you. I thought it was a silly idea from the beginning." Having said her piece, she studied her next bite of food.

Jacob's jaw went slack. He turned to Will, who looked equally amazed at the news.

"Now, see there, it's quite enough to be told just like this," Austin stated. "Oh, wait until June gets a hold of me."

"Well … we certainly didn't expect that," Will said, flatly.

Jacob calculated how long it had been since they last corresponded with their families. Was it possible that all this could have taken place since Jessica's wedding? He finally spoke. "Thank you for telling us, Uncle, but I wouldn't worry about Mother. I'm sure she'll be too taken with our arrival to notice if we're surprised or not," Jacob stated. "I can't believe my parents would take on such a journey. They never spoke of this to *me*." His last comment was mostly for himself. His father and mother had a life beyond his own knowledge or understanding of them.

Just then his uncle stood. "Why don't we go into my study and have a real drink?"

They followed him to the room just off the parlor. Jacob looked back to see his aunt brushing off the couch and seat they had just been occupying. He could only smile.

The leather and horsehide covered furnishings in Austin's study were far more comfortable. Jacob and Will sat as he fixed them each a glass of whiskey. Jacob had almost forgotten what it tasted like. He and Will had only found moonshine on the road. Austin refilled their glasses and they savored the second round more slowly while he brought them up to speed on the family's affairs.

"So, there it is, boys," he concluded. "Now, they're expecting me to take you over after I've sent word to them that you've arrived. June's got a banner to put up on the front porch welcoming you back into the fold. She'll be mighty disappointed if she doesn't get to put that banner up and surprise you. So, how do you want to do this?" A short silence followed.

"I don't suppose we could sneak up and surprise the hell out of *her*?" Will suggested, laughter in his voice.

Jacob could only chuckle at the irony of it all. He hadn't taken a moment to think about seeing Jessica. He'd half-listened to Austin talk about her and Frederick; he wasn't prepared to take any of it in. He felt uneasy about seeing her again, yet a part of him hungered to be with her.

"Is my sister at the house now?" Will asked.

Jacob's heart flopped. He drained his glass.

"They were here on Saturday and Sunday for a visit. June wanted Jessica to stay until you arrived, but Frederick didn't much care for the idea. I'm sure she'll return as soon as she knows you're here. She sure is anxious to see you both. I don't think there's been a family gathering that goes by without her and your parents talking about where you two might be."

Jacob wished she hadn't put herself through the worry. She would not appreciate the man he'd become. She wasn't at his parents' house . . . maybe somehow he would be able to avoid her. He decided that his and Will's stay in Clermont City would now be drastically cut short.

"Why don't I leave you boys to talk it over between yourselves and let me know what you come up with," Austin said, then drained the last drop from his glass and left the room.

Jacob's insides revolted against the liquor. He coughed, acid burning his throat. It felt as if he and Will had walked into a trap.

"Christ! I wasn't prepared for this," Will said.

"What will we tell them we're doing?" Jacob asked.

"I don't know," Will admitted. He looked at Jacob and bit his lip. "Well, I suppose we can tell them how we did so well with Keaton we were able to go out on our own, and that we killed a couple of guys in the process, and we spent most of our money on women and we're ready to kill *each other*... something of that nature."

Jacob stared into the room and couldn't help but see the dark humor in their situation. "Well, let's get this thing over with," he said, not moving from his seat.

Will slapped his thighs and stood. "Come on Jake. It'll be good to see them again, and you can be damn sure we'll get some decent food out of it. What the hell did we just eat?"

Jacob's father was the first to step off the front porch with June all but pushing past him. While he was captured by his mother's embrace he stuck out his hand to shake his father's. Jacob's palm was cold and sweaty and he withdrew first. Will was next and he saw his cousin's expression turn adolescent. *"Two hardened cowboys,"* Jacob mused to himself. When he looked down at his mother, her eyes full of tears, a wave of emotion took him by surprise. The love he had left behind almost two years ago washed over him. He coughed to release the tension stabbing his throat. He stepped back from his mother and looked around barely able to meet his father's eyes which were red rimmed and moist. "This is one hell of a surprise, Father," he said.

"I take it Austin told you," Burt said from the side of his mouth.

"He did. And it's still one hell of a surprise."

"Oh!" June exclaimed. "You both need a shave and haircut before Jessica and Frederick arrive. Burt, give them the name of your man." Then turning to her brother she said, "Austin, these boys are handsome under all that hair! Where's Laura?" Without waiting for an answer she grabbed her son and nephew by their arms. "Come on now you two, I have plenty of food and we need to catch up. Is this a surprise to you or not? Oh, how I wish Thomas and Bethany were here." His mother's energy overwhelmed him and he felt a slight twinge of pity for his father, although he was glad to see them well and happy.

After dinner, Burt finally brought up the subject of his career, as Jacob knew he would. Both he and Will started at once to repeat what Will suggest they say earlier, leaving out the unsavory parts. Then Jacob gave the floor to his cousin.

"We caught on fast to the selling and trade business. Many of the homesteaders appreciated our coming around to sell them what they needed and desired. We eventually went out on our own." Jacob was impressed by Will's smooth delivery. "It's small right now, but I think if we work at it, we can make something of it. We were on our way into California on a few leads when we decided it would be nice to stop in and visit some family. And here you all are!" After his speech Will turned to his cousin with a wide grin. Jacob gave him a slight nod, then looked at his father, who was clearly unimpressed.

The three men retired to Burt's study. "Thanks for sugar-coating it for June's sake, Will," Burt said. "But she's not here and you look like a couple of cowboys instead of salesmen. He turned to Jacob. "Whatever it is you do, son, make sure you don't bring shame to this family."

Jacob couldn't fool his father, and frankly, he didn't want to. But he couldn't tell him what his life was really like. Jessica came to his thoughts and again he wondered what she would think of him now.

After a long bath in the large claw-foot tub, Jacob trimmed his beard and pulled his hair back, securing it with a leather string. He felt almost human again. He let his body succumb to the tiredness that had dogged him lately. He lay on the bed in the guest bedroom, his head on the down pillow, but his mind wouldn't rest. Will was in the next room. It had been a long time since he'd slept without hearing his cousin's snoring. Gazing at the flowered ceiling, he wondered how strange it was that someone took the time to paint a ceiling. *How did I get here*? He couldn't believe he'd traveled this far only to receive a lecture from his father about his future. He was his own man now. He resolved to make himself a success.

His mind wandered to the times when Will would spend the night at his house or he would spend the night at Will's. They would stay up half the night planning all the great adventures they would take when they were older, then act them out the next day. He yearned to go back to that time when their childish fantasies would always turn out in their favor, just before they were called in for supper. He kept his thoughts away from Jessica. Seeing her would take all his strength. What was she like now? Had Frederick turned her into a female version of himself? He turned on his side punching the pillow with a curse. As he went over the day's events the mattress underneath him invited his body and mind to relax. Finally, he drifted off.

The next morning Jacob was groggy from the previous evening's heavy food and wine and it took strong coffee to bring him around. He rocked in the chair on the porch surveying his parent's front yard and the land beyond it while his mother bustled inside like a squirrel gathering nuts. The scent of roses entwined among the picket fence lingered in the air. He closed his eyes and let the sweet aroma waft over him.

The distant sound of horse's hooves took him from his serenity. The wheels of the carriage crunching on the dry gravel made him sit up and take notice. It was fancier than most and he wondered who his mother had invited over. It came around the circular driveway and stopped at the gate. Jacob stood up, ready to say hello to whomever it was.

The driver opened the door and assisted a finely dressed young woman down the short step. Once on solid ground, she lifted her head to him. He took each step off the porch as if he didn't trust his legs. Slowly he approached her, his heart in his throat. This was the moment he longed for and dreaded. He tried to calm his tense body, he refused to give in to his emotions. He was a man now, his youth lost to the trails. He had the rationale of an adult not a love-struck puppy. His chin was raised as he looked her up and down. A smile came to his face. She was standing within feet of him; a dream come true. His mind said to give her a peck on the cheek, his heart wanted to take her to him and devour every inch of her.

Chapter Thirty-three

Jessica stood just inside the gate of her aunt's home. Her feet were leaden and her heart beat in her head like a bass drum keeping time. Jacob looked different than the last time she saw him. His lanky body had filled out with muscle and the strength of his presence gave her pause. He smiled and she saw the youthful man she loved. She spoke his name. He took a step forward and she rushed into his arms, holding onto him as if he might not be real.

Jacob took her face in his hands, his kiss deep and full of love. A love that haunted her every day. She welcomed him in with a rush of ecstasy that ran through her entire being. He gently pulled himself away and she saw tears in his eyes as he wiped her wet cheeks. They stood close while examining each other. She began to laugh, releasing the tension of the moment.

He whispered, "God, I missed you."

She could barely speak as she whispered back, "I missed you too."

Jessica knew they couldn't stay like this, but she ached to spend the rest of her life in his arms. She reluctantly pulled away. Sam came around with her cases. She touched Jacob's arm. "We should go inside," she said softly. Jessica took a deep breath and turned to the house as June came running out.

"Jessica!" her aunt exclaimed. "I didn't expect you until tomorrow. Is he not a handsome sight to see? Oh, you should have seen him before he trimmed his beard. My Lord, what a fright! I don't think Will has touched a bit of his own whiskers, so be prepared. Isn't this just wonderful? No matter the timing, I'm so happy you're here." She hurried into the house before them.

Jacob pulled her into him and stole another kiss. She held on tightly until Sam entered the foyer. She felt the heat in her face as she turned to the driver who waited for her instructions. "Thank you Sam, that will be all," she said. He bowed his head and left. Jessica watched him go and contemplated what he may have seen. Jacob brushed up against her and she was taken back to their reunion. She looked into his brown eyes and smiled.

Her uncle entered from his study and welcomed his niece. "Burt, go wake up Will and tell him his sister is here," June insisted.

"I'm sure he's heard you, June. He'll be down in his own time," Burt said.

Before long Will appeared in the parlor. "Hello, Jess!" He grabbed her off the floor and swung her around. "It's good to see you."

"Will!" Jessica laughed as he set her back down. She began to cry and he hugged her again more tenderly. "I missed you," she said as she leaned into his chest.

"I missed you too, Sis. You sure are a beautiful sight." Will gave Jacob a hard stare as he continued. "I happened to be at the window when your carriage arrived."

Jessica felt the flush of heat rise into her face; her brother had witnessed their reunion. She pulled away. "Yes, my husband arrives tomorrow," she heard herself say. Jessica hooked her arm around her aunt's thick forearm and guided her to the dining table. "Auntie, the food smells delicious," she said, then looked over her shoulder at her brother and Jacob. "Shall we eat?"

The family lingered at the table, reminiscing and sharing their present lives. Jessica was distracted by what thoughts her brother might be thinking. He gave no sign of discord with her but she noticed that he looked severely at Jacob during the entire meal. She sipped her tea as her cousin and brother talked of their adventures.

"Will," Jacob said. "Tell them about the time we met up with that cougar. I thought he was going to kill us for sure."

"Oh my!" June gasped.

Will amused them with his story, concluding with, "we tried to make ourselves look dangerous and he finally took off with a growl. I guess he wasn't too hungry. I doubt we actually scared him off." Then he quickly changed the subject. "Jess, how's that husband of yours?"

"He's fine," Jessica wiped her mouth with her napkin. "He's been working at the San Francisco Savings and Loan as a financial investor. He helps people "expand" their money, as he likes to say. He's quite good at it. Perhaps tomorrow you can talk to him about your own business investments."

"We might have a few extra pennies to throw in the bank," Will said amusingly.

The heat of the day and generous meal made Will and Jacob as lazy as tired pups. June showed them her vegetable garden, tilled and ready for next year's planting. "The men I hired did a fine job of it, wouldn't you agree?" She beamed. Burt showed off his woodworking shed. "I have a woodworker teaching me a few things," he said as he showed them the rugged beginnings of a tobacco pipe.

Later that day, Jessica, Will and Jacob sprawled on the green grass under a large weeping willow near the garden. The turned-up earth had crusted over and a breeze swirled up dust like tiny tornados, but the long sweeping bows of the willow kept the grime away. Jessica inhaled the aroma of good earth and sweet eucalyptus. If she were alone, she would have lounged on the cotton quilt and let sleep take her to a garden of dreams. She sat with her legs to one side, her full yellow print skirt around her. She felt like a child again, free from the weight of the world. She smiled at Jacob when Will was busy swatting a fly. Her eyes eager to relate to him her love. The three talked of younger days and each one teased the other for doing this or that, which now seemed so long ago.

"Boy, if we're reminiscing at our age, what are we going to be like when we really get old?" Will remarked.

"We'll just have a lot more to remember and talk about," Jessica said. She tried to hold onto the moment, before it too became a distant memory. She touched a finger to her damp upper lip and caught Jacob looking at her. He shook his head slightly and closed his eyes. She was so aroused by his simple gesture she had to put a hand to her waist to hold back her desire. Her brother spoke to her and the wave of lust that nearly crashed onto shore went back out to sea. "I'm sorry, what did you say?"

"I was asking you about your trip across the country. Aunt June said you traveled alone. How did Father permit such a thing?"

She straightened her back. "It's not what you think. It was all planned. Frederick just wanted to have everything ready for me when I arrived here, and he did. Our house is lovely. I had an earful from Father, and still do in every letter he sends. Mother's better about it, though she's not over it either." Her brother and cousin exchanged questioning looks.

"Was it a good journey for you or not?" Jacob asked further.

"There was some discomfort, but doesn't all travel have its bit of discomfort somewhere along the way?" she replied. "It was a little over a week and it went by quickly . . ." Her words trailed off as she swept a piece of grass from her skirt. She wondered why she couldn't tell them of her hardship coming to this place and the life she now led, part in public, part in secret. But they would only challenge Frederick, who would take out his frustration on her. She wrapped her shawl around her shoulders. Was the late summer breeze sharpening?

"All right," Will conceded. "We're all here now, that's all that matters."

She smiled at Jacob. He *was* here with her and the moment,

however brief, was just as she had dreamed it would be. Jessica relaxed and the September heat returned to her body.

"And how *is* the old man?" Will asked about his father.

"He's fine, I suppose. Mother hinted he may be working too hard. He hasn't found a replacement for Uncle Burt, and since Frederick decided to … He's been taking on too many cases lately, even though the business would do just as well with a lighter load," she said, shaking her head. "He's become even more stubborn."

"I can imagine him becoming a martyr in his old age," Will replied. "I just hope he doesn't run himself into the ground trying to prove he can keep the business going by himself."

Jessica sighed in agreement. "Jacob, your parents are happy here. They're trying to get our parents out here as well. I doubt they will succeed, but I do think it would be good for Father."

"Do you really want them close, Jess?" Will asked. "By God, I can't think of it!"

"Oh Will, you're too hard on them," Jessica replied, yet her feelings mirrored her brother's. How would she be able to keep up her charade with both sets of parents asking about her marriage and her mother hounding her about grandchildren? She didn't have much freedom in her life and having her parents near meant she would have even less. She relished the woman she was covertly becoming. "But I agree, they are a bit stifling."

The day turned to evening as the sun dipped behind the eucalyptus. The reddish light peeking through the boughs cast a magical glow. Jessica closed her eyes at the ache to be alone with Jacob welled up in her.

"I'm going to the house," Will announced. "Are you two joining me?"

"We'll be along," Jacob said.

"Jake," Will implored.

"We'll be along, I said." Will walked away.

Jessica tucked a loose strand of hair behind her ear and looked up at her true love. Jacob locked onto her eyes and they were lost in their own world.

He took her hand in his. "What is your life really like, Jess?" he asked.

She paused, contemplating what to divulge. "I have a decent life."

He chuckled. "Decent? That's not good nor bad, but some horrible purgatory."

She squeezed his hand and drew closer. "I want you to know that I love you and I've never stopped. I've tried. It's been …" she turned away, blinking away stinging tears.

Jacob put his arm around her and she succumbed to his touch. "I know, I know," he whispered. "It's been difficult for me, as well. I almost backed out of coming here. I didn't know if I could bear seeing you, only to walk away again. I love you, Jess."

Her body quaked and he embraced her. She nestled into him and he stroked her hair, yet she couldn't relax. The shelter of the trees that kept them out of sight of her aunt's house was too tempting. She moved to rise and Jacob quickly helped her to her feet. She brushed her skirt and shook out the quilt. Jacob tucked the quilt under his arm.

"May I see you tonight?" he asked, almost in a whisper.

"Yes," she answered quietly. Her heart quickened. Her bold response alarmed her. She wiped the bead of sweat from her brow. His body moved closer and he offered his arm. She hooked her arm around his and they walked back without another word.

Jacob could barely keep his anticipation in check. He paced the room he shared with Will. It was larger than the other guest room, with two narrow beds, and a small table and lamp between them. The cheery wallpaper and large window reminded him of his childhood home and indeed, he felt as careless as a teenager. He reviewed the consequences of his planned actions, but they hardly seemed to matter. He had gotten used to living life on the edge. He settled on the end of the bed rubbing his whiskers nervously. Jessica was in the room he had just occupied. She would rest her body in the bed he had laid in. He ran his fingers through his long hair. He took a breath, then turned to see his cousin fluff a pillow and place it under his head.

"Don't get used to this, cuz," he said to Will. "I have no intention of staying here. We need to make some money."

"Relax, Jake. Let me just get a few more nights' sleep and more of June's food and I think I'll be ready to go back to selling my soul again," Will replied sourly.

For a small price they had secured the guns and other items left from their recent trades in the safe at the saloon in town. Their cash traveled with them. They kept it out of sight, neatly tucked away in their packs. It was just enough to allow them to continue on, yet not enough to give them much incentive to keep doing what they had grown weary of. They had to find it in themselves to stick with it, and with each other, until they could hatch a better plan.

"If we head into the northern interior we might be able to make some easy dough," Will began. "Plenty of farmers who need guns. Maybe some Indians, too. If we make enough, let's come back and invest with Freddie."

"We'll see," Jacob replied. "Let's stay away from unfriendly territories. I'm not up for any confrontations. We'll ask around. I don't know about Frederick though; I don't trust him."

Will pulled himself up from his cozy spot and cleared his throat. "You have to let her go. Stop imagining that this might all turn out for the best, because it won't."

The stinging weight of Will's words cut sharply into Jacob's gut. He placed his elbows on his knees and studied the floor. He knew what it took for his cousin to knock on that beehive. "Hey, I'm the one who wants to move on as fast as possible. Besides this has nothing to do with you," he said quietly.

"Nothing? She's my sister and you're my ..."

"Will, you're the last person I want to have this conversation with. Let's just say we come from two different places on the subject and leave it at that."

Will scratched his chin. "You haven't made it easy."

There was a soft knock at the door. Jacob slapped his knees and went to see who it was. Standing in front of him in an ivory colored robe was Jessica. *Or was it an angel?* Her dark, hair shone over her shoulders, her creamy skin glowed in the lamplight. Her beauty threatened to sweep him away. He gripped the frame of the door.

"I just wanted to say goodnight," she said. "I had a wonderful day. I'll never forget it. I can't tell you how happy I am to see you both safe." With that she gave him a kiss on the cheek and returned to her room across the hall.

Jacob stood as helpless as a newborn babe. "Good night," he mumbled.

Waiting for Will to fall asleep didn't take long. Once the snoring began, Jacob lifted his body from under the covers and quietly left the room. He stood in the hallway facing her door, giving himself every excuse not to enter and every reason was defeated by his overwhelming need for her. He slowly turned the knob and opened the door. She immediately sat up. She peeled back the covers, exposing her body in the dim light of a candle. Her naked body was as if polished out of stone. Every round curve lead to another, her calves, her hips, her breast. She was perfect. He entered the room and locked the door. He removed his clothes, then slid under the blanket and embraced her warmth, the scent of her hitting his head with a lusty explosion. He could barely control himself as his hands found all the parts of her he longed to touch, while his lips and tongue tasted her soft and sweet mouth and neck. His mind was numb and only the sensation of them together filled him. She touched his manhood and he was beyond weak, beyond anything he felt was real. He wanted, needed to be in her and for her to take him in.

Their love lifted them from the confinements of their lives and only their heavy breath exchanged into each other could be heard in their hushed lovemaking, the rhythm of their dance flowing into the night.

Finally, Jacob lay back spent, satisfied beyond his imagining. Slowly he turned to her and cupped her slight body into his. "Are you comfortable?" he asked.

"I've dreamed of this moment. I know it's wrong, Jacob, but I prayed for it to happen."

Jacob gently squeezed her feeling the strong beat of her heart under his hand. "I don't want to hear that it's wrong. This is only a moment in time. We're together for only a brief moment. I'll take that, but I won't say that it's wrong."

She turned to look up at him. "What will become of us?" she asked. "What can we do?"

"I don't know," he whispered. He let out a puff of air. Why couldn't he find a solution? His frustration broke into his state of nirvana. She resumed her position and he felt her soft backside against his body. He held her tight to him, the wetness of her tears dampening his arm. His lips touched her moist cheek. "I'm sorry," he said. Her only response was a sob. He cradled her until she fell asleep, then he carefully lifted himself from the bed and quietly went back to his room. It was nearing dawn.

To his great relief Will was still snoring. Jacob sat on the edge of the bed, staring straight ahead, his mind struggling to comprehend his irresponsible actions. It was no use. The perfume of her lingered on his skin and he could only breath in its sweetness, letting it take up residency in his being.

Jessica lifted her eyes as Jacob left her bed and quietly closed the door behind him. The wave she had held back for so long rose to drown her. She rolled over and wept into her pillow, heaving sobs so great her stomach hurt. She felt the cruelty of the world as her broken heart wrestled with her anger. She pounded her fist against the mattress, once, twice, over and over until her arm felt as weak as her ability to change her life. If only she could run into the hills and scream to the world to hear her heart. Finally, she wiped her face with the sheet, pulled the coverlet around her and went to the open window. The air was cool. The grey-blue world was silent but for a few chirping birds. This peaceful stillness penetrated her forlorn spirit and she returned to the bed where the heady smell of Jacob's body surrounded her. She lay on her back, her arm covering her wet face. Then a thought rushed to her so loud and foreboding she couldn't move. He hadn't pulled out of her at the crucial moment.

Oh, dear God.

Jessica woke with a start. She went to the window where the early morning light heralded a new day. She could feel him still with her, the taste of him in her mouth, her anguish was freshly ignited. His words filled her heart. He said he would not feel shame for his actions. It seemed easier for Jacob. She wondered what his life was like. Could she abandon her life to join him in his? What about Will? Frederick? Aunt June? The hopelessness tortured her at every turn.

She rubbed the back of her aching neck and returned to bed. She relived their lovemaking and it soothed her, if only for now; Frederick would be arriving today.

Chapter Thirty-four

Frederick had torn himself away from Molly's warm bed and perfumed body to travel to Clermont City, where he was expected to be overjoyed to see Will and Jacob. It was hardly the case. Neither he nor his mistress was happy about the interruption. Yet, his wife's rush to get to her aunt's home did allow them to be together for an unexpected visit.

Frederick's secretary, Annabelle Albright, arranged for the lovers to be together regularly under the guise of Frederick working hard for his investors. He had set Molly up in a tiny one-bedroom apartment not far from the bank. It was convenient for him, although it was not the level of accommodation she was used to. At least he had allowed her to furnish it as she pleased, which she did with all the finery she could find within the city until it resembled a cramped palace. Blue velvet on heavy wood chairs and ivory satin curtains. Chandeliers. Cut glass vases filled with hothouse flowers. Thick wool on the floor and oil paintings on the walls. He felt that his generosity was enough to keep her satisfied. When she did complain he would buy her a bracelet or necklace to silence her. He would remind her of her own words whenever she became restless.

Frederick's life—split between his wife and mistress, the whores in Chinatown and a night of gambling—was filled with his plans to expand his personal wealth, including a few not-so-legitimate dealings to speed up the process. Several of his transactions involved taking large sums of money from investors and placing them into his own personal safe, which he would then use to invest in highly profitable enterprises for himself. The monthly reports would show his clients that their investments were making some strides, giving them confidence in his ability to choose wisely, when all along most of the sizable profits were going into his own pockets. When any of the investors decided to withdraw, he would find someone else willing to take their place. There was never a shortage of persons who yearned for the pot of gold at the end of the rainbow, no matter how sunny the skies were above their heads. Greed, he concluded, was a vein that ran through every human's body, and he was more than happy to tap into it. His conscience remained clear however, since he never took from the poor; he let the bank he worked for do that. He hadn't the expertise or the stomach for loans and mortgages.

Frederick shifted in discomfort. His stiff waistcoat and the carriage's jostling teased his patience. Finally, the horses turned onto the gravel drive in front of the Stanford's home. Sam came around and opened the door. Frederick stepped down and was greeted by his wife.

"Hello, Frederick. How was your trip?" Jessica asked as she raised on her toes to give him a peck on his cheek.

"Long and uncomfortable," he replied. He noticed his wife was flush and flittering. What mischief had she and her cousin indulged in? He threw the thought from his head. Burt and June were there, as well as her brother. *Take it easy. Don't let your mind play tricks.*

He wasn't sure what to expect from this gathering, but he resolved to comment on Jacob's behavior toward his wife if he felt it was out of line in any way. It was one thing for him to hold his tongue when he was courting Jessica, but it was another matter as her husband. He cursed this turn of events. He had figured her brother and cousin to be long gone.

Frederick and Jessica entered the parlor where, to Frederick's dismay, Sophie and her family were seated. Carl was nibbling on a biscuit and Sophie was talking loudly about some woman's gaudy hat. Their boys sat fidgeting like two mischievous raccoons. Frederick cringed.

"Boys, say hello your cousin Frederick," said Sophie. When the boys didn't respond, Sophie became shrill. "*WilliamFranklinRaymond*, I said greet your cousin!" The boys mumbled a hello. Frederick in turn greeted all with dignity and grace, especially Will and Jacob. He couldn't help but notice how the two had graduated into their manhood. Will was as friendly to him as before and Jacob was as distant.

"Frederick, we are so pleased you were able to get away," said June.

"I am quite busy, but this is a special occasion," he replied.

Frederick had no interest in June's prattle. He focused on his wife and Jacob, watching their interaction. He noticed a certain restraint in his wife and a cool confidence in Jacob. It made him uneasy. He saw nothing to make a fuss over, but his suspicions put him on guard, making him uncomfortable in his own skin. At supper he continued his observations, but could hardly concentrate with Sophie's ongoing chatter.

"So, Jacob, is there a special lady in your life?" she asked.

"Not at the moment, Sophie," Jacob answered.

"Well, that's a shame. She put a long finger to her pursed mouth and looked up at the ceiling. "Hmm, let me think." With a sudden burst of thought she exclaimed, "I've got it! There are a few young ladies in my cribbage club who might fill the bill. Auntie, we must have them over while Jake and Will are here," she proclaimed. "Will, you might as benefit as well."

"Yes," June said without hesitation. "We can serve those fish puffs you found in your new cookbook."

"Mother, I don't think that's a good idea," Jacob said, looking at Jessica.

Frederick's chest burned. "Jessica, you might want to help Sophie with her generous offer." He turned to Jacob. "My wife knows of many eligible ladies to add to the list. There comes a time when a man needs to settle into matrimony. You are nearing twenty-five now?"

"I'll be the judge of my own needs," Jacob replied. The discussion came to an abrupt end.

"My dear," Burt said to his wife, "I can speak for all of us when I say bravo to another fine feast!" He then addressed the men. "Shall we leave the ladies to what they do best? Let's retire to my study, where we can discuss important things, like the fine art of smoking cigars."

The men were all for his suggestion. They rose as one and left the table.

June and Sophie retreated to June's kitchen, but Jessica did not follow. Instead she found her own retreat in one of the white rocking chairs on the front porch. She wanted nothing to do with their scheming. She had just sat down when Jacob stepped out and took the chair beside her.

"No cigars?" she asked, her pulse beating a little faster.

"It's not my type of tobacco," he answered.

It occurred to her that he had developed preferences she knew nothing about. The tiny scar over his eyebrow that wasn't there the last time she saw him, and the small string of turquoise beads he wore around his tanned neck, were all indications of a life beyond her reach. Who was he now? The young man she had known was gone and he looked as if he were of a different world entirely. Last night he was feral in his expression of love. She had welcomed it with all her heart, but in the full light of day, she was confused about his true intentions.

She looked over at him. "Last night was different from what I remembered it being with you," she said in a whisper. "You didn't . . ."

"Jess, not now," he replied.

She turned away. Her fingers tapped on the arm of the rocker. She moved it back and forward. Her agitation grew. Who was she giving her heart to? She remembered the article she had read on the train and gathered the courage to ask him about it.

"Jacob, I read about Keaton and the camp," she said as she studied his face.

His look of shock raised her curiosity.

"What? When?" he asked.

"On my train trip out here. It was in one of the local papers we got in Wyoming. I read that Mr. Keaton was killed, and the campsite burned."

"Jesus," he muttered. "Why didn't you tell me this before? What else did it say?"

"I'm telling you now. It didn't say much more. Only that they were considered outlaws and were tracked down." In a low voice she asked, "Were you and Will with him at that time?"

"No," he answered.

"Did you leave the group before this happened?"

"Yep."

She put a hand over her chest. "Oh, I'm so relieved to hear that. What an awful thing. It's what I had figured all along, but I was so scared, Jacob." Her voice cracked, then she stopped the rocker and came closer. "Were you aware of this, that this was an illegal business?"

"Jess, it doesn't matter."

"Why do you think it happened? Have you been able to talk with any of the other men? Were there survivors? Why were they in a camp and not a hotel?"

"What are you, some kind of inspector?" he asked, without humor. "I told you it doesn't matter. We left the group. We're here aren't we?"

Jessica pulled back. "Jacob, I was only concerned. What is your life like? Why do you look as if you haven't eaten or slept or taken care of yourself? Will looks the same as you. What's this all about?"

"Jess, you have to know I'm not living a simple life. You can't be worried about me or Will. You have a good life and I want you to live it and be happy, not burdened with worry over something you can't do a damn thing about. God knows, I don't need that."

She paused to let the rattled-off words sink in. His assumptions, though right, made her angry. "So, you're not worth worrying about?" It was more a statement than a question. She crossed her arms over her chest and huffed. "What do you take me for, one of your 'ladies' that you bedded down with last night? One who thinks you'll be coming back for her and now you feel you have to give some kind of heroic speech before you leave?"

Jacob gave out a short uneasy laugh. "Where the hell did you get that notion, and since when do you talk like that?"

"I suppose we both have changed," she said looking away. "I know you think I live a secluded life away from the real world, but I don't." She came back to him trying to read his expression.

"And what are your adventures these days?" he asked.

She balked. "Don't you condescend to me, Jacob Stanford!"

"All right, all right. I'm sorry, Jess. What are your days like?"

She brushed her skirt and wished she hadn't raised her voice to him in such a childish way. She resumed her adult posture. "I've been very fortunate to be able take art lessons from an old bohemian woman in the Tenderloin," she answered.

"Tenderloin?"

"Yes, it's a dangerous and fascinating place in the city. I've learned a lot from my teacher and the other students. I'm creating art. Not lady's art, but real, emotional art."

"Now, do I have to worry about *you*? Because I don't need that either," he replied.

"Jacob, did you even hear me?" she asked.

"Yes, I heard you, Jess. I want you to play it safe though. Not just in the city, but with Frederick. Promise me you won't let him hurt you."

"Whatever gave you that idea?" she asked.

"I don't know, Jess. It's just a feeling."

She sighed and her body softened. "You needn't worry about the art lessons. Frederick found out I was leaving the house for classes and he hired a teacher to come by to give me instruction. Mr. Calais is an old man with shaky hands. He teaches a method I hardly care for. I still managed to take a lesson once in a while from Lenny, my teacher, but now Frederick has the staff watching my every move. I miss her and the other students." She heard the sadness in her tone and wished she could manage herself better. But this was Jacob and she had longed to pour out her heart to him. It was easier in her daydreams.

"My God, Jess, it sounds as if you're a prisoner. Do you get out at all except for these trips to my parent's home?"

"I do, but it's to the park or an afternoon tea with the wives of his clients. Other social events …"

"Promise me you won't let him hurt you."

"Jacob, he hardly does …" she began.

Jacob snapped his head toward her. "He hardly does *what*?"

"He has a temper to be sure. I've learned to avoid arousing it."

"Jesus. Promise me Jessica. You will protect yourself won't you?"

Jessica wanted to scream, *"How? How do I protect myself besides behaving like an obedient child?"* She looked down and nodded her head. "I promise," she whispered.

There was a weighty pause. Then Jacob reached over and rested his hand on her arm. "You know how I feel about you."

"Do I?" she asked.

He leaned over his chair to meet her ear. "Doesn't last night prove anything to you?"

"It proves what a man will do to satisfy his own needs." Jessica felt a splash of dizziness from her forwardness.

"I like how you've changed," he said with a grin

She was confused, yet she felt a smile rise on her lips and her worries subside. He had seen her for the woman she was becoming. She felt a deeper relationship between them emerging. Her heart begged to ask him where do they go from here, but she knew he would have no answer. "Jacob, what will you do now?" she asked.

"Will and I are leaving in a few days. It was never our plan to stay long. We have our business to attend to."

Her dream of him staying, to be a part of her life, dissolved. She had to press on, to try and keep him near. "But why not find a business here?" she asked.

Jacob settled back in his chair, gazing out beyond the front yard. "I'm not ready for a stable life as you seem to think I am. Will you have me settled?" He looked at her and continued. "A clerk or banker? Farmer? A single gentleman or married with a few off spring? Maybe Sophie will find a good match."

His sarcasm riled her. "Why are you mocking my intentions?"

"I'm not, I'm trying to tell you that our worlds are different, Jess."

"I would live very fine in your world. The freedom you have would be a welcomed change for me, matter a fact," she said. "And you need not give me that silly grin."

Frederick stirred uneasily in Burt's study. The conversation bored him and he noticed Jacob was not in the room. He didn't care for what his instincts were telling him and decided to go looking for his wife. He came to the porch and saw the two of them locked in attention to each other. He decided to put an end to their meeting.

"My dear, why aren't you in the kitchen with the other women?" he asked, as patiently as he could.

Jacob stood and excused himself, heading into the house. Frederick followed him. "We're happy you're back," he said. Then he grabbed Jacob's arm. "Don't break my wife's heart, as you did before." Jacob jerked away. "It doesn't fare well for our marriage and to be honest with you, I'm tired of hearing about you and Will, as if you were some kind of heroes. By the looks of it, you could hardly rub two nickels together."

"You don't look worse off for any of it, I'd say," Jacob replied with steel in his eyes. "I'm sure it's *you* who will eventually break her heart, and it will be hell to pay when I find out. And I don't need to be rich to own a gun," he warned. Just then Jessica entered the foyer. Frederick stepped back.

"What's going on?" she asked. Her eyes darted back and forth between the men.

"Your cousin seems to think I'm intent on breaking your heart." Frederick chuckled.

"Frederick, please," she begged.

"I think I'm due for a night in town, excuse me." And Jacob was gone.

"Do you think you're fooling me?" Frederick lashed out in barely concealed rage. "Sitting with him under the guise of two cousins having a charming little visit? How would your dear aunt react to your feelings toward each other? Hmm?"

"Oh! Your jealousy is getting the best of you now, and I would be most pleased if *you* would show the same respect and allow me to visit with my family," she said.

Her tone was more than he could take. He caught her arm and jerked her towards him. He brushed the strands of hair from her face, his rage turning to desire. "My jealousy is your doing, my love." He pulled her closer and kissed her pursed lips.

"Stop it. Someone will see us." She squirmed in his arms so he held on tighter.

"Good, I hope someone sees how much in love we are," he whispered in her ear then began to suck on her lobe. She tore away and he laughed.

Just then one of Sophie's boys came barreling through the front door. "Mother! Cousin Jessica and Frederick are kissing!" he boomed.

"Billy! That's not very nice, now go back outside," Jessica reprimanded him. Billy ran past them like a naughty puppy.

"Those brats will grow up as lawless as they are now," Frederick commented impatiently. "Now, where were we?" he asked.

"Nowhere," she replied stiffly.

"Very well, behave this way while we are here, but you'll soon have to come back to *our* life and resume your duties as my wife. Make your mind up to do so, my dear. This is intolerable. Your brother and cousin are leaving and unless you plan to go with them, I suggest you stop this foolishness over him." Frederick seethed. "What do you have to say? And spare me your sarcasm," he commanded as he stood over her.

"You're right. I am being a fool," she said meekly. "I promise I will try to behave more *tolerably*."

She exasperated him with her manipulations. It was a lost battle and again he wondered why he cared so much. "We're leaving tomorrow. I have to get back to the bank."

"Frederick, I don't want to leave so soon. Please go on without me."

"Have you no sense of what you are saying?" he shouted. "Shall we just call this a draw? Then we can both be free to reside with the ones we truly love." Frederick took a step back. The slip of his tongue startled him. He'd over-stepped the barriers he had so carefully built up in his new life. He tried to backtrack. "I mean to say, if you're not careful, I may seek the company of someone else, whomever that may be. After all, you don't expect me to stand by and see my wife betray me like this, do you?"

"I'm sorry, Frederick. Of course I would never want you to do such a thing."

"Very well then, we'll go home and put this behind us." For the time being, he was in the clear, however fragile his footing.

Chapter Thirty-five

Jessica entered the kitchen, rubbing her arm. Her aunt looked at her with concern. "What is it, dear?" June asked. "Has something upset you?"

Jessica hugged her. "Thank you for such a lovely stay, Auntie."

"You know the pleasure is all mine," her aunt replied. "Are you all right my dear?"

Jessica smiled reassuringly at Sophie. She didn't want any gossip spread about. "I'm very well, Auntie," she replied.

"What's wrong with your arm?" Sophie asked.

"Oh, I brushed against the corner as I came in the kitchen. Silly of me. Not looking where I'm going."

"You do seem distracted today, Jessica," Sophie commented. "Perhaps it's the sudden visit of your brother and cousin. I know this whole family affair has me at a disadvantage. I'm just not used to so many strangers, even if we are kin."

While Sophie fanned herself, Jessica addressed her aunt. "Auntie, would you join me in the parlor for a cup of tea before bedtime?"

"That sounds delightful, Jessica," her aunt replied.

Jessica wrapped her white robe around her. "Aunt June and I won't visit too long," she said to Frederick, who was already in bed.

"I'll be waiting," he replied. "And by the way, I seem to detect a slight scent," he said as he smelled the sheet under him. "It doesn't smell like you, or me. Were you alone last night?"

"Frederick, please. I will not engage in such vulgarity," she replied. Her hands began to shake and she wrapped her robe tighter. She left the room feigning contempt, but her face felt hot and adrenaline coursed through her veins. She was a racehorse with nowhere to run.

She hurried downstairs, listening for Frederick's footsteps behind her. She paused at the foot of the stairs and looked back; he wasn't following her. She slowed her pace as she went to the parlor where Aunt June was waiting. It was late and everyone had gone to bed, except Jacob; he had yet to return from town. The gas lamps had been dimmed, and the crackle of the fireplace gave some warmth to the chilly night. June stood over a small table preparing the tea.

Jessica sat on the blue-striped Chesterfield and her aunt handed her a cup of tea. She inhaled the chamomile and honey scent. The relaxing herb was a balm on her frayed emotions. Her aunt sat down beside her. "What's wrong, Jessica? I'm your aunt, but as your mother isn't here, I have a duty to serve as her replacement."

What she was about to reveal to her aunt she would never reveal to her own mother. Her aunt had a much broader view of life. June put down her cup and held Jessica's hand. Jessica cleared her throat, fighting back her tears. She set down her own cup. She bit her lip and took a deep breath. "Auntie, I'm not happy in my marriage. Actually, I'm very unhappy." The words came tumbling out no longer able to be stopped.

Stunned, Aunt June sat back, releasing Jessica's hand. "How is this true?" she asked. "Frederick is a perfect gentleman. Yes, he's vain, but he's a man after all." She pondered the situation. "Though I've enjoyed all the years being with your uncle, I know that marriage can be difficult at times. Perhaps ... children would soften him. I don't mean to pry, but it has been quite a while since your wedding day."

Jessica lowered her head. She had no explanation for her aunt's curiosity. She herself was curious that she had not yet conceived; Frederick took no precautions. "I suppose I have to try harder." It became clear to her what she had known all along; her family wouldn't understand her plight. She would have to be more direct. She tried again.

"It's not what it seems," she said, then paused before revealing the whole truth. "He's a bully and treats me as if I were a child." She brushed the tears from her cheeks. "He grabbed my arm just today. It wasn't the first time he's been rough with me."

"Oh my," June responded, bringing her hand to her mouth. "This is very upsetting. If you are being mistreated, then your uncle and I will see to it that you are safe."

"Oh, Auntie, please don't say anything right now. I just wanted to ask you how I become a more agreeable wife."

June clasped her hand around both of hers. "I promise I will keep your confidence, but now you must promise me that if he hurts you, you will come to me and your uncle. Do you vow to do this, Jessica?

"Yes, Auntie. Thank you." Jessica dissolved into tears. "I'm sorry to be such a disappointment."

"Look at me, my child," her aunt said.

Jessica raised her head.

"I'll hear no such thing," June said sternly. "I may not have much worldly experience, but women talk to each other. I've heard of women who have suffered under the hand of their husbands. I pray you will not have to live with such a horrid thing. It would break my heart."

"What will I do if I have to leave him? What will become of me? My social standing? My art?"

"Your art? What has that to do with this?" June asked.

"It's my life."

"I see. Well, let's just take this one step at a time, shall we? And for now, it will be between you and me."

Jessica felt as if a weight had been lifted from her. Yet the unknown of her future frightened her. Instead of returning to her room, she waited for her aunt to go to bed then she retreated to her uncle's study. She was not ready to lie beside her husband.

Jacob entered the quiet house. A small lamp was lit on the foyer table. He used it to find his way upstairs. As he walked quietly through the downstairs a light caught his eye. His father's study. He knocked on the door, then opened it.

"Father?" he inquired. And there was Jessica curled up on the small couch, her robe wrapped around her, as if cowering from a nightmare. The room was cold and the flickering light created strange, disquieting shadows. "Jess? What is this?"

She immediately sat up. "Jacob? My Lord, you frightened me."

"Why are you sleeping here? What has he done?" he demanded. "I'm too drunk to give a shit about what happens to him, Jess. I'll kill him, I swear it!"

Jessica bolted from the couch and grabbed his arm, forcing him to stop. She pulled him down to sit. Reluctantly, he gave in and collapsed beside her. "You *are* drunk," she reprimanded. "I'm fine. I just wanted to be alone for a while."

"Don't give me that. Leave him, damn it and come with me," he said. His words were slurred. He pulled her close to him and began to kiss her lips. He wanted to make love to her with all his might.

"Jacob, stop."

Through the haze of drink and desire he whispered into her ear, "Come with me, Jess. Leave that bastard and come with me. I love you, I want you with me."

She pulled away from him. All at once it became clear to him what the drink had made him say and do. He rose shakily and the room tilted. "I don't know what I'm saying. I'm so sorry." He found the door and left.

Jessica lay down and gathered her robe around her again. His invitation tempted her, as did his sudden kiss. She breathed in the scent of alcohol remaining in the air and wanted to take it in as if taking in a part of him. She blew out the lamp, closed her eyes and tried to sleep, dreaming she was in his embrace. As the black night slowly turned to the grayness of dawn, Jessica woke and crept upstairs.

Frederick turned over and looked up at her, his hazel eyes half open. "Come here," he said. His tone was soft.

She hesitated, then got into bed with him. He took her in and she felt the heat from his sleeping body. In the morning light she came to her senses. Frederick still offered her the financial safety of a marriage, and she had neither the courage nor the money to leave him. She put her head on his chest, letting him stroke her hair.

"I was a brute yesterday, please forgive me. It will never happen again." He embraced her and kissed the top of her head.

She turned her body to face the door as Frederick cupped his body around her. Jacob was only across the hall. How odd she felt. Her world was split in two.

They slept through what was left of the early dawn, and in the bright morning they silently got ready to go downstairs. Jessica gave a meek smile as Frederick left to go down before her. "I'll take that as a sign of your forgiveness, my love," he said. She nodded, her mouth forcing a smile, her emotions heavy.

In the hallway Jessica turned to close the bedroom door behind her. She heard another door open. Jacob stood tall staring down at her. She shook her head and he wrapped his arms around her. "I was drunk and careless last night," he said hoarsely. "Please forgive me."

The second time she was asked for her forgiveness and the day had just begun. "Nothing to forgive. I must go down now, Jacob."

"I'll be down in a few minutes."

Drawing in her desires, she entered the dining room where the rest of the family waited. Frederick gave her a hooded stare. She sat down without a word.

"My, aren't we a somber group this morning," June reflected. "I know you boys will come back soon, and we can all be together again like this." No one seemed to know what to say to their hopeful hostess.

After breakfast it was time for Jessica and Frederick to leave. Sam had already arrived and was upstairs collecting their luggage. Jessica watched nervously as Frederick followed Sam. She was about to go upstairs when Will took her arm and led her outside into the bright sunlight.

"I will miss you," he said.

"Take good care of yourself, Will, and if you're looking for a wife, you'd better do something with this." She tugged at his long straight ponytail.

He laughed and gave her a bear hug. "She'll have to love me just the way I am, sis."

They were soon joined by their aunt and uncle. Jessica said her goodbyes. Her aunt gave her a quick but solid nod of assurance, which Jessica returned with a weak smile. Will accompanied them back into the house and Jessica waited anxiously for Jacob to come out. Her emotions ran high and her pulse beat in her throat. Instead of Jacob, Sam came out with her luggage.

"Where is my husband?" she asked. Sam commented that Mr. Moore was still upstairs then he began to load the back of the carriage.

It was a warm September morning. The fireplaces back in Connecticut would be lit and running until spring, but here she felt the gentleness of the weather touch her face. If only her spirit could embrace its peace. Sam retreated back into the house just as Jacob came out.

Jessica walked to the other side of the carriage beyond anyone's notice, and he followed. They looked into each other's eyes and he took her hand. His ivory colored shirt was tucked neatly into black trousers, and the strand of blue beads around his neck instead of a tie. His beard was trimmed and his hair was combed and pulled back. She caught a whiff of his soap, spicy and clean. He looked like an eager suitor. Her heart swelled.

"Here we are again," he said.

"Yes, here we are," she replied.

"Don't worry, Jess. You're not rid of me yet."

"Please, be safe and come back soon," she said.

"I will, if only for you."

"I'll be here, Jacob. Know that I'll be here. Write to me. Send your letters to your mother and I will get them. I will send my letters to the nearest postal office, wherever you are. You can write to me anytime, anytime at all."

"Jess, I can't write to you. It's just better if I don't," he said.

Her tense shoulders lowered, it was her last string of hope to have him by her side no matter how far apart they were; she felt adrift. He touched her cheek. "I love you." His voice was low and filled with hurt.

With her bottom lip trembling and her eyes filling with tears she whispered, "I love you, too." Jacob gave her a kiss, hardly a peck, and she wanted more.

"Come on, let me help you into the carriage," he said.

She got in just as Frederick was on his way out of the house, with Will alongside. "Goodbye, Freddie. I'll come see you when I'm rich, and let you manage my millions," Will said.

"I'll look forward to it, Will, and while we're still young?" Frederick answered.

"One can only hope," Will jest.

"Take care, Jacob, until we meet again," Frederick said.

"Until we meet again," Jacob replied.

As they drove away, Jessica waved at the men she was leaving behind. Jacob stood at the gate, straight and handsome. She drew a picture in her mind of him, one she would remember for the rest of her life.

Chapter Thirty-six

Jessica finished up her purchases at the boutiques on Market Street. The Christmas season was upon her and she was in good spirits. She was pregnant and her belly was only slightly protruded. It was her secret to keep hidden as long as she could.

She smiled to herself. The doctor had even advised her to wait until her fourth month, possibly the middle of January, before announcing the pregnancy. She took his advice and extended it to include her husband. She was not ready to give in to committing to Frederick for the rest of her life. Being with Jacob in September had opened possibilities within her. The sin of adultery did not disturb her sense of integrity as much as it willed her to find a way to release herself as Frederick's wife.

Divorce. The word had lingered on her tongue for weeks, until she learned she was pregnant. She prayed it was Jacob's child she carried, yet she couldn't be certain. She had to steady herself each time the thought entered her mind; their lovemaking might have created a child.

"These will look lovely on your delicate hands, Madame," the sales clerk said.

"Oh, they're not for me. They're a Christmas present for my housekeeper," Jessica replied, noting the look of surprise on the clerk's face.

"A very lucky woman, indeed, to have such a generous employer," the woman responded as she wrapped the beige, kid leather gloves in red paper.

Jessica placed the package into her woven basket, alongside the other carefully chosen gifts. She was delighted to have found the gloves she'd been searching for. She put on her own gloves and brought up the fur collar on her flared white wool cape, preparing to face the cold, wet December afternoon. As she stepped out the door, snowflakes danced into the shop.

"The winter is a strange one this year," the clerk said from behind the counter. "They say we may even have a white Christmas!"

"Yes, imagine that." Jessica stepped outside. The crisp air brought memories of winters in Connecticut and made her heart swell with a childlike anticipation of the holiday season. She looked up and down the street at the festive sight. The lampposts held large swags of evergreens, eucalyptus and holly, accentuated by wide red ribbons; even the trolley cars were decorated with ribbons and greenery. Store windows sparkled, each display more elaborate than the next. Jingle bells on the horses' reins provided a musical accompaniment for the swirling white flakes. The light grey sky held the magic of expectation.

An older couple walked by and they all marveled at the unusual weather. As they moved past her, she caught sight of a man across the street. He looked remarkably like Frederick, who would never find a reason to visit the shops in this part of town with its boutiques of hats and shoes and lady's undergarments. She squinted to get a better view of the man. Indeed, it was her husband. She stepped back into the shop's doorway, the skirt of her deep maroon dress catching the dusting of snow around its hem. She leaned ever so slightly and spied to see which shop he would enter. Was he searching for a gift for her? She had been so distant from him since the Fall, but he *had* treated her more gently. Her aunt might be right - a child could soften him further. She touched her belly and a warmth filled her chest.

She continued to watch. He stood in front of the little storefront, then he began to pace. Her imagination filled in the gaps.

She anticipated someone coming out and handing him a beautifully adorned package just for her. It would be an affectionate gesture. Instead, he turned to greet a tall, redheaded woman walking gracefully out of the store laden with several boxes and bags. Frederick immediately unburdened this elegant lady, and she in turn wrapped her arm around his and they kissed.

Jessica jerked back feeling the door to the shop hit her. She stepped forward again and peeked out from her shelter. A carriage pulled up beside the couple and Sam got out to help with the packages. They entered the coach and were whisked away. *Sam?* The feeling of deep betrayal extended to the hired help. She felt as if she were watching a horrible dream.

The shop door opened with a whishing sound. "May I help you?" Jessica turned to find the woman who had sold her the gloves looking at her curiously.

"No, thank you. I was just leaving," she said.

She walked aimlessly down the street her labored breath noticeable in the cold air. The wind pricked her wet eyes. She took out her handkerchief and patted them gently. She looked around in near panic. Finally, she found a bench and sat down to collect herself, she wouldn't fall apart here. She remembered where to take the omnibus. The outside world was no longer cheerful and wondrous, but cold and lonely. Would her home be any different?

"Welcome home, Mum, can you believe this bit of snow? I feel as if I'm back in England," Hannah chirped. "How was your shopping? I can see you've done a fair bit of it. Shall I get Kevin to bring in the rest?"

"No. This is all there is. I'm tired, I think I'll go upstairs and rest a while."

Jessica reached her room, closed the door and collapsed onto her bed. So many questions invaded her mind, but all answers led to one conclusion: Frederick had taken a mistress. Her shock turned to anger. She threw a pillow from her bed and shouted at the world beyond the large windows. "I hate you!" She caught herself -, she'd been told that being upset could produce an unhealthy child.

Sitting back on her bed, she propped her head on one hand and turned her thoughts to resolution. Her husband had proven to be an adulterer. She could leave him now. Her bold decision withered as she wondered how she would be able to substantiate her claims, then raise a child on her own. Then a horrible reality invaded her thoughts, he might take the child. By law he had every right to do so. She briskly wiped tears from her cheeks. She wouldn't let that happen. Her body shook as she rose and rushed to the door.

She found Hannah in the conservatory. Surely if Sam was in on the affair, Hannah and Kevin would be also. They would testify on her behalf. Hannah first claimed ignorance but then she hesitated, her face turning bright pink. She looked at her shoes.

"Hannah?" Jessica said sternly.

"I've made a friend of a housekeeper whose sister cleans Mr. Moore's office at the bank," Hannah began. "She says his secretary, Miss Albright, complains on occasion that she's tired of arranging all of Mr. Moore's more delicate appointments, and that it causes her more work than she is being compensated for. She mentioned that a woman *friend* of Mr. Moore was the cause of her complaint," Hannah revealed. "Oh, Mum, I'm so sorry."

Jessica paused to take in Hannah's revelation. "I saw Sam helping them into the carriage. What more do you know, Hannah? I'll need evidence."

Hannah put her hand to her mouth. "Oh, Mum don't do anything out of temper."

"Never mind what I do. I need your help. And Kevin's, too."

"Yes, Mum. We'll do what we can. I mean to say, we *are* in Mr. Moore's employ. What about our reputations and our jobs?"

Hannah's comments stunned her. She crossed her arms. "I see where your loyalty is."

"No, no, it's not like that, Mum. It's just that if Kevin and me get sacked from this job we have nothing!"

Jessica lifted her skirt from the floor giving her feet plenty of freedom to storm away. "Tell Miss Benton I will have dinner in my room." She turned sharply but not before spying Hannah make a curtsy.

"Save your curtsying for Mr. Moore," she stated.

Frederick was glad to be home. It had been a full day and he still had a stack of work from the office to complete, though now he would be able to finish it with a drink by his side and a loosened collar. He sat down at his desk and began to organize his papers.

After a while he noticed the outside light dimming and he turned up the gas lamps on the wall behind him. He took out his watch; it was nearly dinner and he hadn't seen his wife. He pulled on the rope that rang the bell for the housekeeper.

Soon there was a knock on the door. "Yes, come in," Frederick answered. He felt a presence standing in the threshold, but he did not look up from the papers on his desk.

"Where is my wife?" he asked.

"Mrs. Moore is dining in her room this evening."

Frederick finally glanced up at the young English maid. "What for? Is she ill?" He wondered if the stomach ailments she had several weeks ago had returned.

"No, she isn't *ill,* sir," Hannah answered. "I don't want to speak out of turn, sir, but she's quite upset."

"Very well," he replied, returning to his work. She curtsied and closed the door behind her. Frederick leaned his elbows on the desk and clasped his hands under his chin. He gathered her upset had something to do with him. He decided to go investigate.

Frederick knocked lightly on his wife's bedroom door. "Jessica, may I come in?" he asked, but only as a formality; she never said no, and he never expected her to. He heard nothing. He knocked again.

"Yes, come in." He barely heard her reply.

She stood by the bay of tall windows. Her straight back to him, one hand on the heavy damask drapery. "My dear?" he asked softly. "Have you received bad news?"

She slowly turned around. "Yes, yes I have. Very bad news indeed."

"I'm so sorry, what is it?" Frederick replied.

She took a step closer to him as she smoothed her bodice on either side and brought herself up to her entire five-foot four-inch height. "It seems my devoted husband is devoted to another woman." Her chin lifted as she spoke.

Frederick felt a stinging sensation in the pit of his stomach. He scratched his forehead and smirked. Before answering he needed to know the details of what she knew so he could unravel it successfully. He lectured himself to remain unfazed, while his mind was alert to the vast abyss that lay in front of him. "What are you talking about? Surely you've been misinformed, my love," he began.

"No. I have not," she answered dryly.

"Then who, who would have you believe such a thing?" he asked.

"You," she responded.

Frederick placed his hands behind his back and rocked on his heels. He was confident he had done nothing to reveal his secret, and he had paid Sam handsomely to keep it as well. "Me, my dear?"

"Yes, *my dear,* you."

He felt her accusing eyes penetrate him. His arms fell by his side. He could feel his anger swell. "Jessica, I'm tired, please do not play games with me. Tell me what this is about."

"I know you thought I was staying in today," he heard her say. "But I got into the Christmas spirit and decided to visit the shops, the boutiques to be exact." Her clues offered him his answer and he cursed under his breath.

"I bought some very nice things for Hannah and Kevin. And oh, you should see the tea towels I purchased for Aunt June," she continued to his dismay.

"Stop," he said.

She continued. "And what did you and your lady purchase today? Anything for *me*?"

Frederick could feel his blood pressure rising. "No, I bought only presents for her."

Before he knew it, his face stung with the might of her slap. He caught her slim wrist. His need to stay in his marriage prevented him from throwing her against the wall. He was acutely aware that he could break her arm and he released it. His pulse throbbed between his ears, as he retreated to the opposite end of the room.

"My God, how could this be my fault?" she cried to him. "Your anger frightens me!"

He was still shaken by his sudden fit of violence. He calmed his breathing and gained his composure. "Sit down and I'll tell you the truth of it," he said. He hoped his story would suffice.

Jessica's hand was tingling from the slap she had given her husband. She rubbed her hands together as she sat down in the carved wood corner chair, its fluffy, rose color cushion providing little comfort. When Frederick concluded she was stunned by his story. The woman he seemed so happy with in town was simply the wife of a deceased friend and they had just been in a moment of gaiety, nothing more.

"I knew you would be jealous if you found out I was helping her, so I kept it from you," he continued to explain.

She felt sick to her stomach and this time it wasn't the nausea of pregnancy. His story was weak at best. She stood and returned to peering out the windows. "She is your mistress. I will go to my Aunt's house tomorrow. I will send for my things shortly after."

"Jessica, you don't have to leave. I'll go to my club until we sort this out," he said softly.

Holding back her anger made her tremble. She knew if she let herself go, she would become hysterical and he would think she had lost her mind. Perhaps he would become violent again. She couldn't take that chance for herself and the baby. She turned to him. Although she had many questions she asked him only one. "Is she your true love?"

"Let's not get into the subject of 'true love' my dear, we both know where your heart lies," he said, touching the side of face.

"I don't want to be married to you," she said.

"You *are* my wife, damn it! I will not divorce you. What will people say? How could you even entertain such a thought?"

She returned a cold stare.

"You have only yourself as a witness to my infidelity," he said. "You can prove nothing. This is *not* over."

"Not over? How can you think I would stay with you after this?"

He cocked his head slightly to the side and said to her, "*I* stayed with *you*."

Jessica felt her chest tighten. Had he somehow found out about her night with Jacob? She backed into the window as he approached her.

He gently took her hand. "My love, let's talk about this rationally."

"I think it will be best if I go to my aunt's home," Jessica answered, quietly.

She walked around him and left the room. She went to her studio and sat on the pink tufted chaise, gazing out of the little windows of the French doors. The rear of the house seemed to have turned its back on her. This life in a beautifully dressed home, with all the advantages and privileges, had come with too high a price. She could not turn a blind eye to a husband's infidelity, as some women preferred to do, but her integrity seemed to be a burden now, and she wished for the simplicity of ignorance.

She had fallen from grace as his wife with her own infidelity. She shook her head and wondered how her world had become so complicated. She wished for a life free of Frederick and his society. She retreated into her fantasy with her and Jacob and a baby, but it could not help her escape from reality. At barely twenty-two years of age she would be divorced and burdened with a child. Again, her future frightened her. Perhaps Frederick would come to his senses and give up his mistress if he knew about the baby. She felt overwhelmingly protective of her unborn child; it swayed her decision.

Jessica looked up at the flower painted ceiling. Though the room paled in comparison to her grand bedroom in San Francisco, she felt safe and secure here. The unknown loomed over her. She tossed and turned in the large bed. The days had been long and tiring and her body ached, especially her back.

It had been only a week since she discovered Frederick's infidelity. The telegram she sent to her aunt offered no clues to her request for an extended visit, but her aunt had welcomed her without question. "This is a good time for you to be here. I'll be baking for the Ladies Guild Christmas event. You'll be a great help to me." June had also smoothed over her uncle's confusion. "Sometimes a woman needs to be with her family," June said when he questioned why his niece would be staying with them indefinitely.

The winter sky darkened early and her body longed for sleep yet she found no rest. She wore only her nightdress — anything else felt too confining. She ran her hand over the firm bulge of her growing belly. The ache in her back moved to her lower abdomen. She gently moved her hand over the bump as the growing pain made her lightheaded. She needed water or a biscuit. As she rose to get her robe a sharp pain stabbed her back and embraced her belly like the thorns of a berry bush. The pressure in her lower body seized her. The bedroom tilted and she fell to the floor. She brought herself to sit up. She went to the bed and sat on the edge panting with each rising fit of pain. They came in short intense waves each one sharper than the next. She rushed to the water closet shouting, "Auntie! Auntie!"

With her bleeding heart came the blood of her womb. A small mass dropped from between her legs to the cold tile. She looked down at the ball of blood and flesh and cried out. There was a knock on the bathroom door and her aunt was in front of her.

"Oh dear God!" June reached out, her face crumpling in despair.

"Auntie what's happening?" Jessica cried. Her legs were like jelly, yet she felt frozen in place.

June ran to the cupboard and retrieved a towel. She wrapped up the expelled fetus. "You poor child!" she crooned. "I'll have your uncle get the doctor. Let me help you to bed. You must lie down now."

Jessica felt weak and disoriented. She lay in bed, crestfallen and confused.

Doctor Grant took the remains with him to be examined but assured Jessica that these things happen and not to blame herself. "It's nature's way," he said.

But she did blame herself. Her greed for freedom, her greed for Jacob. She had brought this on. She mourned their lost child and berated herself for not staying with Frederick. A battle raged inside her each thought fighting the next. Her head tossed on the pillow, one way then the other. She desperately wanted to turn back time and have their baby in her protective body again. The laudanum the doctor gave her was making her drowsy. She couldn't fight any longer. She drifted into a deep, comforting sleep.

Chapter Thirty-seven

As the blossoms of spring emerged Jessica's dark grief began to lighten. She picked up her watercolor paints and brushes with renewed enthusiasm, using her memories of Lenny and her instructions as an inspiration. She promised herself that one day, she would paint like that again. For now, the softness of the watercolors eased her mind as she rendered the landscapes around her. Bell Park was just off the main street of town and it offered her peace and a place to create her art. The rolling manicured lawn surrounded a gazebo with trellised roses. There was a path with a flowered arbor, a stream under a wooden walking bridge. The solace she found there gave way to healing, which then gave way to determination. Jessica kept hidden the independence that was budding inside her. Throughout the winter, the stirring energy fueled her spirit. Someday she would take her talents beyond the boundaries she was forced to adhere to.

The room with the two beds served as her temporary studio. She made it work until she could find her own place to live and study her art. Her aunt and uncle did not speak of the miscarriage except to say that it was God's will. Jessica was thankful for their discretion, especially concerning her parents. "There's no need to bring grief to them," her aunt stated. Yet, Jessica felt painfully alone with her own grief. The silence, the large and lonely silence surrounded her. "Time heals all," her aunt would say. She would embrace those words however out of reach it felt at the moment.

Jessica stretched her arms above her head. The light from the afternoon sun filtered into her 'studio' tempting her to go outside. She put away her paints, deciding a walk into town would do her good. As she came to the East end of downtown she discovered a small art gallery wedged in between two of the clapboard stores. A stout man with a thick mustache and curly light brown hair stood behind a tall reception desk, his head just above its top. "May I help you?" he asked.

She approached him. "Are you the curator?"

"Yes, I'm Mr. Talbot and you are interested in one of the paintings?"

Jessica straightened her back. "No, I'm interested in selling my own paintings here."

Mr. Talbot looked sideways then back to her. "I'm afraid I'm not open to new artists at this time. Good day, Madame." His head disappeared behind the desk.

She was not about to let him off that easily. "Mr. Talbot, I work in watercolors and oils and I feel my paintings would appeal to a female patron. Besides, I notice that many people come through Clermont City on their way to other places, surely they would want a rendition of our fine town to take with them. I would love to show you my work. Please, consider me."

Mr. Talbot rose, looking down his long nose at her. "Hmm, tourist? I like the idea of it, but I won't make my gallery a cheap attraction." Jessica nodded her head in agreement. "Very well, I will first have to take a look at your work, no promises."

"Thank you, Mr. Talbot! I'll bring them to you later today if that's all right? Good day!" She rushed out of the gallery.

"Madame!" She heard him call after her. "I didn't catch your name."

Jessica stopped in her tracks and turned around. "Oh, yes, my name is Jessica, Miss Jessica Messing."

Three days later her paintings were in the Talbot Gallery. Four small paintings and two larger ones, all watercolors. Mr. Talbot was not ready for her grittier oil paintings. Later that week she ventured to the next town of Lamont, with her aunt. She heard of a general store that displayed works of art. Again she gave her speech to the owner of the store. "If you can produce some paintings of Lamont in a good light, why I think I would be interested," Mr. Jenkins, the shop owner said. Jessica was thrilled at her new commission. Although Lamont had less tourist appeal, she was eager to take up the challenge of showing its best features.

That evening Jessica lay in bed, her arms behind her head. She studied the ceiling, but her mind was on Jacob. Her promising career buoyed her sagging spirits yet she ached deep inside for him and their baby. When would she see him again? Surely he would come back someday. She rolled over on her side and placed a hand on her belly. Tears pricked her cheeks.

Chapter Thirty-eight

Jacob wrote in the small tent, struggling to see his own writing on the yellowed paper by the unsteady light of a kerosene lamp. The rain dripped from the tent's open flap, filling his heart with loneliness. He hadn't seen Jessica since his and Will's surprise visit and it felt as if a lifetime had passed, yet he couldn't erase from his mind their time together. He pressed the lead pencil hard on the wrinkled pages as he poured out his life to her.

Dear Jessica,

I said I wouldn't write to you, but I find I can no longer keep to that. I miss you. Knowing I will not be able to receive a response from you hurts me, but it is for my sanity that I talk to you.

The trails have been unforgiving and my life is in great need of change. To be honest with you, Jess, I'm not as legitimate as I had professed to be and keeping that from you seems impossible for me now. I told you not to worry for Will and me, but you have every cause to. I'm sorry, but I need to feel your worry, your concern, or at least know you are thinking of me.

Since we left that September day, we've traveled up the coast of Oregon, then further east where we came upon tribes of Indians warring with each other. They needed the weapons we had to offer, and we needed the money. I should have known that nothing would be that easy. . .

Jacob paused and stared into the dancing flame trapped inside the lantern's glass chimney, remembering. Regretting.

South Central Oregon, January 1887

Jacob took from his shirt pocket the piece of paper with directions to the spot where their next trade would take place. The Klamath Reservation was a vast land of rugged terrain filled with flat expanses, valleys, plateaus and rivers that snaked along its hills. The mist and drizzling rain surrounded them in a small clearing marked on the map. He looked ahead at the stand of tall firs and cedars also marked out. Somewhere in there was a band of settlers looking to buy weapons and ammo. The man who had scribbled out the map in the saloon last night told him his gang was heading up to the Grande Ronde Reservation up in Northern Oregon. "The government might have let those redskins have that land but we want it back!" the man proclaimed followed by a grizzly sneer. It gave Jacob an uneasy feeling; just last week they'd sold guns and ammunition to three members of the Tillamook tribe who had unlawfully ventured south from their Reservation. Jacob asked no questions; he didn't want to know.

Their horses trudged through the thick under layer of ferns, salal and broken branches. The map said to stay north and Jacob consulted his compass several times. The sweet scent of the pine trees gave him little comfort. After nearly an hour, they came to another clearing where ten or more men on horseback waited. They wore cowboy hats, thick, heavy cotton coats, worn leather riding gloves, and leather chaps. Their beards ran down their chests. One of them finally spoke.

"I see you found your way," he said to Jacob. "These men and I want to make a clean deal, and that means we don't want any trouble with the government." They all sat tall upon their horses, their guns in clear sight.

"I told you last night that we're not with the government," Jacob said. "We have eight rifles, and six pistols. They're all in ready condition, ammo included."

"All right," the leader said. "Now, get down from your horses."

Jacob looked at Will and nodded once. The leader laughed sharply. He gave a signal to his men and everyone dismounted. Jacob counted the cash while the men examined their guns. He placed the hundred dollars in his pack. It wasn't their biggest cash deal, nor their smallest.

No sooner had Will and Jacob rode away the sound of gunshots rang out like pops of firecrackers. "What the hell? Are they already fighting over the guns?" Will asked.

"I don't know, but this doesn't sound good." Jacob looked back. Through the trees he caught glimpses of riders on Mustangs; they were Indians. One rider wheeled around toward them. Jacob was startled. The bone in the rider's nose and shells draped on his neck and chest was indicative to the dress of the Tillamook People. His heart beat fast. How could they have found them? The battle cries and gunshots broke through the peace of the forest.

Without a word Jacob and Will immediately pushed their own horses into a gallop. Shouts silenced by bullets spurred Jacob to ride as fast as Otis would take him.

They rode until the chaos was well behind him. The trail became unfamiliar and Jacob realized they were not heading back the same way. A faint light ahead indicated that they had reached some sort of clearing but not the one they had come from. He turned to Will to get his take on the situation. The blood rushed to his head; there was nothing but forest behind him; his cousin was nowhere in sight. He stopped and began to search wildly in the low light. He turned and headed back to retrace his escape, his adrenaline surging.

Will's horse came trotting toward him without its rider. The animal was stained with blood. "Christ!" Jacob shouted. He looked around for a low branch in which to secure Drake. Then he returned to where he had just ridden. He feverishly searched the ground as the gunshots became loud and clear again, with the cries of triumph and defeat. Finally, in the underbrush a familiar figure lay still.

Jacob flew off his horse and trembled as he lifted his cousin's torso. Will's shirt was wet with blood. With his heart in his throat, he felt his cousin's neck for a pulse. He was alive. Jacob quickly removed the coat and shirt from the limp body and tied the shirt around Will's chest. The wound was on his side with no indication of a bullet hole. It gave Jacob hope that he had been grazed and not shot straight through. As he tended to Will, he discovered another bloody shot in his arm. He took the bandanna from his cousin's head and tied it tightly around the wounded arm. The flow of blood slowed to a steady weeping.

Jacob rode to Drake and led the horse back to Will. He inhaled deeply and hoisted Will's heavy body across Drake's back while trying to steady the spooked animal. He found the rope in his pack and tied it to the horse's halter. Finally, he was able to mount his own horse. "All right, Otis, you gotta help me here," Jacob said to his trusted quarter horse. He pulled on Drake and the horse reluctantly walked with his master draped over his back. "Steady, boy, that's it, come on now." Otis wanted to investigate Drake's new circumstances and Jacob had a time keeping him riding forward as he continued to encourage Drake. He made slow progress as Drake would stop and start in fits.

Finally, he emerged from the forest and soon came upon a small village. On first inspection it looked deserted, but for the smoldering fire pit in the middle of a circle of dwellings. Little pole buildings, the sides and roofs covered in swathes of bark looked uninhabited. As he dismounted an old woman came running out of one of the dwellings. He could see she was one of the native people.

"No, no, no!" she cried, flailing her arms. "You go! Go!" She ran up to Jacob, striking him with her fists. He barred himself from the onslaught.

"I need help!" he shouted at her. "Where is your doctor, your medicine man?"

"You go! You go!" she continued her chant, her feet kicking up dust around her small, deer hide covered body.

He walked past her and knocked on the first door he came to. A skin-covered wooden frame flung open, causing him to step back. The woman standing in front of him gestured for him to leave, then immediately slammed it shut. He stepped away only to see an old man approaching him from across the circle.

"You go! Go!" the elder cried out in a feeble voice, and waved his arms and hands at Will's still body as if to shoo away any evil spirits. Then he and the old woman began to talk in their native tongue. Drake whinnied and moved sideways, clearing anxious to get rid of his pack. Jacob neared his breaking point.

"Jesus Christ!" he shouted and looked around in despair and frustration. He checked Will's pulse. Still there, but weak. He had to continue on, there was no time to waste. He got back on his horse and with his injured cousin in tow, Jacob rode from the unwelcoming village. His thoughts and emotions were swimming in his head, as he tried to piece together where he was. He felt the sting of tears run down his anguished face.

"Oye! Hey! Escucha!" he heard from behind him. He turned around to see a young man running after him.

The man spoke in a thick Spanish accent, nearly out of breath. "I can help."

Jacob followed in guarded relief until they arrived at an old shack in back of one of the dwellings. They carefully laid Will on a long, wooden table in the middle of the small room. To one side an old dresser had various size bottles on top of it and a large jar of liquid that held scissors and other implements. The cramped space was tidy for its rundown state.

"Do you speak English? Are you a doctor?" Jacob asked.

"*Claro, claro!* Yes!" the man answered nodding his head. "Fortez is my name." He impatiently moved Jacob aside as he took several yards of narrow cloth out of one of the drawers. He untied the blood soaked shirt and scarf. "What in the name of God are you two doing way out here? This is no place for you!" he proclaimed, but before Jacob could respond he flung his hand in the air, "*No quiero oirlo.*"

Jacob watched intently as the doctor examined his patient. He wondered briefly how the Spanish doctor came to be here.

"You were smart to tie these," Fortez said. "I cannot do much for him, but I can put fresh bandages on these wounds. They do not look too deep." The doctor plunged a finger into Will's wounds. "I feel no bullets in here."

The room spun and Jacob's stomach flopped; he had to turn away. His mind fled to the time he himself had to examine an arm for bullets. He had been braver with Caleb, now he reeled with dizziness; this was his own blood, his own wound.

"Doc Middleman in Medford can stitch him up," the doctor said. "I am afraid I am all out of thread and needles. If you can tell the good doctor we need help here in Wolf Village, I would be very grateful to you, amigo. Now, I will set him up to weather the trip." He looked directly at Jacob and shook his head. "Not promising."

"How far is it from here?" Jacob asked.

"About three and a half miles. It will take you over an hour, maybe two and it'll be rough on your amigo."

Will moaned and briefly opened his eyes, then fell out of consciousness again.

Jacob had to stop and sharpen the tip of the pencil with a penknife. He shook out his sore hand, cramped from the intensity of his writing, and bent over the paper once again.

I don't think I've ever been more scared in all my life, Jess. The road seemed to go on forever. This town of Medford was beginning to look as if it never existed and Will would die right beside me, slumped over his horse, but I got us there ...

Jacob managed to get them to Medford, Oregon, a civilized town with many houses on a stretch of mostly flat land. The center of town had shops, a large hotel, a theater, a post office, a sheriff's office and Doc Middleman's practice. As the winter sun dipped behind the distant snow-capped mountains he looked for Will's last hope. He finally reached his destination.

The townspeople stared with hushed comments as he called out to the doctor while still mounted on Otis. Drake shifted impatiently.

Doc Middleman's response was quick yet agitated. He went to work on Will in his well-stock patient's room.

"He's lucky those gun shots weren't deep. Looks as if the bullets landed somewhere else," the doctor said dryly. "But he's lost some flesh and a lot of blood." He handed Jacob cotton pads and some rubbing alcohol. "This isn't the first time I've seen this. Some make it, and some don't," the doctor said as he shook his head. "Redress them if the bandages get too bloody, but clean your hands first. I'll take these stitches out in a few weeks. He should regain consciousness now that the bleeding has stopped. If he doesn't, then it might be too late to do anything."

Jacob took in every word as he stood aside. The doctor washed his hands and dried them on a clean towel. He went to a cabinet and handed Jacob a small brown vial.

"Here's something for the pain. If he does wake up he'll be feeling plenty of it. Give him a teaspoon or so before he becomes too uncomfortable, but no more than four times a day."

Jacob took the vial. "What is this stuff?"

"It's a combination of morphine, cannabis, and alcohol among other things."

Jacob thought of Caleb and his wounded arm.

"Doctor Fortez helped you with this?" Doc Middleman asked.

"Yes," Jacob said, then he remembered the doctor's request. "He wanted me to tell you that they are in great need of supplies, needles and thread, that's why he couldn't stitch him up."

Dr. Middleman grinned. "Oh, your friend here would be glad of that. Carlos is not known for his good mending," he said. "All right then, he can stay here tonight, then the hotel across the street will have to be your home until he's well enough to ride. That'll take about three weeks, if there are no complications. By the looks of it, son, you surely can't afford to have me nurse him back to health. Once he's moved to his room, I'll send my nurse assistant to check on him."

"Can I sit with him?"

"Go ahead, but don't touch him. Infection is the cause for most of these things going bad." Doc Middleman cautioned then left the room.

Jacob pulled a chair next to the bed and looked at his cousin's ashen face. An acute feeling of guilt struck his heart. He didn't understand the feeling; after all, his cousin was willing to take the chances. He never had to bend his arm to do so. Still, he felt responsible for him. Their lives had always been inextricably linked, with Jacob as the voice of reason. Nowadays he felt that Will was just as much in that role as himself and he had come to rely on it.

"Don't die on me," Jacob said softly, swallowing his emotions. He took Will's hand and held onto it until he gave into his exhaustion and left to make arrangements at the hotel, leaving his cousin's fate in the hands of God.

It took most of our earnings to pay the doctor and to get a room where Will could convalesce. I took a job at the town's saloon. Will healed slower than I thought he would. We always knew our line of work was dangerous, but I guess we never thought to put away for a rainy day, so to speak.

It was going on the second week of their arrival into Medford and Jacob was getting ready for his shift at the Towne Saloon. He combed his hair and made himself decent for work. Will was sitting up in bed, his strength slowly returning.

"Jake, do you think this is our punishment for selling illegal guns?" Will asked with a wince as he tried to sit up straighter.

"Probably. Just heal up so we can get the hell out of here."

"Have you seen Mi?" Will asked.

It had been two days since Doc Middleman's assistant had come to call on him and Jacob knew he was missing her attention. He saw the look on his cousin's face whenever Mi wrapped his bandages, humming a soothing tune. He understood how Will could be attracted to the young woman. Her black hair was severely pulled back into a ponytail that ran down her back, exposing her pretty, oval face and wide set eyes. Her pleasing smile had offered Jacob comfort in those first critical days when he wasn't sure if his cousin would live or die. She and Will were falling in love and Jacob had to make sure he got well soon; the petite American-born Chinese woman was not in their plan. "Your nurse is probably on her way," Jacob replied.

"Can you believe how she became a nursing student? With her Chinese parents owning a restaurant, with little money?" Will asked Jacob.

"Yes, Will, so you've said."

"She's made it on her own, as a Chinese girl. She's almost a full-fledged nurse. I think that's damn smart of her!" Will exclaimed. He grimaced and put a hand to his arm.

"Take it easy," Jacob said. He turned back to the mirror to adjust the tie he was given to wear. "I hate this fuckin' job." He had only been a barkeep at the Towne Saloon for a week and he ached for his freedom.

"I like her, Jake."

"Yep," Jacob answered sourly. "Why wouldn't you, with all that attention?"

"Jealous?"

"Don't get attached to her. You know damn well we can't stay here. I want to get back to California. This goddamn tie!" He whipped the black string off his neck and tried again.

"Just because you can't have the one you love, don't deny me a chance," Will muttered.

Jacob ignored him. "I've got to go. If she brings up soup, save some for me." He turned for the door.

"I'll save you some soup if you save me some liquor," Will replied with an impish grin.

"I'll see what I can do." Jacob returned the smile. He was happy to see his cousin coming back to himself. As he walked down the hall to the stairs, Mi was reaching the top step.

"Hello Jacob," she said.

"He's been waiting for you. Oh, and by the way, he's not sticking around here, so don't make him too comfortable, if you know what I mean."

"Your cousin and I have developed a very nice friendship. I think who he befriends is none of your business," Mi replied.

"It is my business. So, like I said, don't get too comfortable together."

Will is still getting over his wounded arm and aching heart, Jacob wrote. *His nursemaid wasn't as interested in him as he was in her. They both seem to realize the circumstances. I'm glad for your brother coming to his senses.*

We're in Portland right now and we'll be heading to the Oregon coast. Our travels may take us back to California, but I can't make any promises. The landscape here is beautiful and I think you would make a fine painting from it.

Will is hell-bent on us becoming real entrepreneurs and we may enter the export/import business. Who knows, Jess I may become legitimate after all.

I don't know why I'm telling you all this. I needed to get some of this off my chest, but mostly, I don't want you harboring any illusions of who I am. Next time we meet, whenever that is, I will be myself, even at the risk of your disapproval, though I pray it's not too great.

I never stop thinking about you, although I have tried. I miss your smile and your lips and our bodies close together. No one has captured my heart as you have and I fear no one ever will. Our future together is bleak as it has always been, maybe someday we may find happiness together, in another time and place.

Be well, All my love, Jacob

Jacob placed the letter in the envelope along with a token of his love and sealed it. He wanted his words to reach her and at the same time he knew if he reread what he wrote, he would tear up the pages. His future looked uncertain but he was determined to make something of himself. With Will's suggestion that they get into a legitimate business, he felt a glimmer of hope. Mostly he wanted to prove to Jessica and his family that he could be a success. At the moment, he felt little of the man he envisioned himself to be.

The rain subsided and he emerged from the tent to find Will sitting under a tree, a blanket draped over his head. Jacob lit a cigarette and joined his cousin. "How would we get into this trading business anyway?" He handed Will the cigarette and Will lit his own with the burning end.

"I think an import business may be the way to go," Will answered. "We've been picking up trinkets here and there to sell and trade. We seem to be pretty good at it. We'll take our experience to San Francisco and open up our storefront there."

"We could offer exotic treasures from the Far East." Jacob pondered the possibilities. "Yep, San Francisco would be the place. We'll have to study the shipping business. Do you think we can do this?" He noticed Will's expression harden. "What is it?" Jacob asked.

"San Francisco."

Jacob knew what his cousin was trying to say. He took a drag of his cigarette and blew out the smoke. "We'll both be too busy to think of anything else but the success of our company." He caught Will's raised eyebrow. "There are some things that are my business alone," Jacob warned him.

Will pulled on his cigarette. "And what would we call ourselves?" he asked.

Jacob thought for a moment. "How about J&W Imports?"

Will took another drag of his cigarette and blew out the smoke, mocking his cousin. "How about W&J Imports?"

"A game of poker?" Jacob answered.

"Now that's the way to settle things," Will replied.

While they played the last hand to determine their company's name, Jacob noticed Will was distracted. "Something else on your mind?"

"You're not going to like this," Will said, shuffling the deck his usual three times in a row. He dealt their hands.

Jacob took up his cards and arranged them. "What now?"

"Mi."

"What about her?"

"I told you she had no interest in me, but…. The truth is, we're in love."

Jacob slapped down his cards and snuffed out his cigarette. "Where does she fit into our plan? And why the hell did you lie to me?"

"Sorry. I knew you would get angry. I don't know where she fits in, but she'll have to. I promised her I'd make something of myself then return to get her. She'll continue to stay with the Middleman's until then."

A particular light came into Will's eyes as he spoke of Mi. For the first time, Jacob saw in another man what he so desired for himself. It disturbed him, but he had no time to think about it now. Will's revelation was a blow he didn't see coming.

"She's Chinese, Will," he said.

"I know what her race she is, Jacob. It doesn't matter to us."

"It sure as hell will matter to her family, our family *and* society."

"You should talk about affecting our family and society, cousin." Will retorted.

Jacob crossed his legs and arms. "Jesus Will, let it be."

"There's one other thing." Will lowered his head and scratched his messy hair. His blue eyes looked up from under his brows. A sheepish grin curled his lips.

"Don't tell me," Jacob pleaded. "My God, we were only there for a few months!"

"Doc Middleman confirmed before we left to come up here."

"Son-of-a -bitch, Will!" Jacob sprang up and hurled a branch into the air.

"Her family lives in Portland and she wants me to ask her father for permission for us to be married. She isn't going to tell them about her pregnancy."

"So that's why you dragged us up here? No business deal, just your own selfish pursuits?" Jacob regretted his words as soon as they were out of his mouth. From the expression on Will's face he knew he'd hurt his cousin, who was more like a brother. "Damn it, Will," he said quietly.

"I'm sorry, Jake, but I won't let her go. I understand now what it's like to love someone. I've never had that feeling for anyone," Will said. "Not even you," he remarked with a smirk.

Jacob shook his aching head. "We've got some travels ahead of us before we can think of settling and here you are strapped with a wife and kid."

"The Middleman's will take care of her while I'm away."

"We need to stick to our plans to make J&W Imports a success even with this latest goddamned twist of fate," Jacob said.

"J&W Imports? What about, W and …" Will began.

Jacob gave his cousin a hard look.

"J&W Imports it is!" Will exclaimed. "I told Mi all about the plan. She'll make a good wife and mother, Jake. Hey, I'm going to be a father. Sooner than I hoped, but that's life, isn't it?"

"God help you. God help us," Jacob replied.

Chapter Thirty-nine

Jessica had spent the warm spring afternoon sketching the impressive City Hall. Clermont City had once been on track to become a large railroad city. Instead the railroad had been diverted to Oakland and the city hall and post office buildings remained as a reminder of opportunities lost.

As she strolled down the street she thought of the bigger city just thirty minutes north. Although Oakland had very few galleries, she was anxious to visit the Gates Gallery and meet the owner, a woman.

When she arrived home she changed into a housedress, releasing herself from her boned corset, allowing the air to dry her sweaty chest. She sat on the porch of her aunt and uncle's home. Her home now. She opened her sketchbook. But instead of drawing, she began making notes to plan a trip into Oakland. She would need a chaperone and the money for the stagecoach. She was lost in the plan when the whistling of the mailman interrupted her. He opened the gate and came down the walk.

"Good day, Miss. It sure is a lovely one," he said to her then handed over the mail.

"Yes, it is," she replied. "Thank you, Mr. Benson."

As she leafed through the cards and letters, a bulky envelope grabbed her attention. It was from Jacob, addressed to her. She immediately opened it and a short string of turquoise beads landed in her lap. She recognized them as the ones Jacob wore around his neck. The tender spot in her heart that held her love for him expanded. She breathed in deeply.

She felt the smooth roundness of the bluish green beads as they draped around her fingers. She brought them to her nose. A faint smell of his neck. Her eyes closed and she was whisked away to his strong, tense body. She returned to earth with an effort. She untied the thin rawhide and placed the strand around her neck, the weight of it on her flesh. She placed a hand on them and closed her eyes. Then she impatiently unfolded his letter and began to read of his heart, his life and his remorse. She was relieved that her brother had been spared his life. Their dangerous experience made her ache with worry. Mostly, she wanted to soothe Jacob's troubled life with her love. When she came to the end of his letter she started again from the beginning. Her faith in him renewed. His love for her was strong and wanting. It was a sign that someday, in some way, they would be together.

Jessica placed the letter back into the envelope. Anxious now, she could hardly wait for her uncle to arrive home.

Burt entered his study, with Jessica right behind him. "Sit, and let's talk about this at a legal standpoint," he said. "According to the law, you may divorce, but only under extreme duress and or adultery. Proof must be solid and even with that, you will gain nothing from his worth. You will be as penniless as you were when you married him. You will maintain your part of inheritance from your father once he has passed, but God forbid that for now.

"I see," Jessica replied. She bowed her head. *Whatever it takes.*

"Yes, that is the fact of the matter, my dear. I haven't even touched on the social aspects. I'm sure you don't need to be reminded that a divorced woman is considered less than a whole human being."

"I'm still who I am. He's the adulterer. Besides, I think Hannah and Kevin can back up my claim. No one in Clermont City has to know."

Burt rubbed the back of his neck. "I suppose. Are you willing to keep up such a charade? Think of the embarrassment this might cause your aunt at her clubs if someone was to find out. She's already bragged about her married niece and successful nephew. My standing at the land company could be tainted as well."

Her guilt threatened to strangle her. She brought her fingers to her mouth. "I … I didn't think about it. My marriage seems so distant to me now." She looked at her uncle with an idea. "Perhaps another, unmarried niece has emerged?"

Burt began to pace in front of her. "Well, let's not think of things that haven't happened. Your parents must be informed immediately. I'm not sure they would agree to any of this." He scratched his head. "My whole-hearted suggestion to you, Jessica is to remain married and claim that you are a widow."

Jessica looked up at her uncle. "A widow?" she asked. "I don't know if I could do such a thing. I would be pitied."

"Better to be pitied as a victim of fate than scorned as a failed wife," he replied.

Jessica bent forward in her chair and cupped her face. She knew she had no choice if she were to continue her life free from Frederick. The thought of living another lie disturbed her. She stood up. "Uncle Burt, could the marriage simply be dissolved as if it never took place?"

"My dear, I will help you as much as I can, but you must face the facts. A divorce or even a hint of it will be a terrible stain on you and your family. Perhaps the practice is more accepted here, but certainly Hartford would have a field day with the gossip and your parents may not be as welcome in certain circles."

Jessica looked around her uncle's study. The spring sun dappled across the wood planked floor. It warmed the room with its soft amber light. It warmed her as well giving her a ray of hope. She felt the comfort of Jacob's beads under her high-necked blouse, it emboldened her. "I've made my decision," she said. "I will refer to myself as Miss Messing. Petition for the divorce, Uncle."

"Please think on this," her uncle pleaded.

"I will be a single woman. Nothing less." She could feel the tingle of nerves rise up her spin and hit the back of her neck. It made her head jerk slightly and she brought her hand to her cheek. "Hartford is very far away; my life is here."

"Very well," Burt replied. He took a deep breath. "We will continue to refer to you as our not-yet-married niece. I doubt anyone will be as uncouth as to challenge it. We will inform the rest of the family here. It will be difficult to keep Sophie quiet, but I'll let your Aunt take care of that. Have you written to your parents of your situation?"

Jessica looked away. "No."

"I figured you hadn't. The letters from your mother to June mention nothing about your affairs and you know she would surely have something to say on the matter."

"That's what I dread," Jessica said. Then she had an equally upsetting thought. "What about Frederick?" she asked her uncle.

"I will deal with him," Burt said. "I had heard some disturbing rumors about his dealings at the bank, so I decided to investigate. It seems he's in plenty of hot water at The First National. Something to do with his unfair trades. I'm not sure how far reaching the implications will be. He may even be charged criminally."

Jessica put her hand to her mouth. "My goodness, Uncle, I had no idea." She listened as her uncle became the lawyer he once was. She shook her head in disbelief. Her thoughts were scattered, looking back to what might have been clues of his dirty deals then to the present and how Frederick could profoundly affect her future.

"It could go against you if you had any knowledge of it and failed to report it. Think carefully, Jessica."

She paced the floor searching her mind for anything she might have suspected. The only thought that kept coming to her was his infidelity. She faced her uncle. "No, I have no knowledge of this," she answered.

"Very well," he said. "Then we shall proceed with the charge of infidelity. You said you may have witnesses. That will help our case."

Jessica took her handkerchief from her skirt pocket and wiped her eyes and nose.

"You're forced to age faster than you should, my dear," her uncle said.

Jessica reached out to him. His large, strong hands enveloped her small, shaking hands. She looked up at the tall, gentle man, his compassionate expression gave her comfort.

"You are a brave woman. You will get through this. I will try to persuade him to give you a certain sum of money. You'll need something, after all."

"I know you will do your best, Uncle. Thank you so much."

"I can only promise my part in it, however, society will be your judge and jury."

Jessica retreated to the parlor with her decision like weights on her shoulders. Her body felt tired. She sat down on the chair near an open window. The spring air drifted in carrying scents of bay trees, wild rose and sage. She breathed in and let out a sigh. A time of renewal back in Hartford, where the tulips and jonquils would be giving their brightness, the promise of summer to come. Here the season was already heating up as her life was heating up to the point of boiling over with anticipation. She fingered the beads at her neck. If she couldn't have Jacob on her own terms, at least they would be able to see each other without the cloud of adultery hanging over her head. She gazed out the window to the place she last saw him. He stood so still as he waved goodbye, so accepting of his fate. She rested her chin on the top of the overstuffed chair and wondered what he would think of her getting a divorce. Would he come back to be with her? So many questions without answers. She gathered her skirt to rise from her meditative perch, perhaps a painting of the garden would clear her head. The thought already had a soothing effect on her. She went to her studio and claimed the basket she had of supplies for her field painting sessions. Her aunt was whistling a tune as she snuck by the kitchen and out the back way.

Chapter Forty

Frederick opened the large safe in his office that held all of his liquid assets. His time at the First National Bank of San Francisco had run out and his off-the-books practices were rapidly catching up with him. He would have to move his money to a hidden location. He placed a large brown satchel under the opening of the safe and began to fill it with the stacks of paper bills, and silver coins. The gold bricks would go into a sturdy suitcase he had recently purchased for this purpose. At a knock on the door, he pushed the remaining money back into his safe and closed the heavy steel door.

"Who is it?" he barked.

"Mr. Moore?" Hannah chirped, "Mr. Burt Stanford is here to see you."

Frederick's mind reeled. *What in God's name…?* He straightened his desk, then called for Hannah. "See him through," he said to her.

A minute later, Burt stood in front of Frederick, briefcase in hand.

"Why, Burt, this is an unexpected visit," Frederick said graciously as he stuck out his hand. He felt the weak handshake from his uncle-in-law and it gave him a feeling of foreboding. "Coming all the way from Clermont City. Or do you have business in San Francisco?"

"I'll get right to the matter," Burt said. He brought his briefcase in front of him and held the handle with both hands.

Frederick didn't like the way he was coming off; something was up. "Please do," he said.

"My niece has informed me of your infidelity and she has asked me to start divorce proceedings." Frederick didn't flinch. He chose not to even reply. "She has witnesses," Burt continued. "Your very employees. I will be asking for their depositions in the next few days."

"I have nothing to hide," Frederick said. "I'm surprised you would believe some employee, and not a member of your own family."

"I've also investigated your dealings with the bank."

Frederick could feel the beads of sweat forming below his nose. He swept a finger across his lip and kept his composure.

"I discussed the matter with one of the bank's owners, in fact," Burt continued.

"I've done nothing wrong," Fredrick protested.

"Frederick, the bank's manager, Mr. Harding has proof of your illegal transactions. How long did you think you could turn a profit for yourself using bank customers' money?" Burt's voice rose as he spoke.

"How dare you come to my home and disrespect me!" Frederick went around to his desk. He planted both hands on the polished wood top and leaned forward. Burt's face was a reflection of his rage. He slowly sat and relaxed his shoulders. He could not allow himself to lose control. "Forgive my outburst. Talk of divorce is a serious matter, I'm unprepared to deal with it."

Burt cleared his throat. "Let us both keep our heads," he said. "Even if the bank's efforts are a pointless pursuit, there will be questions you'll have to answer. I'm willing to bet they'll find more than you want them to."

Frederick knew Burt was trying to unnerve him, but he was determined not to fall for this lawyer's tactics. He said nothing, letting the man continue.

"I am willing to talk to the bank on your behalf as a champion for your integrity. There will be a price, however," Burt stated.

"And what price is that?" Frederick demanded. "I suppose you want a cut of the …" He bit back the rest of his words, regretting immediately his panicked indiscretion.

"Just as I thought," Burt said. He laid his briefcase on the desk and opened it. He handed a paper to Frederick. "I don't need your dirty money, Frederick, but my niece requests a divorce. Sign here and the matter will be taken care of at the bank. Jessica and her family will begin the proceedings to be free of you. I might add that you are to offer the bank your immediate resignation."

Frederick snatched the paper from Burt's hand. He read the agreement for divorce and laughed bitterly. "She has no proof," he said, handing the document to Burt.

"The judge will decide that," Burt replied. "There is also a matter of giving my niece a monetary settlement. Two thousand dollars should cover her time as your wife."

"Two thousand dollars? Are you mad?" Frederick knew that Burt was in uncharted waters. The law would provide nothing to his wife.

"Your unscrupulous work has certainly increased your wealth," Burt replied. "But unless you wish to be shamefully run through the legal system because of it, I suggest you accept my offer. Then you may consort with whatever devils you wish to."

"This is bloody blackmail, and I won't stand for any part of it. I ask you to leave now." Frederick commanded. He stood and turned to his office window. Outside was a view of Jessica's abandoned art studio. His thoughts went to the first time he had entered it after she left. He had found only her paint-stained apron draped over the pink chaise he had once made love to her on. He recalled how he had lifted the apron gingerly as if it might hurt him and, in fact, it had. His ego was pained; her arrow had hit its mark. Turning back to Burt, he spoke as if in a dream, "I suppose you wouldn't believe me, if I told you I loved her, and still do."

"Frederick, don't be a fool." Burt spoke with a softened tone

"Some of your clients have already talked to the bank's investigators. They're getting ready to raid your office and your home. Take my offer and I promise you, I will do what I can to prevent you from going to jail."

Burt pleaded. "My niece deserves none of this scandal."

Frederick thought a moment. His pride only slightly giving way to his greed, he said quietly, "Very well, I agree to your terms and concede to a divorce, but only on the grounds that we were both unfaithful." Frederick waited for Burt's fury.

"What are you saying?" Burt lashed out. "I've heard of revenge, but to concoct such a lie just to help yourself. My God, have you truly come to this?"

"Oh yes," Frederick replied. "I forgot how clever they were in keeping it from you, and the rest of the family, and how stupid you all were for not suspecting. My, how families keep secrets, some of which they are not even aware of." He made sure Burt was as uncomfortable as he could make him.

"Talk sense, man!" Burt shouted.

"I will leave it at this: your niece has long had an affair of the heart and I have a document from one Doctor Grant that proves they consummated their relationship during our marriage. Why should I take the full burden of a scandal, while she also betrayed me?" His anger rose from the thought of his wife with Burt's son, and he mentally ripped her apron apart.

"I don't believe you. Doctor Grant assisted her after the miscarriage. I thought she might have informed you of this. Are you saying the child was not yours?"

Frederick decided to spare him the torture. A scandal would only complicate his own affairs. He'd get his revenge some other time. "Being the gentleman that I am, I will not discuss the matter with you further. I will say this my secret is worth more than two thousand."

"Now who is the blackmailer? Play your games, Frederick, but I doubt if my niece will consent to this. I implore you to take responsibility for your actions and if you truly want to live up to being a gentleman, act accordingly. Here are the rest of the documents. Have them back to me by tomorrow, or I can assure you, the police will come knocking at your door instead of me. Good day."

Frederick let Burt show himself out, and then returned to his safe, transferring the remaining cash to the leather bag. He struggled to organize his thoughts. First, he'd take the cash to his secretary's apartment. His faithful Annabelle would be his new conquest and eventually provide him with an ally who wouldn't think of betraying him. He knew she would eagerly welcome his advances and his prosperity.

He leaned against the cold steel safe, stabbed by sadness. Jessica had carried another man's child. Jacob's child. He threw the paper bills into the leather bag then hurled the loaded case across the room scattering his money along the desk and onto the floor.

Chapter Forty-one

Jessica arrived at Frederick's home. Her fear at meeting him face-to-face was great, but her need for his silence was greater. Her uncle Burt had revealed to her, most hesitantly, what Frederick had said about her own infidelity and the suggestion of another man's child. His droll dismissal of the accusation gave Jessica no comfort. She needed to hear from Frederick that he would make no such claims again. She feared that her estranged husband could indeed ruin her life forever and her dreams of becoming an artist of worth would dissolve. Who would buy a painting from an adulterer? She also thought of her family. Shame and guilt rose to the surface and she struggled again to put her love for Jacob in a place far away from those dark feelings.

Today she stood on the front porch of the decorated house she had once called home, feeling apprehensive about her decision. She thought of Jacob with a protective heart. If they were to have any future at all she would have to be brave. She stamped her feet to get her legs to stop shaking. Her thoughts could not find a balance. *Stay with Frederick and forgo all this nonsense, he will provide stability.* What woman truly had her freedom? *No, I must hold my ground so that Jacob and I could have a chance, if only in our own private world.*

Hannah answered the door. "Oh, Mum!" she exclaimed. "You've

come back. I missed you so." She stepped to the side to allow Jessica to enter.

Jessica was so pleased to see her former maid, a lump of longing formed in her throat. However, she couldn't allow sentiment to sway her. "It's lovely to see you, Hannah. I'm here to discuss some matters with Mr. Moore."

"I'll inform him you're here, Mum," Hannah replied.

Jessica saw Hannah about to curtsy, but catch herself. She watched the young woman hurry away. She looked around the large foyer and peered into the parlor. The home was still a pleasant and bright place; perhaps she could find it in herself to forgive Frederick and rejoin him here. Her shoulders rose as a shiver went up her spine, the room tilted. She tugged on her gloves and straightened her purse strings. Her nerves would not get the best of her.

Finally, Hannah instructed her to enter Frederick's office. Her smile and wide blue eyes indicated a degree of hope. Jessica shook her head and Hannah nodded sadly.

Frederick stood in the doorway. Jessica had forgotten how imposing his presence could be. "Welcome," Frederick said, not unkindly. He stepped forward and took her hand. She let him hold her gloved hand, comforted that the fullness of her deep blue skirt hid her shaking legs and the waistcoat over her ruffled blouse hid her pounding heart. The moment was awkward and he released her hand. The mere touch of him made her slightly ill.

She entered his study at his bidding and sat down. She sat on the edge of one of the carved wooden high-back chairs placed in front of his large desk, her hands folded on her lap. He took the seat facing her. She wondered if he had the chairs arranged in this fashion on purpose. He leaned back and crossed his long legs. "Now what do I attribute this great pleasure?" he asked. "Your telegram gave no indication of your intentions."

His tone was repugnant to her. This once handsome and gallant man had become utterly vile. He knew he held her future and he seemed bent on making her squirm. She could even smell liquor on his breath. She was brief and to the point. "Frederick, what will it take for you to keep your opinions of my relationship with Jacob to yourself?"

"Such assertiveness!" he said as he came forward. He frowned. "I'm not impressed, my love. So very unladylike, I must say."

Jessica ignored the barb. She was determined to have this meeting go her way. "What is your answer?" she asked.

Frederick gave a laugh. He stood and looked down at her. "You thought it appropriate to expose my infidelity. Now I'm supposed to keep your own infidelity secret? A child? My dear, you are in an awkward situation. Was the miscarriage a misfortune or was it deliberate?"

Jessica felt the blood leave her head. The room spun. She clenched the arm of the chair.

After a deep breath she found her confidence. "Why would I get rid of a child from the one and only man I've ever loved? I suppose it could have been yours. No matter, I lost *my* child."

"It certainly wasn't mine. For you see, I have not the ability to provide such a blessing."

"What? Why didn't you tell me this?" Her back tightened and she rose slightly off her seat. "How do you know?"

"Doctors, doctors and more doctors. Scarlet fever." He looked down his nose at her. "And to be vulgar, as you know me to be at times, no woman I've bedded has ever come down with the condition."

She turned away, stabbed by a sudden sadness; it was Jacob's child. "I see," she replied. Her purpose for coming here was renewed. Before she could rise and stand with him he was bent over her, a hand on each arm of the chair.

"Continue to be my wife and all this goes away. There are children who need a good home and here we sit in one. Your uncle will help me get out from under this misunderstanding at the bank and we can live as they say- happily ever after."

She looked into his softened eyes and moved to rise. He took one arm away and she had to meet his chest to get around him.

She decided to stand near the door. "Is it money? I can take far less than what my uncle has in mind."

Frederick laughed again. "It all comes down to money. As it should, my dear. Tell me what has your lover to offer you? He's a rogue and by some accounts an outlaw."

Jessica refused to take the bait. "Money is your life. Tell me how much."

"Will he provide you with all this?" Frederick asked as he waved his arms around the room. The gesture seemed childish to her. She let him continue. "You used my money as you used me; a cover for your incestuous affair. What will you live on now, the measly pennies you get for your art?" He continued to test her steel.

"Love and art hold greater value than money," Jessica replied. She refused to let him taint what was in her heart. He came closer.

"Good luck living off either one," he said with amusement. He reached out and put his arm around her waist pulling her into him. She tried to get away, but his grip prevented her from escaping. "I won't hurt you, my love. I thought since we are about to end our marriage that perhaps we might kiss and be friends. Your bedroom is as you left it." He kissed her cheek. Jessica felt the tepid moisture touch her face, the liquor-tainted sweat rising from his body.

She pulled her head back, away from his lips. "Frederick, please let me go. My uncle can still ruin you." With that she was freed. She wiped her face and straightened up, pulling on the hem of her waistcoat. "I'll ask again. What will it take?"

Frederick put a finger to his lips and slowly drew it around his mouth. "You still tempt me. It's a shame your immorality excludes me."

Jessica went for the door opening it to her escape. His hand caught it and slammed it shut. He abruptly turned her to face him, then pressed himself against her. She pushed him back, her head swirling with fear. He regained his balance and laughed. Again he put the full strength of his body into hers while he forced her arms to her sides. The doorknob pressed against her lower back. His hand was on her wrist while his other hand squeezed her face. He kissed her hard on the lips. "No!" she tried to shout. She struggled to reach for the knob with her free hand but he caught it and now she was his prisoner. Her face throbbed.

"Just one more dalliance?" he asked, almost pleading.

She twisted her head away from his advancing lips. His open mouth was on her cheek then his tongue was thrusting into her mouth. For a moment her fear tightened her throat and she could barely send up a squeak. He shoved her away with such a force her head slammed against the door. She took in several quaking breaths before she felt herself being swung around, into the wall. She cried out, "Hannah! Help!"

"Shut up!" he roared. "My household needs none of your shrill drama!"

She felt him lift her skirt from behind with one hand while his other pressed her face against the wall. "Hannah! Help! Help!" She tried to scream but her mouth barely moved.

She saw the door come ajar, then his foot immediately slammed it. He threw her to the side and she toppled to the floor. He turned the lock under the knob and panic struck her like a bolt of lightning. She dared not yell to Hannah, it would surely add to his rage. It took her a moment to stand again. She shook uncontrollably. Frederick had retreated behind his desk. His heavy breath and hooded eyes made him seem demonic. A moment of dark silence passed. She had to abandon her plan. She went for the door.

He spoke clearly. "I will give you five hundred dollars, not a penny more," he stated.

She turned and saw him flipping through papers. She had seen this strange sort of calm in him. Next he would be caressing her with words of regret. She would not, could not, wait a second longer. Her back tightened and she inhaled and let out a trembling breath. She untied her handbag, her wrist throbbing, and extracted the folded piece of paper. The edges of it caught on the striped material. Determined to get hold of herself, she tugged it free. “Write the figure down and sign it.” The paper vibrated as her arm extended it to him while she tried to remain as far from the desk as possible. She felt like a frightened mouse, but she was almost free.

“You came prepared, for what it’s worth,” he said, wiping his mouth. He leaned over his desk and snatched the paper from her. He scribbled with such violence, she thought he’d shred the paper with his pen. “You are more foolish than I could ever imagine.”

“I will have my uncle revise the amount from two thousand to five hundred and add your agreement to never discredit me. He will send you the amended documents.

Frederick rubbed his chin. “I see,” he said. “Well then, I shall never utter another word of you, your family or anyone you are associated with.” He brushed off his vest with the back of his hand. “No court or judge would listen to the ranting of a silly girl. I am well rid of you, you bloody whore.” He picked up the signed paper and waved it teasingly in front of her.

Jessica lunged forward and grabbed it. She had succeeded in doing what she came to do. She rushed to the door, unlocking it as fast as her cold nervous hands could turn the latch. She ran down the hall, her legs barely able to support her. She opened the stained glass front door and without looking back, rushed to her waiting carriage. Her thoughts went to his mistress.

Now she can live in this prison with that madman.

Chapter Forty-two

A week after her ordeal with Frederick, Jessica still trembled when she revisited the scene in her mind. She tried to reconcile the purpose with the trauma, but she cursed herself for even attempting to see him. What would she tell her uncle? Today as she faced him and her aunt, she once again told herself that her life depended on the deal she made with Frederick.

"Uncle," she began. "I know this seems out of line to you, but I saw Frederick and I offered to take a lesser settlement for his silence on such delicate matters. I've come to peace with it and I will find great joy in my freedom." She handed him the paper Frederick had signed.

Burt looked at it. "I don't know what to say. I'm sorry you didn't consult with me first. Five hundred dollars?"

June chimed in. "Oh my, that is a tidy sum, but it won't be enough to support your next endeavors. A lady needs certain adornments to attract a man. She must be seen at certain clubs and social events. I assume you have thought of remarrying as soon as possible. We can only keep up this charade for so long." She began to wring her hands.

"I ask only that I may stay here until I can make a living with my paintings. Then, I feel I will be able to perhaps have a small place of my own."

"Jessica, you may stay here as long as you wish," her aunt said, turning to her husband. "We would never let you live on your own. You'll stay until you marry again."

"Auntie, I hope I won't disappoint you too greatly, but I have no intentions of finding another husband."

"I would hate to see you as a spinster," June replied. "You are much too talented and beautiful for that sort of life." She raised her teacup to her lips and looked at the floor.

Jessica looked at her uncle. He sat with his brows knitted and his arms folded across his chest. "Uncle?" she asked.

He cleared his throat. "My dear niece, why was it necessary to make such a bargain?"

Jessica had thought about the answer to that question. "I couldn't let him scandalize me or our family. I knew I could persuade him with money. It's all the power I had to keep this … to keep what lies festering in him quiet."

"I see," her uncle said. She flushed, afraid her actions had spoken too loudly. "He was ready to concede," her uncle went on. Jessica teared up. "My dear, I know this ordeal has taken a great toll on you. I feel, and I know your aunt will agree, that you need to rest. Stay out of society for a while and I'll see what I can do to reinstate the original agreement."

"Your uncle is right, Jessica," her aunt insisted. "A good rest and you'll think more clearly."

Jessica had taken up a sword in her mind and heart to defend her decision. She had come too far to back down from life now. "I know Frederick. I did what I believe to be the best course of action. It isn't that I don't appreciate all your help, Uncle. Truly, I do. But this … this false accusation."

"What false accusation?" June asked.

"Nothing, nothing," Burt replied to his wife. "Frederick was being vengeful. I thought nothing of it and you should follow my lead on this."

Jessica kissed first her aunt then her uncle on the cheek. "Thank you both for your support and love. I will live here until I find my own home."

The judge's small chambers in the Clermont City Courthouse gave Jessica a great sense of relief. She was glad she didn't have to go through the divorce court. Her uncle's acquaintance with Judge Meed offered her a more private proceeding. The judge sat behind a heavy wooden desk, his chair rising behind him like a throne. His meticulously groomed young clerk sat behind a much smaller, plain desk on the same side of the room. Jessica stood with her uncle in front of them as they waited for Frederick, the thud of her heartbeat drumming in her ears. She shifted her weight to release the tension in her spine.

Time ticked by. Frederick was not only late, but after thirty minutes the judge concluded that he was absent from the proceedings. She was able to breathe again. She studied Judge Meed's every move. He looked over the papers in front of him. Hannah had given her affidavit, but Kevin refused to. Jessica prayed it would be enough. He went back to the former pages he had consulted then leafed through others. Then he rose and went to a row of thick gold embossed books and took one off the shelf. She watched with anticipation as he settled back behind his desk. She could feel the sweat underneath her cream-colored blouse and light brown waistcoat. To Jessica's great relief the judge began to sign the last pages. She waited with hands clasped in front of her, but her insides were a jumble of anxiety and hope.

The judge handed the papers to the clerk, who stamped several. Judge Meed spoke to Burt. "The record will show that the marriage of Frederick Bennett Moore to your client Jessica Elisabeth Moore is dissolved under the laws of California."

Jessica turned to her uncle, tears welling in her eyes. She brought her hand to her waist and slightly bent forward. He nodded to her. She was eager to thank him and the judge. Her uncle touched her sleeve and shook his head. She got the message and remained still.

The judge turned to Jessica. "The circumstances under which

I grant this divorce here and not in a courtroom full of jurors is as follows: your uncle's credible standing in the law back in New England, and Mr. Moore's lack of defense in this case. I also, just now, took into account his disrespect of the Court. I will take his absence as an admission of guilt to the charges of infidelity. As is stated in the formal decree, Mr. Moore retains full custody of all his and your assets and all of the assets you brought into the marriage and was provided within the privileged state of matrimony excluding your personal belongings such as clothes, etcetera. Is this clear to you, Mrs. Moore?"

"Yes," Jessica stated soundly.

"Now as to this paper he signed with the amount you shall receive is entirely between you and him. Is that clear? I will uphold the non-slander agreement however, and only if at the time you provide definitive proof of it to the court."

"Yes," she stated.

The judge nodded to Burt, dropping his tone of authority. "We must get together for a drink. I'd love to share stories with you."

"Yes, soon. Thank you, Judge Meed," Burt replied.

Jessica left the courthouse feeling a heavy burden had been lifted from her. She grabbed her uncle. "Oh, Uncle Burt! I'm free!"

He returned her hug and she heard him say in her ear, "But penniless, my dear."

Jessica received the letter that she had been nervously anticipating for days since she had written to her parents of her changed circumstances. She pulled up her skirt and sat on the bed in the flower ceiling room that had become her small hideaway. She looked at the front of the envelope. Seeing her mother's beautifully even script always made her homesick. She hoped that the words written inside wouldn't be too stinging. She took a deep breath and read its contents.

My Dearest Daughter,

Your father and I are overwhelmed with shock and grief by your news. How could such a thing have happened? He cannot even put pen to paper to express his disappointment. We have no doubt that you tried your best, but we fear you have given up on your marriage too soon.

I cannot bring myself to tell anyone of these most unfortunate events. As far as Hartford is concerned, you are still married to a successful businessman.

I thank God your aunt and uncle are there for you. Your father will write to my brother about funding your needs until you are married again, which we hope will be soon. My own daughter! How could you do this to us?

Please, keep us informed of your progress. I would hope your aunt will find some decent gentlemen among her associations there. We are ready to have you come home, but will wait for further news from your uncle.

With love, as always,

Mother

Jessica tore the letter in two and buried her face in a pillow. Her mother's heartless words ripped into like a knife. They had abandoned her. She wiped her tears only to have more stream down her face. A knock on the door startled her.

"It's Auntie."

"Come in," Jessica replied.

Her aunt sat on the bed and Jessica collapsed into her arms.

"Now, now, it can't be all that bad. Tell me what your mother had to say."

Jessica sat up and searched for the two pieces of paper on the bed. She handed them over and watched as her aunt pieced the letter together without judgment. She read its contents.

"Well, I think they are in shock. It's only the first letter since the news. Give them time."

Jessica took back the torn pages. "Yes, I suppose it is a shock." She sniffled. "I'm still myself, Auntie. Doesn't that account for anything?"

"Jessica, you are a good person, beautiful and gifted. Yes, it accounts for much!"

Jessica felt her aunt's love and acceptance, which buoyed her. She would need to hold her head up high and continue to make her way. But for now she felt as weak as a kitten.

Chapter Forty-three

As the weeks passed, Jessica sensed that the world did not care as much about her as she feared it would; not in Clermont City anyway. No one seemed to mind that Miss Messing was content to remain unmarried, though several of her aunt's friends knew gentlemen to whom they were desperate to introduce her. She politely declined their invitations.

She wrote to her parents and thanked them for their offer of money. She ended her letter telling them that she was doing fine and that her art was beginning to bring her some income. She wanted to tell them how free she felt, but she knew they wouldn't understand. The letter that followed from her mother contained a note of one hundred dollars and questions about her social status. She put the money into the account her uncle had helped her open. Her own account. She was delighted to add to it from the sale of her art whenever possible. She worked diligently to provide worthy, sellable pieces. Neither of the galleries she showed in was grand. The space in Lamont's general store was even smaller than the slender Talbot Gallery and it was on the same side of the street with the town saloon. It was only the beginning. She continued to dream of the day she would show her work in Jilly's Gallery in San Francisco, or perhaps a place in the heart of New York City. When she was daring to dream further she saw her paintings boldly displayed in her hometown of Hartford.

Her daydreams became a daily mantra for her future, until she walked into Talbot's Gallery to deliver her paintings, which were often displayed in the back on a small table. She would try to move the framed art to the front without Mr. Talbot's notice, but each time she returned they had been moved again to the back.

Recently Mr. Talbot asked her if she would join him and his wife on a trip up to Oakland. "I know you've wanted to visit the Gallery there. They're having a showing." With a smile that went from ear to ear, she gladly accepted his invitation.

The stagecoach left early in the morning, rocking along in a merry fashion. Mrs. Talbot seemed to be less inclined to enjoy the trip and sighed heavily once they reached Oakland's stagecoach station. From there they hailed a cab to Gate's Gallery. Jessica's thoughts went to the time she arrived in Oakland from Connecticut. Her appearance in shambles, she hadn't bothered to look around. She had only seen the train tracks that seemed to sprout from the city in every direction, anxious to be on one of them heading to her new home. She was most content to be where she was in life and not the innocent young woman who had arrived with barely a piece of clothing to her name. Now she surveyed a city that was hailed as the place to be. The shop-lined streets of 7th and Broadway were abundant with merchandise and luxury hotels and restaurants she had read about. A fresh food market filled with buyers, sidewalks bustling with people. Finally, they arrived at the gallery. Jessica was helped out of the cab and as she stepped down, her eyes were drawn to the large windows framed ornately with creamy swirls of wooden carvings. She could hear a woman at the door welcoming patrons inside. She was able to peek in the windows where colorful art was arranged on massive white walls. The sight reconfirmed her heart's desire to be an artist.

Jessica followed Mr. and Mrs. Talbot with great anticipation.

She had chosen her dress from the collection she had once worn in San Francisco society. It was more formal than her usual attire. She was glad of her choice for most of the other women were dressed in the same manner. She straightened her flower and feathered bonnet, adjusted her green paisley waistcoat and smoothed her lace-paneled skirt. They joined the line of patrons and waited there turn to enter the gallery.

"Welcome, welcome." Jessica heard the woman say at the front of the line. It rang a familiar tone. She tried to peer around the woman in front of her whose large frame and feather adorned hat blocked her view. She moved further out of line but there were more feathered hats and full skirts keeping her from satisfying her curiosity. When it came time to be welcomed she was taken aback.

"Why, Jessica!" Jilly exclaimed. She grabbed her hand, their skirts colliding as Jilly whisked her away from the door and into the gallery, abandoning the other patrons.

Heat flared into Jessica's cheeks. Her breathing became shallow. She fought for composure. "Jilly, what a nice surprise."

"Where on earth have you been these past months? I heard from Margret Peterson that you no longer live with your husband. Lenny hasn't seen you either. What has become of our budding artist?"

Jilly was creating a scene. Luckily the gallery had partitions and not everyone was in earshot. "I've been living with my aunt and uncle. Frederick and I are … I mean to say we had some …" She wrung her gloved hands, searching for the Talbots.

"I see," Jilly replied. She leaned in closer and talked in Jessica's ear. "Not that it matters to me, but some in your previous circle find it distasteful. Margret Peterson is here, as matter a fact. This could get uncomfortable for you."

Jessica caught on that her 'previous circle' had already heard of the divorce. She smiled as Margret approached. She had two choices: To be polite and rejoin the Talbots, or she could stand proud and honest. She didn't know which one she would choose until after Margret spoke.

"Jessica." Margret began. "Hello, my dear." She looked her up and down as if she was inspecting a piece of meat for dinner. "How have you been?" she asked with a slight tilt of her head and a sad pucker of her mouth. "I do not envy you and here you have the courage to come out in a most public way. I mean it's just … well I could never."

"Hello, Margret. It's nice to see you. I'm very well. As you know I have divorced my husband and I have devoted my life to my art. I'm here to see these wonderful works by such talented artist. Such inspiration. How have you been?" She brought her hands in front of her skirt and waited, a smile plastered on her face. She wouldn't even blink.

"I … I have been very well myself," Margret replied. "The dinners and luncheons have been taking so much of my time. We had the mayor over just the other night and some of the city council were eager to dine with us. My husband is such an asset as you know. San Francisco adores him." She said and gave a small laugh.

"I'm sure it's very fulfilling for you, Margret." Jessica turned to Jilly. "Would you relay a message to Lenny for me? Tell her what I have said to you both here today and anyone else who asks. And Jilly, I'd love to get together with you and hear about your gallery. I must join my companions now. Excuse me." Jessica turned and heard Jilly say, "Yes, by all means and Margret let out a huff.

The Talbots were viewing a set of paintings. "Jessica, these remind me of your oils," Mr. Talbot whispered as she drew closer to him and his wife. "We must promote you here. Leave it to me." She smiled and remained close while she glanced around for any signs of Jilly and Margret. She caught sight of them talking closely with a few other women. They were surely gossiping about her. She shook her head to clear the thought. She swore to herself that someday her art would hang in such a gallery, signed *Miss Jessica Messing.*

She studied the paintings around her. Each group had several of one artist's work and each seemed to have a theme: Impressionism. She squinted her eyes as Mr. Talbot instructed, yet the work still looked messy. "I get the idea," she said. "Yet I'm not sure how one could achieve such painting when all it is are dabs."

"Ah, the realism painter in you cannot see the value of such art," Mr. Talbot commented as he stroked his whiskers.

"Yes, I suppose," she replied. She leaned in closer to discover the secret behind the brushstrokes. She thought of Lenny and her constant reminder to stay loose with her paintings. She cocked an eyebrow. Maybe she could learn a lesson from this type of art. It took her mind away from the unexpected meeting with Jilly and Margret, but not for long. Margret's appraisal stirred up her fears. She had to confess it disturbed her more than she wanted it to. She reminded herself of her life at present. The one person she knew would understand was Lenny. It was Lenny she most wanted to confide in. Her thought went no further; she heard Mr. Talbot promising his wife they would find a restaurant very soon.

Jessica entered the eatery at the end of Broadway along with the Talbots. Perhaps a bite to eat would lift her spirits. The owner of the Gate's Gallery hadn't been present. It added to the disappointment already residing in her. As they sat in front of a window watching the many passersby and waiting for their lunch of salmon and vegetables Mr. Talbot said he would try to talk to the owner about her paintings. The thought brought lightness back into her heart. This was the reason for her trip here.

She sat back with relief as the stagecoach made its way back to Clermont City. She had managed to escape further interactions with Jilly and Margret, or had they managed to escape from her?

Jessica took her uncle's carriage to Mr. Talbot's gallery with her latest rendition of the town park. It was one of many of her paintings of the scenic area but from a different angle. People traveling through town especially liked the small paintings. She called to the back room of the gallery. When Mr. Talbot didn't immediately reply, she went in search of him. Through the open door in a small room at the far end of the building, she found him looking around at the empty space with his chin resting in his hand.

"Mr. Talbot?"

"Hello, Miss Messing! Why, I didn't hear you come in," he said.

Jessica looked around and had an idea. She set her framed paintings against the gray concrete wall. "Mr. Talbot, do you mind me asking what use you have for this space?"

"Why, that's what I'm trying to figure out," he replied. "I have plenty of storage upstairs."

Jessica knew she had to act quickly before he decided. "Mr. Talbot, would you consider having me rent this space from you? I'm painting more in oils and I'm afraid my aunt can't tolerate the smell any longer."

Mr. Talbot looked it over from side to side. "Why, it's hardly a room at all," he replied.

"It's fine for me," she said. "What do you say?"

He rubbed his chin. "I suppose you can pay me out of your commissions. Say, three dollars a week?"

Jessica calculated the cost against her commissions. "Two dollars?"

"Two twenty-five a week and you've got yourself a studio, for what it's worth," he answered.

"It's a deal! Shall we shake on it?" She stuck her hand out. He gently shook the tips of her gloved fingers. Jessica looked down at his scant handshake. "I suppose that will do," she said. "I'll move in right away."

The cramped nine by ten-foot space was like a palace to Jessica. It had a small window and its own entrance from the back of the building. The alley was a place for old carts and over ripe fruit from the small grocery store nearby. Today it smelled of rotting oranges.

Broken frames and packing newspaper were stacked haphazardly alongside her door. She gathered the garbage and placed it in a pile away from her entrance. A good sweeping and she was ready to move in. She gave a quick survey of the frames, perhaps she could mend some for her art. She brought in her large stand up easel and a table to hold her paints and a place to work on her watercolors. She fit a chair against the wall. She unrolled the thread worn cotton carpet her aunt had brought from the attic for her to use in the bedroom. It was stained with her paints, yet it added warmth and authenticity to the space. Jessica looked around. A hook for her smock would complete her studio. It would have to be mounted on the inside of the door; the walls were made of concrete blocks. The window was barely twelve by eight inches, but she was elated that it opened. A small curtain perhaps.

There was one last thing she had to do. She reached into her pocket and took out Jacob's necklace. She kissed the beaded strand and looped it over the top post of her easel.

Jessica put the last touches on a piece she had been working on for days. She had fallen in love with her little studio and spent most of her time creating the art that truly inspired her. The June heat kept her from closing the back door however stinky it got. The cool concrete studio gave some relief. The pots of fragrant flowers she placed at the entrance just outside helped to curb the smell. She was learning to accept this part of the deal. The door that led back into the gallery was locked from the other side and she had placed several of her canvases against it.

Mr. Talbot came around the back to peek at her progress. "He turned his head with a wrinkled nose and a loud sniff. "I'll get Jonas to remove that rubbage, Miss Messing." He walked in and admired her work. "I could get a good price for this," he said. "But I must say, your watercolors are selling very well. I hope you don't abandon them altogether."

"I wouldn't think of it," Jessica replied as she continued to dab the reddish-orange color onto the canvas. "Could you really sell my oils?"

He shook his head. "Not in my gallery. They're too provocative for a lady. I'm sure I would lose some customers, and that wouldn't go well for either one of us."

Jessica stopped her work as Mr. Talbot began to examine the painting in front of him: a young woman, dressed in tattered clothing walking barefooted through small puddles of mud, a child clinging to her with a rag doll in its hand.

"This is too sad," he finally said. Then he paused before continuing. "Life is difficult," he began. "You and I live in a small, clean town, away from hardship. My wife is in four different clubs. Your aunt attends some of them. But I will tell you, your art is a story of the less fortunate. There is a market for that sort of gritty realism." With his palms together he said, "I pray that you also paint a little dog in a park or children standing in front of a church. Perhaps these lighter subjects in oils?"

Jessica smiled. "Of course."

"I've talked to the owner of the Gates Gallery," he said. Jessica froze waiting for the next words to come out of his mouth. "She seems open to the idea. She's difficult to deal with. I mean to say, she's picky about what she displays. I am also discerning about what I have in my gallery, yet people's tastes run a bit broader in the larger cities, so we shall see. I suggest …"

With mouth agape Jessica hugged the man who had helped her gain her independence.

"Yes, well, as I was about to say," he began, as he pulled away, flustered. "You will have to change your name."

She tilted her head. "My name? I've signed them with my full name, Miss Jessica Messing."

The little man rolled his eyes. "I've been meaning to tell you, the 'Miss' isn't necessary unless you are advertising for a husband.

Jessica's heart skipped a beat. "Oh, I didn't think of it that way." Her mind rushed to think how she would delicately conceal that part of her signature.

"It's J. Lingerhoph from now on," she heard him say bringing her out of her thoughts.

"It has a certain ring to it; don't you think?" he said with a satisfied look on his face.

Jessica didn't know what to think of having to change her name to sell her art. She chuckled with amusement at his suggestion. "Who will know I've done these paintings?"

"You and I," he replied. "We will assume you are a male artist in oils, and you can remain a gentile lady artist in watercolors. I'll say I receive J. Lingerhoph's works from abroad and feel it would do well in a larger gallery. And please, Miss Messing, don't try making watercolors gloomy. This trend is quite disturbing. After all, I'm here to make a profit from my artists' work. And I can tell you, as a male artist you will see more money. Which I will take a small fee from, of course."

She pursed her lips and squinted her eyes. This would take some thought. She could certainly use more income. Perhaps she might make enough to find a room to rent, a place to call her own. She realized the freedom in such a disguise. She could paint as a man, as bold as she pleased. She nodded at Mr. Talbot. They shook on it; this time it was a real handshake. Mr. Talbot left. She could sense his satisfaction.

Alone, Jessica trembled with anticipation at the thought of breaking some sort of artistic law by not revealing her real name. She cupped her hand to her mouth, barely covering the broad smile on her face.

Jacob's strand of beads hung from her easel. She unbuttoned her high collar and placed them around her neck. She retrieved her brush and without re-buttoning her collar, she continued to paint. The open door let in a breeze mixed with the stench of the garbage and the heady smell of lilies.

Chapter Forty-four

Jacob arrived in Clermont City. He'd left Will and pregnant Mi in Oregon to carry on the business. So far they had traveled within the state, but he'd been eager to dive into importing. However, their funds were still not up to par and life had shown no mercy. Jacob wanted to get away and find perspective. He decided he needed to see Jessica. This time it would be without the fanfare of last summer.

He wrote to arrange the meeting, hoping she would receive the letter from his mother before his arrival. Jacob knew he was taking the risk of having Frederick find out, but he had taken many risks in his life and for far lesser reasons.

Jacob waited for what seemed like hours on the wooden bench in the park, until the midday heat made him restless. His mind ran in disturbing directions. *She was in San Francisco with her husband. My letter never reached her.* Thinking he had made a foolish and wasteful mistake he decided to abandon his plan. He walked towards the bridge that led back to his horse. A woman stood at the end of the curved overpass. His heart rose in his chest threatening to choke him. They walked toward each other and met in the middle.

Jacob took Jessica's hand and felt it tremble under his. He cupped it with his other hand and gazed into her dark, soulful brown eyes. "You look beautiful," he said.

"I'm happy, Jacob," Jessica replied. "I can't believe you're here."

Her hand grasped his. Her smile melted his heart, yet her peace dismayed him. "How have you come to such happiness? Frederick?" he asked. He never felt more vulnerable.

Jessica laughed. "No, not at all. He's no longer my husband. I'm a divorced woman."

Jacob was dumbstruck. "Oh. I didn't expect to hear that." He searched for a private spot and spied an empty bench shaded by a large tree. "Let's sit over there. You must tell me all about it."

She gave a summary of her life since they'd last seen each other. Her struggles, her victories, her art and studio.

"You are a marvel," he stated. "If not for the fact that … I mean, if we were free to, I would ask you to …" he stopped short, not wanting to ruin the moment.

"Yes, I'm afraid we were born in the same family cabbage patch," she mused.

He smiled and lifted one eyebrow. "I thought we went over that at one time … long ago." He wanted to disappear into her laughter. He watched her beautiful eyes peering into the distance.

"I feel as free as a woman can be these days," she said.

"I'm happy for you," he replied, wanting to say so much more.

"It's a lovely feeling," she continued, turning back to him. "Though my parents have made it clear that I'm a great disappointment to them. Along with your parents, they're holding their breaths until I find another husband."

"I'm sure my parents are holding their breaths for me, too," he said with a gentle smile. "Are you looking to marry again?" he asked.

She looked away and he waited, his mind and heart needing to hear her answer. "Not at the moment," she replied. It was sufficient for him, for now.

"Your brother has not disappointed," he said. "Will is probably getting married soon."

"My brother has found a wife?" Jessica asked.

Her wide-eyed expression delighted Jacob. "It's Mi, the woman who nursed him back to health."

"Yes, the Chinese woman you mentioned in your letter. I must say we are a trio of misfits," she exclaimed with a laugh.

Although Jacob welcomed her levity, he became self-conscious at the mention of his letter. He cleared his throat. "Apparently Mi had more feelings for him than either had let on."

"Is she of good standing?" Jessica asked.

"Her family owns a Chinese restaurant in Portland. They rejected her after she told them she was intent on marrying a non-Chinese. Her father nearly shot Will and the two of us had to run for our lives!"

"Oh, the poor girl. The world is so unfair."

Jacob looked at her. "Yes, it is." Jessica smiled as he entwined his fingers around hers. "Here's the bigger news: she's pregnant."

Jessica gasped. "Oh my!"

Jacob gave her a moment to take in the information about Will. "Jessica," he began. "I'm striving to make something of myself. Will and I are going into a legitimate business. It will take a while, but I'm confident it will be a success. You have compelled me to do better. I want you to be proud of me, Jess." He nervously waited for her response.

Jessica leaned back. "I'm already proud of you, of your spirit and your courage. What you must have gone through out there in the wilderness, and … and still do."

Her words touched him deeply. He was not what he wanted her to see. He lowered his head. "You must already know that I brought every bit of it on myself. I have no reason to complain or be proud of what I've done." He looked into her eager eyes. "What I'm trying to tell you is that someday, I will be worthy of a woman like you."

She pursed her lips and he wanted to devour them. "I see," she said. "Am I so worthy? A divorced woman? A painter?"

"Jess, don't look at me that way. You're everything I want! I don't care if you're a divorced woman. Hell, I'm very happy to hear that you are!"

Their eyes locked and they were again lost in each other. A place Jessica felt she had come home to. She couldn't have wished for more than to be sitting beside her true love, his eyes looking into hers. His hair was short and neat. His clothes were new and he looked less rugged than the last time she saw him. She was relieved. "You look well, Jacob."

He glanced at his pants and polished boots. "I cleaned up for you." He laughed then she noticed a sly smile come over his face.

"What is it?" she asked.

"Well … you said you have a studio? Is it … private?"

She lowered her head with a smile and her cheeks felt warm. Smoothing her skirt, her eyes set on the crease she was straightening, she shyly replied, "Yes."

He cleared his throat. "I would very much like to see your art studio, Cousin."

Jessica looked around as if the world had read her mind. Desire bloomed in her and she willed herself to be composed. "I could show you the new piece I've been working on," she said.

He stood up and offered her his arm. She took it with dignity and gave him a polite, charming smile. "Oh, Cousin it is good of you to take an interest in my hobby," she remarked as two women walked by and nodded to them.

He came closer to her and whispered in her ear, "I take an interest in *you*."

The warmth of his breath was about to undo her when he pulled her along, laughing.

Her feet practically left the ground. The moment of heavy desire had been lightened. She could walk to her studio without feeling as if she was about to explode.

Jacob looked around the concrete-walled space. Jessica was happy the garbage had been removed regularly and the place smelled only of art supplies and summer flowers. She was proud of her space. "Is this some kind of a root cellar?" he asked with a chuckle.

Jessica furrowed her brows and glanced at the unfinished walls. "It's my art studio, Jacob," she replied flatly.

His accepting nod and kind smile released the tension in her. He inspected her canvases, some with splashes of color, some prepped for color, one half-finished, another almost completed. Then to the watercolor painting on a small angled easel propped on a table. "You've always had the talent, Jess," he remarked. "I hope you're making some pennies from these."

"Pennies?" she asked. "Why, I'll have you know I make more than mere pennies."

There was a glint in Jacob's eyes. "Are you going to tease me?" she asked coyly.

Jacob raked his hand through his hair. "I'm proud of you Jess," he said and stood closer to her now. He bent down and put his mouth to her ear. "Is there a lock to that door?"

She nodded and slowly turned the darkened brass ring, the pulse of her blood surging through her body. He walked up behind her and placed his hands on her waist. She gave a soft moan. She turned around and met his mouth. His full, warm mouth. A puff of air escaped his shirt and the musk of him made her legs go weak. The thin carpet was splatter with paint. The hard chair in the corner was the only place to sit.

He slid his body across her chest and reached over for the chair swinging it to set it down before them.

Jessica's breath caught as Jacob sat upright on the wooden seat. He spread his long legs and she stood between them and leaned her body over him her hands on the back of the chair. She watched his fingers unbutton her blouse, then her camisole laces, exposing her chest. She leaned in closer and he gently kissed each breast. Her mind swirled in a whirlpool of emotion. His kisses were sweet and unhurried. She unbuttoned his shirt. He kicked off his boots and lifted his hips for her to release him from his pants. She undid her skirt and it fell to the floor and her foot threw it out of the way. No corset to untie and no pantaloons to remove. She slid her pink satin pant to the side and straddled him on the chair. Their giggles muffled by their strong passionate kisses. Soon they were in the world they had created so long ago. The chair rocked hard. It tipped and Jessica braced herself for impact when Jacob brought her gently to the floor. Her body felt the hard concrete beneath the thin carpet. She did not care. She let the timelessness of their love take her to a place where there were no rules, no judgments, only freedom.

She sighed with contentment, resting her head on his chest. It rose and fell with his breathing. His smooth skin and delicious smell were all hers. Then a sudden wave of sadness struck her. It rose like an unwelcome friend, one she had bargained with many times, one she knew would never completely leave her be; grief. Jacob must have felt the tightening of her body for he pulled away. "What is it, Jess?"

She stared up at him. "Oh, Jacob."

"Jess?"

She lowered her head onto his chest, her harbored feelings now untethered, the sting of tears like sparks in her eyes and nose. "Our baby did not make it into this world." She waited for his response, barely able to breathe. A moment passed and he did not move. She wanted fall into the earth.

Jacob raised up on one elbow. "What are you saying?" His expression was one of confusion and disbelief. Her skin went cold. He took her body into his. "I'm so sorry. God, I'm so sorry. Please forgive me, Jess. I wasn't here for you." She relaxed into him letting his strong arms take some of her sadness away. He rocked her and they wept together. She heard him mumble, "I love you."

"Jacob, let's always be together, in our own way," she whispered in a hiccup of emotion.

His warm hand caressed her face. "Yes, always," he vowed. His quiet, deep voice etched the words onto her soul.

A soft breeze wafted through the small window, whispering the promise of another summer.

THE END

Acknowledgements

There is no way I could have published a book that I am proud of without the help of others. Thank you to all the beta readers who took the time to read my first, second, and third drafts. Your honesty and encouragement gave me wings. To my first editors Carrie and Susan who plodded through my whole 265,000 word trilogy. Your help and advice was the beginning of my awakening as a writer. A special thanks to my editor Julie Christine Johnson. Her accomplishments are many and include her own works; In Another Life and The Crows of Beara. She is a skillful editor. Julie, you showed me what a story should look and feel and taste like. It turned the corner for me as a writer. You gave me the self-confidence and the strength to continue until I got it right. What a joy it is to work with you!

Last but never least is my family. Loving thanks to my wonderful daughters Star and Heidi for their love and support. You always encouraged me to move forward. Thank you Beth, my sister, my friend, my soulmate. You helped to shape the tone of my book by making me see things I would never have thought of looking for. Thank you Nathan for always asking me when my book will get published so you can read it. How does a four-year-old care about such things? You did and you still do. Someday you will finally be old enough to read Memaw's book. Thank you to the rest of my grandchildren, Dylan, Liam, Miles, and Dalila. Without knowing it you inspire me to be the best I can be. Thank you to my husband, Jeff. My life took a turn and there you were. Loving, understanding, honest and forever supporting my dreams. Thank you Wilson and Tommy for understanding why I was sometimes late feeding you. I know cats don't like that.

I am so grateful to have such love and support surrounding me.

Veronica Mahara is the maiden name of Veronica Stoneman who lives with her husband and two cats surrounded by her family and the beauty of the Pacific Northwest.

CPSIA information can be obtained
at www.ICGtesting.com
Printed in the USA
FFHW02n0655041018
48687760-52701FF

9 781732 371200